BABY BE MINE

Also by Paige Toon

Lucy in the Sky
Johnny Be Good
Chasing Daisy
Pictures of Lily
One Perfect Summer
One Perfect Christmas
The Longest Holiday

Paige Toon

BABY BE MINE

**SIMON &
SCHUSTER**

London · New York · Sydney · Toronto · New Delhi

A CBS COMPANY

First published in Great Britain by Simon and Schuster UK Ltd, 2011
A CBS COMPANY
This paperback edition, 2013

Copyright © Paige Toon, 2011

5 7 9 10 8 6

Simon & Schuster UK Ltd
1ˢᵗ Floor
222 Gray's Inn Road
London
WC1X 8HB

www.simonandschuster.co.uk

Simon & Schuster Australia, Sydney

Simon & Schuster India, New Delhi

A CIP catalogue copy for this book is available
from the British Library.

ISBN: 978-1-47112-958-2
eBook ISBN: 978-1-84983-127-7

Typeset by Hewer Text UK Ltd, Edinburgh
Printed and bound in Great Britain by CPI Group (UK) Ltd, Croydon, CR0 4YY

For Idha
MY baby
Love you, little one

Prologue

'He's not mine, is he?'

That's the question I fear the most.

You see, I have a secret. My son is not fathered by my boyfriend, but by one of the most famous people alive. And he doesn't even know it.

My boyfriend doesn't know, either. No one does. That's the only way it can be. It's a crushing burden to carry, but it's mine to carry and mine alone.

I'm terrified, so terrified that the truth will come out. Because my son doesn't look like my boyfriend. He looks like his rockstar father. And sooner or later, the world is going to realise . . .

Chapter 1

'Happy birthday to you,
Happy birthday to you,
Happy birthday, dear Barney,
Happy birthday to you.'

I'm singing this very quietly so as not to wake him. He's had a busy day with his nanny, grandad and me, and now he's crashed out in his cot. He's going to grow out of it soon. I can't believe my baby has just turned one. It's frightening how time flies.

Bit of a bummer that his daddy wasn't here today. I say that flippantly, but inside I'm not happy. Not happy at all. Then, suddenly, I'm fine again. It's the guilt. It balances out the anger. I can't stay cross with Christian for long. That word: 'Daddy'. It's a lie. I'm a liar. And I hate myself for it.

I can hear my parents clattering away in the bathroom next door. They'll be in bed soon, and then I'll have the living room to myself. I'm getting the urge again. My head is prickling with the thought of it. It will be the first time I've done it in six months. The last time was when Christian and I had a big fight.

That was before I knew. Before I knew for sure. But I'd suspected it for a long time.

Oh, Christian . . . What have I done?

One year and nine months ago, I had sex with my boyfriend's best friend. It sounds horrendous when you say it like that. Don't get me wrong, it is horrendous. But there was a history there. I was in love with Johnny. I was in love with him first.

I look back once more to my sleeping baby, who is no longer a baby. I lean over his cot and kiss him softly on his forehead as tears fill my eyes.

I'm so sorry, my darling. I don't know what to do.

If I told Christian now and he threw us out, as of course he would, how would my son be affected? Would he remember the person who was his father for the first year of his life? Christian is away such a lot at the moment that we're almost getting used to life without him. Maybe it wouldn't be such an upheaval. Maybe it would be okay. Oh, who am I kidding?

I think my parents have finally retired to bed. I get up and quietly walk out of my bedroom into the living room. My laptop screen is dark, the screensaver having switched itself off hours ago. I take a seat on the sofa and pull the computer onto my lap. My head is prickling again. I shouldn't be doing this.

'I thought you were in bed?'

I almost jump out of my skin at the sound of my mum's voice. 'You frightened me!'

'Sorry, I wanted a glass of water.'

I quickly push down the laptop lid and put the computer back on the side-table, the urge momentarily quashed. 'I was just checking my emails,' I lie as I get up and join my mum in the kitchen.

3

'Can't you do that in the morning?' she asks, pulling a bottle of water out of the fridge. 'You've had a busy day,' she adds.

'I know, I know,' I brush her off, not enjoying being told what to do, especially now that I'm a responsible parent myself. Allegedly.

'Have you spoken to Christian?' she asks as she decants water into a tumbler.

'No, I haven't called him back yet,' I admit.

'Don't you think you should? I'm sure he'd like to know about Barney's birthday.'

I bite my tongue and take the bottle from her, pouring a drink for myself. 'I will,' I reply shortly.

'Good,' she says annoyingly.

I follow her out of the kitchen and switch off all the lights, taking one last look at my laptop sitting silently on the side-table in the living room.

You'll keep . . .

I follow my mum down the corridor to the bedrooms. She and Dad are sleeping in Barney's room to the left of the bathroom, while he and his cot have been temporarily relocated into my bedroom on the right.

'Night, night.' Mum turns back to give me a peck on the cheek.

'Night,' I reply, and go into my bedroom.

I shut the door and take a deep breath before exhaling as quietly as I can. My iPhone is charging on my bedside table. I see that there's another message from Christian:

Boarding now. Will ring when I land

I feel bad. I should have called him earlier. I'm surprised to discover I'm looking forward to seeing him.

Why am I surprised? He's my boyfriend. I love him.

I know why: it's the guilt. It's poisonous. And deep down I know that it's going to be the death of our little family.

Chapter 2

'Hello, there!'

I hear Mum's cheerful voice echoing through the walls. I'm in the bathroom and, from the sounds of it, my dad has just arrived home from the airport with Christian.

'Hi!' Christian replies. 'Hey . . .' There's silence as I picture him scooping up Barney into his arms for a warm, cuddly hug. I quickly towel myself dry – I didn't think they'd be back so soon.

'Where's Meg?' Christian asks.

'In the shower,' my mum replies.

'Have a nice lie-in, did she?' Christian says and I frown as they all chuckle at my expense. It's six thirty in the evening and I've been on my feet all day. A moment later there's a knock at the door.

'Meg?'

'I'm coming,' I reply tetchily.

'Unlock the door.'

Still frowning, I do as he says.

'Hey!' He beams as he enters the steam-filled bathroom, but his face falls when he sees my expression. 'What's up?'

'Nothing.' I wrap the towel around my still-damp body.

'Can I have a hug?' he asks warily as he opens his arms and cocks his head to one side.

'Sure.' I grudgingly step forward and his arms embrace me.

'Mmm,' he murmurs into my wet hair. 'I missed you.'

'Did you?'

He pulls away and gives me a look. 'Of course I did. I hoped you'd change your mind about coming to get me.'

'Sorry,' I say and genuinely mean it. I've been having second thoughts all day about whether or not I should go to the airport myself. 'I thought I'd better do Barney's dinner and get things back to normal after yesterday's mayhem. Dad offered; I didn't think you'd mind.'

'You're still pissed off at me for not getting home in time.' It's not a question. I shrug. 'I did try. I couldn't help it,' he says. 'Anyway, it's not like Barney would have missed me; he's only one.'

I'll have to remember you said that if you discover the truth about him anytime soon . . .

I nod towards the door. 'Better go and get dressed.'

He turns away and I follow him into the bedroom. 'How was yesterday?' he asks, sitting down on the bed and watching me as I open the wardrobe.

'It was good,' I reply, taking a navy-blue and white polka-dot maxidress out of the wardrobe and slipping it over my head. 'I don't think he knew what hit him with all the toys your parents sent. And he loved the balloons and candles. Did you bring him anything back?'

He grins. 'Yep.'

'What?'

'A dumper truck.' He's still grinning cheekily.

'What's so funny?' I smile. 'Did you bring *me* something back?'

'You'll have to wait and see.'

'It's Pebbles, isn't it?' He laughs as I clamber onto his knees and throw my arms around him. He collapses back on the bed.

Pebbles is a type of American cereal. It's supposed to be for kids, but Christian and I both have a sweet tooth and we became addicted to the multicoloured rice crispy things when we spent time in the States a few years ago.

Christian rolls me off his body onto the bed next to him and stares into my eyes. I stare back into his: a darker shade of brown than mine. His black hair falls across his eye-line and I reach over and push it away. He needs a haircut.

He leans forward and kisses me on the lips. I sit back up again.

'I'm going to get the bed wet.' I indicate my damp hair.

'Fuck the bed,' he says, a tad exasperated.

'Oi, don't swear!' I chastise.

'He's not in earshot, is he?' He's talking about Barney.

'It doesn't matter,' I reply firmly. 'You've got to get out of the habit.'

Christian swears more than anyone else I know. I've been trying to get him to clean up his act ever since our baby was born.

'He can't even talk yet,' he mutters, getting up from the bed with a sigh.

I move on. 'How was your flight? Flights, I mean.'

We live in a little village called Cucugnan in the French Pyrenees, so Christian had to fly via the UK from Los Angeles and then onto our nearest airport, Perpignan, which is twenty-five kilometres away. With the winding mountain roads it takes a good forty-five minutes to travel to Cucugnan.

'Both fine. The LA one was an hour delayed, but I still managed to find time at Heathrow to buy some Krispy Kremes.'

'I hope you didn't eat them all . . .' I say of the doughnuts.

'Only six.'

'Six out of twelve?'

'I'm joking. I managed to stop at three, so there are nine left for you lot.'

'Bugger the others,' I joke.

We used to live in Belsize Park in north London – in fact, Christian still owns his house there – but a few months ago, his friend offered us a reduced rental price on his holiday home in the south of France and we jumped at the chance to take a break from grey old London. My parents actually live in the south of France themselves, in Grasse, about four and a half hours' drive away. I'm not working at the moment, and as for Christian, he's a full-time writer, so he can work anywhere – and he does.

'How was your trip?' I ask. 'Did you get much done?'

'A fair bit.'

'Anything interesting happen?'

'The gig was good. Scott whisked a couple of groupies away to his hotel room afterwards.'

'Threesome.' I roll my eyes.

'Yeah, been there, done that.' He glances at me and gives me a wry little smile. 'I'm going to hang out with Barney. See you in a min.'

He leaves the bedroom and I turn to look at myself in the mirror on the dressing table.

Johnny . . .

I grab my hairdryer and start to blast my shoulder-length, straight blonde hair.

Christian used to be a music journalist, but now he's an author. He made his name writing his best friend's – rock star Johnny Jefferson's – biography and his 'been there, done that' comment is a reference to the wild boy's own sexual encounters. Now Christian is working on another biography, this time about American rock group Contour Lines. But there are three guys in the band, which means three times as much work for my writer boyfriend. Plus, as Scott, Niall and Ricky are all based in Los Angeles, Christian has to travel there a lot. I'm dreading this summer when the band goes on tour. I'll never see him.

A memory comes back to me of being on tour with Johnny. The screaming fans, the obsessive groupies, the drink, the drugs . . . Thankfully Christian isn't into any of that stuff. I trust him completely. He can't say the same for me. In fact, he can and does say the same thing about me. The sad thing is, he's severely misguided.

I slam my hairdryer down on the dressing table. I've had enough of facing my own reflection for now.

The sound of laughter brings a smile to my face as I walk down the corridor towards the living room. Christian is tickling a near-hysterical Barney on the sofa.

I lean against the doorframe and watch my boys, Christian with his dark, messy hair and Barney with his blond locks. My smile falters as Barney looks up and spies me, his green eyes piercing in the early evening sunlight. He looks just like his dad. His real dad. How can Christian not see it?

'How about a drink, Mummy?' Christian interrupts my thoughts.

'What do you fancy?'

'Got any of that cheapo cider?'

All the cider is cheap here. Doesn't mean it's not yummy.

'Yep.'

'Right, we're off!' Dad declares, coming into the living room with his car keys dangling from his fingers. Mum follows him in.

'Aah, thanks for coming.' I go to give them both a hug. 'Are you sure you don't want to stay another night? Set off first thing?'

'No, we'd better get going, honey,' Dad replies. 'Your mother's got her ladies coming over for morning tea tomorrow.'

'See you soon, Barney!' Mum calls, but my little boy stays entangled with Christian on the sofa.

'Come and say bye to Nanny and Grandad,' I urge, and Christian heaves himself up, carrying my son's weight with him. The three of us see my parents outside to their car and wave them off, and I experience the usual pang at watching them go. My head starts singing that song, 'Alone Again'. I wish they lived closer. At least they're in the same country. I wonder if I could get them to come and stay next time Christian goes away.

The following day, Christian and I sit by the pool drinking iced lemonade and making our way through a fresh baguette. We took Barney for a walk in his buggy earlier to get him to sleep. He usually naps for about two hours, so Christian and I are taking this opportunity to chill out together.

'This is bliss,' he says, slicing a piece of Camembert for his bread.

'Mmm,' I agree, tilting my head back and gazing up at the blue sky. It's been tipping it down in England for the last four days. It is lovely here. I just wish I had some friends around to enjoy it with.

'When are you going away again?' I pop my sunglasses on top of my head and turn to face him.

'I don't know,' he replies, not looking at me. 'Might be soon.'

'How soon?' I ask with trepidation.

'The band's starting tour rehearsals next week. I should probably be there for that.'

'Next week?' I exclaim. 'Please tell me you're joking.'

'I'm not. Sorry, Meg.' He glances at me sideways, furrowing his brow.

'For pity's sake!' I explode. 'You've only just got back!'

'I know. But I have to do this. I have to make this book work, otherwise I'm fucked.'

I don't bother to tell him off for his language. I put my sunglasses back on and stare moodily at the pool.

'I'm sorry,' he says again.

'Whatever,' I reply.

'You do like it here, don't you?'

'Of course I like it,' I retort. 'I'm just really bored being all by myself.'

'You're not by yourself,' he corrects me, irritatingly. 'You've got Barney.'

'You know what I mean,' I reply crossly. 'I have no social life. I have nothing to do, no friends to see.'

'How can you say you have nothing to do? Look around you! Don't you know how lucky you are?'

'Yes, of course. But I'm lonely!'

'Why don't you get a job?'

'What would I do?'

'I don't know – work in a bakery or something.'

'Oh, yeah, and where am I supposed to put Barney? Out at the back with the ovens?'

'He could go to a nursery.'

I shake my head. 'That's hardly likely to be financially viable, is it?'

'I don't know, Meg, but you said you were bored. I thought maybe you could do with a change of lifestyle.'

'By sticking our son into day care?' I snap.

He sighs. 'Why don't you try taking him to a playgroup or something, then?'

'I don't know of any.'

'There must be a way to find out about them.'

'I don't know anyone at them, though,' I say.

'Isn't that the point? You'd go to meet people.'

'What if no one speaks English?'

'You speak French!'

'An A level doesn't constitute speaking French! Especially when I've barely used the language in the last decade, apart from asking for croissants and baguettes.'

'Well, wouldn't this be a good time to use it? I thought you wanted to brush up.'

'Now you are really annoying me,' I warn.

'Only because you know I'm right,' he replies. 'Stop making excuses for yourself.'

I'm about to storm inside when he puts his hand out to stop me.

'I don't mean to wind you up. I'm trying to help.' He gets to his feet and goes out through the pool gate. I sit there stewing for a minute, but I'm over it by the time he returns with some magazines.

I nod at them. 'Research?'

'Yep. Band interviews.' He dumps them on a table. 'I sat in on a couple of them. It's interesting to see how they've been edited.'

I lean forward and riffle through the stack. Most are serious music journals, but finally I come to an addictively trashy celebrity magazine. My heart jumps, as it always does when I read these sorts of things. I try not to do it very often.

'Mind if I borrow this one?'

'Of course not,' Christian replies.

I lean back in my seat. I have to get through the news and gossip before I can relax. I'm nervous as I turn the pages, barely reading the content. I don't even pause to admire the beach snaps of sexy Scott from Contour Lines. It's only when I finally reach the fashion pages that I can breathe a sigh of relief. No news or gossip about Johnny in this one. I settle myself and begin to browse at a more leisurely pace.

I come to a double-page feature:

WHEN YOU WERE YOUNG . . .
Match the celeb to their childhood pic!

Ooh, I love these quizzes!

And then my heart stops.

Barney. There's a picture of Barney.

No. That's not Barney. I quickly scan the tiny headshots of celebrities running along the bottom of the page and immediately spy what I'm looking for. Johnny Jefferson. Johnny Jefferson as a child looks identical to my son.

I feel the blood draining from my face as my eyes dart towards

Christian, reading in amicable silence beside me. Act normal. Try to act normal, Meg.

My heart is pounding so hard inside my chest, I'm surprised it's not cracking my ribs. I slowly close the magazine and get to my feet.

'Do you want anything?' I ask breezily, holding the offending article behind my back. I can't let him see this. I can't.

'No, thanks,' Christian replies, distracted.

'Back in a tic.' I quickly make my way through the pool gate and down the stone path to the front door.

Holy SHIT!

I hurry into the house and shut the door behind me, leaning up against it in a panic. What the hell am I going to do with this? I look down at the magazine in my now-sweaty hands. I could tear out the page? It's the centre spread, so that could work. No, there's another feature on the back of one of the pages – what if Christian tries to read it and discovers half of it is missing?

I'll have to bin the whole thing. But where? I can't put it in the kitchen bin. I'll have to walk to the big waste bins down the road. It'll take me a few minutes, so I'm going to have to hurry. I run out through the door, hoping Christian doesn't come back inside and notice my absence.

Johnny Jefferson is one of the world's most recognised celebrities. He'd barely turned twenty before his band, Fence, was catapulted into global superstardom. But three years later, when the band split, Johnny spiralled out of control before falling into a dark depression. It was another two years before he was ready to reinvent himself as a solo artist, but when he did, it was one

15

of the most successful comebacks of all time. Now thirty-three, he's had more platinum-selling records than any other rock star in history.

As for my part in all this – well, before I was stupid enough to mix business with pleasure, I worked for Johnny as his personal assistant. Occasionally I can remember the excitement I felt when I got the job; how thrilling it was being able to tell my best friend Bess that I was going to work for him in LA. She screamed so loudly it almost split my eardrums. I wasn't even a very big Johnny Jefferson fan, unlike Bess. She was always into that alternative-rock stuff, but I was more of a pop girl. Of course I grew to love rock music, mostly because I grew to love my boss.

I met Christian when I was working in LA. He'd known Johnny since childhood. They went to school together, lived close to each other in their hometown of Newcastle upon Tyne, and were best friends for over fifteen years until Johnny was stupid enough to sleep with Christian's girlfriend. They eventually patched things up and became mates again, and that's how Christian ended up with the job of writing his famous friend's biography. I liked Christian instantly. He was such a good guy – not like his pal, who treated women appallingly and yet they still came back for more. I was as bad as any of the groupies, and that's not something I can easily admit. It was so hard to resist him. Of course I knew he was gorgeous – I'd seen countless pictures of him in magazines – but I didn't properly understand his attraction until I met him face to face. I still remember that first time. It was outside by the swimming pool at his LA mansion. At six foot two he was taller than I expected him to be, and his green eyes were almost luminous with the light of the pool reflected in them. His dirty-blond hair fell messily around his chin and he had a few freckles across his nose that I'd never noticed in photographs. I was so on edge that I knocked my beach towel into the water and I recall the muscles on his bare arms flexing as he wrung it out. My eyes were drawn to his famous tattoos, etched into his tanned skin with black ink. I soon found out that he is also incredibly charismatic: rooms fall silent when he walks into them, and something is inexplicably lost when he leaves. Plus, he has an astonishing talent for music. It's not hard to understand how I fell for him.

When things crashed and burned with my boss, Christian and I just kind of fell into step with each other. Christian would probably describe that differently. Apparently he'd had feelings for me for a long time.

I am in love with Christian. I don't need to convince myself of that. And I'm not in love with Johnny anymore. But somewhere deep inside there's a part of me that's connected to him. I wish I could disconnect myself for good. But I can't. I will never be able to. Because my son is his son. I feel so sick I could throw up.

Chapter 3

'Bloody hell, it's hot,' Christian says. We're sitting on the beach near Perpignan. Barney is playing with his new dumper truck in the sand a few feet away and Christian is propped up on his elbows to my left. I'm sitting up so I can keep an eye on my little boy.

'I should introduce a swear box,' I say drily. 'Then you'll be sorry.'

'And you'll be rich.'

'Exactly,' I reply with a grin.

'Shall we go for a swim?' Christian turns to Barney, not waiting for me to answer. 'Barney, do you want to go for a swim? Barney?'

He's too engrossed in his truck to even look up.

'You go,' I say. 'I'll stay with him.'

'No, we should go together as a family.'

A wave of nausea passes through me. I've been feeling off colour ever since the other day, when I saw the picture of Johnny as a child. Luckily, Christian hasn't noticed his magazine is missing. I don't suppose a bandmate's beach snaps are particularly crucial to research.

'Come on, Mummy!' Christian says. He's scooped up a giggling Barney and is now holding his hand down to me. I take it and he pulls me to my feet. He turns and runs towards the water with Barney slung over his shoulder. I follow them, smiling.

Together as a family . . .

It occurs to me as I walk across the hot sand, that I've become very good at lying. What a despicable talent to have. It's not something you can boast about, like being good at languages or playing the piano. I'm a good liar. My parents would be so proud.

Christian runs with Barney into the clear blue water, white foam splashing in their wake and, at the same time, a small voice inside my head wonders if maybe I should lay off myself a little bit. It was an accident. A mistake. I didn't mean to hurt anyone. But if I let all these bad feelings continue to eat me up, that's exactly what I'll end up doing: hurting someone. I push these thoughts to the back of my head, unwilling to contemplate them any further at the moment.

'It's cold!' I gasp, wading into the water.

'Go under quickly,' Christian urges, doing just that and ending up with Barney squealing in his ear.

I duck in up to my neck and quickly burst out of the water again.

'Better?' Christian asks.

'No!'

'Go under again.'

'I think I'll stand here for a bit, thanks.'

He casts his eyes heavenwards, then smiles. 'I like your new bikini, by the way.' It's a gold-coloured one from H&M.

'Thanks. Mum took me birthday shopping in Perpignan last week.'

'You look fit. No one would ever be able to tell you've had a kid.'

I laugh. 'Breastfeeding hasn't entirely killed my boobs, then?'

He chuckles. 'No. Unlike hers . . .'

He discreetly nods towards a middle-aged woman nearby who is tanned a deep bronze and has her naked boobs swinging happily past her ribcage.

I giggle and he pulls me down into the water, kissing me on the lips while I simultaneously breathe in sharply.

'I wish you didn't have to go away again,' I say after a while.

'I know.' He changes the subject. 'Do you want to swim to Mummy?' Christian zooms Barney towards me and I catch him, laughing. He can't talk yet, but he can understand quite a lot. I encircle my son's small waist with my hands and bob him up and down in the water as he kicks furiously. Eventually his kicks subside. We rub our noses together.

'You should do this more often,' Christian says.

'I know,' I reply. 'It didn't take very long to get here, did it?'

'Not with me driving,' he replies. 'You'd have to add at least fifteen minutes onto your time.'

Christian loves cars. I still remember the time he borrowed . . . I sigh. I can't even say his name inside my head without flinching.

'What's up?' Christian asks.

I don't bother to lie. 'I was just remembering the time you drove me to Santa Monica beach.'

'In Johnny's Bugatti?'

20

If Christian notices me flinching again, this time he chooses to ignore it.

'Yeah.'

It was shortly after I'd started working for Johnny in Los Angeles. He told Christian and me to take the day off, so we borrowed his Bugatti Veyron – one of the fastest and most expensive cars in the world – and went out for the day. Christian was beside himself at getting to drive the car. Johnny has several supercars in his garage. At least, he used to. I assume he still does.

I wonder if Christian caught up with him while he was in LA. I don't ask. I never ask. Sometimes he offers up the information, but most of the time he keeps their catch-ups to himself. He knows about my history with Johnny. I think he prefers to pretend there is none.

'Shall we go to the beach bar for lunch?' Christian asks.

'Sure.'

We get back to Cucugnan in the early afternoon. Barney has fallen asleep in the car so I transfer him to his cot and then go to the bathroom with the intention of taking a shower. I open the window to let in some air and see that Christian is in the pool.

'Come in, it's beautiful,' he calls.

I didn't bother to get changed out of my bikini for the car journey home so all I have to do is grab Barney's baby monitor and step back into my flip-flops by the front door to avoid scalding my feet on the scorching stone tiles. I wander around to the side of the house, untying my black sarong as I go and trying not to disturb the bees buzzing away at the lavender lining the path. Several yellow butterflies flit around the purple flowers as I pass and I breathe in deeply and smile to myself. At moments like these, it's impossible not to feel happy. I walk to the steps and go in. The cool water of the pool takes my breath away, but it's almost instantly lovely. I swim over to Christian and he puts his hands on my waist. He bends down for a kiss, and for the first time in what seems like ages, I kiss him back.

'I love having sex outside in the hot sun,' he says later.

'You say that like you've done it often.' I tie my sarong back around my waist. Christian is still lying naked on the sunlounger in front of me. It's just as well this house isn't overlooked by the neighbours. Christian smirks.

'What? Have you done it often?' I pry, curious now, but not jealous.

'Once or twice,' he replies with a grin that implies it was substantially more than that.

'Who with? Clare?' That was his last serious girlfriend. 'Actually, I don't want to know,' I decide.

'Haven't you?' He turns the tables on me.

'No.' I rack my brain to be sure. No, not with Johnny. And most certainly not with the other guys I've been out with in my life.

'That's a travesty. I'll have to help you make up for lost time,' he teases.

'That's not going to be easy with Barney around,' I comment, before nodding down at him. 'You should get dressed. He'll be awake soon.'

He sighs. 'Don't you ever wish it was just the two of us?'

'That's a terrible thing to say!' I exclaim.

'I don't mean it terribly. I don't know...' He doesn't continue, instead rising to his feet and putting on his almost-dry swimming trunks.

I stand and stare at him. 'Do you wish we had more time to ourselves?'

'Yeah, just to talk and – you know, without being interrupted. I wish our parents lived closer.'

'It would be nice to have them around to help more,' I agree. 'Are your mum and dad still planning a trip?'

'I think so, but Dad's really busy at work at the moment.'

'Hasn't he found a replacement for Joel yet?'

'No.'

Christian's dad, Eugen, owns an electrical store in Newcastle. He used to run it with Christian's younger brother, Joel, but Joel quit the business recently to go and live with his girlfriend in her native Australia.

'Mum might come out by herself. She's having withdrawal symptoms from her grandson.'

Mandy, his mum, is besotted with Barney. If she knew he wasn't hers... It's too horrendous to contemplate.

'That'd be nice,' I say. I like Christian's mum, feisty though she may be. She's from Newcastle, whereas Christian's dad hails from Sweden. It still impresses me that Christian is bilingual.

I really should practise my French...

A noise comes from the nearby baby monitor.

'I'll get him,' I say, heading inside to retrieve my little sleepy-head. He's lying awake in his cot, staring at the colourful boat mobile above his head. 'Come on, you.' He grips me around my neck with his chubby fingers and presses his face into my shoulder as I walk back down the corridor. A powerful wave of love throbs through me. I can barely imagine my life before he came along. The thought of being without him now . . .

That's not to say I've found motherhood easy. The first few months came as a complete shock. Christian was working so hard and I ended up doing the lion's share of the work – both with the baby and around the house. I cried a lot. I was exhausted beyond belief from getting up in the night to breastfeed, yet I would still lie awake thinking about everything. Even though Barney was born with a head full of dark hair and people said he looked like Christian, I could never be sure. His eyes were blue. Maybe they'd turn brown like Mummy and Daddy's, as everyone presumed, but I used to torment myself that they'd turn green instead. Which of course they did.

Chapter 4

'Did Christian get away okay?' Mum asks a few days later. Christian set off this morning to return to LA for tour rehearsals. He'll be there for a week.

'Yes,' I reply into the receiver. We're talking on the phone.

'Barney will miss him,' Mum says.

'Not as much as I'll miss him.'

'Oh dear, I hope you don't mind me not coming.'

'No, of course not. Don't worry.'

I asked my parents if they'd keep me company while Christian was abroad this time, but Mum had some important bridge game to attend.

'It's a shame he has to be away so often,' she comments. 'I don't like the thought of him mingling with all those sex, drugs and rock 'n' roll types. Why he can't just stick to writing fiction, I don't know.'

'Yes, you do know,' I say with annoyance. 'He didn't get a new book deal.'

'But why? I thought his first one was quite good.'

'I thought it was great!' I hear my dad chip in, in the

background. 'I want to know what happened to Dr Whatshisface!'

'Tell Dad he'll find out in March.'

'You'll find out in March, apparently,' I hear my mum say.

'March?' my dad exclaims. 'That's almost a year away! I thought his next one was coming out in September?'

'Put Dad on,' I tell my mum. She does so. I explain: 'The first one came out last September and flopped, so his publishers want to try releasing the next one in a different season.'

Around the time I found out I was pregnant, Christian's Johnny Jefferson biography was published and was a huge success. His publishers had released it in the autumn against the other heavy hitters in the lead-up to Christmas, and a year later, they assumed his first book in his new crime series would be able to hack it in the same competitive market. They were wrong.

They've pushed back the release of his second book to next March and are yet to offer him a new book deal. His dream of writing fiction has had to be put on hold for now, hence his saying yes to another celebrity biography.

'I'm sure it'll be a huge success!' Dad booms, slightly too buoyantly.

'Thanks, Dad,' I reply, with a small smile that he can't see.

'Give me the phone,' I hear my mum say. She comes back on the line. 'Let me know if you want me to come down on Saturday.'

'No, it's okay, Mum. Christian will be back on Monday so it's probably not worth you making the trip for the sake of a day and a half. I'll take Barney to the beach or to a playground or some-thing. I'll be alright.'

'Call me if you want to chat.'

'I will do if I can find the time,' I promise. We hang up and I sigh loudly. 'Alone Again' . . . That bloody song is driving me nuts. I switch on the radio, hoping to find something else to get stuck in my mind. An instantly recognisable tune fills the living room and a shiver travels all the way up my spine and into my head. I fumble for the off switch, but it's too late. I've heard it now. The damage is done.

That was the song Johnny wrote for me.

He said he loved me. He once told me he'd never loved anyone.

The phone rings, making me jump. I snatch it up.

'Hello?'

'Meg?'

'Bess!' I exclaim. It's so good to hear from my friend.

'Hey, how are you?'

'I'm alright.' I sigh, unable to project enthusiasm into my voice.

'You've heard, then,' she says.

'Heard what?'

'About Johnny?'

Silence.

'Oh, you haven't heard,' she says.

Apart from Christian, Bess is the only other person who knows about my relationship with Johnny – if you can call it that. There were rumours in the industry when I quit working for him so suddenly, but no one knows for sure what happened, and my confidentiality clause prevents me from telling anyone, even if I wanted to. I shouldn't have told Bess, but I couldn't help myself.

'Tell me,' I urge Bess, dread seeping into the pit of my stomach.

She cuts to the chase. 'He and his girlfriend are both in hospital after overdosing.'

My heart jumps.

'It was an accident, apparently.'

I can't speak.

'Meg?'

'I didn't even know he had a girlfriend,' I say dully.

'They met in rehab.'

'Fat lot of good that did them.' I manage a bitter laugh.

'Are you okay?' Bess's voice is hesitant.

'I'm fine,' I reply curtly. 'Nothing to do with me.'

'I know you don't mean that,' she says gently.

'Stop. Just stop,' I warn.

'He's alright,' she says. 'In case you want to know.'

'I don't.'

She continues, 'They're saying he'll be going back into rehab.'

'He should never have left the bloody place,' I mutter. 'Bess, I've got to go. Barney has woken up. I'll speak to you soon.'

'Okay. Lots of love.'

'You too.'

I end the call. The baby monitor is silent. Barney hasn't woken up – that was a lie. Another one.

I stare out of the French windows to the mountains in the distance.

I was right to choose Christian . . . Johnny wouldn't have changed for me.

Or maybe he would have . . .

No. I made the right decision. It's just a tragedy biology made the wrong one.

The baby could have been Christian's. It's possible, even

though we used protection. I wanted it to be Christian's. I knew Johnny would have run a mile if I'd told him I was pregnant and that the baby was his, or at least might have been his. The same sentence would have probably gone down equally as well with Christian: 'Hey, honey, you know that kid you've always wanted? Well, get this! I'm knocked up! And the good news is, it *might* be yours!' I don't think so. Christian would have joined Johnny on his marathon to get as far away from me as possible. Don't get me wrong: I would have deserved it. But my baby wouldn't have. And I wanted to give my child the best possible upbringing I could hope for. Christian is a good dad – when he's around. Johnny would have been a terrible one.

I'd better not turn on the radio for the next few days. They'll be playing his songs incessantly as a result of this. I should leave the telly off, too. I glance at my laptop. No. No. No.

My resolve lasts until late that evening, when Barney is tucked up in bed and I still haven't heard from Christian. He was supposed to call me when he landed, but he hasn't, and I've allowed my bitterness to eat away at me so it's easier to justify my actions. I turn on my laptop, my head tingling with anticipation.

Google: Johnny Jefferson.

Millions of hits come up. I nervously click on the first news link:

Superstar Johnny Jefferson and his partner, Dana Reed, have been hospitalised following a suspected overdose. The pair were discovered yesterday morning at Jefferson's Beverly Hills mansion. His manager confirmed that the overdose was accidental.

Stupid, stupid idiot!

How could he do this to himself?

I saw at first hand the effects drugs had on Johnny. It got to a point where he was in such a bad way that I could bear it no longer. I took him to a house in the Yorkshire Dales in the north of England and made him go cold turkey. It wasn't the smartest idea I'd ever had, but it worked. For a while, at least.

A memory comes back to me of sitting in front of the log fire in the house. His green eyes staring into mine, his lips trailing down my neck . . . I shiver.

Stop. Stop thinking about it.

I can't.

His warm chest pressing into me . . . my fingers tracing the tattoo across his navel: '*I hurt myself today, to see if I still feel . . .*'

'Johnny Cash lyric,' he explained.

'You wouldn't ever hurt yourself now, would you, Johnny?'

Stupid, stupid!

Another memory slams into me, this time about when he came to see me after he found out I was dating Christian.

'Nutmeg . . .'

That was my nickname. The name he gave to me.

He runs his thumb down the side of my neck.

'Stop it!' I bat his hand away. 'Why are you doing this? I'm happy, Johnny. I like Christian.'

'There!' He practically shouts, pointing at me. 'You said "like"!'

I step backwards. 'I love him,' I say determinedly.

He shakes his head and leans back against the corridor wall. 'You said "like",' he says again, this time more slowly. 'You *love* me.'

*　　*　　*

Sobs well up inside me.

I still love him. I love him even now.

I cry my heart out, stifling the noise with my fingers so as not to wake my little boy. Oh, God, what am I going to do?

It's too late . . . It's too late . . .

I cry for a long, long time, curled up on the sofa as the sun dips below the horizon and the mountains change in colour from sunset orange to pitch black. Eventually my tears subside, but my curiosity doesn't. I want to find out about Dana Reed.

I click on another link.

They met in rehab back in March during Johnny's third stint there. Relationships in rehab are discouraged, but Johnny and Dana flouted that rule. There's a picture of them coming out of a club in the early hours of the morning a few weeks ago. She has long, dark hair and is wearing a lot of make-up: black eyeliner around her eyes, heavy metallic black eye shadow and red lipstick. Her skin is pale, considering she lives in LA, and Johnny towers above her so she must be petite. She's beautiful, in a rock-chick kind of way. She suits him, I realise, and jealousy surges through me. I angrily rub away my tears and read on.

She's an up-and-coming singer songwriter who, according to the music press, is the Next Big Thing. She's twenty-five, eight years younger than Johnny and a year younger than me. They haven't been apart since they met – there have been no rumours of Johnny messing around. 'Could she finally be The One?' one journalist asks. 'They're a bad influence on each other. It will all end in tears,' another states.

They got that right.

I'm done. I've had enough. I push the laptop lid down and put the machine back on the side-table before wearily getting to my feet.

That's the reason why I don't do this very often.

Chapter 5

The next morning, Barney rouses me from a deep sleep. I lie there in bed, as exhaustion weighs down every part of my body. I would give anything to be able to stay here all day, but, after a while, his happy babbling turns into whining and I drag myself from bed and stumble through to him.

'Good morning.' I try to sound bright and breezy.

His face breaks into a toothy grin and all my bad feelings instantly evaporate. He's the most important person in my life. I can't fall back into that black hole. I lift him up onto the baby-change station in his room and proceed to change his nappy.

Last night seems surreal. I feel strangely detached about the whole thing now. Johnny's just another idiotic celebrity to end up in hospital after a drug overdose. Of course I don't still love him.

Weight lifts from my stomach. I smile down at Barney – a genuine smile.

'Shall we go up into the village and get some croissants for breakfast?' I don't expect him to answer, but I like talking to him in any case.

I throw on some shorts and a T-shirt and quickly get Barney dressed before buckling him into his buggy and bumping him down the stone steps to the front gate. Cucugnan is a beautiful, medieval village situated on a hill. Said hill is small in comparison to the mountains that encircle it, but it certainly doesn't feel like it as I manoeuvre the buggy up the steep road towards the village centre. We pass the town hall and post office on the left, and a bar and a couple of shops on the right and then the road starts to wind as we make our way up to the seventeenth-century windmill at the top of the hill. Sometimes there's a break between the buildings and I can see the mountains beyond. I use these viewpoints as an excuse to catch my breath and let the burning sensation in my thighs die down. No wonder Christian was able to comment on my figure the other day – these hills are hardcore.

Long before we reach our destination we can hear the machinery whirring and chugging as it grinds the flour. The bakery is located right underneath the old windmill and it looks like something out of *Elle Deco* with its wooden beams and cupboards painted in neutral tones. Classy blackboards detail current specials, and cakes, biscuits, bread and almond meringues are laid out on display tables at the entrance. I go inside to order, then return to the bright sunlight with our purchase. There are bench tables outside, but instead of sitting at one we head past the windmill and around the corner to the rocks at the very top of the hill. I have to park the buggy with the brake on and carry Barney and our breakfast the rest of the way. I pause for a moment when I realise there's a blonde girl sitting on the dry yellow grass in the distance. She has her back to us and is facing the surrounding mountains. It dawns on me that she's doing yoga.

I reluctantly drag my eyes away and sit on a rock, nursing Barney on my lap. The morning sun is casting a glow over the mountains and down below there's a patchwork of lime-green vineyards and the small village cemetery. Opening the paper bag from the bakery, I pull out a biscuit – I forgot they do croissants only on weekends – and hand Barney a small piece. We can have some proper breakfast when we get back home.

This area is full of crumbly old castles. I stare up at the Château de Quéribus on top of a mountain peak. Sometimes I feel like I've been transported back in time to a place where Aragorn is king, and elves and goblins roam the land. Yes, I know *The Lord of The Rings* is fictional, but, honestly, living here it's hard to believe it. Anyway, Aragon did rule this land. Aragon as in Spain, not Aragorn as in sexy Viggo Mortensen. I've read up on my history, I'll have you know. There's nothing else to do here.

Joke.

Barney wriggles on my lap. I suppose we should set off home.

I get to my feet and turn around, clocking the lone blonde doing yoga. I feel envious. What it must be like to sit up here doing yoga with no concerns, no big secrets that could destroy a family . . . It's so beautiful here, so inspirational.

I wonder why Christian never comes up here to write.

Johnny would . . .

I scramble over the rocks with Barney in my arms and buckle him back into his buggy. Then I set off down the steep hill towards home, trying not to think about anything.

It's quicker on the return journey, although my arms feel like they're being pulled out of their sockets with the weight of the buggy and gravity. I'm going to end up like Barney's favourite Mr Men character: Mr Tickle with his 'extraordinary long arms'.

The smile on my face suddenly feels like it's been slapped off and I come to an abrupt stop outside a shop. Johnny's face blazes out from multiple newspapers. I stare, sickened, at the front-page photos of him leaving hospital.

He looks awful, pale and deathly. He's not wearing his trade-mark sunglasses and it doesn't help his appearance. I don't imagine he had his sunglasses on when they found him.

I put my head down and push on, but the image won't leave me. Thoughts buzz around my mind like persistent blowflies.

I wonder who did find him. Would it have been his lovely cook, Rosa? I was so fond of her – and she adored Johnny. It would have killed her to see him like that. Or perhaps it was one of his security guards. Then there was Santiago, the pool boy, who became a friend of mine. I wonder what happened to him after I left.

Barney falls asleep on the way home and I should wake him so I don't mess up his routine, but I don't have the energy. I park him in the hallway and slump onto the sofa in the living room, crossing my arms over my face and lying there for a while, trying to let my mind go blank. Fat chance.

Eventually I get up and go outside and around the corner to the pool. I kick off my shoes and stand on the first step, staring at the water sparkling in the hot sunshine. And then I'm back in LA again, looking down at the spectacular view of the City of Angels from Johnny's super-cool mansion. It was my first day. Johnny was supposed to be away on a writing trip, but he turned up after I'd fallen asleep by the pool.

'Is this what I pay you for?' he drawled. Later he removed his black T-shirt to reveal a toned, tanned torso decorated with the occasional tattoo and I'd thought: maybe I have a crush on Johnny Jefferson, after all.

I wonder if he's okay. I get a sudden image inside my head of me calling him to ask if he's alright.

Crazy! I could never do that.

But I want to.

I wonder if Christian has spoken to him. I should ring him and ask.

No! You can have nothing to do with Johnny Jefferson – ever again!

I'm a mess. I can't bear this.

I wish Bess hadn't told me. But then I still would have seen it on the front of those newspapers today, not to mention heard it on the telly and on the radio. There's no escaping news this huge about a star so big.

I wonder if Christian has seen him. They've been best friends for years. He wouldn't have stayed away, surely. How is Christian feeling? He must be upset by all of this. I should call him. I *should* call him.

I go back inside and pick up the phone before I can talk myself out of it. Christian answers on the fourth ring.

'Hello?'

'It's me.'

'Hi.' He sounds tired.

'Are you okay?' I ask.

'I'm knackered,' he replies. 'Have you seen the news about Johnny?'

Good, I don't have to ask. 'Yes. Have you spoken to him?'

'I'm at his house now.'

I wasn't expecting that. I don't know how to feel about it. I feel like I should be there, too. The three of us, how we used to be, when it was all platonic and I was just nice, dependable Meg.

'It's the same old shit, Meg. Only this time he's got an accomplice.'

'Have you met her?' I ask of Dana.

'I've met her in the past, yeah.'

During another visit he failed to mention. I try not to let it bother me.

'What's she like?'

'Full of herself. I think she fancies the pair of them as being the next Kurt and Courtney. It's a fucking joke. I'm sick of it!'

'Hey . . .' I say gently.

'Yeah, I know, he's my oldest friend and all that, but when's it going to end? I've had it up to my eyeballs.'

'Who are you talking to?' I hear Johnny ask in the background and my heart jumps into my throat.

'I've gotta go,' Christian says brusquely to me. 'I'll call you later.' He hangs up.

Later I text Christian, asking him to call me back when he has a chance. It's seven o'clock the following morning before he finally does.

'I'm off to bed,' he tells me. 'It's been a long day.'

'What time is it there?' I ask groggily. Barney is having a rare lie-in.

'Eleven.'

I prop myself up on my pillows. 'How's Johnny?' It feels strange to say his name out loud – especially to Christian.

'He's feeling a bit better. He's going to go back into rehab tomorrow.'

'That's good.'

'Yeah. I'm not sure if his heart is really in it, but it's better than nothing.'

'Is she going to go, too?'

'Who knows? Probably. I think it's only her manager who kept her away from him today.'

'How's Bill?' Bill is Johnny's manager.

'He's fine. Water off a duck's back. You know Bill.'

Yes, I do. In fact, he probably looks upon this as good publicity. Not that Johnny needs any more publicity.

'Who found him?' I ask.

'Rosa.'

Aah, so it *was* Rosa. 'How is she?'

'Quiet.'

'That's worrying,' I comment. Rosa used to be anything but. 'What actually happened? How did he do it?'

'He reckons he took a dodgy "e", but he'd mixed a few things. It could have been anything.'

'Did she take the same drugs?'

'Seems so.' Christian sighs. 'Listen, Meg, I'd better get some sleep. Johnny wants me to wake him up early if we're going to do this rehab thing.'

'Are you staying at his house?' I ask in surprise. I'd assumed he'd gone back to his hotel.

'Yep. In the gold room, as usual.'

It's the room he always used to stay in. I remember Johnny once telling him he could have any room he wanted: 'Except for Meg's. Keep your hands off my staff.'

It seems like another lifetime away.

Then I'm transported again, into *my* room. My room was

white, all white. The windows looked out onto green, leafy trees, and inside there was a super-king-sized bed with a pure white bedspread, floor-to-ceiling white lacquer wardrobes and an enormous en suite with dazzling white stone lining every surface . . . It was beautiful.

'I want you to come back to LA with me as my girlfriend, Meg. Come and live with me.'

I shake my head quickly, trying to rid myself of the memory, but I can't. Suddenly I'm looking into his piercing green eyes and he's asking me to leave Christian and choose him instead.

It was everything I'd ever wanted – once. To be the girl that changed Johnny Jefferson's wild-boy ways. But he'd left it too late. And now it seems that there's no end to his downward spiral.

Chapter 6

Christian returns the following week. I've kept tabs on the internet so that I can avoid constantly asking my boyfriend for news about my former lover, but all has been quiet. Dana went to her parents' place in Montana to recuperate, and Johnny has been holed up in rehab. Christian cracked on with his work and we settled back into our unconventional routine.

In the middle of June, Bess calls to ask if Christian, Barney and I fancy meeting her in Barcelona for her birthday at the end of the month. I broach the subject with Christian over coffee outside on the terrace. 'We still haven't been and it's only a couple of hours away.'

The corners of Christian's mouth turn down. 'Contour Lines will have started the European leg of their tour by then. I've been meaning to tell you.'

'Oh.'

'Sorry,' he says. 'But you and Barney could go?'

Within days, Bess has booked her flight to Barcelona, and Christian has surprised me with a weekend's stay for Bess, Barney and me at one of the city's top hotels.

He's due to fly out to Austria on Monday, but a phone call on Friday night completely scuppers those plans. As soon as I see his face, I know instantly that something is wrong. Very wrong.

'What?' he asks.

Johnny? Is it Johnny?

'Oh, no . . .' He clutches the receiver with shaking fingers, his face creased with pain.

'What's wrong?' I ask urgently, sick to the pit of my stomach.

He doesn't answer, too caught up in what the person on the other end of the line is saying.

Christian drops the phone to the floor with a clatter and buries his face in his hands. I quickly pick it up and speak into the receiver.

'Hello? Who is this?'

'It's Anton.' Christian's older brother. He sounds upset.

'What's wrong?'

'It's Mum.'

His next words send a chill through me: 'She's dead.'

Mandy Pettersson was killed simply crossing the road. She had nipped out between a small break in the traffic and didn't see the motorcycle that hit her – it wasn't even going very fast – but the impact knocked her into the path of an oncoming lorry. She died instantly.

'I'm so sorry,' I tell Anton, going to Christian and putting my arm around his broad shoulders. He's staring ahead in a daze. 'Do you know when the funeral will be?'

'No, not yet. Joel has to get back here from Australia. Call me tomorrow; we should know more then.'

'Okay, I will. How is your dad?'

Anton's voice breaks. 'He's in shock.'

'I'll let you go,' I say gently, rubbing Christian's arm.

'Okay. Bye,' he manages to say before hanging up.

I turn to look at Christian. He meets my eyes and his instantly fill with tears.

'I'm so sorry,' I say, and then he breaks down. I hug him tightly while he sobs into my shoulder. 'I'm so sorry.'

Two days later, we drive to Barcelona. Not to enjoy a mini-break, but to fly home to the UK. There aren't any direct flights from Perpignan and this was the next best option. We've left Barney with my parents in France. It's the first time I've been away from him and already I hate it. I'll stay in Newcastle with Christian's family for only a few days before flying home to him. Christian will need to be there for at least another week to support his dad and brothers.

It's a bright, sunny day when we touch down at Newcastle airport, in total contrast to how we're both feeling. The funeral is the day after tomorrow and we've opted to hire a car, refusing Anton's offer of a lift because we figure he's got enough on his plate. We're staying at Christian's house in Longbenton, which is about a twenty-minute drive east from the airport and ten minutes north of Newcastle upon Tyne. Christian is silent as he navigates the roads. He's barely spoken since he found out. It's a good thing that Barney isn't here. He may be only young, but I'm sure he understands that something isn't right with Daddy. It's heartbreaking to think that my son won't remember Mandy when he's older, especially considering how much she loved him. A lump forms in my throat as Christian pulls up outside his childhood home.

I still remember the first time I came here. Anton was getting married to Vanessa, and Mandy had given Christian grief about not bringing a guest to the wedding. He'd just broken up with his girlfriend and that had messed up the table plan, apparently, so he invited me to keep his mum off his back. We were only housemates at the time, but Mandy put us in his bedroom together, convinced we were more than friends. Christian was mortified, but I found the whole thing amusing.

Oh, it's so sad . . .

We walk up the front path towards the semi-detached, red-brick house. Anton opens the door to us, his face weary. It always surprises me how different Christian looks to his brothers. Anton and Joel take after their dad: distinctly Swedish-looking with blond hair and blue eyes. Christian, with his dark looks, took after his mum.

Anton gives me a hug, then turns to embrace his brother.

'Dad's in the living room,' he says, breaking away.

'How is he?' Christian asks quietly.

'The same,' comes the reply.

Hours pass and I don't know what to do with myself. Christian's dad can barely speak. He sits in the living room, staring at photos of Mandy with tears trailing down his cheeks. Anton has had to leave to get home to Vanessa, who's eight months pregnant. I decide that my role will be tea-maker, and experience a sting when I remember that Mandy never used to let anyone else into her kitchen – to make toast, tea or whatever. She always did everything. I don't know how Eugen, Christian's dad, will cope now she's gone.

The next morning, Joel returns from Australia, sans girlfriend. He's always been a joker, but there's no laughing today.

The funeral is tomorrow. Guests are coming back to the house afterwards so I busy myself cleaning and taking care of the catering. In the afternoon, Christian joins me on a trip to the supermarket – he needs to escape the house. I try to stay upbeat for him, but it's hard. That night he faces away from me in bed and I know he wants to be left alone, but the following morning he comes into the kitchen while I'm making sandwiches and wraps his arms around my waist from behind.

'Thank you,' he murmurs into my hair. I turn around and give him a hug, pressing my face into his chest. I hate seeing him so sad.

It's Tuesday, the day of the funeral. We travel to the cemetery in a procession of black cars and walk into the church behind the pallbearers: friends and colleagues of Christian and his brothers. Mandy's coffin is shiny and black with a wreath of white flowers on the top. There's a framed photo of her on the altar, a snapshot of her laughing, as she so often did. The casket is closed. Her injuries were too severe to permit an open one.

Everyone is in tears during the service and I'm thankful that Barney isn't here. He wouldn't understand such sadness at his age, but as I sit next to Vanessa, her hands cradling her bump, I miss him intensely. It's like there's a hole in my heart, where he should be.

I once used to say the same thing about Johnny.

I reach across and squeeze Christian's hand. He squeezes mine back, hard.

After the service we return to Eugen's house for the wake. I reprise my role of caterer and spend the next two hours with a tray superglued to my hand as I offer sandwiches and sausage rolls to friends and family. I'm glad to have something to do. Eventually people begin to leave. I refuse Vanessa's offer of help and insist she goes home to put her feet up, and finally only Joel, Christian and Eugen remain. I make them tea to take into the living room and then go into the kitchen to clear up, promising Christian that I'm happy to do the task by myself. To be honest, I want be alone for a while. I don't know Christian's family well. Many of them came from Sweden and don't speak much English. Christian is bilingual so he's had no trouble conversing, but the small talk for me has been exhausting, however unkind it feels to admit that.

I scrape the remnants of food off plates and stack the dishwasher. I set it going and then pause for a moment to lean against the sink and remember Mandy. I can almost hear her laughing.

The doorbell rings, snapping me back to life.

'I'll get it,' I call into the living room, the murmur of male voices halting briefly. I can see an outline of a person through the stained-glass door and wonder who would call at this hour after a funeral. It's only eight o'clock, but everyone went home ages ago. I open the door and my heart almost beats out of my chest when I see Johnny standing there.

I stare up at him in shock. He seems taller than I remember, even though I know he's six foot two compared to my five-foot-seven-inch frame, and somehow he also appears broader. The fact that he's wearing a chunky black coat in the middle of summer could have something to do with it. His face is tanned and his dark blond hair is as dishevelled as it ever was, falling to just below his chin. Even in the lacklustre light of the hallway, his eyes have an intense greenness to them.

He mirrors my shocked expression, but quickly gets himself

together. 'Are you going to let me in, or what?' He glances over his shoulder with an air of impatience.

I find my voice. 'Of course, yes.' He'll be worried that the press have tailed him. I step aside and look down at his beaten-up Chelsea boots as he walks over the threshold, the smell of fresh cigarette smoke wafting past me. What am I going to say to him?

'Where's Christian?' he asks, not meeting my eyes. I'm caught off guard by the bluntness of his tone.

'In the living room,' I reply, shutting the door behind him. I begin to follow him, but something makes me stop. Heart still in my throat, I go instead to the kitchen, trying to block out the sound of Johnny's now warm and sympathetic voice as he greets his oldest friend.

I face the kitchen sink, clutching the edge of the countertop. My hands are shaking.

Snap out of it, Meg. Snap out of it.

I force myself to reach for a glass, with the intention of washing it, but I have to rest my hand back on the countertop. I feel too weak to move. I need to sit down, but I daren't move my feet.

I haven't seen him for almost two years and he's treating me like a stranger. No, worse: he's treating me like an enemy.

I want to get away from here.

No. I want to stay. I want to see him again.

I hear footsteps behind me and I spin around, expecting it to be Johnny, but it's Christian.

'Are you alright?' he asks, concerned.

'Yes, yes, I'm fine,' I reply quickly, blood rushing into my face. 'How are you?'

'I'm okay,' he says slowly. 'Would you mind making Johnny a cup of coffee?'

'Of course, yes.' Like a woman possessed, I clatter a cup out of the cupboard and switch on the coffee machine.

'Are you sure you don't want a hand out here?' Christian indicates the mess in the kitchen. The plates may be in the dishwasher, but there are still loads of glasses to wash by hand, not to mention serving bowls and trays.

'No, no, I'm fine,' I reply, dementedly trying to shake a coffee capsule out of the large jar beside the Nespresso machine.

'Why don't we do the rest in the morning?' Christian suggests. 'I'll help you. Come into the living room. You haven't seen Johnny for ages.'

'No, I'm fine,' I say again, continuing to shake the jar like a nutcase until I manage to retrieve one of the extra-strong blends.

'Okay. Only if you're su—'

'I'm sure,' I cut him off. 'I'll bring his coffee through in a minute.'

He leaves, but my pace doesn't slow. I lift up the lever and insert the capsule, then push it back down again and press the green button. Black coffee begins to fill the cup. Black, no sugar. I remember.

There's pressure against my head. I feel like I'm in a vice.

I take the cup with my shaking fingers and, on autopilot, enter the living room. Johnny is relaxing in an armchair in the far corner. He's taken off his coat and is wearing skinny black jeans and a faded black T-shirt with a yellow spark plug on the front. It looks vintage and is tight against his torso. He's leaning back, one foot resting on the opposite knee, but he sits up as I approach. His fingers touch mine as I try to relinquish the cup. I almost drop it.

'Whoa,' he says.

'Sorry,' I murmur, turning around and going back through to the kitchen.

'Do you need some help out there?' Joel calls after me.

'No, it's okay,' I call back.

My fingers are burning. For a moment I put it down to the heat of the coffee cup, but then I realise Johnny's touch is to blame.

I stand in front of the sink for at least five minutes before I feel able to get on with the washing-up. After a short while, Christian returns.

'Come and sit down,' he urges.

'No, no, it's okay. I'd rather get it done.'

'Meg,' he says firmly. 'I insist.' He switches on the kettle. 'I'll make you a cuppa. It'll be the first time I've been allowed to make one in this kitchen in thirty-three years.'

We glance at each other and both our features soften. He takes my hands and looks at me directly.

'It's okay,' he says. 'I know this is hard for you.'

'It can't be easy for you, either,' I reply. Whoever wants to be in the same room as their girlfriend and their girlfriend's ex? Chuck in the fact that the ex is the person-in-question's best mate and it's even higher on one's list of things to avoid.

Christian shrugs. 'We were going to have to do this sometime. He's my oldest friend and you're my girlfriend, the mother of my child. On that subject, I want him to meet Barney one day, too. I think enough water has passed under the bridge . . .'

The vice cranks up its pressure on my head. The kettle boils, thankfully distracting him from the look of pain on my face.

Joel makes room for me on the sofa so I sit between him and

Christian. My legs are bare; I'm wearing a black dress and I took my heels off ages ago. Detached from reality, I feel strangely relieved that I painted my toenails before we left France. I stare down at my mug. It's bright yellow and there's a small chip on the rim. It's one of the old, non-matching mugs that have been in Christian's family for years. The nice ones are all in the dishwasher.

'I heard the news about you ending up in hospital, son.' My eyes shoot towards Johnny as Eugen speaks these words. 'Not good, my boy, not good,' Christian's dad continues.

Johnny shifts in his seat. I try to tear my eyes away, back to my chipped yellow mug, but I can't. They're fixed on him.

'It was a stupid mistake,' he says.

'Mistake?' Eugen scoffs. 'Come on, now.'

I get the feeling that Eugen doesn't cut Johnny any slack, no matter how rich or successful he's become since he and Christian were little.

'Ah, man . . .' Johnny leans forward to rest his elbows on his knees. 'Not a mistake, but, well, stupid.' His accent has an American twang to it, but he's still unmistakably a British lad from up north.

'You got that right,' Eugen snaps.

Johnny says nothing, and it seems that he respects Christian's old man. I've never seen them together before.

'Yeah, aren't you supposed to be still in rehab in LA?' Joel chips in.

'I got a day pass,' Johnny drawls in his direction.

'I hope you're going back,' Eugen interrupts.

Johnny shrugs. 'Maybe.'

'No "maybe" about it,' barks Eugen.

Christian nudges me and I glance at him to see a small smirk on his face. This exchange doesn't go unnoticed by Johnny, who raises his eyebrows at Christian. He doesn't look at me.

'How's it going with Contour Lines?' Johnny asks Christian.

'You trying to change the subject?' Christian teases.

'Damn right I am,' Johnny replies, pursing his lips at Eugen.

Christian chuckles and launches into an easy conversation. I'm vaguely pleased for him and his family that they have this distraction, even though I'm finding it hard to manage the simple task of sipping my tea. Johnny is steadfastly avoiding eye contact with me.

After a while, Eugen sighs. 'I think I'm going to turn in.' He heaves himself out of his chair. Johnny crosses the room to shake his hand.

'I really am sorry,' he says, awkwardly folding his arms in front of himself.

'I know you are,' Eugen replies, looking down.

'I wish I could have made the funeral,' Johnny adds, looking more sincere than I think I've ever seen him.

'Don't worry,' Eugen replies. 'I understand. No more getting into trouble!'

'Yeah, okay.'

'If Mandy were here she'd give you a battering.' We all smile sadly at the thought, then Eugen sniffs. 'I'm sorry,' he says, his eyes filling with tears. He brushes them away, but they make their descent down his cheeks. 'I'll see you all in the morning,' he says.

On a sudden impulse, I stand up. 'Let me see you upstairs.' I take his hand.

'No, no,' he brushes me off.

'Please,' I insist. I want to tidy up a bit and make his bed for him, even though he's about to get into it. More than anything, I don't want him to walk into his marital bedroom alone on the night of his wife's funeral.

'You're a good girl,' he says, squeezing my hand and letting it go. I glance at Johnny and at that exact same moment, he locks eyes with me, sending shockwaves down my spine. We quickly look away from each other as Christian gets to his feet.

'Thanks, love,' he murmurs, rubbing my arm affectionately.

I turn away and hurry up the stairs, leaving Eugen to say good-night to his sons.

Johnny used to call me a good girl. Maybe I was, once. Not anymore. Eugen is sadly mistaken.

When I return to the living room, fifteen minutes later, Christian and Johnny are alone. I hear a clinking sound coming from the kitchen and realise that Joel is washing up the last of the glasses.

'Sit down,' Christian commands, before I can leave the room. 'You've done enough today.'

I take a deep breath and do as he says. Upstairs, my whole body felt awash with exhaustion. I probably should have gone to bed myself, but the pull to return to the living room was too strong.

'I've been telling Johnny about our pad in Cucugnan,' Christian says. 'I said he should come to see us sometime.'

'Oh, right,' I manage to choke out. Johnny is watching my reaction. Hopefully he knows me well enough to understand he's not welcome.

'Are you working, Meg?' Johnny asks, and I sense that he's trying to act normal for Christian's sake.

'No. Being a mum keeps me busy enough,' I reply, trying to inject some nonchalance into my tone. I should feel pleased that he's not avoiding eye contact anymore, but I feel disconcerted instead.

'She won't trust anyone else with Barney,' Christian explains, patting my knee.

'Where is he at the moment?' Johnny asks.

'With Meg's parents,' Christian replies. 'Toddlers and funerals don't really mix.'

'How old is he now?' Johnny enquires, as though making polite conversation.

'He's just turned one.' Thankfully, Christian answers again, because my entire body has gone rigid.

'Oh, happy birthday for whenever,' Johnny says, nonplussed. 'I should have sent a card.'

The sound of breaking glass comes from the kitchen, followed in quick succession by Joel cursing. Christian puts his arm out to hold me back. 'I'll go,' he says. I grip his hand tightly – I don't want to be left alone with the man who was once the love of my life – but Christian gently extricates himself, gets to his feet and leaves the room.

I stay where I am, racked with tension. Johnny is the one to break the awkward silence.

'Terrible about Mrs Pettersson,' he says.

'Awful.' At last, something we agree on. Hang on . . . 'Mrs Pettersson?' I tease. 'Didn't you call her Mandy?'

He shrugs. 'No.'

'What about Eugen?'

'No. He's always been Mr Pettersson to me.'

'That's hilarious.'

'It's not that funny.'

'It is pretty funny.'

'Why?'

'You're thirty-three. I can't believe you're not on first-name terms.'

'You remember how old I am.' He raises one eyebrow.

'Don't read anything into it,' I reply cuttingly, the smile gone from my face. 'You're the same age as my boyfriend.'

We fall silent. Joel and Christian sound like they're still cleaning up the glass in the kitchen.

'Where's your girlfriend?' I ask drily.

'At her parents',' he replies.

'She hasn't bothered going back to rehab, then?'

He shakes his head and the corners of his lips turn down.

'I don't know why *you* bother, quite frankly,' I comment.

'Yeah, alright, Meg,' he snaps. 'I didn't come here to get a lecture.'

'Why did you come?' The retort comes naturally, but I immediately feel stupid. He came because he's known Christian's family his entire life, of course. Johnny gives me a hard look and doesn't dignify my question with an answer. I'm aghast to find myself blushing.

Christian walks back into the room and slumps on the sofa next to me. I tuck my knees up underneath myself and cosy in closer to him. Johnny averts his gaze and pushes his hair back off his face. He yawns.

'You must be jet-lagged,' Christian says. 'Where are you staying?'

Johnny pats his pocket. 'Don't know. Some place in the city centre. Lena sorted it for me.'

Lena? She must be his current PA and I'm guessing his accommodation details are on the phone in his pocket. I feel a prickle of jealousy. I wonder what she's like, if she's better at her job than me. If he's attracted to her . . .

'I should probably get a cab.' Johnny drags me out of my internal monologue.

'You can crash here, if you like,' Christian says. 'Sofa's free.' He grins, but I can see that he's tired. 'But of course I won't be offended if you opt for five-star luxury instead.'

Johnny smiles back at him. 'Thanks for the offer.'

Sarcasm?

'When are you going back to Froggy Land?' Johnny asks, his eyes flitting between Christian and me.

Christian answers. 'Meg's flying home tomorrow, but I'm sticking around for a few more days. What about you? When are you going back to LA?'

'Tomorrow afty,' Johnny replies.

'Private jet?' Christian checks.

'Yep.'

'EasyJet.' Christian winks and jabs his thumb my way.

'It's not easyJet, actually,' I say of the low-budget airline.

'Alright, darling, don't be pedantic,' he says good-naturedly. 'So what shall we do, get some sheets out or order a cab?'

Again Johnny's eyes flit towards me. 'I'll stay,' he says after a moment. 'It'd be good to catch up properly tomorrow. If that's alright.'

'Of course it is,' Christian replies.

I stand up. 'I'll get the bedding together.'

'Meg,' Christian says, a touch infuriated. 'I can do it.'

'It's fine,' I reply, leaving the room. When I return

downstairs, the kitchen is empty and it appears Joel has gone to bed.

'Thanks for coming,' I hear Christian say from the living room.

I pause at the door and listen for a moment.

'I wish I could have made the funeral. Didn't think your family would thank me if I brought the press circus with me by accident.'

'I know. Dad really appreciates you coming, too.'

'It's good to see him again.'

'You took his mind off things for a bit.'

'I hope so.' Pause. 'How are you holding up?'

Another pause. 'I'm . . . okay. I miss her, though, you know?'

'I know.'

There's weight to that sentence. Because Johnny does know, of course. He lost his mother when he was barely a teenager.

Christian sniffs. 'Oh, fuck,' he mutters. 'I thought I was all cried-out.'

My heart goes out to him, but my feet are rooted to the spot.

'I'm sorry, mate,' Johnny says softly. 'I'm going to miss her, too.'

They both fall silent.

'Where's Meg with my fucking sheets?' Johnny jokes, trying to clear the air.

Christian laughs. 'She's been a gem these last few days. I don't know what I would have done without her.'

I wait to hear how Johnny will respond to that, but he says nothing. I step quietly back into the kitchen and then bustle through to the living room.

'Here you go,' I say. Johnny comes to take the sheets from me.

'I'll do it,' he says, not meeting my eyes.

'Alright, Johnny boy,' Christian says, gently guiding me to the door. 'See you in the morning.'

'Goodnight,' I say.

'See you in the morning.' I notice Johnny replies to Christian, but not to me.

Chapter 7

I wake up in the middle of the night. I feel groggy and my mind is a jumble of thoughts. I'd been having a dream about being absolutely parched and asking Johnny to pass me a bottle of water from the fridge. He did and then laughed when I couldn't open it. I tried desperately to twist off the top, and then his laughter died and he stared at me furiously and watched as I failed.

I realise now that I'm thirsty for real. I climb out of bed and put on my dressing gown, then carefully navigate the stairs and head into the kitchen. The house is dark. The time on the oven says it's two thirty-three a.m. I go to the fridge and open it. Light spills out as I reach in for a jug of filtered water. I pour some into a glass and gulp down a few mouthfuls, before refilling my glass and returning the jug to the fridge. I freeze as I get a whiff of cigarette smoke.

'Johnny?' I whisper. 'Is that you?' I close the fridge door and poke my head into the living room. I can see by the light on the TV's LCD display that the sofa is empty. I hear the front door close gently and suddenly I'm face to face with Johnny.

'What the fuck?' he curses in a loud whisper. 'You scared the living daylights out of me!'

'Shh!' I berate him. 'I was getting a glass of water. I smelled the smoke,' I explain.

'Jesus!' He's still freaked out.

'Sorry,' I say. 'What are you doing up at this time?'

'Body clock's buggered up,' he says.

'Do you want anything? Glass of water?'

'No, I'm alright.'

'Okay. Goodnight, then.' I turn to go.

'Meg!' He calls me back.

'What?'

'Stay and talk to me for a while.'

I pause. My head tells me that I should go back upstairs, back to my Christian, but I find myself being pulled in the opposite direction and hate myself for it. I sit in Eugen's armchair while Johnny returns to his makeshift bed on the sofa. He's wearing his jeans and T-shirt from earlier.

'What do you want to talk about?' I ask uneasily.

He sighs. 'I was just . . . thinking about you,' he says carefully. 'It's been a long time.'

I nod.

'Too long,' he adds.

'It's been a while,' I agree.

'You seem happy.' He sounds sincere.

'I am,' I tell him. Most of the time.

He smiles at me sadly. 'It's weird being back in this house. Staying here without Mrs Pettersson around.'

'Did you know her well?'

'I haven't seen her much in recent years, but she looked after

59

me, you know, when my mum got sick.' His mum died of cancer. 'I used to come and stay over when mum was in hospital. I'll never forget that.'

My heart goes out to him. Johnny rarely talks about his mother's death to anyone. It feels strangely natural to have him talk about her again to me. It must be to do with the darkness, the night – it's catapulted us back to the way we once were.

'I'm sorry. I didn't realise.'

'It's okay. How could you?' He pauses. 'Rosa always asks Christian about you.'

'Does she?'

'At least, she used to,' he adds. 'She quit.' He shrugs and tries to appear indifferent, but I can tell that he's hurting.

'She found you after the overdose, didn't she?' He glances up at me and nods slightly. 'It doesn't surprise me that she quit,' I continue.

He looks down again. 'I guess enough was enough for her.'

'That's very sad,' I say and mean it. 'She was part of the family.'

'I know.' He takes a deep breath and exhales loudly.

'What about everyone else? I often think of them.'

'Lewis, Samuel, Ted and Sandy are all still there.' Sandy was the maid. The first three make up the security team.

'What about Santiago?'

'I knew you meant him,' he says with a slight smile.

'He was a friend!' My voice rises. I don't know why I sound defensive. He may have come to Johnny's house only once a week to tend to the gardens and treat the pool, but I sometimes found myself chatting to him for hours.

'Yeah,' he replies. 'He's still there. Still smoking behind the garage . . .'

Once, when I was really stressed, Santiago gave me one of his cigarettes. Johnny saw and went bananas. He hated to think about anyone else corrupting me in any small way – I think he was actually jealous. That night he came into my room and into my bed . . . I shiver inadvertently.

'You never became a smoker, then,' Johnny continues.

'Of course not,' I retort. 'I'm a mum. Anyway, it's a filthy habit,' I add with raised eyebrows.

He smirks. 'Can't argue with that.'

'You should quit,' I say.

'There are a lot of things I should give up, Nutmeg, but I rarely do.' He stretches his arms over his head and smiles at me and it takes me a moment to realise he's just called me Nutmeg, the term of affection he used for me.

I come to my senses with a start. 'I'd better get back to bed before Christian misses me.'

'Of course.'

'Don't get up,' I tell him, but he's already on his feet. He meets me by the door and leans against the doorframe. I suddenly feel jittery.

'I'm glad you're happy,' he murmurs, looking into my eyes. 'You deserve it.' He touches my arm, briefly, tenderly. Lost for words, I turn away and hurry up the stairs.

Chapter 8

I finally fall asleep around dawn, when daylight has already started seeping under the blinds. Christian wakes me unintentionally at around seven o'clock in the morning.

'Sorry,' he says. He's pulling on his jeans. 'Go back to sleep.'

'No, it's okay. I'm awake.'

He comes over to the bed to take my hand. 'I wish I could come home with you today.'

I look up at him in sympathy. 'How long do you think you should stay?'

'I guess I'll play it by ear. Dad's a bit of a mess.'

He's not telling me anything I don't already know.

'I'm going to head downstairs. Please stay in bed,' he urges. 'We don't have to leave for the airport for two hours.'

'No, I'm coming down.'

He shakes his head in amused frustration and leaves the room. I climb out of bed and pull on some jeans and a purple top. I make a concerted effort not to bother with make-up. The guilt is well and truly back.

What the hell was I thinking, going into a room alone with

him? What would Christian think? Actually, Christian would probably approve. He wants us all to be friends. He's fallen out before with Johnny and they always patch things up. Thankfully, he and Christian weren't speaking at the time I fell pregnant, so Johnny couldn't put two and two together with his dates. It took them about a year to get back on good terms, and by then Barney had already been born. But Johnny turning up yesterday for such a momentous occasion will certainly cement their friendship. Unfortunately.

I trot downstairs and into the kitchen, noticing on my way that the living room door is closed.

'He still asleep?' I ask Christian.

'Yep.' He's making a coffee. 'Want one?'

'Sure,' I reply. I look around the kitchen. Joel did a good job of finishing up. We hear someone coming down the stairs and both turn to see Eugen enter the room. He looks weary.

'Alright, Dad?' Christian says.

'Alright, son.'

'How did you sleep?' I ask.

'Not too bad. Took a pill,' he admits.

'Want a coffee?' Christian asks him.

'That'd be good.' Eugen heads towards the living room.

'Johnny's asleep in there.'

Eugen turns around with a start.

'What?' he asks.

'Johnny's asleep on the sofa,' Christian explains.

'Can't he afford a bleedin' hotel with all his money?' he barks. It's the perkiest I've seen him in days.

'I'm awake!' Johnny shouts groggily from behind closed doors.

'Aah, he's awake,' Eugen says with satisfaction and goes through to the living room.

'Couldn't sleep with all that racket,' we hear Johnny mutter for Eugen's benefit and Christian and I glance at each other and smile.

'I'd better make him one, too,' Christian says as an aside to me. 'Didn't see him drink anything last night, did you?'

'No.'

'Unless he raided the booze cabinet after we went to bed.'

'I don't think so.' I try to keep my voice steady as I continue. 'I came downstairs last night to get a glass of water and he was outside having a ciggie. We chatted for a while.' I've got nothing to hide, I tell myself.

'Did you?' Christian looks interested. 'What did you talk about?'

'Not much. He told me Rosa had quit.'

'Oh,' he says. 'That's a shame.'

'You didn't know?'

'No. Must've just happened.'

'Morning.' An exhausted-looking Johnny emerges at the doorway.

'Hey,' Christian says. 'Heard you didn't sleep too well?'

Johnny glances at me in surprise, but quickly recovers. I don't suppose he thought I'd tell Christian about our night-time chat. 'No. How are you? Alright?' He comes over to Christian and puts his hand on his shoulder. I worry the sympathy could have adverse effects, but Christian shrugs.

'Pretty shit, but I'll be alright.' He laughs half-heartedly.

Johnny gives him a sympathetic nod and pulls out a crumpled packet of cigarettes from his jeans pocket. He shakes out a fag and puts it between his lips.

'I might just . . .' He indicates the door with his thumb.

'. . . pop outside for a cancer stick?' Christian finishes his sentence.

'You got that right,' I snort.

'Yeah, alright, Meg.' Johnny pats my arm good-naturedly as he walks past. Christian smiles at me.

'What?' I say, when Johnny has gone.

'See?' he says. 'I told you we could all be friends again.'

'I don't know about that,' I mutter. But hope stirs inside me. I rarely admit it to myself, but I miss Johnny. I miss being a part of his life: his crazy, nutty, fast-paced life. I miss him.

Er, *Barney?*

Reality hits and a feeling of fear – a feeling I know so well – grips my throat and stomach. I can never be a part of his life. I can never let him meet Barney. For a moment there, I forgot that I'd slept with him, that I'd fallen pregnant with his child. For a moment, I forgot that everything was so complicated.

I turn away from Christian so he can't see my face as all my positive feelings are crushed to death.

I tell Christian I don't want breakfast and go upstairs to pack my bags. I take my time. I have a shower and put on some make-up in the attempt to make myself feel half-decent again. I carefully pack my things and then tidy the room for Christian. I feel so sad for him. I wish I didn't have to leave him alone.

Everyone is in the living room when I return downstairs and I feel self-conscious and on edge.

'Ready?' Christian asks.

'Yes,' I reply.

'Are your bags upstairs?'

I nod.

'I'll go and get them.' He leaves the room and I try to find somewhere to turn my attention. I look at Eugen and give him a small smile.

'Have you got any pics of your boy?' Johnny asks and my whole head starts to itch as though imaginary ants are crawling around under a thin layer of skin.

'Er, no,' I manage to respond.

'Christian doesn't either,' he says, rolling his eyes.

My relief is temporary.

'I do!' Eugen interrupts. I stare at him in horror as he reaches behind for one of the photo albums he's been trawling through since we got here. Johnny takes the album and starts to flick through it.

In what feels like the distant background I can hear Christian lugging my suitcase and carry-on bag down the stairs, but I'm frozen.

'What've you got there?' Christian asks perkily, going to join Johnny. 'Aah, baby pics,' he says, glancing over Johnny's shoulder.

'He's a looker,' Johnny says, grinning at his friend. 'Got your hair, mate.'

Oh, thank God. Barney is just a baby in the photos.

Christian laughs. 'He's got Meg's now.'

I find my voice. 'Come on, Christian, we should go.'

'Right you are,' he says.

'Haven't you got any recent ones?' Johnny asks Eugen.

I tense up again, but he shakes his head. 'No. Mandy—' He clears his throat. 'There are some on her computer.'

'Don't worry about it,' Johnny says quickly, not wanting to set him off again.

I say my goodbyes to Eugen and Joel.

'Thanks for all your help, sis,' Joel jokes as I turn away from him to hug Eugen.

'Yes, thank you,' Eugen says, with tears in his eyes.

'It was the least I could do,' I reply as tears start to fill mine.

'I'll see you out,' Johnny says and I don't argue. I feel awkward enough looking at him, let alone hugging or kissing or doing neither of those things in front of Christian's family.

Christian leads the way to the front door and opens it. 'I'll put these in the boot,' he says tactfully, hauling the bags over the threshold and down the front steps.

I look up at Johnny. 'See ya.'

He gives me a sad smile. 'Bye, Meg.'

At least he didn't call me Nutmeg again. I tell myself it's for the best. I turn away.

'Hey,' he says with surprise. 'Is this Mandy and Barney?'

I whip around and there, on the hallstand, is a close-up photo of Mandy and Barney. A recent photo. Johnny picks it up. I want to scream, 'NO!' but it's too late.

I hear the car boot slam. 'All set,' Christian calls. I stare at Johnny in shock as he studies the picture and then everything turns to slow motion as his eyes meet mine. He looks stunned, like I've just punched him in the face. And if the similarity between him and Barney isn't already clear enough, the look on my face will have instantly confirmed his suspicion.

I flee down the steps and climb into the car. Christian, oblivious, starts the ignition. I look out of the window at

Johnny, who's still staring after me, and silently beg him to keep quiet, to not say anything to Christian when he gets back from the airport, and then I face ahead and try to still my beating heart.

Chapter 9

Text me when you land

Oh my God, what does that mean? I've wanted to call Christian during every minute of the two-and-a-half-hour flight to Barcelona, but when I'm finally allowed to switch my phone back on, this is the message from him that greets me.

I grip my phone with white knuckles and call him. It rings and rings before reverting to voicemail.

Text me when you land . . .

Why? Has Johnny told him that he thinks Barney is his? I try him again as I'm waiting for my suitcase and again when I reach our car in the parking lot. I can't think straight, and I need to concentrate on driving this journey that I'm supposed to be doing again in just two days' time for Bess's birthday. That trip no longer feels appropriate. I must speak to her.

Christian rings me himself when I've exited the motorway and have started winding my way through the mountains towards Cucugnan. I pull over and take the call, my voice shaking as I answer.

'Hello?'

'Five missed calls!' he practically shouts. I couldn't resist pressing redial another two times on the motorway. 'Are you alright?' he adds, and, thank God, he sounds normal.

'I'm fine,' I reply as some of the tension evaporates. 'But you wanted me to call you when I landed and I wasn't sure why.'

'I said "text", you divvy. I just wanted to check you got there safely.'

'Oh!'

Dur . . . He wouldn't ask me to merely text if it were something serious. I did say I couldn't think straight.

'Are you home yet?' he asks.

'No, not yet. How are you?' I ask. 'Why didn't you answer your phone?'

'I forgot to take it with me. Dad wanted me to go with him to see his solicitor. I've only just seen your missed calls.'

'Aah.' I so want to ask about Johnny, but I keep my focus on Christian. 'How did the meeting go?'

'Oh . . .' He sounds sad. 'It was just a formality, but it's still not easy.'

'Of course not,' I say sympathetically. 'I wish I could have gone with you.'

'I miss you,' he replies and I wish I could hug him down the phone.

'I miss you, too,' I say softly. I try to hang onto this warm, compassionate feeling, but my dark side drags my thoughts, kicking and screaming, towards Johnny. Finally I give in. 'Is Johnny still with you?'

'No,' Christian replies. 'That was a bit weird. He left when I took you to the airport.'

I swallow. 'Did he?'

'Yeah.' He humphs. 'I was only gone half an hour, I thought he'd at least hang around to say goodbye.'

Oh, God. He knows. He knows.

'How odd,' I manage to say.

'You know what he's like.'

'Mmm. Well, give your dad and Joel my love.'

'I will do. You should get back on the road,' he adds. 'Call me tonight?'

'Yes, will do.'

'Love you.'

'I love you, too.'

'Bye.'

I stare out through the front window.

Johnny left suddenly because he knows Barney is his. I wonder if I can convince him he's wrong.

It occurs to me that Johnny might convince himself of that. He doesn't want a child, for goodness' sake. Why would he want to get involved when he's so clearly not cut out for fatherhood? Surely he wouldn't do that to Christian, either.

I have a sudden compulsive urge to hurt myself, to punish myself for what I've done. I take a few deep breaths and try to think about my son laughing, and even though that image is – and probably always will be – tainted by the knowledge of this overbearing secret that is no longer a secret, it does calm me slightly. I put the car into drive, indicate and pull away from the kerb.

Barney is with my parents on the terrace when I turn into the driveway. It looks like they've been outside under the shade of the umbrella waiting for me. Barney starts to squeak with excitement before I've even unbuckled my seat belt. The badness fades away and is replaced with an overwhelming sense of love and happiness. I run up the steps, not caring that my bare legs are brushing against the lavender with all its bees buzzing around. If I get stung, so what? I want to hold my son. My mum passes him over, laughing at our obvious delight to be with each other. I hug him tightly and then kiss his plump lips over and over again until he's in hysterics. My face aches from smiling so much.

Whatever happens, happens, I tell myself. But Barney is mine and always will be.

Chapter 10

My parents leave the following day and Christian convinces me not to cancel the trip to Barcelona. I don't tell Bess that I considered not going, because when I speak to her on Thursday night, she's so excited about donning her brand-new swimming costume and leaping in the rooftop pool that I don't want to dampen her enthusiasm.

'What time does your flight come in?' I ask her.

'About midday, so I'll see you at the hotel.'

'I was wondering if I should swing by the airport to pick you up.'

'Don't be daft,' she says. 'I'll jump in a cab. You check in and get the champers on ice for me. I can't bloody wait!'

Traumatic though the last week has been, it's impossible for her enthusiasm not to rub off on me. Which is just as well, because I don't want to ruin her birthday by being miserable.

Barney and I set off the following morning in time for his nap. He falls asleep before we've even hit the next town. I plug my iPod into the stereo and try to relax as I navigate Christian's black Alfa Romeo through the Pyrenees. Scraggly trees cling onto the rocky cliff faces and wildflowers pepper the sides of roads as crazy cyclists huff past us up the steep hills. We pass over glittering green rivers and through villages with old stone bell towers and the ever-present boulangeries, charcuteries and pharmacies. Wooden shutters on creamy houses are painted cornflower blue, and all the time the sun beats down from the cloudless sky. Just like Bess, I start to daydream about that rooftop pool.

The journey takes only two hours so we arrive around noon. I park the car in the underground car park across from the hotel and lug our bags towards the lift while single-handedly pushing the buggy. I'm glad I packed light. It's a skill I had to learn when I became a mother and realised I wasn't built like an octopus. We emerge into daylight and find ourselves in a square. Directly opposite us is a beautiful cathedral. I stand under the shade of a tree and try to accustom myself to the stifling heat as I point out the 'big church' to Barney, but he's more interested in the yellow flowers that have fallen like confetti onto the ground from the tree over our heads.

The Grand Hotel Central lobby is dark, sensuous and blissfully cool. We check in and take the lift to the seventh floor. There are stairs directly from here to the rooftop bar. Our suite is huge. The sofa bed has already been made up in one room, and next door is a giant super-king-sized bed with a large bathroom equipped with shower and bathtub. Excitement swells through me and I remember with a small smile that this is remarkably similar to how I felt when I first saw my bedroom in Johnny's house. How young I seemed back then. How old and jaded I feel now. But not right now. Right now, I feel young and free and I can't wait to see my best friend and have a proper girls' weekend, even if we do have a male toddler in tow . . .

I get us changed and lather us both with suncream and then we walk out of the room and push open the door to the outside stairs. The heat hits us again as we climb the wooden steps to the pool and Skybar. The first thing I see is the infinity pool, clear and blue and so inviting I feel like plonking Barney on a sunlounger and diving right in. We have a bird's-eye view over Barcelona's rooftops, and it's a mishmash of beautiful old churches and haphazard rooftop terraces with television aerials and satellite dishes. Cranes spike upwards and penetrate the city's skyline and the low murmur of building works creates a background noise that isn't unpleasant. A flock of birds swirl around the hazy blue sky and planes fly to and from Barcelona airport.

Hurry up, Bess!

I carry Barney across the wooden deck and up a few more stairs to a raised platform under a white awning. Small pines line one side of the top deck and the bar is at the other side. I sit Barney on the black sofa seat beside me and give him a packet of rice cakes to keep him entertained. I'll take him swimming in a minute, but for now I just want to soak up the atmosphere.

Bikini-clad model types laze on sunloungers beside the pool. For a moment, I wonder if I'll be able to pluck up the courage to go swimming in front of them, but one look at my gleeful son tells me that of course I will. I remember going to the Mondrian Hotel's Skybar in LA – funny that the two bars have the same name. I never would have gone swimming there in front of all those beautiful people, but being a mother has made me feel strangely less self-conscious.

Across the other side of the bar the lift doors open and Bess steps out.

'MEG!' she squeals, and several people turn to look at my friend. Her sumptuous curves are encased in an army-green tankini and her dark hair swings around her shoulders as she waves enthusiastically. I wave back and moments later I'm in her arms and she's squeezing me half to death, both of us giggling our heads off.

'This is amazing!' she yells, not caring in the least that we're causing a bit of a disturbance.

'Isn't it?' I reply, as she turns to hug my slightly overawed son.

'I brought you a prezzie!' She reaches into her beach bag and pulls out a sticker book. 'Does he like stickers?' she asks me.

'We'll soon find out,' I reply, smiling. 'I cannot believe you used the lift! The stairs are only there!'

'I know.' She winks. 'I wanted to make a grand entrance.'

'That you certainly did.'

'Where's your drink?' she asks, looking around with alarm.

'I haven't been to the bar yet.'

She tuts.

'We've only just arrived!'

'Never mind,' she brushes me off. 'Bellinis?'

'I'll get them.'

'No, I'll get them,' she insists. 'Have you seen the barman?'

I laugh and, like a whirlwind, she's off again. My thoughts flicker towards Mandy and Christian and I'm momentarily swamped by grief. I'm going to have to make a real effort to conceal my emotions from Bess. I look over at her flirting with the sexy Spanish bartender and can't help but smile again. It's so good to see her.

'Get this down ya,' Bess says a little while later, handing me a champagne glass full of Prosecco mixed with peach juice. 'Cheers!'

'Happy birthday!' I exclaim.

'It's tomorrow.'

'I know.' I grin at her as she turns to Barney.

'I can't believe how much you've grown!' He looks distracted as he tears a yellow digger sticker in half. 'Not quite getting the hang of those yet, then,' she jokes. 'His hair has gone blonder,' she comments. 'You look just like Mummy!' she says to Barney. She studies my son's face before glancing swiftly at me. My heart is in my throat for a moment, but Bess pinches Barney's chubby cheek and takes a sip of her drink.

'We'll go for a swim in a little while.' I pat my son's arm and try to sound breezy, but inside I'm shaken.

By the time we return to our suite, I'm feeling chilled out again.

'I can't believe Christian booked this place for us,' Bess says enthusiastically. 'That was so, so nice of him.'

'I know.' I beam. 'He's a sweetie.'

'How is he? I'm so sorry about his mum, that's terrible news.'

'Shocking. I think he might still be in shock. I don't know if it's properly sunk in.'

'How awful.' She shakes her head sadly.

'I must call him later,' I add.

'I'll look after Barney if you want to call him now?'

'Actually, I might do that quickly. Do you mind?'

'Of course not!'

I go into the adjoining room and find my phone before sliding the doors shut.

'Hey, you,' I say warmly when he answers. 'How's it all going?'

'Not too bad,' he replies with a small sigh. 'Dad hasn't looked at any photos today, so that's a step in the right direction.'

I murmur with sympathy.

'How are you?' he asks. 'Cheer me up. How's your room?'

'It's amazing,' I say earnestly. 'Thank you so much.'

He chuckles softly. 'You're welcome. What are you up to?'

'We've been for a swim and now we're getting ready for an early dinner. I'm hoping Barney will fall asleep in the buggy after that so we can stay out for a while. You know how he sleeps through anything when he's knackered.'

'Good luck. I wish I could be there.'

'I wish you could be, too,' I say sadly. 'Have you booked your return flight home yet?'

'No.' Another sigh. 'I think I'm going to fly straight into Berlin for the band's next show.'

'When?'

'Tomorrow.'

'Are you sure?' I ask worriedly. 'Isn't that a bit too soon?'

'I don't think so. Joel's going to be here for a couple of weeks, and Dad won't let us help him clear away any of Mum's things yet. I'll have to come back in a month or two anyway, so I should get back to work.'

'How long will you be away?'

'Could be another week or two.'

'Oh.'

'Well, I missed the tour's opening night so I've got a bit of catching up to do. Maybe I'll only need ten days.'

That still seems like forever to me.

'Okay.'

'You don't mind, do you?'

I take a deep breath. He's already been through so much. 'No,' I reply. 'It's fine.' But inside I'm disappointed.

Thankfully, it doesn't take long for Bess to lift my spirits. She's cracked open the complimentary champers in the minibar and has poured me a glass.

'I shouldn't really drink any more,' I say solemnly. 'I'm a mother now.'

'Bollocks to that!' She chinks my glass. I grin and then cough as the fizzy bubbles hit the back of my throat.

'You alright, love?' Bess asks wryly. 'You don't drink much these days, do you?'

'Not as much as I used to,' I admit.

'We'll soon rectify that,' she jokes. 'How was Christian?'

'Relieved that his dad has stopped trawling through photo albums of his mum,' I reply with a sad smile as I put my champagne glass down on a table. 'He also told me he's going to join Contour Lines on tour instead of coming home again.'

'Oh no,' she says.

'Mmm,' I reply unhappily.

'Sounds like you need a night out on the town!'

'I couldn't agree with you more. Let's get ready.'

'Good plan.' She turns to rummage through her suitcase. 'Ooh, I forgot about this.' She plucks out a box-shaped parcel brightly wrapped in paper decorated with rocket ships. 'Barney!'

'You've just given him a present!' I exclaim as my little boy leaves his torn-apart stickers for a moment and comes crawling over.

'This is his birthday present – I only sent him something small last month,' Bess replies.

'You didn't have to do that,' I chide. 'But that's very sweet, thank you.'

'You won't thank me when he opens it.' She gives me a cheeky grin and helps Barney remove the paper to reveal a white toy bunny. 'I've already put some batteries in it,' she says, taking it out of the box and switching it on. The thing squeaks into life immediately before doing a sudden back-flip and landing on its feet again. A delighted Barney picks it up.

'That is seriously going to do my head in,' I joke, as the fluffy rabbit keeps on squeaking.

'The joys of parenthood,' Bess says smugly. 'Now, help me decide what to wear.'

'Come into my bedroom,' I urge. 'In fact, why don't you sleep in there with me? We'll put the travel cot in this room so we can chat and watch telly without waking Barney up.'

'Alright, as long as you keep your hands to yourself,' she warns. 'I know your type.'

I shake my head in amusement and we relocate her bags to the adjoining room.

We used to live together and it's lovely to be able to get ready for a night out, just like old times. Barney entertains himself with his new toy while I quickly unpack. Bess refuses to do so, even though the clothes in her suitcase already look like they've been in a jumble sale.

'I'm only here for two days, you nutcase. You're too bloody organised, that's your problem.'

'Yeah, yeah,' I reply. 'Right, what's it going to be?' I hold up my outfit options.

'The jeans and sparkly top,' she decides. 'Save the black dress for my birthday tomorrow night.'

'Good call.'

It's almost four o'clock in the afternoon by the time we leave the hotel, but the sun overhead is still beating down from above and there's no shade even as we walk between the tall buildings of Plaça de la Cucurulla. Luckily there's a slight breeze to take the edge off the heat and the shops are air-conditioned, so Bess uses that as an excuse to go into them and trawl through the merchandise.

'Lots of shoe shops,' she comments. 'I'm right in my element.'

Bess loves shoes.

We wander down Las Ramblas. There are crowds of people gathered around a stall as we approach and I soon realise it's a pet shop, right out in the open. Barney is beside himself, gleefully pointing out rabbits, hamsters, mice, birds, tortoises and even chipmunks.

'That is so out of order,' Bess complains. 'Look at all those poor animals!'

'They seem happy enough,' I try to convince her. She drags me away, much to Barney's dismay, but moments later we happen upon another pet stall.

'This stretch is full of them!' Bess exclaims. It's true. One look ahead confirms this part of the city is animal mad.

'You can't get away from them,' I say. 'So let's let Barney . . . Oh my God, that is the cutest hamster I've ever seen.'

'Meg,' she warns.

'No, seriously. I think I have to buy it.'

'Meg, no,' Bess says firmly.

'But I want it,' I say like a small child.

'You can't have it,' she replies like a mean old mummy. She gently eases me away, taking control of the buggy at the same time. My son continues to point at the critters like a little maniac.

'Please,' I beg. 'Just one tiny little hamster?'

'No,' Bess tells me. 'You've already got Barney.'

I stop and stare at her, trying to keep a straight face. 'Are you comparing my son to a rodent?'

She tries to keep a straight face also. 'You once told me Barney was the best pet you'd ever had.'

Now I laugh out loud. 'That was when he was a baby. He seemed a bit like an animal then.'

She giggles. 'Call yourself a mother.'

'Obviously I was joking!' I slap her arm.

'Bin ladies!' she screeches, as we turn to cross the busy road. I follow her gaze to see two blonde female refuse collectors, who are bloody gorgeous.

'This city is bonkers,' I say as we both stand there and watch them in awe.

'I love it. Come on.' She drags me away. We head down a side street as the city's bells ring out to announce it's five o'clock. I suggest we look for somewhere to eat before Barney gets over-tired and after a while we happen across a pretty tapas restaurant called Bar Lobo. Herbs in terracotta pots adorn the wooden tables outside, and the metal chairs are painted in muted tones of green and grey.

'Too hot,' Bess complains, dragging me towards the door. 'I know I'm a traitor to the Brit abroad. I should be sitting outside getting prawn crackered, but I need air-con,' she says.

'Prawn crackered?' I laugh as I follow her.

'Pink like a prawn and, you know, all crispy.'

'Crispy prawn wonton? Prawn toast?'

She grins over her shoulder at me. 'Prawn crackered sounds better.'

Inside there's a big, open bar and kitchen and lots more seating. Dozens of oversized Chinese lanterns hang from the ceiling. It's very trendy. We take a seat at a table and a waiter brings over some menus. We order a bottle of sparkling water to quench our thirst before starting on something more serious.

'It is such a beautiful city,' Bess comments. 'This is the second time you've been here, right? The first time was when you went on tour with Johnny?'

'Mmm.'

This is the city where I saw him take drugs for the first time. My mum had just told me my grandmother had died. Upset, I went to confide in Johnny and walked into his room to see him snorting a line of coke. I was stunned. How naive I was back then.

Suddenly I don't feel quite so happy to be back in Barcelona.

'So, he walked out of rehab,' she says drily.

'To come to Christian's mum's funeral,' I reveal.

'No shit?'

I nod.

'How did you feel, seeing him again?'

'It was strange,' I admit. A waiter comes over, interrupting us. We apologise for not consulting our menus yet and get down to the business of food.

'I'll tell you later,' I say.

Bess nods back, understanding that for now, at least, this conversation is over.

* * *

Later, much later, after we've wandered the streets of the Gothic Quarter near our hotel and Barney has fallen asleep in his buggy, we find a couple of outdoor seats at a bar and order two glasses of Prosecco.

'I've been very patient,' Bess says mock seriously, her face lit by the tea lights on the table. 'But now it's time to talk about Johnny.'

I sigh. 'Do we have to?'

'Meg, don't clam up,' she says firmly. 'I know you. And you know you can talk to me about anything.'

'True,' I say quietly.

'So what was it like, seeing him again?'

I concentrate on the earlier part of seeing Johnny, and simultaneously try to forget about the look on his face when he saw the photo of Barney with Mandy.

'I told you, it was strange.'

'Go on.'

I fill her in on the initial shock at opening the door to him and how he acted like he barely knew me. I tell her about how supportive Christian was and how Johnny put on an act in front of him. Eventually I get to the part about me coming downstairs in the middle of the night.

'He was . . . different,' I reveal. 'More like the Johnny I used to know.'

'Oh no,' she says, shaking her head.

'Bess, cut it out. I don't mean I felt the same way about him as I did back then.'

'Are you sure about that?'

'Definitely!' I exclaim, trying to convince her. 'I mean, look at him; he's a mess. Has he even gone back into rehab?'

'Not that I know of,' she says. 'But he always *was* a mess, Meg. That didn't stop you back then.'

'I'm not the same person I used to be.'

She examines me across the table. 'I believe you.'

'What about you?' I change the subject. 'Anyone on the scene?'

'I had a drunken snog with some bloke in a bar last weekend, but that's about it.'

Envy racks me for a moment. The idea of being able to go out on the pull again, snog guys I fancy . . . I've hardly ever done that. I've gone from boyfriend to boyfriend, with not enough space in between. Now I'm tied in for good. Not that we're married. Christian doesn't believe in marriage. I'm not sure if I do or not. I always thought I did, but I can kind of see his point. Why do we need a piece of paper to validate our relationship?

Barney stirs in his buggy and lets out a small squeak.

Bess giggles. 'He sounded like a hamster then.'

I smirk. 'We should get back. He's going to wake me up at the crack of dawn.'

'Sure thing.' She flags down a waiter and asks for the bill.

The next day, we go to see Gaudi's Sagrada Família, and it still takes my breath away, even though it's half covered with scaffolding. Bess holds Barney's hand as he toddles along the top of walls and it makes me smile to watch them. After lunch we wander aimlessly around the city, down by the harbour, through the shops. Bess points wildly at a shop with a familiar red H&M logo gracing the front.

'Ooh, ooh, ooh, Hennes!' she squeals, pulling me in that direction.

'Hennes?' I ask in disbelief, pulling her back. 'You've got Hennes in England!'

'Yeah, but it's different abroad.'

'Bess, no, don't be silly.'

'Don't tell me you don't want to go into Hennes.'

'Of course I don't.' I giggle. 'I had a Hennes fix a few weeks ago in Perpignan.'

She laughs. 'I knew I recognised your bikini! Come on, it's my birthday, I can do what I want to . . .'

Forty minutes later, we emerge with more shopping bags to add to our already quite impressive collection.

'Right, I think we should quit while we're ahead,' I say.

'Rooftop pool?' she suggests.

'Sounds like a plan.'

Everyone takes children out at all hours here, so I feel only slightly guilty about going for drinks again while Barney sleeps in his buggy beside us. We've found a gorgeous bar not far from the hotel and are sitting right at the back in black velvet seats. The lighting is warm and inviting. Bess fingers the sterling silver and crystal charm bracelet that I gave her this morning for her birthday.

'Do you like it?' I ask again.

'I love it,' she gushes as the waitress brings our drinks and some nibbles.

'Happy birthday!' I exclaim as we chink glasses for what feels like the hundredth time in twenty-four hours. 'This has been the nicest weekend,' I say, and I mean it. I've even managed to half convince myself that everything will be alright – that things will continue as they always have done, because there's no way Johnny will interfere if it means him becoming a father.

'I'm glad you've enjoyed it,' she says, looking down, and for a split second I get an uncomfortable feeling in the pit of my stomach. I choose to ignore it.

I'm halfway through a story about the latest annoying thing my annoying older sister, Susan, has said, when I realise that Bess isn't really listening.

'Are you alright?' I ask her.

'Hey?' She sits up straighter.

'What did I just say?'

'"As if a child should know how to say please and thank you when they've only just turned one."'

'Oh, okay, then, so you were listening.'

Apparently, Susan told my mum I should have taught Barney better manners by now, which is just ridiculous. She and her annoying husband, Tony, don't have children, and they act like spoiled children themselves most of the time, even though they're eight years older than me. I don't get on very well with my sister, as you might've guessed. Luckily I don't have to see her often.

'Yes,' Bess says, then: 'No, I wasn't really. I just heard that part.'

'What's on your mind?' I pry, as the uncomfortable feeling returns.

She glances at Barney in the buggy. She looks shifty.

'He's asleep, don't worry,' I say, curious now.

'No, it's not that.'

'What is it, then?'

She's not meeting my eyes and suddenly the discomfort swells into nausea. I stare at her, the smile long gone from my face. I wait for her to speak.

'I didn't know if I should say anything,' she says, edgily.

'Then don't,' I reply quickly, willing her to shut up.

She turns to look again at my son, sleeping peacefully.

'Don't,' I repeat, my voice firmer. I was wrong to lower my guard. I'm remembering Bess's face when she first saw Barney on the rooftop deck yesterday. It's the same look she's giving him now.

'He doesn't look like Christian.'

'I know. He takes after me.' I force a tinkling laugh.

'He doesn't look like you, either,' she says seriously. She reaches into her bag and carefully pulls out a celebrity magazine. I know before I even see the front cover that it's the same magazine that I threw out, the one with a picture of Johnny as a child inside.

I bury my face in my hands, my stomach churning horrendously.

'I saw this a few weeks ago,' she says.

'I've seen it,' I mumble. 'You don't have to show me.'

'I thought they looked similar,' she continues. 'But I didn't realise how similar until I saw Barney yesterday. I didn't know whether or not to talk to you about it, but you're my best friend. How could I not?'

I don't say anything.

'Meg? Please look at me.'

I let my hands fall to my lap, my face expressionless. She stares at me for a long time, a mixture of sympathy and concern written all over her features. But none of it gets through to me. I feel dead inside.

'I'm right, aren't I?' she asks.

'Right about what?' I say slowly, wanting her to spell it out, not just to be sure about what she's saying, but to make it harder for her. I'm certainly not going to help make it any easier for her. A feeling of dislike for my so-called best friend is starting to invade me. I know that's unfair, but it's how I feel. I hate her for discovering the truth.

'Does Christian know?' she continues.

'Does Christian know what?' I spit venomously.

'Meg.' She reaches out to touch my arm, but I snatch it away.

'Get off!' I all but shout, shocking myself at how out of control I feel. I glance quickly at Barney, but he doesn't stir.

'He's Johnny's, isn't he?' Bess whispers, and I can hear her perfectly, even with music playing in the background. 'He looks just like him.'

I meet her eyes and then I crumble. A lump comes out of nowhere to lodge itself in my throat and the tears come. Bess touches my arm again, but I pull it away, not so violently this time.

'You know you can trust me,' she says.

I didn't think I could trust anyone with this, but it's all going wrong. It's going the way I thought it would, but still I hoped that I could get away with it.

Bess regards me with sadness. 'Have you always known?'

I shake my head and whisper, 'No.'

'What happened?'

I take a deep breath. Then I take another one. Soon I'm able to speak, but it's not without difficulty. 'It was when Johnny came back to try to convince me to go to LA with him. He wanted me to leave Christian. I refused.' I look at her and she nods, urging me to go on. 'I didn't have the will to stop when he

89

started to kiss me. He has . . . a hold over me. I feel drugged when I'm around him. At least, I used to.'

'I know.' She takes my hand and squeezes it.

'I used to torment myself,' I say, now a little manically. 'My pregnancy . . . I used to torment myself with ludicrous scenarios, like what if Christian and I had more children and one of them needed a bone-marrow transplant in the future. Siblings are the most likely candidates for a good match, but what if the doctors discovered that they were only half-siblings? And what if my son or daughter died as a result of my mistake?'

There's pity in Bess's eyes as I continue to ramble.

'Or what if we couldn't have any more children and Christian found out he was infertile and always had been? I literally drove myself nuts contemplating it all. But I thought Barney could have been Christian's. I tried to convince myself. Christian is a good dad.'

The lump gets bigger.

'Does he know?' Bess asks the question for the second time.

'No. And you can't tell him,' I say fervently. 'You can't ever, ever tell him.'

'Meg . . .'

'No, Bess, no.'

'He'll find out. How can he not?'

I start to feel slightly hysterical. 'I don't know. I don't know why he hasn't realised already. I don't know what to do.'

'You have to tell him.'

'How can I do that? It would destroy him!'

'He needs to know the truth.'

'Why? What good will the truth do any of us? Barney is used to having Christian as his daddy; he's used to him! Christian loves Barney. And you know what Johnny's like – what sort of a father would he make?'

Bess shakes her head, sadly. 'It's not about Johnny and Christian. I mean, of course it is, but you have to think of Barney.'

'I do think of Barney!' I cry, as sobs well up inside me. 'I think of him every minute of every day!'

'I know you do. You're a great mum. But this is not about him *now*; it's about him in the future. He won't remember this time when he's older. Sad as it is, he won't remember that Christian was his dad.'

I brush away at my tears, but they keep falling.

Bess continues, 'You have to sort this out before he's old enough to remember. It's the kindest thing to do. I'm sorry.'

I nod, through blurry eyes. 'I know. I know you're right,' I choke out.

'You have to tell him soon. You have to promise me you'll tell him soon.'

Abruptly, my tears stop. I stare ahead in subdued silence.

The next day, I can't look at Bess. She takes Barney down to breakfast while I lie on the bed and stare into space. Eventually I get up and pack our things. I try to put on a brave face when they return, but it's hard.

I drive Bess to the airport. We don't speak in the car, apart from Bess pointing out things to Barney. I pull up in front of Departures and turn to her. I still can't look her in the eyes. She leans across and hugs me tightly, but I barely have the strength to return it.

'You'll be okay,' she whispers into my hair. 'It will all be okay. These things happen for a reason.'

I pull away, trying to stay strong.

'Bye, Barney,' she says to my little boy, strapped into his car seat in the back. 'He's beautiful, Meg,' she says to me sincerely. 'You're lucky to have him.'

I nod quickly, but can't stop the tears from filling my eyes.

'Bye,' I say quietly, meeting her gaze for a millisecond.

'Keep in touch,' she urges, and closes the door behind her. I drive away before she reaches the sliding doors.

Chapter 11

'Go to sleep, Barney,' I say to him when he starts to grizzle. I don't have the energy or the patience to deal with him on the car journey home. I hope he naps soon. I need to think.

Christian is away for approximately another week and a half. It's probably a good thing. I'll need that time to prepare. He won't want us to hang around once he finds out the truth. I'll need to pack up our things and decide where to go. We could stay with Mum and Dad for a while. I'll have to tell them what I've done. At least Mandy isn't around to discover Barney isn't her grandson.

I instantly feel dirty and disgusted with myself. How could I ever regard her death as a positive?

Barney drops off after a while, giving me the peace I need. The more I think about it, the more I know that Bess is right. I have to sort this out before my baby gets any older. If Bess worked it out, any of our other friends could do exactly the same. In fact, blind though Christian has been so far, if Barney and Johnny ever do meet, surely even Christian will find it impossible to ignore their similarities. It's better for Barney that his life is disrupted now, before he's old enough to fully understand or remember.

But, God . . . My poor, poor Christian. He's already dealing with the death of his mother – how much can one person cope with before they break?

I feel like I'm close to breaking point myself, but this is nothing compared to what he's going through with his family's bereavement.

Do I really have to do this?

Yes. Yes, I do.

Bess calls me that night, after I've put Barney to bed. I've been walking around in a daze all day, unable to perk myself up, even though I know my mood has been affecting my son. I take the phone to the sofa and lie down in the darkness. I'm glad to have someone to talk to.

'I wanted to check you're alright,' she says.

'No. I'm anything but,' I tell her, my eyes welling up. 'I can't bear the thought of hurting him like this.'

'You haven't spoken to him yet?'

'No. I don't know how I'll keep up the act, but I don't want to drag him home early.'

'He's going to know something's wrong,' she says gently. 'It's better that you tell him sooner rather than later, even if that does mean him ducking out of work early, so to speak.'

'Oh, God . . .' I start to cry.

'I don't know how you've lived with this secret all this time,' she says in a kind voice. 'It must have been awful.'

'Don't feel sorry for me. I deserve everything I get.'

'Hey . . .' she says soothingly. 'I know you probably can't see any light at the end of the tunnel, but you couldn't have gone on carrying this burden around. It would have worn you down in the end, even if the truth hadn't come out.'

I take a deep breath and try to stop crying. What she's saying makes sense.

'Bess, I think I'm going to go.'

'Okay,' she says. 'You take care. Call me if you want to talk. I'll ring again tomorrow.'

'Okay.' I hang up and take another deep breath. I reach for a tissue to dab at my eyes and then I blow my nose. I feel utterly wretched. I go to the French windows and open them up to let in the warm night air. If the mosquitoes choose to attack me, so be it. I want to see the mountains and I don't want to see them behind glass. The sun has set behind me so the peaks ahead are dark. In the far-off distance I can hear a motorcycle screaming around the bends.

I wonder what Christian is doing. I look at my watch: it's nine thirty. He's probably backstage at a Contour Lines concert, pen and paper at the ready. The sound of the motor-cycle is getting closer. Moments later, the machine roars into view at the bottom of our hill. Then it stops. The rider is star-ing in my direction, the low murmur of the ticking-over engine audible from here. How strange. Suddenly the person revs up the engine and starts to storm up our hill. And then stops again. Right outside our house. The terrace lights are on, but I'm standing here in the darkness, so I don't think anyone can see me. My heart starts to beat faster. I don't have a good feeling about this. The rider climbs off the bike and pushes it into our driveway, and then goes out of sight. Barney is asleep and I'm here alone. Did I lock the front door? I don't know. I quickly run across the living room and check that the door is bolted. It is. Are all the windows closed? Yes.

BANG, BANG, BANG!

The person's at the door!

'MEG!'

Johnny?

'Johnny?' I ask through the wood.

'Open up!' he shouts, pounding at the door once again.

Stunned, I unlock the door and pull it towards me. Johnny is standing there, his helmet under his arm.

'He's mine, isn't he?' he demands to know.

I stare at him. His face is anguished.

He pushes past me into the house. 'I want to see him.'

I come to life. 'No. NO.' I close the door behind him. 'What the hell were you thinking, turning up out of the blue like this? Christian could have been here!'

'What the hell was I thinking?' He looks at me, incredulous. 'Sorry, did you just ask me what the hell was *I* thinking?'

I ignore him. 'Please keep your voice down. Come through to the living room.'

'I want to see my son,' he says slowly, adamantly.

I turn to look at him, a deadly calm settling over me. 'You can't. He's asleep.'

He looks tortured. 'So he *is* mine.'

'Come through to the living room,' I repeat.

He dumps his helmet on the sofa and slumps down, burying his head in his hands.

'Can I get you a drink?' I ask. I feel detached from my body, or rather, detached from my emotions. I feel robotic, calm, in control, yet at the same time this is totally surreal. This isn't happening to me. It's like I'm in a dream.

Johnny doesn't answer, so I leave him there and go into the kitchen. I switch on the kettle and put two teaspoons of instant coffee into a mug. We don't have a coffee machine, so it'll have to do. I bring it back through to him and put it on a coaster on the coffee table. I have a feeling it might stay there for some time. I sit on the sofa perpendicular to him, and then I wait. It's not long before he raises his tormented eyes and stares at me. He looks pale, tired. He hasn't shaved in days – not since I saw him at Christian's parents' house, I imagine.

'I want to hear it from you,' he says quietly. 'Is he mine?'

I nod. 'It would seem that way.'

'Has Christian always known?'

'No.' I pause. 'I'm telling him when he gets back.'

'You won't have long to wait,' Johnny says. 'Contrary to popular opinion,' he adds, mildly sarcastically, 'I wouldn't have turned up out of the blue, even if I do only have a window of a day.'

'A day?' I ask, panicked. 'He's not coming back until the week after next!'

Johnny closes his eyes, irritated with himself, and then opens them again. 'He was going to surprise you. I wasn't supposed to tell you.'

'Oh, God . . . He's back tomorrow?'

Johnny nods.

So now I have even less time to prepare, to pack up all our belongings, to speak to my parents . . .

He sighs deeply. 'How could you let this happen, Meg?'

Rage rushes through me. 'How could *I* let this happen? I seem to remember there were two of us there when you forced me to have sex with you!'

'I didn't force you to have sex with me!' he scoffs, getting to his feet.

'You may as well have, coming into my bedroom like that when I was getting changed! What the hell were you thinking?'

'Here we go again: what the hell was I thinking?' he says irately, pacing the room. 'What the hell were *you* thinking, not telling me you were pregnant? I had a right to know!' He points at me angrily. 'I *waited* for you, Meg! I waited three months for you! You could have told me! We might have been able to work it out.'

I laugh, bitterly. 'Are you living in fucking cuckoo land? *Look at you!* You're a mess! Who the fuck would want *you* to be a father?' Ker-ching goes the swear box.

He glares at me. Seconds pass before he speaks. 'That's not your choice to make.'

'I thought he could have been Christian's,' I say, a slight tremor to my voice.

'How long did it take you to work out that he wasn't? Anyone with half a brain can see that he's mine. I don't know how Christian hasn't worked it out – I thought he was brighter than that!'

'Don't you *dare* speak about him like that! He doesn't deserve it.'

'Oh, fuck,' he mutters, pushing his hands through his hair and collapsing back on the sofa, the desolation returning. 'He's never going to forgive me for this.'

'No. I don't imagine he will,' I say.

Johnny looks up. 'Well, he's sure as hell not going to forgive you!'

'Are you kidding me? Do you think I don't know that? Barney is going to lose his father over this! Christian is going to lose the son he thinks is his! I may as well cut him open, tear out his heart and rip it into shreds!'

I snatch at the Kleenex box and empty it of its last three tissues. Johnny lets me cry. When I calm down he's looking at me gravely.

'I want to see him, Meg.'

I nod, my resolve gone. 'But you can't wake him up.'

'I won't.'

I lead him down the corridor to Barney's bedroom and push open the door. Johnny is so close I can feel his body heat. Barney is fast asleep in his cot, his face lit by the glow of his night light.

I step back while Johnny tentatively approaches. Tears trek down my cheeks and I brush them away as he stares at my son. He reaches down and strokes my boy's face.

'Okay,' I say quietly. 'That's enough.'

I lead the way out and start to walk back down the corridor, but I realise there are no footsteps behind me. I turn around to see Johnny standing outside Barney's room, his green eyes glistening.

'What's he like?' His voice sounds croaky.

I smile sadly. 'He's the best. He's very funny, very sweet, a real little character. Come away from his room,' I urge.

'I want to meet him properly,' he warns when we reach the hallway. His face is deadly serious.

I nod. 'But I have to speak to Christian first. Please,' I implore. 'Please give us some time.'

He takes a deep breath and exhales loudly. 'I'll wait for you to call me,' he says firmly. 'But make it sooner rather than later.'

That doesn't feel like a promise; it feels like a threat.

Chapter 12

Today. Today is the day. I've hardly slept a wink, and the little sleep I did get was plagued by horrible nightmares. There are dark circles under my eyes, and I look so pale I might as well have been living in the Antarctic, not the south of France. Christian will probably joke that I've partied too hard in Barcelona. If only he knew.

I don't know what time he's returning. I haven't had a chance to pack up all of our things, but I have started to put aside some essentials to get us through the next few days. I don't want a suitcase to greet Christian when he arrives – that would make it impossible to hold off explaining until Barney is in bed. I was hoping I'd have time to tell my parents, to ask them to look after my son while I talk to Christian, but it's all going so fast. I can't believe this is happening.

Christian calls me on my mobile at two o'clock in the afternoon.

'Hello?' I answer the phone, too surprised to sound shaken. Isn't he coming home today, after all?

'Hey!' he says. 'Where are you?'

'At home,' I reply. 'Where are you?' There's a jaunty knock at the door. 'Hang on,' I say. 'Someone's here.' It occurs to me that it might be Johnny returning. Terrified at that thought, I open the door to see a beaming Christian standing on the terrace, his phone at his ear.

'Boo!' he shouts, grabbing me around my waist and swinging me full circle, his phone pressing into my skin through my flimsy dress. He kisses me squarely on the lips and puts me down on the baking-hot terrace. I'm too taken aback to say or do anything other than hop, barefooted, back inside to the cool stone floor.

He laughs. 'Sorry.'

'I didn't think you were coming home until next week!' I exclaim.

'I'm back for only two days,' he cautions. 'Then I have to go away again, but the band is taking a break and, after everything that's happened recently, I needed to come home and chill out for a bit and see my little family.' He seems so happy, like the weight from his mother's death has momentarily lifted off his shoulders. 'Where's Barney?' he asks.

'Still asleep. He'll wake up soon.'

'I'm bloody boiling!' he says. 'Let's grab our swimmers and go to the lake.'

I stare at his excited face and despise myself for having to put on a pretence for the rest of the day. Then again, what's one more lie?

'Okay,' I say.

There's a lake not far from here, down a beaten track off one of the mountain roads. Only the locals know about it, but Christian's friend let us in on the secret when we first moved here.

We pull into the car park. Christian hired a car to bring him from the airport and he got upgraded to an Alfa Romeo 159 Sportwagon, which is the next size up from the Alfa that he currently owns. He has to return it in two days when he flies out to join the band at the next concert, but he's really pleased to be getting an extended test drive because he's been thinking about getting us a bigger car. His delight is just another nail in my coffin: there won't be any need for a bigger car now.

The air-con has barely had a chance to kick in, but the heat when I open the car door makes it hard to breathe. The lake shimmers behind the trees as Christian leads the way across a small stream via stepping stones. Barney is in his arms.

We normally approach the lake via a wider stream and a grassy bank, but now we reach a concrete platform that looks down at the lake below us, deep and green and crystal clear. There are some teenagers dive-bombing into the water nearby. There are no steps here and it's a drop of about six feet. I don't think I'd fancy it even if I didn't have Barney to think about. Christian looks at me with a cheeky grin on his face.

'Can I?'

'Can you what?'

'Can I jump in and meet you over there?' He indicates the bank in the distance.

I smile at him. 'Of course you can.'

He hands me Barney and the two of us stand and watch as 'Daddy' takes a running jump and dive-bombs into the water, creating quite a tidal wave. Christian rises to the surface, gasping at the cold temperature. It's impossible not to laugh.

'Whoa! That was amazing!' He looks like a child on Christmas Day.

It's at times like these that I remember why I love him.

My throat aches and my nose starts to itch. I turn away and head towards the wider stream, stepping extra carefully so I don't drop my son.

I remember why I love him . . . What a strange expression. Surely you always know why you love someone? Is it possible to forget? Sometimes in my darkest moments I wonder if I actually love Christian at all. That's a terrible thing to say, but it's true. I'm fond of him – very, very fond of him – and I like him immensely, but love?

I loved Johnny. I loved him passionately. I just didn't like him very much.

I see Christian walking across the grass to meet us on the other side of the stream. The rocks are sharp underneath my feet, but I'm wearing flip-flops so it's not too treacherous. I am struggling to carry Barney and our bags, though, so I'm glad Christian has come to help. He grins at me as he waits at the muddy exit to the stream. His dark hair is dripping wet and his broad torso sports quite an impressive tan. He's looking better than he ever has, with happiness and contentment etched into his face.

I do love him. Right now, right this second, I love him so much that my heart aches. Because I know I'm going to lose him.

'Let me take that from you,' he says, grappling for Barney and my beach bag. 'You should do that next time,' he adds. 'It was so much fun.'

'It looked it,' I reply.

'Let's go up to the waterfall,' he suggests.

'Okay.'

I try to hold back my tears as I follow him across the grass to a tiny dirt track behind a dilapidated old stone building. The narrow pathway requires some concentration – there's a hefty drop into the lake below – but eventually it widens and we reach some sandy-coloured rocks below a waterfall. Christian holds Barney while I lower myself into the water with a sharp intake of breath. The hotter I am, the colder the water feels, but I'm desperate to cool down. It must be forty degrees today. Christian hands me Barney and I dip him up and down. He gasps and wriggles in my grasp and I can't help giggling.

'How was Barcelona?' Christian asks, sliding into the water beside me.

'Good,' I reply. 'The hotel was stunning. Thank you again for that.'

'You're welcome.' He smiles. 'We'll have to go back there sometime, just the two of us. Well, three of us . . . Maybe for your birthday in October.'

'Mmm.'

I can't do this. I just can't.

'You alright?' he asks.

'Me? Yeah, I'm fine.'

'You seem a bit . . . off.'

'I don't feel that well.' At least that part's the truth.

'Coming down with something?' He presses his hand to my forehead.

I shrug and turn away, not wanting him to be kind. 'I don't know. I'll be okay.' I hope.

By the time Barney is in bed that night, I'm feeling so tense and ill that I'm actually dizzy with it. The fact that I've barely touched a morsel of food all day doesn't help.

'Are you still feeling rotten?' Christian asks sympathetically.

This is it. This is it.

I nod, not meeting his eyes. Don't be a coward, Meg. I drag them up to look at him.

'Do you want me to make you some toast or something?' he asks.

I shake my head slowly. I open my mouth to speak, but nothing comes out.

'What?' he asks, his brow furrowing.

'I . . .' Again the words fail to come.

'Come and sit down.' He takes my hand and leads me to the sofa. His touch is warm and comforting. I gently detach myself and go to sit on the other sofa. He stares at me in bewilderment.

'You won't want to be near me in a minute,' I manage to say. 'You should sit down.'

He does, hesitantly. All of the happiness and contentment from earlier has gone. Now he looks worried and confused.

I glance down at my hands and then up at his face. I haven't rehearsed this. Why haven't I rehearsed this? I had enough time to do that. I don't know where to start, what to say. How can I break such awful news to someone so inherently decent?

Christian speaks first. 'It's Johnny, isn't it?'

His question takes me aback. It is, in a way.

'You're still in love with him, aren't you?' he says flatly.

'No.' I shake my head vehemently. 'No! No, I'm not.'

'Then what is it?'

Oh, God . . . Oh, God . . .

For a moment, I wish I had that magazine. I could have put it in front of him with a picture of Barney and that would have revealed the truth in an instant. But no, I should start at the beginning. I might not get a chance to explain otherwise.

'I have to tell you something.' I finally find my voice. 'And I'm so sorry. So very, very sorry.'

'What is it? This is driving me mad.'

'I'm sorry,' I say again. 'I'm so sorry about your mum and what you've already been through. I can't believe what I'm about to say . . .'

'Meg.' His tone is firm.

I take a deep breath and then it comes to me, the way I'm going to tell it. 'A bit under two years ago, Johnny came to the house and tried to persuade me to leave you and to choose him instead.'

Christian nods tensely, willing me to go on.

'I refused,' I tell him. 'But . . . I'm so sorry.'

'What?' he practically shouts.

'We slept together.'

'Oh, fuck,' he curses, dragging his hands through his hair and slumping back on the sofa. He glares at me.

I haven't even started yet . . .

'Did you fuck him at my parents' place last week?' he spits.

'No!' I exclaim. 'Of course not! It was just the one time. It's never happened since.'

Some of his anger dissipates, and I sense that he would have forgiven me for this as it was quite a long time ago. But he will never forgive me for what I'm about to say next.

My eyes well up. 'I fell pregnant.' I stare at him and he stares back at me, not comprehending, not yet. Tears start to trail down my cheeks.

'What do you mean?' He's confused. 'You had an abortion?'

I shake my head, very, very slowly, not taking my eyes from his. Then, suddenly, he gets it.

The look on his face . . . It will haunt me for the rest of my life.

'Barney?' he whispers. 'Barney is his?'

'I'm sorry.'

'No, no, no . . . NO!' He starts to pull at his hair, scratch at his face. 'NO!'

'I'm sorry.'

He leaps to his feet and stalks towards the balcony window. I stay seated, giving him space.

'No,' he says again. 'No.' He turns on me. 'When did you find out? Have you always known?'

'No!' Words flood out of my mouth as I try to explain. 'I wasn't sure. I wanted him to be yours. I hoped he would be born with dark hair, and when he was, I cried with relief! But now . . .' I stare at him miserably. 'Now he doesn't look like you at all.'

Christian regards me with hatred in his eyes. He's never looked at me like this before and I deserve it, even though it's cutting me to the bone.

'Does Johnny know?'

'He worked it out.'

'When?'

'In Newcastle. As we were leaving. He saw a picture of Barney with your mum . . .'

'I'm going to fucking kill him.'

'Christian, I'm so sorry.'

'I'M GOING TO FUCKING KILL HIM!'

Christian stands with his back to me, facing the mountains, breathing heavily. And then suddenly he puts his face in his hands and starts to sob. It's the most awful, heart-wrenching thing I will ever hear. I hurry over to him and put my hands on his shuddering back, but he violently pushes me off.

'I've started packing some things,' I say quietly. 'We'll go to my parents in the morning if you'll just let us stay tonight. I don't want to wake Barney if that's at all possible.'

His sobs stop abruptly and he looks at me in disbelief.

'You're leaving me? You're not fucking leaving me! You're not taking my son away from me. He's my son!' He aggressively points down the corridor and then turns his finger on me. 'That bastard might've fucked you, but I raised him and YOU'RE NOT TAKING HIM AWAY!'

'Okay, okay!' I put my hands up to calm him. 'I will do whatever you want me to do. I love you.'

He stares at me, his eyes wide and his shoulders visibly moving up and down with every breath.

'I love you,' I say again, willing him to believe it, hoping it will somehow dull the pain.

His face crumples and this time I can't give him space. I throw my arms around his neck and he gives in, crying into my shoulder.

'I'm so sorry. I'm so sorry.' I say it over and over again. I'll never stop saying it.

'I don't want you to go,' he says in a muffled voice and I almost dare to hope that it will all be alright, that somehow we will work this out.

'I won't go,' I promise. 'I won't leave you. I'm here for as long as you want me. I'm so sorry.'

'Have you told your parents?'

'No.'

'Does anyone else know?'

I hesitate before owning up. 'Bess worked it out in Barcelona.'

'For fuck's sake!'

'She won't tell anyone,' I add quickly.

'Good. Don't tell your parents. I don't want anyone else to know.'

'Okay,' I say, because I don't want to hurt him anymore. But this is going to be complicated. Johnny is aware of Barney's existence now. I can't imagine how this is going to pan out, but there's one thing I'm certain of: there's more heartbreak to come.

Chapter 13

Christian cancels his trip to join the band, claiming there's no way he can concentrate on work now. I don't know how we get through the next few days, but we do.

His devastation is crushing, though. He can barely look at Barney without crying. It's the most horrible thing to witness and I hate myself more and more with every hour that passes. I think Barney is confused. He's acting fairly normally, but sometimes he regards his father with wariness. I hope with all my heart that we can get through this, but I'm far from convinced that we can.

Christian won't look at me. He won't touch me. He won't come to bed with me. He sleeps on the sofa – refusing to let me sleep there – and speaks to me amicably enough when Barney is around. When Barney isn't there, he hardly speaks to me at all. He doesn't want to know any more details about what happened. He doesn't care that this lie has been killing me. He sniggered when I told him I didn't want to hurt him, but mostly his pain is pure, not poisoned by sarcasm or cruelty. Not yet, anyway.

I still haven't called Johnny. I know that I have to. I just don't know how. I've already been so deceitful and I don't want to cause Christian any more pain, but we're going to have to go there soon. Johnny won't wait forever.

After six days, Christian tells me he has to return his rental car, because the rental company have started to charge him extra money for his upgrade. He needs to drop it off at Toulouse airport, which is two hours away, so I offer to follow him in our car to save him from catching a train back. He nods curtly, and I tentatively ask if we should relocate Barney's car seat to my car.

'No,' he snaps. 'He can ride with me.'

It feels strange driving his Alfa without Barney in the back. I don't like it. I don't like it at all. Christian drives faster than me around the winding mountain roads – he always has – but I'm struggling to keep him in my sights and I don't feel as in control as I should be. What if something happens to me? Who would look after my son?

I put my foot on the brake pedal to slow myself down. If he drives away from me, so be it. I'll find my own way.

He speeds around the corners and out of sight. I wish he'd slow down. What if he crashes and kills Barney? Suddenly I'm overcome with panic. I want to catch them up, even though I feel dizzy. I should pull over, but what if he kills himself and my son with him? Up ahead I see Christian's rental car and I realise he's slowed down, waiting for me. I take several deep breaths and try to compose myself, but it takes me a good ten minutes before I return to normal. Finally we hit the motorway and I relax.

When am I going to call Johnny?

Hang on, *how* am I going to call Johnny?

That second thought hasn't even occurred to me until now. I doubt Johnny has the same mobile number that he had when I worked for him – he lost his phone twice during that time and I assume that's fairly standard behaviour. Everyone used to go through his PA, but I don't fancy calling her. What was her name? Lena, that's it. How would I convince Lena that my message is one she should definitely pass on? I wonder if she even knows who I am. 'Meg Stiles. I used to work for Johnny.' The ghost of another PA before her. Again I wonder if he's come onto her, too, just like he did with Paola, his PA before me. Envy jabs at me and I'm revolted by myself. How can I feel envy after everything I've been through, after everything I'm putting Christian through?

Well, he won't have shagged her if she's still working there. I doubt it, anyway.

Christian will have his private number. But I can't see that going down too well.

My phone beeps and I wonder if it's Christian trying to tell me something. I keep my eyes on the road and rummage around in my handbag until I find it. I give the screen a quick glance to see if it's from Christian, but there's no caller ID – only a telephone number. I return my attention to the road but, moments later, curiosity gets the better of me and I slow down and take a look at the message.

Have you told him yet?

Johnny? My heart skips a beat. It must be from him. That's so weird. So weird. I was only just thinking of him.

The weirdness continues to plague me as we drive on. What should I say? I can't text and drive. I mean, I can, but I shouldn't. Anyway, he can wait.

What should I say? What should I say?

'Yes'?

No, that won't do. I'll have to explain, to stop him from contacting me again. Something along the lines of: 'Yes. It's been awful. Please give us more time to adjust. I'll text you soon.'

That sounds about right, but like I said, he'll have to wait.

I try to keep my resolve, but the urge to text him back keeps itch, itch, itching at me until I can hardly keep from scratching it. I'm about to give in when Christian pulls into a petrol station. We're near the airport so he needs to refuel. Immensely relieved, I drive into a parking space and snatch up my phone. I type out the message and throw the phone back into my handbag.

Ping!

Another message.

Christian is still filling the car. I pick up my phone and read it:

How soon?

Oh, for pity's sake. Leave us alone! No, I won't reply. I won't. Bugger it.

I don't know, Johnny. Have some respect!

My phone starts to ring.

'What?' I snap.

'Are you taking the fucking piss?' Johnny asks down the line.

'I can't talk now,' I reply crossly. 'You're going to have to wait!'

'I've waited long enough, thank you very much. Two fucking years I've waited.'

'Well, then, what's another week?' I say sarcastically.

'A week,' he replies smugly. 'A week it is, then.'

He hangs up on me. The bastard hangs up on me. Bloody hell.

I glance up to see Christian getting back in the car, having already paid for his fuel. I start up the engine and follow him out.

That evening, Christian doesn't offer to help with any part of Barney's bedtime routine. He sits in front of the telly watching *Top Gear* so I get on with Barney's bath, milk, story and bed. Afterwards I walk across the hall with my head down, scratching my elbow absent-mindedly as I wonder if Christian will talk to me tonight. I reach the living room and glance first at the television and then at my boyfriend, and then I stop in my tracks when I see the look on his face. He has my phone in his hand and is glaring at me accusingly.

'What the fuck is this about?' He holds up the phone.

'I was going to tell you,' I say hurriedly.

'Don't make me laugh.'

'I was!' My voice rises. 'I was!'

'What were you going to tell me? That you and this bastard have been having cosy little chats with each other behind my back?'

'We haven't been! He texted me earlier—'

115

My sentence is cut short by Christian hurling my phone in a fury across the room. It narrowly misses my face, clonking against the wall and clattering to the floor. In despair I pick it up and discover that my phone has a crack straight across the screen.

'You broke my phone!' I wail, unable to keep my cool.

'You're lucky I didn't break your nose.'

I stare at him in shock and his face instantly mirrors mine.

'I didn't mean that,' he says quickly. 'Of course I didn't mean that.'

A cry from Barney's room startles us both into action.

'I'll go,' I say, leaving the room.

It takes me a few minutes to settle him before I return with trepidation to the living room. Christian is staring straight ahead. He's switched off the telly.

'I'm sorry I didn't tell you about Johnny contacting me,' I say.

'It's alright,' he brushes me off, and it's clear he's calmed down somewhat. 'I know you would have done eventually,' he concedes. 'So tell me what he said.'

'You read the messages?'

'Yes.'

'You know they weren't "cosy little chats", then.'

He nods. 'He called you – I saw your recent calls,' he explains.

'Yes. Once again, not cosy.' I take a deep breath. 'He wants to . . .' I pause, and then it all comes out in a flurry of words. 'He wants to meet Barney properly.'

Christian's jaw is set in a straight line. 'How do you feel about that?' he asks with some effort.

'I don't like it,' I admit. 'The last thing I want to do is to cause

116

you any pain. Any *more* pain,' I correct myself. 'But I guess this isn't just about you and me anymore.'

He nods abruptly. 'So be it. I want the best thing for Barney. He's still my son.'

'Of course he is,' I say. 'He always will be.'

Chapter 14

'When are you going home again?' I ask Christian two days later.

'I don't know. Dad's still not ready to clear away Mum's things.'

'What about joining the band on tour?'

'Are you trying to get rid of me?' he asks drily.

'No! Of course not.' Do I sound guilty?

'Have you called Johnny yet?'

Yep, he's onto me. 'No.' Don't be a chicken. 'But I should.'

'Well, I'm not going away while all that's going on. I want to be here.'

I take a sip of my drink. We're sitting out on the terrace and have just finished a dinner of pork cooked in cider. I'm trying to make it up to Christian through his stomach, but I've had no compliments for the chef.

'I guess I'd better call him,' I say.

'I guess you'd better.' He takes a gulp of his beer and plonks it down on the table, then he gets to his feet and starts to clear the table. I do the same, following him indoors to the kitchen.

'You don't want to ring him?' I ask hesitantly. I've been

wondering this for a few days now. Christian looks at me like I'm mad. 'No?' I double-check.

'What do you think?' he snaps.

'I just thought . . . well, he's your best friend.'

'Was,' he corrects me. 'There's no way in hell we're getting past this one.'

'But you've been through so much,' I implore. 'This whole situation would be easier—'

'Meg,' he cuts me off. 'No.'

I look down, disheartened. I could but hope. 'I'll call him, then.'

'What, now?'

'If that's okay with you?'

'Yep.' He scrapes the remnants of his dinner into the bin. I walk away, treading carefully over the eggshells that will no doubt line my path for some time to come.

I take my phone and go back out to the terrace, leaving the door open so Christian thinks I don't mind him listening in, even though I do. I dial Johnny's number. My hands begin to shake. He doesn't answer and it goes straight through to voice-mail. I'm dithering about whether or not to leave a message when my phone beeps to let me know there's another call coming in. I look at my handset to see that Johnny is calling me back.

'Hello?' I say.

'What's the plan?' He cuts straight to the chase. 'When am I going to meet the boy?'

'His name is Barney,' I say tersely. 'How soon can you get here?'

'Friday?'

That's two days away.

'Okay,' I say.

'I'll get Lena to contact you with the details,' he says.

'Don't palm me off onto your PA, Johnny,' I say crossly. 'You contact me yourself with the details.'

'Ooh, tetchy,' he says annoyingly, and I detect a hint of amusement beneath his tone. But this isn't funny.

'I mean it,' I add.

'Okay, Nutmeg, I'll text you later.'

'Fine,' I say, but he's already hung up. Damn. He's irritating like that.

I walk back inside to see Christian leaning up against one of the countertops in the kitchen. His face is expressionless.

'He's coming on Friday,' I tell him nervously.

'Great.' Sarcasm, obviously.

'Are you going to be alright with this?'

'Oh, I'm going to be dandy,' Christian says, false-merrily.

The nausea inside my stomach swirls a little more. I've been feeling sick incessantly and I can't imagine how that will ever cease.

Johnny's PA books him into a chateau about an hour's drive away; he's planning on staying in France for four days. He comes to the house on Friday afternoon on the same motorbike as before. Was it really less than a fortnight ago that he was last here? It feels like an age.

Christian has barely left Barney's side all day. He's with him in the pool when Johnny arrives. I'm on the terrace waiting. Again, I hear his motorcycle before I see it. This time he doesn't stop at the bottom of the hill, but zooms around the corner and straight up to our driveway. He pulls in on the gravel and kicks down his foot-stand. I get up and lean over the wall as he climbs off his bike. He looks up at me as he pulls his helmet off, his hair damp with sweat. This is Johnny Jefferson, rock star, father of my child.

'Alright?' he says, unzipping his leather biker jacket. I can see his wet shirt from here.

'Bit hot, are you?'

'Fucking sweltering.' He positions his helmet on his handle-bars and climbs the terrace steps.

'Where did you get your bike from?'

'Brought it from LA on the jet.'

Only in Johnny's world . . .

'Where's Christian?' he asks.

'He's in the pool with Barney.'

He doesn't attempt to hide his surprise. 'He hasn't gone out?'

'No. He wanted to be here. Come inside,' I motion towards the door and Johnny walks past me, removing his jacket and gloves as he goes.

I know that Christian will have heard Johnny arrive, but he's making no attempt to bring Barney to us. He'll make us go to him, and who could blame him?

'Have you spoken to Christian?' I ask, even though I'm pretty sure I know the answer.

'No,' Johnny says.

'Why not?'

'What do you mean, why not?' He frowns. 'I don't think he wants to talk to me, do you?'

I shrug, faking nonchalance. 'I don't suppose you want to talk to him either, but it's not about want, it's about should. Have you even considered apologising?'

He snorts. '"Sorry" ain't gonna cut it.'

'We're not talking about the time you shagged his girlfriend – the *other* time,' I correct myself, because he had sex with one of Christian's girlfriends years ago, way before I came along. 'You didn't say sorry then, either, and it all blew over eventually. But not this time, Johnny. This time he deserves to hear it, even if he never wants to speak to you again.'

He regards me curiously. 'I didn't think he'd forgive you.'

'Neither did I,' I say honestly. 'Anyway, he hasn't, yet. I don't know if he ever will, but we're trying to get through it.'

I hear Barney squealing hysterically. Johnny looks at me quickly.

'Is that him?'

'Yes.'

He shifts from foot to foot.

'You're nervous,' I say, oddly fascinated by the realisation.

He shrugs, but doesn't answer. A minuscule wave of sympathy crashes inside me.

'Come on.'

I lead the way out onto the terrace and down the steps, turning right towards the pool. We can hear Christian's deep voice behind the gate and when I push it open, the wood screeching loudly across the stone, we see Christian drying Barney off at the poolside with a blue and white striped towel. He glares at Johnny before turning his attention back to Barney. My little blond-haired, green-eyed boy glances at his biological father and then looks at me and grins a toothy grin.

'Did you have fun in the pool?' I ask him brightly, intensely aware of Johnny's presence beside me.

Barney pulls away from Christian and stands, wobbling on

the spot, with his arms opened out to me. I whisk him up and give him a cuddle, immediately feeling the dampness of his swimming trunks seeping through my khaki-coloured T-shirt and white shorts. I've dressed casually today; I don't want to look like I've made an effort for Mr Celebrity.

Christian stands up and drops the towel onto a sunlounger. I know that he's struggling to remain calm. If looks could kill, his former best friend would be on his way to the coroner right about now.

Barney presses his cold, wet nose to mine and I can't help but smile, despite the tension surrounding us.

I give Christian a supportive nod and then turn to look at Johnny. He's staring at Barney with a strange expression on his face. I don't know how to describe it: a sort of awe and awkwardness all rolled into one. He can't take his eyes off him.

'Barney, this is Johnny,' I introduce them for want of something else to say.

'Hello,' Johnny says quietly and he reaches out and takes Barney's hand, shaking it slightly.

'You've got a fucking nerve,' Christian growls from behind me. I spin around, the action wrenching Johnny's grasp from Barney's hand. Christian's whole body is rigid and he's breathing heavily. He's close to losing it.

'Calm down,' I urge nervously. 'Shall we all go inside?'

'No,' Christian says bitterly. 'I like it out here.' He sits on the end of a sunlounger and eyes Johnny up and down in his long-sleeved shirt and black jeans. He knows that his enemy will be uncomfortable in this heat, on top of everything else.

'Take a seat,' I tell Johnny in a strained voice, and then I pass

Barney to Christian and unwind the awning so at least we're not sitting in full sun.

Barney starts babbling and Christian manages a half-hearted smile at him.

'How's your hotel?' I ask Johnny, trying to make small talk.

'Yeah, it's fine,' he replies, his eyes on my son.

He's distracted. I've seen him distracted before, but not like this. This is weird. It's one of the weirdest things I've ever seen. He's not the cool, confident rock star that everyone knows; he's just a guy.

He leans forward and rests his elbows on his knees, his head still turned towards Barney. Christian gets to his feet abruptly and takes Barney with him. He sits on the top step of the pool, with his back to us and Barney on his lap. Johnny and I meet each other's eyes and his lips turn down momentarily. He gives me a small shrug.

'Christian, shall we go out somewhere?' I ask. 'Shall we go for a walk into Cucugnan?' He doesn't reply. 'Christian?' I prompt.

'I'm happy here,' he says gruffly.

'Do you want to get some writing done or something while we go?'

Slowly, determinedly, he turns around and gives me a look of such pure hatred that my blood runs cold.

'I. Don't. Fucking. Think. So.'

'Christian . . .' I plead.

Johnny interrupts us. 'Maybe I should go.'

I take a deep breath. 'Yes,' I agree. 'That's probably enough for today.'

He gets to his feet.

'I'll see you out.' I glance at Christian, but he has his back to us again. Neither he nor Johnny says anything as I lead the way out through the screeching pool gate.

Johnny follows me back indoors to get his bike stuff.

'I'm sorry about that,' I say as he puts his leather jacket back on.

He shakes his head and pulls on his gloves. 'Could have been worse.' He stops suddenly and stares ahead as though in a daze, then seems to snap out of it. 'Can I come back tomorrow?' He picks up his helmet and moves towards the door.

'Sure, of course.' I offer him a small smile. 'Hopefully it will be better. I'll talk to Christian toni—'

'Don't,' he interrupts. 'It's okay. I can handle it.'

I open the door and he steps over the threshold. 'I still think it would help if you apologised,' I suggest.

'See you tomorrow, Meg.' He gives me a final look and jogs down the steps.

I'm reluctant to go back out to the pool again because I know the mood that will be waiting for me there, but I force myself to.

'Are you okay?' I ask.

'Take Barney,' Christian says, getting up and handing my son to me. I look at him in surprise, but he doesn't meet my eyes. I follow him back indoors, the sickness and dread kicking up a notch. He goes straight into the bedroom and angrily drags a T-shirt over his head.

'Where are you going?' I ask nervously as he exchanges his swimming trunks for shorts.

'Out.'

I follow him back down the corridor. He snatches the car keys from the ledge.

'Christian,' I say, disappointed. 'Can't we talk about this?'

He doesn't answer, he doesn't look at me, he just slams the door in my face as I stand there, holding my son.

He doesn't come home until eleven o'clock that night. I'm waiting for him on the sofa.

'I thought you'd be asleep,' he mutters.

'I was waiting for you. I was worried.'

'I'm back now. Go to bed,' he commands.

'I'm sorry, Christian. I know this must be hard for you.'

He snorts. 'You haven't got a fucking clue,' he says bitterly.

'I'm sorry,' I say again. I'm not even going to try to convince him I can imagine how he must feel. I get up and go to him. He glares at me as I put my hand on his arm, trying to get through to him.

'I'll do anything I can to make this easier,' I say softly, but he shrugs me off, his chest moving up and down aggressively with every breath.

'Go to bed,' he says warningly.

I close my eyes for a second and take a deep breath and then I look at him and nod. 'Okay.'

I stroke his arm one last time and find his bicep rigid with tension.

'Goodnight,' I say. He doesn't answer.

Chapter 15

How are we going to get through this? I don't see how we can.

Barney's presence improves the atmosphere the following morning, but the pressure is bubbling away below the surface, threatening to burst through at any given time.

We eat breakfast out on the terrace and look at the mountains cast in morning sunlight. There's a slight haze across them today. It probably means it's going to be hot again.

I need to talk to Christian about Johnny, but I feel like my lips are glued together. Christian is saying nothing. I can hear him crunching on his cereal as he stares up at the view. He's having cornflakes this morning, and not even the Crunchy Nut variety. He's not giving in to his sweet tooth. I don't know what this means, but it feels ominous.

Barney is being unusually quiet in his highchair.

I push away my barely touched toast. I don't have an appetite.

'So,' Christian starts, and I can hear the sarcasm even in this one word. 'What exciting things have you got planned today?'

'Please . . .' I give him an imploring look.

He shovels in another spoonful of cornflakes and munches angrily.

I try to speak soothingly. 'I wondered if you might find it easier if we go out.'

'"We", as in you, me and Barney?' he asks jollily and doesn't wait for my answer. 'No, I didn't think so,' he sneers.

I bite my lip and stay silent for a while before continuing, 'I don't know what to do. I want to make this easier for you. I just don't know how,' I admit. He doesn't answer. 'Please, Christian, tell me what to do.'

'How about, don't fuck your boyfriend's best friend? How about that? And if you absolutely *must*,' he says acidly, 'then have him use a fucking condom.'

Barney starts to rap his spoon noisily on the bar of his highchair.

I take him inside to play with his toys, without saying another word.

It's a good twenty minutes before Christian comes indoors. I'm sitting on the living room floor, building blocks with Barney. I look up at him. He seems defeated.

'Go out today,' he says flatly. 'I don't want to see him again anyway.' He's talking about Johnny, of course.

I nod slowly. 'Are you sure?'

'Yes. But go soon before I change my mind.'

I wait until I'm in the car before I call Johnny. 'We're on our way to you,' I say. 'Just me and Barney.'

'Okay,' he replies with surprise. 'Do you know where I'm staying?'

'Yes, Johnny,' I say sardonically. 'Your PA texted me the

details two days ago. We'll be there in an hour.' I end the call and throw my phone into my bag. Now I can concentrate on driving.

To be fair to him, he did tell me his time of arrival himself. But Lena sent me the rest.

I suppose it's best that she knows about me, even if she isn't aware of all the details. I wonder if anyone else is. I wonder if he's told the elusive Dana Reed.

Johnny is staying in a chateau in the hills about forty-five minutes west of Perpignan. It takes me about an hour to get there on the mountain roads and by the time we arrive it's eleven o'clock and Barney is fast asleep. I climb out of the car and look up at the beautiful grey-stone castle surrounded by leafy green trees. I can see why his PA booked him in here, even though one of the hotels in Cucugnan or a nearby town would have been a hell of a lot easier to get to.

I wonder if Lena has hired out the whole thing. I doubt she would have managed it on such short notice – if she did, she's a better PA than I ever was. I think we'll be safe from the paparazzi, in any case. The press in France are slightly less intrusive than those in the US and the UK.

I manage to transfer Barney to his buggy, but getting him across the gravel makes for a bumpy ride. I look around to see if there's anyone who can help me carry the buggy up the steps, but the whole place seems deserted. Maybe Lena is more skilled than I imagined. I pull out my phone and text Johnny to tell him that we're downstairs.

I squint my eyes against the glaring sunshine and peer inside. The front hall is dark and enchanting, long tapestries hanging on the walls. Moments later, I see Johnny jogging down the spiral staircase. He pushes open the gothic doors and emerges into the daylight.

'Hey, how's it going?'

I put my finger to my lips and indicate the buggy.

'Is he asleep?' he whispers.

'Yes. Help me carry him up the steps?'

I put my hands on the handles, but Johnny wraps his arms around the centre of the buggy and takes off with it.

'Are you alright with that?' I whisper loudly after him. That buggy is a nightmare to carry on your own.

'Yep,' he grunts, not bothering to put it down on the floor to cross the stone tiles to the staircase. I follow him up the winding stairs, trying not to look at his tattooed biceps.

We reach a long corridor and Johnny pushes open the first door he comes to.

'No key?' I say wryly.

'No valuables,' he replies.

'I'm not sure souvenir hunters would agree with that,' I say, looking around the spacious suite. Johnny's biker jacket and helmet are lying where he threw them on a seat under the window. The dark-wood shutters are wide open, allowing sunlight to spill into the room, revealing walls of polished ochre and antique furniture. Oil paintings of family members from years gone by hang on the walls. I glance through to the next room to see a large four-poster king-sized bed, made up with a golden silk bedspread.

'Nice room,' I comment.

'It's alright,' he brushes me off. 'Where do you want him?' He indicates Barney.

'Can I park him in the bedroom?'

'Sure.'

'How long does he sleep for?' he asks when I come back through.

'Hopefully another hour,' I tell him, sitting down on one of the sofas. 'He has two hours a day at this age. If he wakes up early, he's usually a grump.' Am I boring him? Oddly, I don't think so.

He sits down on the sofa opposite me and picks up the phone on the side-table next to him. 'Want a drink?'

'I wouldn't mind a latte.'

He dials a number and places an order for room service.

'It's quiet here,' I say. 'Have you got the whole place to yourself?'

'No.' I feel a strange relief. Lena didn't quite manage it, then. 'Only a couple of honeymooners in the rooms upstairs, though,' he explains, picking some fluff off his jeans.

'Have you told Dana about us?' I ask suddenly.

He looks up at me. 'Not yet.'

'But you will?'

He nods. 'Yeah.'

'How do you think she'll take it?'

'She'll cope.' Pause. 'How was Christian last night?'

'Not good,' I admit. 'But I don't want to talk about him.'

'Why not?'

'It feels like I'm betraying him and I've done enough of that already.'

There's a gentle knock at the door. Johnny gets up to answer it. A neatly dressed man comes in with a silver tray and places it on the coffee table between us. Johnny pulls his wallet out of his pocket and hands him a note as he leaves.

I get up and look out of the window. I'd forgotten what it was like living in such luxury. Actually, that's not true. You never forget it once you've experienced it, and I experienced it repeatedly during the eight months I worked for Johnny.

Surreal realisation hits me again. Johnny Jefferson is Barney's father. This changes everything. Life will never be normal again.

I turn around and watch him as he lifts up a silver-coloured coffee cup from the tray and blows at the hot liquid. Steam swirls away from him in a tiny cloud. He's clean-shaven and his hair looks blonder in the sunlight. He's wearing a light-grey T-shirt and I notice that he has a new tattoo on the inside of his arm, just up from his wrist. He glances up at me and his green eyes meet mine. For a split second I feel like I'm falling and I must look shocked because his coffee cup freezes inches from his lips.

'What?' he asks.

'Nothing.' I avert my gaze and go to sit down. 'What do you want to do today?' Try to act normal, for God's sake. I take a sip of my latte.

'It's up to you. I wasn't expecting you to come this way. Did you take the mountain roads or the motorway?'

'Mountain.'

'Me too.' He grins. 'Awesome on the bike.'

I smile back at him, feeling strangely relaxed considering recent – and past – events. 'So, today . . .'

'There's a spa here. Does Barney like swimming?'

'Mmm, he does, actually. Oh. I don't have any swimming gear.'

'We can sort that.' He reaches for the phone again, dials a number and then speaks into the receiver. 'My friend and her son want to use the pool. Can you have someone bring up some swimming costumes?'

I know from experience that the manager here will be pulling out all the stops to impress a client of Johnny's stature. It may seem quiet, but you'd better believe that there are two or three times as many staff as usual buzzing around behind the scenes to make sure everything runs as smoothly as possible for their super-prominent guest.

'And swimming nappies . . .' I suddenly remember.

'And swimming nappies,' he passes on. 'For a one-year-old.' Pause. 'Size ten in the UK, six in the US. I don't know how your sizing works over here.' Pause. 'Thanks.' He hangs up.

I try to mask my surprise that Johnny remembers what size I am.

Within five minutes, there's another knock at the door and we're brought in a selection of designer swimming costumes for me, from bikinis to one-pieces, plus children's swimming trunks and nappies for Barney. I take the collection and go through to the bathroom, reeling slightly.

When I emerge, my chosen bikini on underneath my skirt and top, Johnny is not in the living room. I go through to the bedroom to see him perched on the end of the bed, gazing into the buggy.

He glances up at me as I stand at the doorway. 'Still asleep?' I whisper.

He looks down again. 'I thought I heard a noise.' He gets up and walks towards me. I turn and lead the way back to the sofas.

'Find one you like?' he asks.

'Yep.' I ping the strap poking out from underneath my T-shirt.

133

'Black,' he notes.

'I know, I'm boring.' I cast my eyes heavenwards and sit down.

'Suits you.' He collapses onto the sofa opposite and rests his arm against the back of it. 'Always did.'

Is he mocking me? Barney lets out a sharp cry and I leap to my feet as I always do, even though there's no rush.

'Hello,' I say sweetly, peering into the buggy. He's rubbing at his eyes and looks like he's about to burst into tears. 'Come on.' I unclick his buckles and lift him out. He sleepily buries his head into my neck as I carry him back through to Johnny, then he lifts his head and looks around before cuddling back into me. 'It usually takes him a little while to wake up,' I explain.

Johnny nods, lost for words. His face is that strange mix of emotions again and I notice that he's sitting up a bit straighter.

'We've come to see Johnny,' I say in a high-pitched tone into my son's ear. He doesn't move from his snug position. 'Do you want a biscuit?'

His head shoots up. He might not be able to say the word, but he certainly knows what it means. I smile at Johnny as he passes over the plate that came up with our coffees. Barney takes a biscuit with his chubby fingers and has a small bite, before glancing across the coffee table with mild interest at Johnny.

'Your mum thought you might like to go for a swim,' Johnny suggests hopefully, mimicking my high-pitched tone. I try not to smile.

Barney continues to eat his biscuit without making any indication of having heard him.

'Would you like that?' I ask. He continues to munch. I glance at my watch. It's after twelve. 'Maybe we'll have some lunch first. Shall we go downstairs for a change of scenery?' I ask Johnny before he can pick up the phone again.

'Sure.'

Twenty minutes later, we're downstairs in the sitting room. There's a fireplace to my left already laid out with logs for this evening's blaze, and on the right is a small bar area. More family portraits line the walls and there's an abundance of fresh flowers in large vases. We're seated at a table with Barney between us in a highchair. I've already started the messy business of feeding him. It'll be interesting to see how Johnny copes with this.

'How's your work going?' I ask Johnny. 'Are you writing at the moment?'

'No. Haven't written anything for a while.'

'Too busy partying and ending up in rehab,' I say wryly.

Barney reaches across and tries to grab Johnny's heavy metallic watch.

'No, darling,' I say, catching his arm before he smears tuna mayonnaise all over Johnny's – platinum, probably – timepiece.

'It's okay,' Johnny says, shaking his arm so his watch jangles slightly. I flinch as Barney's grubby fingers grapple with their prize. Johnny unclasps the watch and hands it to him.

'Do you like that? You can have it, if you like.'

'No, baby, give it back to Johnny,' I insist, knowing it probably cost more than our car.

'Why?' Johnny asks. 'It's not like I can't afford it. I want him to have something from me.'

'Buy him a teddy,' I say, taking a baby wipe out of my nappy bag and giving the watch a good polish before handing it back to its owner. I give Barney a plastic car to play with instead.

A waiter interrupts us with our *croque monsieurs*. 'Merci,' I tell him.

When we're alone again, I look across at Johnny. He's distinctly unimpressed.

'What?' I ask.

'I don't like it that he has to call me by my first name.'

I sigh, wearily.

'I don't,' he continues obstinately.

'We can't do anything about that now,' I say calmly. 'It's too soon. Anyway, it's not like he can even say "Daddy" yet.'

'But he will learn. Probably soon. And technically the term applies to me.' Not Christian, he refrains from adding.

'Be patient,' I plead.

'I don't want to be patient,' he bites back.

'Well, of course not.' Sarcasm kicks in. 'You're used to getting everything you want, aren't you?'

Barney grizzles.

'Sorry, baby.' I instantly come out of my mood. I know I'm being a bitch. I glance at Johnny. 'Sorry,' I mouth.

He starts to cut up his toasted ham and cheese sandwich. 'Not everything,' he murmurs.

What's that supposed to mean?

The chateau staff clear the spa area in advance for us so we have the swimming pool to ourselves. It's in a beautiful ornate glass-house and it's heated to just the right temperature.

Despite the fact that Barney is in my arms and consequently covering a large portion of my body, I feel self-conscious as I walk down the steps into the pool. Johnny is already waiting in the water.

'Can he swim yet?' he asks me.

I can't help but laugh. 'He can't even walk.'

'Well, I don't know,' he says defensively.

'No, that's true.' I try to keep a straight face. 'Why would you?'

'Exactly. I haven't been around kids before.'

'You're coping with this far better than I ever thought you would.' I find myself speaking frankly.

He nods slightly, staring at Barney. 'I can't believe how much he looks like me. When did you know?' He gives me an inquisitive look. 'For sure.'

I take a deep breath. 'When his eyes turned green. It was about six months ago, maybe a bit longer.'

'Jesus, Meg,' he breathes.

'Language,' I berate, for want of anything else to say.

'Can I hold him?' he asks, opening up his arms.

'You want to swim to Johnny?' I ask Barney and don't wait for his answer before zooming him at breakneck speed around in a circle and over to his bio-dad. He's giggling by the time he reaches him. Johnny repeats the action and zooms him back to me.

It's not long before I acknowledge to myself that I'm having a nice time, and then, of course, the guilt kicks in.

'I guess we should set off soon,' I say reluctantly.

Johnny's face falls. 'You can't stay a bit longer?'

'We should get back,' I reply. I walk to the steps and climb out, feeling self-conscious again. I grab a towel and quickly wrap it around myself before tending to Barney.

'What are you doing tomorrow?' Johnny asks, reaching for a towel and patting himself dry. He doesn't bother to cover up his body. He's toned and tanned and has been told time and time again that he's one of the fittest guys on the planet, so he's hardly lacking in self-confidence.

'I don't know yet,' I reply, averting my gaze. 'Have you ever been to Carcassonne?' I ask.

'No.'

'It's beautiful,' I enthuse. 'There's a medieval village on top of a hill with views all around. Maybe we could go there for lunch.'

'That'd be great.'

I suddenly get a reality check. 'Um, sorry, I'll actually have to speak to Christian first.' I was getting carried away. 'Let's talk in the morning.'

Later, Johnny walks us out to the car. I put my nappy bag in the front passenger seat and turn around to see him trying to figure out the car seat. 'I'll do that.' He watches over my shoulder as I buckle in my son. 'These things are a nightmare.' I shut the car door and turn around to face him. 'I'm sorry for not telling you about him,' I blurt out. His green eyes study mine for a moment, the smile gone from his lips. He nods abruptly and then pats the car roof with finality.

'Let's move on.'

My nose starts to prickle. 'Okay.' I climb in the car. Johnny raps on the back window and motions for me to put it down.

'Bye, Barney,' he says cheerfully. 'See you tomorrow, okay, buddy?'

It's only when we're driving away that I hear a rattling sound and look back to see Barney playing with Johnny's watch. I smile and shake my head, then make a mental note to hide it in my nappy bag before Christian sees it. It's not worth enraging him anymore tonight.

* * *

The house is empty when we arrive home. I call Christian to let him know we're back, but the phone goes straight through to voicemail. Hopefully he's just out of reception. I leave a message and then get on with Barney's dinner.

By the time Christian's keys sound in the lock at ten o'clock that night, his shrivelled-up dinner in the oven looks almost as bad as I feel.

'Christian?' I call anxiously, getting to my feet. I've been sitting in the living room fearing the worst. 'I was worried something had happened to you.'

He walks into the living room wearily and stares at me.

'I can't do it,' he says.

'Can't do what?'

'I can't do it.'

'You can,' I implore, a lump forming in my throat.

He shakes his head. 'I can't, Meg. I wanted to. I wanted to do the right thing by Barney. But I don't have the strength. He won't remember me—'

'No!' I interrupt.

'He won't,' he continues. 'Not when he's older. Kids adapt very quickly, especially at this age. It's better that I walk away now before it all gets too confusing for him.'

'But I don't want you to leave!' I wail. 'Barney doesn't want you to leave!' I try to get through to him, but he sounds so resolute, like he's thought about this for far too long. 'Please forgive me,' I beg. 'Can't you forgive me?'

He looks at me and there's sorrow in his eyes. For a split second I have hope, but when his answer comes, I know that he means it.

'No.'

My insides turn to stone.

'I'm going to join the band on tour tomorrow,' he continues flatly. 'I can't fuck up another book.' His tone becomes bitter for a moment, before reverting to dull. 'I'll be away for a week. It will give you time to pack up.'

'Please,' I beg again, getting to my feet and going to his side. 'I love you.'

He meets my gaze and the warmth that I usually see in those dark-brown eyes is gone.

'I don't love you,' he says. 'Not anymore. And never, ever again.'

Chapter 16

Christian leaves early the next morning to catch his flight. He has a taxi collect him at five forty-five a.m., before Barney is awake. I stand out on the cold stone doorstep and wave at the cab driver to let him know his passenger is on his way.

Christian is in with Barney. He won't wake him. He doesn't want to say goodbye to his face. He thinks it's better this way. Me, I'm not sure. But it's not my choice; I just have to live with the consequences.

The door opens and Christian comes out, looking crushed. He walks towards me with his head down, but before he reaches the door he breaks down. I try to go to him, but he puts his hand up to keep me away.

'I'm sorry.' I've said it so many times it should be engraved on my tombstone.

He shakes his head and doesn't meet my eyes. I go into the kitchen and get us both some tissues.

'You could change your mind,' I beg.

'No.' He's steadfast. He vigorously wipes away his tears. He takes a deep breath and tries to compose himself before speaking.

'I don't want to lose him.' His voice is wavering. 'But I need some time. I don't know how long—' And then his speech cuts off so I hand him another tissue, my heart full of hope that maybe all is not lost as he dissolves into silent sobs. 'I'll be in touch,' he says, and then he walks through the door and closes it behind him, without looking back.

I collapse onto the floor beneath me and cry so hard I fear my chest will burst. I can't be a mother today. How can I be a mother today?

Barney will wake within the hour. I have no longer than that to wallow in my misery. It's not enough. I need help. Johnny . . .

In a daze I crawl across the floor to my handbag and pull out my phone.

C has left me. Come as soon as you can

I send the text to Johnny's phone and then slump back against the wall as more tears trail aimlessly down my cheeks.

He's gone. Our life together is over.

Images begin to strike me, one after the other. Christian dive-bombing into a crystal-clear lake; Christian laughing so hard that one of the buttons on his slightly-too-tight shirt pops off; Christian staring across the bed at me after we've made love; Christian tickling my son to near hysteria; Christian holding Barney for the first time . . .

I clutch my chest and sob. It hurts so much.

Christian spooning multicoloured kiddie cereal into his mouth; Christian sitting at his desk with his back to me, typing away at his keyboard; Christian shouting in frustration when my baby talk distracts him from his work . . .

My sobs stop abruptly.

Christian storming out in a fury late at night, leaving me holding a screaming three-month-old; Christian staring ahead in a daze in the darkness of our Belsize Park living room after his book sales plummet; Christian missing Barney's first birthday . . .

I wasn't expecting to be bombarded with those memories. It hasn't all been rosy. It's been far from it at times.

I wipe away my tears and blow my nose before taking a deep breath and exhaling slowly.

What did Christian mean, he doesn't want to lose him? He still wants to be in Barney's life? It's this hope that allows me to get up and pull myself together, and by the time Barney awakes at five minutes to seven, I'm able to function as his mother.

Johnny calls me at eight o'clock. He arrives within fifty minutes. I hear his bike, but wait for him to knock at the door instead of going out to meet him. I barely have the energy to stand up.

'You shouldn't drive so fast,' I say flatly, looking at his chin. He hasn't shaved this morning.

'You alright?' Johnny's voice is sympathetic, worried.

I step away from the door to allow him to enter, but I can't meet his eyes.

Barney babbles away in the living room and crawls through to see us. Johnny throws his biker jacket on a chair in the hall and I manage a small smile at my son as Johnny lifts him up into his arms.

'What have you been doing, hey?' He glances through to the living room. 'Building blocks? Come on, let's go.'

I close the front door behind him.

'Do you want a coffee?' I call after him robotically.

'No, I'm fine,' he says over his shoulder.

I go through to the living room and perch on the armrest of the sofa. Johnny sits on the floor with Barney.

He looks up at me. 'Want to talk about it?' he asks quietly.

I shake my head and watch Barney as he tries to put one block on top of the other. Johnny quickly builds a tower and then lets my giggling son topple it.

I feel dead inside.

'Where is he?' Johnny asks.

'He went to join the band on tour.'

'When's he coming back?'

'In a week. I've got a week to pack up, decide where to go.'

'You're moving out?' He sounds surprised. 'Where are you going?'

I shrug. 'I don't know. I haven't spoken to my parents yet.'

'When will you do that?'

'Probably tonight, when Barney is in bed.'

'I can take him out if you want to call them now?'

I look at him again. 'Where would you go?'

'I don't know. Walk up the road, whatever you want. He might like to look at my bike or something.'

'You're not taking him on it,' I say strongly, feeling like a mother again.

'Yeah, right,' he scoffs. 'I may be a moron, but I'm not that much of a moron.'

I smile at him wryly, but at least it's a smile. 'Okay.'

When he's gone, I pick up the phone, a different kind of

dread filling my bones. No one enjoys disappointing their parents, and that's exactly what I'm about to do. I don't bother to go through the usual pleasantries, instead launching straight in.

'I'm afraid I have some news for you and you're not going to like it.'

'What?' Mum's voice is full of apprehension.

'Christian and I have split up.'

'Oh no!'

'What's going on?' I hear my dad ask in the background.

'Shoosh!' my mum snaps and I can imagine her waving her hand at him to keep him at bay.

'Let me tell you why,' I continue.

'Okay . . .'

I take a deep breath and then it all comes out in a rush. 'Barney is not Christian's son; he's Johnny's.'

My mum gasps and then the disappointment comes.

'Oh, Meg . . .'

This phrase is used time and time again as I go on to explain. I feel remarkably calm. Even the tears seem to have dried up.

'What are you going to do?' Mum asks eventually.

'I wondered if we could come and stay with you and Dad for a little while.'

'Well, yes, of course. When?'

'In a couple of days? I need time to pack up, and also Johnny is here.'

'Johnny is there?' she asks in amazement.

'Yes. He knows.'

'How's he taking it?' From the tone of her voice, she's not expecting a positive answer.

145

'Better than I thought he would,' I reply, still taken aback by this fact.

She hesitates before speaking. 'I had no idea about you and Johnny being involved in that way. How on earth did that happen?'

'It's a long story, but we'll have time to talk in a couple of days.'

My dad is obviously chewing at the bit, and we terminate our conversation so my mum can explain. I can picture them both shaking their heads in shock and displeasure. It's a horrible thought, but it's not as awful as I'd imagined. I feel strange. Why? I realise that some of the weight has lifted from my shoulders, and terrible though the truth is, I feel oddly free that it's out there. I take another deep breath. I should call Bess, but I don't have the energy right now. I could start to pack, but I don't have the energy for that, either. I lie down on the sofa and cover my face with my arms. I'm tired, so very tired.

The sound of Johnny's motorbike wakes me up. I leap to my feet, startled. I hurry to the door and out onto the terrace. Barney is sitting on top of the machine. Johnny has hold of him with one hand while he revs the engine with the other.

'You'll scare the life out of him!' I shout in alarm, standing barefoot on the tiles shaded by the table.

'Look at him; he's loving it!' Johnny shouts back, a huge grin on his face. Barney is indeed smiling his head off.

I watch them in bemusement, my hand held in a salute above my eyes to protect myself from the sun. There's a hot wind today and it whips my retro floral cotton dress against my knees. I go back inside and grab Barney's hat before slipping my feet into my silver flip-flops. I join the boys on the driveway.

'Do you like that?' I ask Barney as I pull his hat on. He's too busy playing with the shiny handlebars to take much notice. The bike is a Ducatti. I recognise it as one of the ones Johnny used to have in his garage.

'How did it go with your 'rents?' he asks.

'They're disappointed,' I reply weightily. 'Have you been out here for long? I fell asleep.'

'You must've needed it.'

'I look tired, do I?'

He tilts my chin up with his thumb and forefinger and peers into my bloodshot eyes. My heart quickens.

'Don't answer that,' I say hastily, pulling away. 'How long was I out for?'

He turns his attention back to Barney. 'About an hour and a half. We went for a walk up into the village and came back down about fifteen minutes ago.'

'Did you take the buggy?'

'Hell, no. You won't catch me pushing that thing. He sat on my shoulders.'

I roll my eyes. Good job I put suncream on my son before they left. 'We should probably go inside before we bake.'

'Come on, then.' He lifts Barney up and off the bike before following me into the house.

Needless to say, I don't really feel like taking Johnny for a day trip to Carcassonne. He entertains Barney while I start to pack. Listening to him talking to Barney as they play together in the living room is a good distraction.

147

We don't have many belongings, but it takes longer than you'd expect to pack them up. It's the sorting through what is mine and what is Christian's. I leave Christian with everything that we bought together – everything except for Barney's things. I'm appalled to think of the money Christian has spent on a son he thought was his. I promise myself that one day I'll pay him back. Not that he'd ever want to take money from me.

Johnny sticks around until dinnertime. I can just about manage defrosting some food for Barney, but I can't do adult cooking tonight.

'Takeaway?' he suggests.

'No. Thank you, but I'm not hungry.'

'You should eat something.'

'You should stop being so nice to me because it's freaking me out.'

He chuckles. 'I'm a nice guy.'

'No, you're not.' I give him a look and he raises one eyebrow at me.

'I'll be off, then.'

'You'd better go before it gets dark, anyway,' I say.

'Okay, Mum.'

'I think you'll find my name is Mummy. Now, bugger off,' I joke.

He grins and touches my arm. I step away and pick up his bike gear, then lead the way out to the terrace. I hand him his jacket to put on and place his helmet on the table. He turns to face me.

'You'll be alright, Nutmeg.'

'Let's hope so, JJ.'

'I cannot believe you just called me that.' He takes a cigarette out of the packet in his pocket and lights up.

When I first met Johnny, his actress girlfriend at the time once called him JJ in my presence. He didn't like it.

'How is Serengeti these days?' I ask of his former belle.

'She's married to some old codger. Film producer,' he adds, inhaling deeply and indicating his fag. 'Gagging for this.'

I ignore him. Considering he's a chain-smoker, he hasn't done badly today. I don't want him smoking around Barney. 'This isn't the guy who gave her Footsie, is it?' I ask. Footsie was Serengeti's dog. It used to drive me nuts with its yapping and crapping all over the place. She chose its name because the man who gave it to her had a foot fetish.

'That's the one.' He cocks his head to one side. 'How did you know about him?'

I pretend to zip up my lips. 'Never reveal my sources.'

'Bloody Santiago,' he mutters, taking another drag.

I smirk. Yep, his gardener/pool boy was the one who gave away that information. I wonder if I'll ever see him again.

'Anyway,' I say. 'I'd better feed Barney before he bites my arm off. We'll see you tomorrow?'

'Sure. I don't fly out until the afternoon.' He picks up his helmet and puts it under his arm.

My heart dips. 'I didn't realise it was so soon.'

'I have to get home for a gig Dana's doing,' he explains.

Now my heart plummets. Why? I'm not interested in him. I'd never go there again. Not now, not after everything we've all been through. I guess I'd almost forgotten about his girlfriend. Of course, she's going to complicate things.

'Ah, I see.' I try to keep my voice steady. 'I'd better carry on packing.'

'How's it going?'

'I'll finish by tomorrow. We may set off when you go. Shit.'

Something occurs to me and I don't even chastise myself for swearing.

'What?'

'I don't know how we're going to get there.' How could I be so stupid?

'Isn't that your Alfa out in the driveway?' he asks, confused.

'No, it's Christian's. I can't take that.' I shake my head, adamant. 'I won't take that.'

'Oh. Well, look, I'll sort it.'

'What do you mean, you'll sort it?'

'I'll buy you a car.' He stubs his fag out on the wall.

'Johnny, you're not going to just *buy me a car*,' I say, frowning. 'Actually, we can catch the train. Taxi to train station, yes.' I'm thinking out loud.

'Not with the cot and all your luggage,' he chips in.

Oh.

'We'll be fine,' I say firmly. 'Now, see you tomorrow.'

He winks and pulls on his helmet.

Chapter 17

The car turns up at two o'clock, a dark grey Golf GTI with shiny alloys and leather interiors.

'What did I tell you?' I stare at Johnny, gobsmacked. 'No! You're not buying me a car!'

He rolls his eyes. 'Meg, it's like a drop in the fucking—'

'Don't swear.'

'. . . ocean for me. Take the fu— Take the car.'

'I can't,' I say. 'I can't accept it.'

'Yes, you can,' he says firmly, directing the truck driver to lower the car onto the road with a flick of his finger.

'And you gave Barney the watch, too,' I point out, remembering the platinum timepiece that's still buried in my nappy bag.

'Drop in the ocean, Nutmeg, drop in the ocean.'

'Stop calling me Nutmeg.'

'Why?'

'Just stop.'

He chuckles, infuriatingly. The truck driver gets out of his cab and comes over to us with some paperwork.

'You don't want to make him take it away again,' Johnny says in a soothing tone. 'Think of poor Lena, all the effort she went to, to find it in time.'

I glare at him and take the pen from the driver. Again I wonder what Lena is like, what she must think of me. I turn back to Johnny and point the pen at him accusingly. 'Okay, but I'm paying you back.' I sign my name where the driver indicates.

Johnny grabs Barney and swings him up onto his shoulders. The truck driver holds the keys out to Johnny, but he nods his head in my direction. I take them with building excitement, even though I don't feel like I have the right to be excited about anything right now.

'Come on, let's go and see your mum's new car,' he says over the roar of the truck engine. A sandy cloud of dust puffs in our direction as the truck makes off down the hill. We walk over to the car.

'What's Lena like?' Curiosity has got the better of me.

'She's great,' he enthuses, breaking off to go to the front passenger seat. 'Married,' he adds with a knowing look at me over the car roof.

Married? Relief surges through me, but I'm instantly annoyed with myself.

Johnny climbs in and I follow suit. This car is left-hand drive – Christian's Alfa is right-hand drive because we brought it from the UK – but it shouldn't be too hard to get used to the change.

Barney sits on Johnny's knee and leans forward to press the dials and knobs on the dashboard. I glance at him, so comfortable on the knee of someone he hardly knows. A child's innocence. I hope it's true that young children adapt quickly to new situations. I hope so with all my heart.

* * *

I don't want to stay another night in our house without Christian, so Johnny helps me switch the car seats from Christian's Alfa and load up all our bags – most of which are the plastic shopping variety as only one of our suitcases is actually mine. I've told Barney we're going to stay with Nanny and Grandad, and he's too young to understand it's anything out of the ordinary. Earlier I asked Johnny to take Barney out for a walk while I tidied the house for Christian; it's going to be hard enough for him walking back into it empty. I write him a letter and leave it on the coffee table in the living room. There's nothing in it that I haven't already said, but I want him to have something solid that reminds him how much I love him and how sorry I am. I hope he reads it before tearing it up.

Johnny leaves before we do. He's not the sort to stand and wave goodbye.

'Thank you for all your help this last couple of days,' I say as he sits astride his Ducatti with his helmet still on the handle-bars. I feel awkward trying to convey my appreciation. 'Have a good flight home. I hope Dana's gig goes well.' It's hard to say the last part, but I feel it's necessary.

Johnny nods towards Barney. 'I want to come back and see him again soon.'

'Sure.'

'Your parents are in Grasse, is that what you said?'

'Yes. The nearest airport is Nice.'

'I'll call you next week to sort something out.'

'Okay.' I feel pleased.

He pulls his helmet on, leaving the visor up. 'See ya, buddy,' he says to Barney, ruffling his hair. 'See ya,' he says to me and his green eyes look more intense because that's all I can see of his

Chapter 18

My parents live in a two-storey cream-coloured villa with dark-wood shutters and leafy green vines creeping up the walls. It's situated in the hills south of the medieval town's centre and the view across the valley is spectacular, especially at sunset, which is when Barney and I pull up. He's already dozed off. I'm glad my parents have a travel cot because I should be able to put him straight into it and pray that he stays asleep until morning. Mum, Dad and I have a lot to talk about.

My Barney plan works – just. I take a few minutes to make sure he's settled properly before going downstairs to the living room to discover that Dad has already unpacked most of our belongings from the car.

'Thanks, Dad,' I say quietly.

My mum comes in. 'I didn't know if you'd eat on the way, but I saved some dinner for you just in case.'

'I'm not really hungry,' I tell her.

'Come out to the terrace,' Dad urges. 'You should eat something and I'll get you a glass of wine as well. Red? White?'

'I don't know, whatever's open. Thank you!' I call after him.

155

'So I'll get you some dinner?' Mum persists.

I nod. 'I guess so. Thank you,' I add, feeling compelled to be particularly polite to my parents.

We go outside and sit at the glass table on the stone-tiled terrace. There's a decent-sized rectangular-shaped swimming pool in front of us and, beyond that, neatly mown grass. The property is bordered by trees – palms, pines, lilacs – which offer some privacy from the surrounding villas, but, as we're on a slope, they don't interfere with the view of the valley from the terrace.

'How was the drive?' Dad asks when we're seated. My dad is of medium height and build, with greying brown hair. Just like Mum and me, he also has brown eyes. My mum is slightly taller than him when she wears heels, which isn't very often. Her hair is a darker shade of blonde than mine. They've been married thirty-odd years after meeting in their early twenties. My mum used to work in a dry-cleaner's in Guildford, where we're from. Dad used to get his business suits done there. He worked in a bank – arranging mortgages was his speciality – until he retired a few years ago and they moved here.

'Fine. Good,' I tell him.

'What's with the car?' he asks. 'Bit too nice for a rental, isn't it?'

I swallow my food, hard. 'Johnny bought it for me.'

They both reel backwards and glance at each other with surprise.

'It's not a big deal,' I tell them. 'He insisted. He said it was like a – and I quote – "drop in the ocean".'

'Hmm,' my mum says wryly.

'Well, if he can afford it, why shouldn't he buy my little girl a car? You are the mother of his child, after all.' The cheeriness in my dad's tone is forced. It's clear he's finding it hard to make light of the situation.

'Oh, Meg . . .' my mum says. Here we go.

'I know, Mum,' I respond. 'I don't blame you for being disappointed, but I'm trying to do the right thing, now.'

She nods, tears in her eyes. I look down at my food. I have absolutely zero appetite, but I don't want to let Mum's cooking go to waste.

She shakes her head disapprovingly. 'I knew something was up that time we came to see you in Paris.'

'Nothing had even happened between us then!' I respond indignantly.

'No, but I could see it, the way you were running around after him.'

It was when we were on tour. Johnny went haywire and I had to leave my parents having dinner at the Pompidou centre to go after him.

'It was my job,' I say wearily. 'It had nothing to do with my feelings for him.'

'But, still,' Mum says.

I pick at my food.

'How's Christian?' she asks.

'Not good,' I admit, looking down at the table because I can't face her expression. 'He'll never forgive me.'

'I'm sure that's not true,' Dad says kindly.

'You're wrong about that,' I tell him. 'But thanks, anyway.'

'Goodness me.' Mum sighs. 'Goodness me.'

'What?' I ask, because this is a different tone from the 'Oh, Meg' I've been getting so used to.

'Johnny Jefferson. What will Barbara say?'

Barbara is one of my mum's ex-pat bridge buddies.

'You can't tell her,' I say fervently. 'You can't tell anyone.'

'Well, we're going to have to tell people sometime,' Mum says, slightly put out.

'Not yet. Not until it's right. That goes for Susan and Tony, too,' I say of my older sister and her irritating husband. 'I don't want them blabbing about it to all and sundry.'

'They wouldn't do that,' my mum snaps.

'Yes, they would,' I insist.

'You're going to have to tell them at some point. They're family. They have a right to know.'

'Yes, but we need time to get used to all this. It's a very strange situation for Johnny, too. He wants to spend some time with Barney, get to know him without the press interfering.'

'Has he got any other kids?' Dad asks.

'No!' I exclaim.

He shrugs. 'I just thought, well, these rock stars . . . They often have secret offspring hidden away. They do get around a bit.'

'Dad!' I cry.

'Geoffrey!' Mum cries simultaneously.

My dad looks defensive. 'It wouldn't be that surprising, I didn't think.'

I feel sick again. Can you imagine? If Barney weren't his only illegitimate child . . . If there were more mothers like me out there, that he's been looking after, paying off . . . But, no. I would have known it. I was his PA – he couldn't have kept that from me. Could he? And that look on his face . . . I'm sure Barney is his first. I hope for all our sakes he'll be his last.

158

God, how horrid, though. As if this doesn't feel tainted enough.

'You alright, love?' Dad asks.

'Actually, I'm very tired. Would you mind if I turned in?' I push my chair out from the table.

'Of course not,' Mum says, getting up and taking my plate.

'I'm sorry,' I say.

'It's okay,' she responds brightly. 'Next door's dog can finish it off. He's always hanging around out at the front.'

'I didn't mean my dinner,' I say, 'although I am sorry about that, too. I'm sorry for . . . all this.'

Mum nods. Dad gives me a sympathetic smile and rubs my shoulder.

'These things are put here to challenge us,' he says. 'But you'll make it through. Better the truth comes out now than in a few years.'

'Yes,' Mum agrees.

'I just wish I hadn't done it.' I stare ahead in a daze.

'No, you don't,' Mum says shrewdly.

I look at her with astonishment.

'If you hadn't done it, Barney wouldn't be in our lives. None of us would change that for the world.'

Chapter 19

It smells of flowers, here. Jasmine and roses and lavender. Grasse is the perfume capital of the world, and it's beautiful. I only wish I could enjoy it under better circumstances.

Barney and I have been here for three weeks. Last week, he took his first steps. I felt like both Christian *and* Johnny should have been there, but at least my parents were here to share the moment – even if it was a touch bittersweet.

Barney loves having his doting grandparents around. It's nice to have their company – and their help – but it's also harder in some ways. I feel a bit useless when I'm not running my own household. That sounds very Women's Institute, but it's true. Plus, I have far too much time on my hands to reflect on the mess I've made of things.

I've had no contact with Christian. He doesn't answer my calls. I've only tried him three times, but I daren't call him again. I can't bear to endure the torture of an endlessly ring-ing phone.

*   *   *

True to his word, Johnny calls me soon after we arrive in Grasse. He makes arrangements to come and visit us in the middle of August. My parents are horrified to hear that he's planning on staying in a hotel.

'He can stay here,' my mum insists.

'No!' I hastily brush her off.

'What, is our house not good enough for him? Not five-star enough?' Dad chips in.

'It's not that,' I reply.

'What is it, then?' Mum asks sarkily.

'I don't know . . .' I respond. 'What if people realised he was here?'

'People are far more likely to recognise him if he stays in a hotel,' Mum points out.

'Not if Lena manages to secure all the rooms.'

'Oh, well, if he's got a whole hotel to himself . . . Who'd want to stay in a measly four-bedroom house?' Dad snipes.

'Who's Lena?' Mum asks.

'His PA,' I say as an aside, then to Dad: 'It's not like that.'

'His PA?' Dad changes the subject. 'Is he having it off with her, too?'

'No, Dad!' I cry. 'She's married!'

'Didn't stop him when Christian was around.'

'Christian and I weren't married.' I try to stay cool.

'You may as well have been,' Dad says gruffly. 'Christian was his best friend. If he does that to his best friend, why wouldn't he start on another man's wife?'

'This is why I don't want him here!' I finally erupt. 'You two! All you'd do is nit-pick at him the whole time. It's embarrassing!'

There go my gold stars for good behaviour.

'Oh, dear,' Mum says, entirely unimpressed. My dad humphs.

I close my eyes for a few seconds and open them again. 'I'm sorry. You'll see enough of him when he's here. I'm sure we'll hang out at the house rather than risk being seen around town.'

That seems to pacify them somewhat. God knows why – it's not like they're big Johnny Jefferson fans.

I turn to my dad, all of a sudden overcome with the need to explain something. 'What you said . . . about Johnny stealing his best friend's girl . . . Johnny and I were together first.' It feels important that my parents know this. 'So you could say that Christian stole me from him,' I add stupidly.

'Is that true?' Mum's eyes widen.

'Well, not strictly speaking,' I backtrack. Got a bit carried away. 'We weren't actually together when Christian and I . . . Oh, maybe I don't want to talk about this, after all.'

'Why not? I think we should know the whole shebang,' Mum says indignantly.

Oh, for goodness' sake, I moan inside my head. 'I fell for Johnny, he apparently fell for me, but was scared of commitment . . .' That's the diplomatic way of saying that he came onto women right in front of me and shagged someone I really, really didn't want him to shag. Even now I wince at the memory. I continue, 'I quit my job as his PA, stayed friends with Christian, got together with Christian, then Johnny came back for me.'

My parents lean forward in anticipation.

'Johnny came back for you? What happened next?' Mum pries, addicted to this unexpected gossip fix.

I sigh. 'Johnny and I . . . you know . . .' I give them a look and they shift in their seats. I cannot believe I'm telling them this. 'He wanted me to go back to LA to live with him—'

'*Really?*' Mum interrupts.

'Well, why wouldn't he?' Dad says, puffed up full of misguided pride for his daughter.

'And I said no.'

'Oh.'

That was both of them speaking.

'A month later I found out I was pregnant and the rest is history . . .'

Silence as they contemplate this information.

'You can't tell any of this to Barbara,' I warn my mum.

'As if I would!' she snorts, but I know her.

'And you won't be able to have any of your friends over while he's here,' I tell them strongly. 'In fact, you can't tell anyone that he's here at all.'

'Goodness me, what a palaver,' Mum sniffs. 'I'll have to make up some excuse about us all coming down with something.'

'You don't need to stop seeing your friends,' I say. 'But if you could please go to their houses instead of inviting them here for a few days, that would be grand.'

'Oh, yes, we'd be happy to do that,' Dad says. 'Anything to make the famous rock star feel at home.'

Oh, God, this is going to be a nightmare.

I go to pick up Johnny from Nice airport in the GTI. He flew first class instead of bringing the jet this time – and after a quick conversation on the phone the other night, we agreed that he won't need alternative transport while he's here. We want to keep this whole thing as low-key as possible.

I park the car and go inside to Arrivals, wondering blithely what disguise Johnny will be wearing to make sure he's not recognised. I check his flight's arrival time and see that it has just landed, and then I go to stand behind the barriers.

It starts as a buzz before turning to screams. Flashes are popping off all over the place and people begin to push and shove to get closer to the barriers. I'm being crushed among the throng and I know that all of this can only mean that, one, Johnny is in the vicinity and, two, the disguise didn't work.

The last time I experienced anything like this was when I was travelling with him on tour; but then I was with him and under the protection of his security guards, not being squashed to smithereens by a bunch of perfect strangers.

I push back against the crowd as hard as I can and somehow manage to get away from the people and into fresh air. The screams grow louder and if I follow the light of the flash bulbs I can just make out the top of Johnny's head as he walks through the Arrivals hall. What on earth am I supposed to do now?

He must be surrounded by security, otherwise he'd no longer be walking.

This is hopeless. There's no way he'll be hopping into the Golf under these circumstances. I make a decision to go and get the car and then try to contact him.

One of his security team calls me before I get out of the car park.

'Meet us in Sainte-Hélène, just off the A8. We'll pull up on the approach to town. We're in a black Merc, licence plate . . .' He reels off some numbers, but they go straight in one ear and out of the other. I'm sure I'll know it when I see it.

As soon as I exit the motorway on my way to Sainte-Hélène, I get another call.

'We're being tailed by the paps. Wait at the location while we try to lose them.'

I recognise that voice.

'Is that you, Samuel?' Samuel was one of Johnny's security guards when I worked in LA.

'Hello, Meg Stiles,' he replies in a deep American accent. 'Gotta go. See you in a bit.'

I hang up and smile to myself. It's strange to be back in this world. Strange and momentarily exhilarating.

I wait on the side of the road for twenty minutes before I'm contacted again.

'Have you lost them?' I'm referring to the paparazzi.

'Yeah, but we're no longer near the motorway. Permission to take the subject direct to the location?'

I sigh. All this waiting for nothing. 'Yes, of course,' I reply.

When I finally reach Johnny's hotel, the black Mercedes is nowhere to be seen. I go inside and approach the reception desk. The receptionist – long, dark, silky-smooth hair and immaculately made up – regards me with suspicion.

'*Bonjour*,' I say.

'Hello,' she replies in English.

Fine, if she's going to play it that way. Makes my life a whole lot easier.

'We're fully booked,' she says snootily.

'I know. I'm here to meet someone. Has Mr Jefferson arrived yet?'

She shrugs, playing dumb. 'I don't know who you mean. Who is this "Mr Jefferson"?'

'Johnny Jefferson,' I say, looking her straight in the eye.

'I don't know who this person is that you are speaking of, but

I'm sure that if you are supposed to be meeting him, you would know of his whereabouts.'

Oh, for God's sake. She clearly suspects me of being a demented fan.

'I guess I will have to try calling him again,' I reply, giving her a look through narrowed lashes. I turn and walk away, choosing to ignore whatever it is that she's bitchily muttering under her breath.

Now feeling pretty peeved, I get back into the car and dial his number. I expect Samuel to answer, so when Johnny picks up, sounding happy as Larry, I'm a bit taken aback.

'Where are you?' I ask.

'At your parents' house,' he replies with surprise.

'What are you doing there?' I'm aghast. Johnny with my parents? Alone?

'Didn't you hear Sam? He said he was taking me to the location.'

'The location? I thought he meant the hotel.'

'Crossed wires,' he replies merrily.

'Have you been drinking?' I ask suspiciously.

'Had a few on the plane. And your dad's got a lovely bottle of red on the go, here.'

'Don't drink any more!' I tell him, horrified.

'Why not, Nutmeg? We're having a whale of a time . . .'

Oh, Jesus. 'I'll be there in half an hour!'

'See you later, alligator,' he says happily.

Bollocks.

Chapter 20

Samuel, and whoever else joined Johnny on this jaunty little security mission, have already left by the time I arrive. I don't suppose it would help if their slick black Merc were parked on my parents' driveway in full view of everyone. I wonder if Samuel will be sticking around in France while Johnny's here, or if this was just a one-off due to Johnny catching a commercial flight instead of his private jet. Even if he did have first class all to himself, word can – and clearly did – get around about who was up at the front.

I park the car and hurry inside, full of apprehension. The feeling doesn't ease when I hear what sounds like a mini party going down in the living room. I walk along the corridor towards the noise and see Johnny lounging on the sofa opposite my parents, a half-full glass of red wine in his hand.

'Here she is,' my dad booms, leaping to his feet. The wine in his glass sloshes dangerously close to the edge.

'Hello, darling!' Mum says tipsily. 'Been on a bit of a wild goose chase, we hear.'

'Yes.' Through no fault of my own.

'Hello, Nutmeg.' Johnny waves from across the other side of the room.

'Where's Barney?' I ask, looking around.

'Here we go,' Mum rolls her eyes at Johnny and my dad, then says to me: 'He's still asleep.'

'Still asleep?' I exclaim. 'It's after four o'clock! He'll never go to bed on time.'

'Ooh, she's a whip-cracker,' my mum jokes.

I purse my lips with annoyance.

'He had a late nap,' she explains. 'Your dad had him in the swimming pool and he was having such a lovely time that I didn't want to spoil it by putting him to bed.'

'I'd better go and get him,' I mutter, knowing he's unlikely to be happy about it. He's usually a handful when he sleeps late.

'We weren't sure if you were going to tell us off, so we've kept Johnny inside rather than risk him being seen by anyone,' my dad calls after me in a stage whisper.

'Oh, right,' I reply, turning back. 'I'm sure it's fine to go outside.'

'She says it's fine to go outside.' Dad points at me as he tells Johnny this information, even though Johnny heard me say it himself. 'Ooh, you'll like it out there. We've got a lovely view,' he adds. 'Although I'm sure you've seen lots of lovely views in your time.'

'I've seen a few,' Johnny admits. 'But you can never get bored of a good view, can you, Geoffrey?'

'I quite agree,' my mum chips in.

Er, hello?

'Shall I get Barney?' Mum asks, standing up before I can answer.

168

'Um, yes, okay,' I agree, before looking meaningfully at Johnny. 'Can I have a word, please?'

'Oh, dear,' Mum says over her shoulder as she walks past. She knows that tone. Dad gives Johnny a sympathetic look as he climbs over my dad's feet and out past the sofas.

'In here.' I direct him to the kitchen.

'Alright?' he asks casually.

'No!' I hiss. 'What the hell are you doing, drinking?'

'I'm not an alcoholic, Nutmeg,' he replies, rolling his eyes good-naturedly. 'I just have a little issue with narcotics now and again.' He glances through to the living room to give my dad a whoops-a-daisy kind of look. Thankfully my dad doesn't hear or see.

'What you are, is in denial,' I snap. 'And I'm having none of it while you're around my son – or my parents!' I add.

'Okay, chick.' He puts his hands up and pulls a naughty-boy face at me, before pouring the rest of his red wine down the sink and opening the fridge.

'Can I get you anything?' My mum comes bustling in with Barney in her arms.

'A glass of water would be lovely, Cynthia.'

Cynthia? Geoffrey? Since when were they all on first-name terms?

'Right you are,' Mum says, passing over my son. Barney rubs at his eyes tearfully and suddenly he's all I can think about.

'Are you hungry, baby?' I ask him.

He snuggles into my shoulder.

'Hey, there!' Johnny says brightly, peering at his face. Barney lifts his head up to look at him for a moment before burying his head into my other shoulder, away from Johnny.

'Oh,' Johnny says, disappointed.

'Here you go, Johnny,' my mum interrupts, handing him a glass of water. 'Don't worry about Barney; he's always sleepy when he wakes up,' she adds.

'Especially if he's slept in until after four o'clock,' I mutter.

'Give it a rest, Meg,' Mum snipes.

Okay, so I didn't mutter that quite quietly enough.

'Shall we go out to the terrace?' Dad calls from the living room. Mum glances at me for confirmation.

'Yes, okay,' I agree.

'I'll get us some nibbles,' she says.

'Barney won't eat his dinner if he snacks now,' I point out.

'We won't let him have anything, then.'

'You can't stop a child from eating if it's right there in front of them,' I say.

'Oh, for goodness' sake,' Mum replies. 'We'll all go hungry, in that case!'

I take a deep breath, but can't keep the annoyed tone from my voice. 'Do what you like. Forget it. I'll just give him some rice cakes now.'

'There's an idea,' Mum says. 'I'll get on with the nibbles.'

What is it about my parents that makes me revert to being a moody teenager again? I hate it. Yet here I am, living in their house. This can't go on for much longer.

I walk out of the kitchen. Johnny follows.

'Chill out,' he says soothingly, although it just comes across as irritating to my ears.

'Don't you start,' I turn back and jab my finger at him.

'Hey, hey!' He puts his hands up again, then something catches his eye. 'Fuck me, your parents like potpourri.'

'Language,' I reply automatically before following his gaze. There are several bowls of dried flowers within eyesight – I hadn't really taken them in before. 'Hmm, yes,' I agree. I never really thought of my parents as potpourri types. 'Must be to do with living here. Did you know Grasse is the perfume capital of the world?' I ask.

'Yes, Nutmeg, I read up about it on the plane.' He grins, humouring me.

'I'm surprised you managed to do anything between whiskies,' I say caustically. 'What was with all the security and that fuss at the airport? I thought we were supposed to be keeping this low-key?'

He shrugs. 'You know how these things go.'

'I bloody well do, and they always go haywire when you've been at the booze.'

'Language,' he chides, a twinkle in his eye.

'God, you are so annoying.'

'And you are so cute when you're angry.'

'Don't start with that,' I warn.

'Why not? Anyway, I've got a girlfriend,' he says nonchalantly. 'I'm not starting anything.'

'Is anyone planning on joining me?' my dad calls from the terrace.

'We're on our way.' I give Johnny a look and lead the way outside through the French doors.

'Can I get you a top-up?' my dad asks Johnny, brandishing a bottle of red wine. 'Oh,' he says, spying Johnny's water glass.

'No, thanks, Geoffrey, I've been put in my place.'

'That's no good,' my dad replies, disappointed at losing his drinking partner.

I scratch my head with frustration and sit down. I envisaged this to be difficult in an entirely different way.

'Here we go,' my mum says cheerfully, putting a tray full of nuts, olives and savoury biscuit-type things on the table. Barney is instantly wide awake. 'Here you go, little one.' She passes me a packet of rice cakes. 'You forgot them,' she says to me.

I take them from her and open the packet, but Barney is only interested in the snacks on the table.

'Can't he have a biscuit?' my mum implores, pulling a face.

'They're full of salt,' I point out.

'It doesn't matter, does it?' She frowns. 'One won't hurt him.'

I take a deep breath and stare straight ahead before nodding tautly. I've lost the will to argue.

Johnny offers to drive himself back to his hotel – it turns out Lena insured him on the Golf when she bought it – but, as he's been drinking, I feel I have no choice but to take him myself. When I return to my parents' house, there's another car on the driveway. I'm irked, seeing as I had asked them, very nicely, if they could please not invite their friends around for the duration of Johnny's stay. Maybe someone dropped in unannounced.

I turn my key in the lock and push the door open. My mouth almost hits the floor when I hear my annoying sister Susan's annoying husband Tony's guffawing laugh.

Excuse my French, but WTF?

Aghast, I walk down the corridor to the living room and there, through the double doors to the garden, I see Susan and Tony sitting at the terrace table. I stand and stare. Almost as though sensing my presence, my mum spins around and spots me, simultaneously leaping to her feet.

'*Meg!*' she exclaims, putting her glass of wine on the table and opening her arms wide. She was halfway on the tipsy train to drunk when I left, but now she has clearly reached the station.

'There's my little sister!' Susan booms, going to the effort of standing up. She wouldn't usually bother; Tony doesn't.

'What's going on?' I manage to splutter. 'What are you doing here?'

Susan looks disgruntled. 'That's a nice welcome, isn't it?'

'How? How? Why?' I stutter in my parents' direction.

'What?' Susan demands to know, snappy now. 'I'm allowed a break from London life to come and see my parents, aren't I? What's your problem?'

I ignore her and stare straight at the guilty party. 'Did you tell them he was going to be here?'

My dad looks into his glass. My mum shifts from foot to foot.

'Who?' Tony tries to fake surprise, but he's a terrible liar, amongst other things.

'It sort of slipped out,' my mum admits worriedly.

'How?' I exclaim. 'How did it "sort of slip out"?'

'Excuse me!' Susan interrupts angrily, putting her hands on her hefty hips and shaking her short-ish, curly brown hair. 'I'm your sister. I have a right to know!'

'Did you tell her about Barney?' My eyes open wide as I look at my parents.

'No, no, no,' Mum hastily replies.

'What about Barney?' Susan chips in, her eyes darting between Mum and me.

'Nothing,' we both say simultaneously.

'I only told her that Johnny was coming for a visit,' Mum quickly explains. 'That the two of you were still friends.'

'Why would you do that?' I cry.

'Why shouldn't she? She's my mother!' Susan erupts.

'Because you and Tony would probably turn up on the doorstep unannounced and uninvited! And . . . *surprise!* Here you are!'

'I don't see what the fuss is all about,' she replies, now slightly guiltily. Tony helps himself to another glass of red wine and takes a massive gulp. He's good at getting through booze when he hasn't paid for it.

'Well, you're not going to meet him, if that's what you've planned,' I say furiously. 'There's no way in hell I'm bringing him back here now.'

Susan slams her hand on the table, making everyone jump. 'You are such a bitch!'

I glare at everyone and storm inside to my bedroom, desperately wanting to slam the door, but not enough to warrant waking my son.

I can't believe this! Why? Why did my mum tell them about Johnny? Of course they were going to be here in a shot! I still remember how pissed off Susan was with me for not getting Tony a signed copy of Johnny's album – she didn't care one iota that I'd lost my job and that I was miserable.

What on earth is Johnny going to think?

Chapter 21

I take Barney with me the following day to collect Johnny. I'm quite certain that, knowing my luck, Miss Bitchy on reception won't be working today, so I'm surprised when we go inside to see her sitting there. She glances up and sees me, then goes back to clicking away at her computer. I walk up to the desk. She ignores me.

It suddenly occurs to me that she's playing a computer game. Quick as a flash I lean over the desk and peer at her screen. She is! She's playing Solitaire!

'Aha!' I say triumphantly as she quickly closes the window. 'I knew it!'

'Can I help you?' She tries to put on a front, but I've totally caught her off guard.

'Here to see Johnny,' I reply, grinning like a crazy lady. I'm so delighted to have caught her out that it's put me at ease.

'Johnny?'

She's playing dumb again.

'Look,' I say, putting Barney down on the floor. 'Are you going to call him, or am I?'

'I don't know what you're talking about.' There's no conviction to her behaviour this time, though. She's starting to doubt herself.

I pull out my phone and dial Johnny's number. A couple of rings in, my heart starts beating faster with adrenalin – it would totally take the wind out of my sails if he didn't answer. The receptionist raises one catty eyebrow, then, praise the Lord . . .

'Nutmeg,' he says.

'Get your butt down here,' I reply.

Miss Bitchy's mouth falls open.

'Are you here already?' Johnny asks me.

'Yep. In reception.'

'Why didn't reception call me, then?'

'I don't know,' I say, turning to look at the girl. I peer closely at her nametag. The print is tiny – what use is that? 'Jeannette asked me to call you myself.'

'I didn't!' she squawks. 'I didn't ask you to call!'

'Shh.' I put my hand up to silence her.

'Want to come up?' Johnny says. 'I'm in the penthouse suite.'

'Penthouse suite,' I repeat out loud, flashing Jeannette a sarcastic smile.

'I'm not dressed yet,' Johnny drawls.

'We'll be there in a sec,' I say brightly. 'But put your pants on first, Johnny, I don't want to see you naked.'

I snap my phone shut, cutting off the sound of him chuckling.

'Been there, done that.' I raise one eyebrow at Jeannette, then almost clap my hand over my mouth when I realise what I've just said.

'Come on, Barney.' I try to keep my cool.

Jeannette leaps to her feet. 'I'll take you.'

'No, no, no,' I say sweetly. 'You've already been *so* helpful, and you're clearly *very* busy.' I give her computer a pointed look and then spin around on my heels and lead Barney to the lift.

Johnny opens the door to us. He's wearing jeans, but no shirt.

'I thought I told you to get dressed.'

'You told me to put my pants on.'

'Hmm.'

'Which I did,' he adds with a grin. 'Hello, Barney!' he says cheerfully.

'Look, check this out,' I say proudly, standing Barney on the floor in front of me. He grips my fingers, but I gently extricate myself. 'Go to Johnny,' I urge. Barney takes a few unsteady steps before falling backwards on his nappy-clad bottom.

'Wayhey!' Johnny exclaims, lifting him to his feet again. 'Clever boy.' Barney babbles up at him and toddles towards his guitar, propped up against a wall.

'Thought I might be able to get some writing done,' Johnny explains, still grinning at Barney's achievement.

'That'd be good.' I give him an encouraging nod.

'You're so funny, Nutmeg.' He reaches over and ruffles my hair.

'Get off!' I wave him away. 'Jesus, what am I, your sister?'

He looks sad. 'I never had a sister. Always wanted one.'

'You can have mine, if you like.' I'll get to that news in a minute . . .

He smiles again. 'You sounded chirpy on the phone.'

'Yep. Receptionist downstairs was being a cow.'

His face falls. 'Really?'

'Mmm. Thought I was a stalker, I think.'

'That's crap. Want me to get her fired for you?'

I laugh. 'No, you're alright, thanks.'

'I will,' he says casually.

'Yep, I'm aware of how *powerful* you are,' I say this in a comedy fashion. 'But no need to put people out of work just yet.'

He shrugs. 'Whatever you want.'

'Barney, don't touch that, baby,' I call. He's reached Johnny's guitar.

'It's okay,' Johnny says, going over to him. 'You like this?'

I slump down on one of the ridiculously comfy sofas. Johnny crouches next to Barney and lets him pluck the strings.

'Why don't you play him something?' I suggest.

Most people would modestly decline, but Johnny doesn't. It's refreshing.

He spins his guitar around and sits cross-legged on the floor. His chest is still bare and there's not an ounce of fat on his stomach. Barney watches, fixated as he starts to strum.

'Sing, too,' I urge from my comfy sofa position, smirking now because I'm probably pushing my luck.

Johnny glances up at me and raises one eyebrow before looking back at Barney. He plays a different, jaunty tune.

'Old McDonald had a farm, E-I-E-I-O . . .'

I laugh as Barney starts to clap.

'And on that farm he had a pig. E-I-E-I-O . . .'

Johnny stops playing and chuckles, shaking his head. 'Nah, you can do the nursery rhymes, but I want my son to be raised on real music.'

I watch him, amused, as he starts to play something else. I recognise it, but don't know what it is until he gets to the chorus:

'Hey, Mister Tambourine Man, play a song for me . . .'

'Isn't that about drugs?' I tease over the music. Johnny rolls his eyes and carries on playing. I smile to myself and listen to his deep, beautiful voice. Barney, next to him, is absolutely enthralled. For the first time in way too long, I feel content.

It's at times like this that I remember why I loved Johnny.

A feeling of déjà vu strikes me, and I recall thinking the same thing about Christian only a few weeks ago. I interrupt him before the song comes to an end.

'So,' I say, all business-like. 'We've got a bit of a problem.'

Johnny stops playing and puts his guitar down. 'What?'

'My sister and her husband have besieged us.'

'Hey?'

'My sister, Susan, and her husband, Tony, have landed on my parents' doorstep in search of fame and fortune. *Your* fame and fortune, to be more precise.'

'Ah.'

Barney starts to pluck the guitar strings, distracting Johnny. He strokes his hair affectionately.

'Johnny.' I try to regain his attention.

'What? Oh, yeah. What's the big deal?'

'Have I never told you about my sister before? Scrap that, I know I haven't. She's a pain in the arse. We won't be able to go to the house now. We'll have to hang out here.'

'Why?' He pulls a face. 'Is she going to knife me through the heart?'

'Unlikely,' I say wryly. 'She and Tony will just spend the whole time pretending that they're not interested in you in any way whatsoever and that they don't care that you're some big celebrity – even though they clearly do.'

'So? It's not like I haven't dealt with that sort of thing before.'

'It's embarrassing,' I point out.

'Fuck it. Whoops,' he apologises. 'Don't worry about it, Nutmeg. Let's go and meet them.'

I hesitate. 'Are you sure?'

'Yep.'

'Don't say you haven't been warned.'

'I won't.'

'Okay, then. But play another song first.'

He grins and starts to strum.

'Hey, hey, we're the Monkees . . .'

Barney giggles, and pretty soon I do, too.

'What's his name again?' Johnny asks as he pulls up outside my parents' place. He insisted on driving – way too fast, I might add – *and* I had to give him directions the whole way.

'Tony,' I reply. 'And she's Susan.'

'Got that.' He unclicks his seat belt.

'Oh!' I cry, suddenly remembering a very important piece of information. 'They don't know about Barney.'

'What do you mean?' He turns to look at me with confusion.

'They don't know that Barney is yours.'

'What the hell do they think I'm doing here, then?' he exclaims.

'I guess they think we've stayed friends,' I reply uneasily. 'They never knew about you and me, either,' I add quickly, feeling my face heat up at the thought that he might assume that I bragged about it to anyone.

'This is going to be awkward, then.'

'I'm sorry,' I say. 'I did warn you.'

No reply.

180

'Shall we go back to your hotel?' I ask tetchily. Like I wanted to come here, anyway.

'No, f-f-fudge it,' he corrects himself and instantly smirks at his own ingenuity. 'Let's have some fun.' He climbs out of the car. 'Susan! Tony!' he calls as he opens the front door – my parents rarely lock it.

'Is that him?' I hear my sister squeak in entirely unconcealed surprise.

'Yes,' my dad replies unflappably.

I groan.

'Who? Johnny Jefferson?' Tony asks in disbelief.

Dur . . . Who else, you idiot?

'Yes, it's the one and only!' Johnny cries gleefully down the corridor.

I hurry around the corner just in time to see Johnny engulf Susan in a massive bear hug.

'Tony,' he says affectionately, breaking away from my flabbergasted sister. 'Come here, you.' Over Johnny's shoulder, Tony gives Susan a look of unparalleled incredulity. Susan looks like she's going to burst. Even more than she usually does.

Oh, dear, I've obviously got the bitch in me today. I blame Jeannette the receptionist.

'We were about to have lunch,' my mum says, beaming at this turn of events.

'Great, Cynthia! I'm starving,' Johnny says, clapping his hands together. I give him a wry look and he winks at me as we head outside to the terrace table.

'That was totally over the top,' I say later, much to Johnny's amusement. He's about to drive himself back to the hotel in the

GTI. By some miracle, he didn't drink anything alcoholic today. I'm standing on the driveway, talking to him through the window.

'What that was, Nutmeg, was fun.'

'Will you stop calling me Nutmeg?' I ask.

'Nope.'

'No, I didn't think you would.' I roll my eyes at him. 'God only knows what Susan and Tony would be like if they found out Barney was yours.'

'If?' Johnny queries. 'Don't you mean, *when*?'

My lips turn down and I shrug.

'We are going to tell them, aren't we?' he says, in a tone that implies we'd bloody well better.

'Fine, if you want it plastered all over the tabloids.'

'They wouldn't do that,' he scoffs.

'You don't know my sister.'

'I know that she's your *sister*,' he replies. 'I don't believe she'd sell a story about you.'

'Hmm, maybe not. But I still don't want to tell her yet.' I regard him curiously. 'Have you told Dana?'

'Nope.'

'When are you planning on doing that?'

'When the time's right. She's already peeved at me for disappearing out of LA for days on end.'

'What have you told her you're doing?'

He shrugs. 'Writing.'

He always did use to disappear on impromptu writing trips. I remember feeling horribly insecure about it. I shudder at the memory of that girl; that girl I used to be. I'll never let myself get in a position like that, ever again.

'Right, you'd better be off,' I say.

'Yep.' He turns the key in the ignition. 'See you in the morning?'

'We'll be waiting.' I cast a look over my shoulder at the house, then turn back to him and say with widened, crazy eyes, 'We will *all* be waiting . . .'

He shakes his head with amusement before driving away.

Chapter 22

Johnny doesn't turn up until after one o'clock the following day and it nearly drives Susan and Tony around the bend. I can see them continually checking their watches. Even my parents are distracted.

'Why don't you go out for the day?' I suggest at about eleven o'clock to annoy them.

'No, we're happy here, thank you,' Susan replies tersely, but forty-five minutes later, she erupts. 'Where the hell is he?'

I shrug. 'This is what he's like.' Although, inside, I'm getting a little bit irate myself. What the hell has he been doing all morning? I tried calling him earlier, to no avail. I hope he's not nursing a hangover. I'll be really pissed off.

Sure enough, when he does finally turn up, it's in dark sunglasses and looking the worse for wear. I answer the door to him.

'You've been drinking.' It's not a question.

'And?'

'This isn't a bloody holiday, Johnny. You're here to get to know Barney.'

'I am getting to know him,' he replies unapologetically.

'I don't want you drinking around my son!' I'm starting to get worked up.

'I'm not drinking around *my* son,' he replies.

'What are you doing, boozing on your own, anyway? That should be the clearest sign to you that you've got a problem.'

'Who said I was drinking on my own?' he asks.

My mouth shuts abruptly.

'Where's Barney?' He eases me to one side and steps over the threshold.

'Outside.'

He starts to saunter in that direction and I find I'm lost for words.

As soon as they heard the knock at the door, Susan and Tony leaped into their 'casual' positions. Susan is now lying on a sunlounger, with one leg propped up to try to make her frame look smaller. It's not really working.

'Good morning!' Tony says with forced cheerfulness. 'Or should I say, good afternoon?' He strokes his weak chin in an attempt to be comical and then flicks his limp brown hair back before giggling hysterically.

'Did you have a nice lie-in?' Susan asks huskily.

Johnny gives them a slight nod of acknowledgement, but doesn't pay them any additional attention as he walks past. He joins Barney on the grass under the shade of an umbrella and silently proceeds to push one of his plastic toy cars around. Barney makes a grab for it and Johnny smiles a small smile. It's blatantly obvious to me that he's nursing quite a hangover. I go indoors to the medicine cabinet and return to the shade of the umbrella, this time accompanied by a glass of water and painkillers. I hand them to Johnny without comment. He takes them without looking at me.

'Have you been to a perfume factory yet?' Susan asks Johnny brightly.

'Nope.' He shakes his head.

'Oh, you must go,' she says. 'Maybe we could all go today?'

'Perfume's not really my thing,' Johnny drawls, clearly not keen to engage in conversation. Susan is having none of it.

'Not your thing? It's not about that; it's just really interesting to see how they make it. Isn't it, Tony?' She nudges him hard.

'Oh, yes,' he complies. 'Very interesting. We should go. Shouldn't we?' He looks at Susan.

'Yes. We should all go.' Susan gazes meaningfully at Johnny, but he ignores her. 'Or we could all just stay here and enjoy the sunshine,' she adds, false breezily.

Johnny murmurs under his breath, 'Get me away from here.'

'You want to go out?' I ask him quietly.

'Need.'

Twenty-five minutes later we're in the car. I'm driving. Johnny is silent in the seat next to me.

'Where do you want to go?'

'I don't care.'

It was a nightmare getting away. When I announced that we were going for a drive, Susan decided it was an excellent idea and that she and Tony should join us, even though she'd already promised to go with Mum and Dad to a perfume factory. She then suggested driving behind us in their car, and when I knocked that idea on the head, she accused me of being selfish.

I walked out at that point. Ooh, it's going to be fun around the dinner table this evening.

We drive around for half an hour before Barney becomes grizzly.

'Can you entertain him?' I ask Johnny.

'My head,' he mumbles.

'Look, what do you want to do?' I snap. 'I can't just drive around all day – Barney will go bananas.'

'Won't he sleep?'

'No, he's already had his nap this morning.'

Silence.

'Shall I take you back to your hotel?' I ask crossly, expecting him to say no and consequently perk up.

'Yeah, that might be an idea,' he replies instead.

Angrily, I do a U-turn and begin to make my way there.

'Will you swing by and pick me up tomorrow?' he asks me when he gets out of the car.

'What time?' I can't keep the unimpressed tone from my voice.

'Not too early.'

'Ten o'clock?'

'Eleven?'

'Whatever. Shut the door.'

He does and I drive off.

I can hear my sister's raised voice before I even open the front door.

'Can you keep it down?' I ask irritably, indicating Barney.

'Where's Johnny?' Susan demands to know.

'I took him back to his hotel,' I reply.

'Why?' she cries.

'He was hungover,' I respond. 'Not very good company.'

'Speak for yourself,' she replies.

'Oh, would you please get over it!' I exclaim.

'Meg, that's enough.' My dad frowns at me. He doesn't often tell me off, but when he does it really hits home.

My mum comes to take Barney from me. 'No, it's alright,' I say, clutching hold of him. 'I don't have anything more to say.'

I go to bed early that night, feigning illness. My mum puts Barney to sleep. I don't want company. I just want to be on my own. I have a deep sadness inside me and I don't want to do anything other than dwell in my own misery for a while. I'll feel better in the morning. I'm sure I will.

Chapter 23

I'm sitting in my bedroom with the phone pressed painfully hard against my ear. My stomach is a knot of tension and anxiety. I'm calling Christian again. It's the fourth time in three days. But he's not answering. He's still not answering.

Johnny left a week ago after a whirlwind trip. I was sorry to see him go. Being around him made for a nice escape from reality, but now I'm back in the real world, and I miss Christian.

Aside from everything else, he was my friend. Plus, of course, he was Barney's father. Barney still seems completely unaware of – and unaffected by – Christian's absence. I'm thankful for that, at least.

I stare down at the receiver and end the call, my ear burning from the pressure of having the phone pressed up against it. I wonder what he's doing. I wonder if he's doing this exact same thing right now: staring down at his phone. I wish he wasn't refusing to answer it.

Susan and Tony went home a few days ago and, despite the fact that their brush with celebrity made them more unbearable than usual, I even miss them. They talked about Johnny

189

incessantly after he left – even Mum and Dad were on a strange, Johnny-related high. They all forgave him for refusing to grace them with his presence that day. I think they've chosen to erase the negative parts of his stay from their memories so they can reminisce about their time with him with untainted affection.

I come out of my bedroom to hear the unmistakable sound of Johnny's singing coming from my dad's study. Frowning, I wander down the corridor to the room at the end. My dad is sitting in front of his small stereo, staring down at a CD case. I stand there for a moment, listening. I recognise this song. It's one of the album tracks Johnny was writing when I worked for him. I listened to his CD only once – during one of the dark moments I had when I was pregnant with Barney. The track comes to an end and the next song starts to play.

'Hi, Dad!' I say brightly, making him jump. He looks guilty. 'I didn't know you owned any of Johnny's CDs?'

'I, er, found this one in town. I thought it might be nice to hear some of his work – you know, seeing as he's part of the family.'

'Fair enough,' I say, trying to block out the lyrics about the 'brown-eyed girl'. When this single was released, I remember coming across a music review which said Johnny was paying a tongue-in-cheek tribute to the Van Morrison song. But this is the song he wrote for me. *I'm* the brown-eyed girl.

'Turn it down, Dad, I don't want to hear this,' I say cheerfully.

'Why not?' he asks, furrowing his brow. 'I like it.'

'Yeah, me, too, but I've heard it too many times.'

That part's the truth. When Johnny asked me to go back to LA with him and I said no, he told me he'd wait for me for three months. One month later, I found out I was pregnant. My decision to stay with Christian seemed pretty clear-cut after that, but sometimes, late at night, I would doubt it. When Johnny's single came out I would play it over and over, not only to torment myself, but also to question whether I was doing the right thing. I only truly decided to cut my losses with Johnny on the day that I had my twelve-week scan. I hadn't told Christian I was pregnant, so I went alone to the hospital. Seeing that tiny grey and black jellybean shape on the monitor . . . its heartbeat . . . In the first three months, it hadn't seemed real, but now there was my baby, right there on that screen. And it hit me there and then – with an impact as hard as a slap across the face – that the first person I wanted to tell was Johnny.

If I hadn't walked past the newsagent's inside the hospital, maybe it would have all turned out differently. But I did, and there on the front of one of the tabloids was a picture of Johnny with his arm around a girl – a girl I knew. The headline read: 'Going to put a ring on it'. I stopped dead in my tracks and snatched up the paper. It was a trashy story about Johnny finally falling in love, and the girl he was with was the same one he slept with in LA. She was the final straw for me back then. And here she was again. It was a message: my three months were up. He was moving on. I remember standing there, clutching my stomach as I read this stupidly speculative story – which turned out to be totally untrue because he never did settle down with her – and finally my breathing slowed and I calmly put the paper back where I found it. Then I went home and told Christian my news.

I take a deep breath as the memory of all of this comes back to me now.

'When's he coming to stay again?' Dad asks casually.

'I don't know.'

'You should call him, invite him again. He can stay with us next time.'

'Mmm, maybe.'

My dad turns the music back up before I leave the room.

My parents' love affair with Johnny takes a nosedive a week later when there's a picture of him looking wasted in one of the papers.

'He's looking a bit the worse for wear,' my dad sniffs. 'Who's this lass, here?' He points to Dana, who's dressed all in black and is hanging off Johnny with her arm around his neck. Her dark eye make-up looks smudged – maybe the panda-bear look is fashionable these days.

'Dana Reed,' I explain unhappily. 'She's his girlfriend.'

'I didn't know he had a girlfriend,' my mum says.

'I did tell you about her,' I say.

'No, you didn't,' she bats back.

'I'm sure I did.'

'You didn't,' she insists. Oh, I give up. 'Well, that's a shame,' she says, putting the paper back on the table with disgust. My dad picks it up again and brings it closer to his face to study it.

'She's quite a looker, isn't she?' he muses.

My mum snatches the paper back. 'Too much make-up,' she decides.

'I thought he wasn't supposed to be drinking anymore?' Dad chips in.

'I'm not his keeper. I can't force him not to drink,' I say.

'You managed to stop him when he was here,' my dad says.

'That was different.'

'When's he coming to stay again?'

'I don't know, Dad . . .'

Two days later there's another story about him. Another party, another picture of him looking wasted on the arm of Dana Reed. The press speculate it's only a matter of time before he ends up back in rehab.

'Have you spoken to him yet?' Dad demands to know.

'No,' I say firmly.

'I think you should call him, give him a revving.'

'What he does with his life is his own business,' I reply, trying to keep calm. The truth is, I'm feeling sick again.

'He's the father of your son,' Dad barks crossly. 'His life is your business, now.'

'I don't want to talk about this in front of Barney,' I reply as an excuse. I take my son and go outside to the garden.

Dad slaps a different newspaper in front of me at breakfast the following day. He jabs his finger at a small story in the gossip column. Tensing up, I scan the words and discover Johnny and Dana took an impromptu dip in a pool at an after-show party for a hot new band, and this was after doing seven shots of whisky in a row.

'This sort of behaviour is not on.' My mum pulls a face. 'You should talk to him about it.'

'You don't know Johnny very well if you think I can do that,' I reply wryly, trying to ignore my churning stomach.

'Have you heard from him?' Dad chips in.

'Not since you last asked me about it,' I reply, putting the paper back on the table.

'I hope we're not going to be greeted with a story like this every day,' my mum says.

'Don't read the tabloids. That's what I've learned to do.' I continue to eat my Coco Pops and try to pretend that all this doesn't bother me.

'We can't not read the papers,' my dad scoffs.

'You can *not* read the tabloids,' I reply, raising my eyebrows. 'You never used to.'

They've been buying them these last few weeks. It's not hard to guess why.

'I like the tabloids,' Mum says. 'They're a bit of fun.'

I glance down at the paper on the table. This doesn't feel like fun to me.

That night I try calling Christian again. He doesn't answer.

Chapter 24

'I don't remember these roads,' Johnny says from the driver's seat.

It's the end of September and we've arranged to go away on a trip together, just the three of us. My parents weren't at all happy with the idea of Barney and me going off with Johnny alone, and they made their concerns known when there was another story about him in the papers, but I was insistent. Barney needs to spend some time with his dad. His real dad. And who knows where Johnny's crazy life will take him in the months and years to come. We have to make the most of our time when he's not touring or working or doing God knows what while we still have it.

'You didn't drive them,' I remark. 'You were too trolleyed at the time. Slow down!' I cry.

'Wicked.' He chuckles as he takes another corner at breakneck speed. 'God, I miss this.'

'What?'

'Driving around these country lanes. I bloody love it up north.'

We're in the Yorkshire Dales, almost at our destination. We're going to the house where I took Johnny over two and a half years ago – that time when I forced him to go cold turkey. It's private, secluded and familiar. It's perfect.

'It looks different to how I remember it,' he muses a while later, as we reach the cottage at the end of a long dirt track.

'It was the middle of winter then. This is more how I remember it from my childhood.' I came here with my parents once after my sister had left for university. I was only about ten.

I look up at the grey-stone two-storey cottage. It's surrounded by a drystone wall and there's a green, grassy hill sloping away behind the house. I remember coming out of the cottage one day – the morning after I'd slept with Johnny – to see him sitting at the top, strumming his guitar. That was when he wrote my song. Butterflies swarm through me.

Johnny retrieves our bags from the boot while I get Barney out of his car seat.

'We'd better make sure we keep the doors closed,' I say, trying to act normal. 'We wouldn't want him falling in that stream in the garden.'

'No,' Johnny agrees, slamming the boot shut and meeting my eyes over the roof of the car. I force myself to look at my son and smile, trying to ignore the shivery feeling inside.

Barney and I take the front room facing the track, while Johnny takes the room looking up at the hill. It's the same way it was two and a half years ago, and there's no need to change things. We've brought our own travel cot so I assemble it while Johnny entertains Barney, and then I trot downstairs to an empty house. I go out through the back door in search of my boys, and then jolt to a stop when I realise I've just called them 'my boys', like I used to with Christian.

I take a deep breath and continue on my search. I find them in the garden. The last time we were here it was leafless and muddy. Now the trees are full of leaves which are just starting to turn and it's beautiful. There's heather in the garden in gorgeous pinky-purple bloom, and elsewhere pretty white flowers break up the greenery. I inhale deeply and feel at peace for a brief moment. Then I think of Christian again.

Last week, I had what I thought was a brainwave. I'd totally forgotten that we had a landline in Cucugnan because we hardly ever used it. I found the number in my contacts and called it, feeling both hopeful and fearful. A man answered, and it wasn't Christian.

'Who's that?' I asked, perturbed.

'Who's this?' he replied.

It suddenly dawned on me. 'Is that you, Jed?'

'Meg?'

'Hi.' Jed is the friend we rented the house from. 'Is Christian there?'

'No.' Jed sounded confused. 'He went back to the UK. I thought you knew.'

'No.' My head felt fuzzy.

'Yeah. And I'm, you know, just having a break from all the madness back home before my September rental comes in,' he explained casually, but I wasn't really listening. Christian had gone. He'd left France. I don't know why this made everything seem so much more final, but my insides felt like they'd been put in a tumble dryer.

'Okay, thanks for letting me know,' I said in a monotone voice.

'Hey, are you okay?' he asked, suddenly curious.

'I'm fine, thanks. I've got to go.'

'Oka—'

'Bye,' I interrupted, ending the call.

I don't know what I'll say to Christian when we do finally speak. If and when that day ever comes.

Johnny and Barney are standing on the small bridge in the garden overlooking the stream.

'What are you up to?' I call.

'I'm going to make him a paper boat,' Johnny calls back. I smile as I wander towards them, folding my arms across my chest. There's a chill in the air. Summer may be raging on in the south of France, but it's officially over in England.

I reach down and pick up three sticks. 'Race ya,' I say to Johnny, handing him one and Barney the other.

'Hang on a sec,' Johnny replies, giving me a sardonic look. 'Let me check the aerodynamics of that one, first, please.' I roll my eyes and hand him my stick. 'Sneaky,' he murmurs, swapping my stick for his.

'Happy now?' I ask, raising my eyebrows. 'Or would you like to check Barney's, too?'

'Hmm.' Johnny regards Barney's stick through narrowed eyes. 'I suppose he can have that one.'

'That's nice of you, seeing as he's only one, and all.' I shake my head at him. 'Right . . .' I show Barney how to hold his stick over the edge of the bridge before throwing it in, and then we all rush to the other side to see whose comes through first.

'I won! I won!' Johnny cries.

'Yes, you beat the baby. Well done.' I smirk at him and he chuckles. I wonder if Barney should start to call him Daddy . . .

That thought came to me out of nowhere. But no, it's too soon.

'I should probably get on with dinner,' I say.

'I hope your cooking has improved from the last time we came here,' Johnny responds.

'You ungrateful sod,' I remark. 'We're having a Spaghetti Bolognese ready meal, for your information.' We stocked up on food at the service station on the way here.

'Man, I miss Rosa.'

He immediately looks a little taken aback at his own declaration. I don't think he meant to say it out loud, to admit to anyone how much he cared for his beloved cook. I give him a sympathetic smile.

'There's no chance of her returning?'

He shakes his head. 'Come on,' he says to Barney. 'Let's find some more sticks.'

I turn and head back inside.

'Messy eater,' Johnny says at dinner. Half of Barney's spaghetti is on the floor.

'This is nothing,' I reply. 'You should have seen him when he'd just started solids.'

It's a flyaway comment, but I immediately realise it's an insensitive one. I look up at Johnny to see him watching Barney thoughtfully.

'So,' I say with a wry smile, trying to change the subject. 'What have you told Dana this time?'

'The truth,' Johnny replies without a beat.

'Seriously?' I'm shocked. I thought he was going to say he'd told her he was writing or away on business, or had used some other excuse. 'You've told her about Barney?' I double-check.

'Yes.' He stares at me directly. I find it unnerving, but try not to show it.

'Wow. What did she say?'

'She was pretty cool with it.' He pushes his plate of half-eaten spaghetti into the centre of the table.

'Was she?'

'Yep.' He abruptly gets to his feet, the wooden legs of his chair screeching across the stone floor. 'Gonna nip outside for a fag.'

'Okay,' I say in a small voice.

Why doesn't this feel like good news?

'Do you remember this?' Johnny asks me that evening when I come downstairs after settling Barney. He's holding up a jigsaw box with a picture on the front of a litter of multicoloured kittens in a basket.

I smile. 'Yes, I do.'

There's no television in the cottage, so last time we were here we spent a decent chunk of our time playing board games.

'Are you up for it?' he asks.

I pull out a chair and sit down. 'Go on, then.'

He opens the box and tips the pieces out onto the table.

'First, you've got to do the corners,' I say, teasing him because this is what he said to me the last time we did this puzzle, as if I didn't know how to do a jigsaw. 'Then the edges,' I add for extra effect.

'Are you taking the piss?' he asks and my smirk turns into a giggle.

'Maybe a little bit.'

'I think more than a little bit, babe.' He reaches across to my side of the table and retrieves a corner.

We work in amicable silence for a while until he says, 'Chuck us that piece of ginger pussy,' and I collapse into more giggles.

'You have got such a dirty mind,' he mutters. 'What happened to my good girl?' His green eyes confront me for a moment across the table and my stomach flips.

'I think she's long gone,' I joke drily, looking down at the puzzle as my heart hammers away inside my chest. This is not right.

'Don't say that, Nutmeg.'

'Don't call me Nutmeg.' It's a knee-jerk response, but this time he leans back in his chair and folds his arms, eyeing me across the table.

'Why don't you like it?'

I shrug awkwardly. 'I don't mind it, really. What do you call Lena?'

'Lena,' he replies.

'Is that her real name?'

'Isn't it good enough for you?'

'Yeah, it's a nice name.'

'I didn't think her partner would appreciate it if I changed it to something else.'

'No, probably not.' I smile. 'How long has she been working for you?'

'Couple of years now.'

'You like her, then?'

'Not in that way.' He raises one eyebrow at me and I'm horrified to find myself blushing. It doesn't escape his notice. 'Aah, my little Nutmeg,' he says with amusement.

Oh, God, what is happening to me? I feel like the tables of power are turning. I don't want him to have this control over me again. I should go to bed. Right now.

'Ciggie break.' He stands up, stealing my opportunity to leave the table first.

'I'm going to hit the sack,' I tell him, a touch too quickly.

'Right you are,' he replies, opening the door. 'Night.' He shuts it behind him.

Upstairs I sit in my darkened bedroom and stare out of the window. I forgot to pull the curtains earlier and now I can see that there's a full moon tonight.

Maybe it was a mistake coming back here. There are too many memories. Good memories – and bad. Is it affecting Johnny, too? He doesn't seem to be bothered by it, but then Johnny hardly ever seems to be bothered by anything.

I go to the window and see his cigarette outside in the night. He puts it to his lips and inhales, lighting his face with an orange glow. Then he looks up and I pause, my fingers clutching the curtain fabric, not sure if he can see me or not. I nod down to him, just in case, and pull the curtains closed.

Chapter 25

'Good afternoon,' I say to Johnny when he emerges the following morning.

'What's the time?' he asks in confusion.

'Almost ten o'clock.'

'Christ, this is early for me. What time were you up?'

'Six thirty,' I reply chirpily. 'I'm absolutely knackered!'

He gives me a wry grin and rubs at the sleep in his eyes.

'I could get up early tomorrow. Give you a lie-in.'

I turn to him in surprise. 'Really?'

'Sure.'

Then I think of all the practicalities of breakfast and nappy changes and getting Barney dressed, and actually it feels like harder work trying to explain it all than just getting out of bed and doing it myself.

'We'll see,' I say, making him a coffee and handing it over.

'Don't you think I can cope?' He blows steam off the top.

'It's not that,' I reply.

'Don't look a gift horse in the mouth.'

'No, you're right, I shouldn't.' I glance down at the countertop.

'Did Christian help much with Barney?' he asks casually.

'I don't want to talk about him,' I reply, then feel mean.

Johnny shrugs and wanders to the door, reaching into his jeans pocket for his fags. He shuts the door behind him. After a minute, I go to the window and open it, leaning out.

'Have you ever thought about giving up?'

'Nope.' He inhales deeply.

'You haven't had a drink since you've been here.'

'Drink isn't my problem,' he says.

'How did you come to that conclusion?' I ask, unimpressed. 'It always used to be.'

'It's the drugs that keep ending me back in rehab.'

'And the drink,' I add. 'What do your counsellors say?'

'They're full of shit.' He shudders. 'God, I hate that place.'

'Not enough to stop you from going back there.'

'I'm not going back again,' he replies resolutely.

'Why don't you give up the booze, then? I would have thought it's a slippery slope.'

His face breaks into a grin. 'You're so cute, Nutmeg.'

'Don't start that again, and don't change the subject, Johnny. You know you can talk to me about this.'

'What makes you think that?'

'Who else do you have to talk to about it?'

'My girlfriend,' he replies bluntly, stubbing out his cigarette.

'Your drug-addicted girlfriend?' I ask pointedly, trying to ignore the sting.

'You know nothing about Dana.'

I know it hurts to hear him defend her.

'Is it serious?' I find myself asking.

'You could say that,' he replies.

204

'Do you love her?' A buzzing starts up inside my head, but Johnny never gets to answer that question because Barney lets out an almighty cry from the living room. I run through to where I'd left him playing on the floor. His face is bright red and tears are pouring down his cheeks. He's clutching the back of his head with his hand. I scoop him up and cuddle him. Johnny joins me a moment later.

'What happened?' he asks with alarm.

'I think he must've fallen over,' I say loudly over the noise of crying.

Johnny holds his arms out in an offer to take him, but I clutch Barney to my chest and shake my head. Eventually his cries subside.

'He'll be tired,' I say. 'I should take him for a walk to get him to sleep.'

Johnny nods, looking slightly helpless. I quickly get my things together and put Barney in the buggy before heading out of the cottage and down the dirt track.

It's quiet outside, and I need the peace to think. I stride purposefully down the road as thoughts whizz around my head. I shouldn't be here. It was safer in France with my parents around. Maybe I should cut this trip short and go back early.

No. I can't let him get to me. I can't believe I'm letting him get to me.

I swallow the lump in my throat and glance into the buggy. Barney is starting to doze off, but I don't want to go back to the cottage yet. Or maybe I do. And therein lies the problem.

Johnny's bedroom door is closed when I return. I transfer Barney to his cot and go downstairs with my book. I lie on the sofa, looking at the words but not taking them in.

I wonder what he's doing.

After an hour, I can stand it no longer. I go upstairs on the pretence of checking on Barney. Johnny's door is still closed and there's no sound coming from inside. He's probably gone back to bed. Barney is still fast asleep. I return downstairs, but can't be bothered to try to read. I decide to make an early start on dinner. Fifteen minutes later, I hear footsteps on the stairs and look around with surprise to see Johnny carrying Barney into the kitchen.

'Did he wake up?' I ask, going over to them. 'Oh, God, I forgot to bring his monitor downstairs!'

'You're a terrible mother,' Johnny jokes, handing him over to me.

'Where have you been?' I ask.

'Chilling out in my room. Trying to write.'

'You like writing here.' I place Barney on the floor with a wooden spoon and a saucepan to bang it on. He immediately starts making a racket.

'Must be the fresh air,' Johnny replies sardonically, then: 'Jesus, please tell me you're not cooking?'

I whack him on his stomach and he clutches it in fake agony. 'You'll get what you're given and you'll act happy about it.'

He grins and leans his elbows against the counter behind him. He hasn't done the buttons up at the bottom of his dark-blue-almost-black shirt and I catch a glimpse of his navel with the Johnny Cash lyric tattooed across it. I look up to find him watching me.

'Need a hand?' he asks.

'You can chop that carrot,' I reply, handing him a knife but not meeting his eyes.

This is not right . . . This is not right . . .

'What are we having?' he asks.

'Chicken stew.'

I wait for the teasing remark, but it doesn't come.

'Next!' he calls after a minute.

I pass him the celery and he cracks on with the job.

'Who needs Rosa?' I say with a small smile.

He laughs quietly and shakes his head.

'If only your fans could see you now . . .' I add: 'Super-cool rock god Johnny Jefferson chopping vegetables.'

'Meg, did you just call me a super-cool rock god?'

I laugh. 'I've called you that before, remember?'

'I do remember,' he replies.

An image suddenly fills my head of me encircling his waist with my arms and smiling up at him, as if we've been together for years.

'Anything else?' he asks, dragging me away from my strange vision.

'Um, can you just entertain Barney for a while?' I try to focus on trimming the chicken breasts.

'Sure. Come on, buddy, let's go into the garden.'

He goes out of the back door and I put the knife down on the countertop, trying to get my breath back.

Barney wakes up early again the following morning. I bring him into bed with me, desperately hoping he'll fall back asleep, but he's having none of it. I'm shattered, and so confused about all the thoughts that have been endlessly spinning around my mind.

There's a knock at my bedroom door.

'Come in?'

I pull the covers over my chest because my vest top is a little revealing, and an extremely sleepy-looking Johnny appears around the corner.

'I'll take him.' His voice sounds gruff. He's wearing a white T-shirt, which he probably slept in, and denim jeans, which he's obviously just pulled on. No shoes or socks.

'Are you sure?' I ask hopefully. Despite yesterday's reservations, all I want to do now is close my eyes and sleep for a week.

He nods. 'Yep.' He comes around to the other side of the bed and reaches down for Barney.

'Go and play with Johnny,' I say. *Daddy . . .*

Johnny lifts him up and carries him out of the room.

'Wake me if you need me!' I call. Damn. Breakfast. I leap out of bed and go to the door. 'Will you give him breakfast?'

'Rice Krispies,' he calls back. He's halfway down the stairs already.

'And can you warm up so—'

'Milk. Yep.'

I pause, half in and half out of my bedroom door.

'Go back to bed,' he shouts.

'Okay.' I smile and shut the door before doing as I'm told.

It's nine o'clock before I wake again. I could sleep for another hour at least, but I should get up. For a minute, though, I just lie in bed and stare at the ceiling.

Did I make the right decision?

I can't believe I'm asking myself this question, but I keep seeing Johnny playing with Barney and helping me in the kitchen last night . . . This could have been my life, my simple, domesticated, uncomplicated life.

Uncomplicated? Am I insane? I know what he's like, and, anyway, it's too late.

I climb out of bed and pull on my dressing gown. I'm about to go downstairs, but I pause and go into the bathroom instead. I might shower and get dressed first.

'Good afternoon,' Johnny says when I emerge.

'Ha ha,' I reply acerbically. 'How's it all been?' I survey the mess in the kitchen.

'Fine,' he says, scratching his stubble.

'Couldn't be bothered to shave this morning?'

'I haven't had a second to myself!' he exclaims. 'Anyway, you don't care if I shave or not.'

'True,' I concede with a smile. 'Thanks for the lie-in.' My tone is sincere.

'Anytime.'

'You mean that?' I open my eyes wide with pretend delight.

'Ha ha,' he mimics, patting his pocket and nodding towards the door.

'You're officially off duty,' I say and start to tidy the kitchen. I seem to be smiling more these days.

I bet Christian isn't smiling.

And at that thought, neither am I anymore. It seems all I have to do is think of Christian and I'm brought back down to earth with a bump. I wonder if that will ever change.

After a while, Johnny comes back inside.

'You're wearing make-up,' he notes.

'Oh, yeah,' I brush him off. 'I don't usually bother, but I felt a bit more human after the extra sleep.' I force a laugh and hope he doesn't see through me.

I tried not to make an effort after my shower, but I couldn't stop my fingers from reaching into my cosmetics case.

I turn back to Johnny. 'Why don't we go out for the day?'

Johnny lights a fire that night, just like when we came here in the middle of winter. It's a strange feeling coming downstairs and seeing him sitting there in front of the fireplace, watching the flames. It brings back old memories. I instantly feel nervous. I should sit at the table and carry on with the jigsaw puzzle, but I'm drawn instead to the place where Johnny is.

I thought I was over him.

It's clear I was wrong.

He doesn't turn to look at me as I slide down beside him, our backs leaning up against the sofa. I wonder if he's remembering the same thing as me. This was where we made love for the first time.

'That was nice today.' I force myself to make conversation.

'Mmm.'

'Barney likes you.'

He stares ahead at the flickering flames.

'Are you alright?' I feel compelled to ask.

He says nothing for a minute, then: 'I'm going to miss him.'

I take a deep breath and exhale slowly. 'It's good that you're spending this time with him.'

'I want to spend more time with him. I don't want him to forget me.'

I fold my arms and focus on the heat. It's a little overbearing, but I don't want to move away.

'We've still got a few more days,' I say, turning to face him. 'Will you come back to France soon?'

'Of course. If that's where you're going to be.'

'You think I should move out of my parents'?'

He looks at me, his eyes even more intense in this light. 'Don't you?'

He still hasn't shaved. My gaze wanders to his jaw, to the stubble gracing it, and then back up to his luminous green eyes. 'I guess so.' I know I should look away, but I'm finding it impossible. Abruptly, he turns his head towards the flames. It snaps me out of whatever strange mood I was entering into. I quickly stand up.

'I'm going to bed.'

'Already?' He looks up at me with surprise, then glances at his watch. 'It's only eight o'clock.'

'I know. I'm knackered,' I stutter.

'You had a lie-in,' he points out.

'I want to read my book. It's a really good one,' I lie.

I couldn't tell you if it was good or bad; I've barely been able to take in one sentence since I've been here.

'Fair enough.' He turns back to the fire.

'Night,' I say.

'Night.'

One foot in front of the other, Meg, one foot in front of the other.

I reach the bathroom and go inside, closing the door and leaning up against it. I should leave. I should get out of here. This is wrong, so wrong. I can't go down this path again. I don't know if my head would survive it, and my heart clearly still hasn't recovered from last time. What is it about him?

211

I need to meet Dana. That's what I need to do. I need a short, sharp, reality check. Meet his girlfriend and let it sink in that he's off-limits. He's obviously into her. This relationship is different for him, I think. I instantly feel jealous and hate myself for it.

Chapter 26

I wake up at six o'clock the following morning, despite the fact that I've tossed and turned all night. I feel jittery. I want to see him.

I need to meet his girlfriend.

I sigh and climb out of bed. Johnny won't be up for hours. I can't bear it. Yes, I can! I pull on my dressing gown and head to the bathroom, then suddenly halt in my tracks. My song . . .

I step quietly down the stairs and walk into the living room to see Johnny sitting on the sofa, quietly strumming his guitar. He has an unlit cigarette hanging from his lips. I clear my throat and his head whips around.

'You're up early,' he says, leaning his guitar against the sofa.

'I could say the same thing about you,' I say. Should I comment on the fact that he was playing my song? He doesn't look guilty.

He sighs and leans his head back against the sofa, taking the cigarette from his mouth and tapping the filter end on his thigh. 'I've gotta go back to LA, babe.'

'Why?' I sink down onto the sofa next to him.

'Dana's freaking out.'

'About Barney?'

He shakes his head. 'Nah, I don't think so. Danger of relapse. She needs me.'

'Oh.' A lump forms in my throat and I try to swallow it. He is serious about her. Scarily serious. 'When will you leave?'

'As soon as Lena can organise a car and ticket. Today.'

'We've got a car,' I say, confused. It's sitting out there on the driveway, a nice little BMW lent to us by a dealer.

'I'm not going to take that from you,' he says, frowning.

'I don't want to stay here without you,' I reply automatically.

His brow furrows. 'Really?' He's surprised and I wish I hadn't revealed that.

'We'll go back to France,' I say.

He regards me for a moment before speaking. 'Okay. I'll ask Lena to sort it.'

'Thanks.' I go to get up, but he grabs my wrist and pulls me back down again.

'Meg . . .' he says.

'Yes?'

He pauses for a moment, as if an idea has just struck him and he's unsure about whether or not to go on.

'Tell me,' I press him, curious now.

His words come out in a rush. 'Come back to LA with me.'

'What?'

'You and Barney. Come back to LA with me.' He sits up with excitement, running with the idea now. 'You could have your own rooms, you'd have your own life, but I'd get to see him every day. He would *know* me.'

'Don't be ridiculous.'

'I'm not.' He shakes his head fervently.

214

'What about my parents? They haven't exactly enjoyed reading about you in the papers, recently.'

'Yeah, but surely they still want what's best for Barney.'

'You think this is what's best for Barney?'

'Yes. I do, actually. He's my son. I'm his dad. He should be with me.'

I take a gulp of air. 'What about Dana?'

'What about her?'

'Don't you think you should talk to her about this?'

'How do you know I haven't?'

'Have you?'

Pause. 'No.'

I look at him sadly. 'I can't, Johnny.'

He takes my hands and stares into my eyes, pleading with me. 'Yes, you can.'

I detach my hands. 'No, I can't, Johnny. I can't go back there again.'

'It wouldn't be the same as before,' he tries to reason with me.

'How do you know? It might be even worse, with you two getting off your heads on drugs . . . I can't put Barney into a situation like that.'

'I won't relapse again. I promise you.'

'I thought addicts weren't supposed to make promises like that.'

He shakes his head. 'How did you get to be so smart?'

'I'm not smart. Just one look at my crazy, fucked-up life should tell you that.'

'Language . . .'

We smile at each other sadly.

'You're not fucked-up, Meg. It's time to move on. You've got a son, an amazing son. *I've* got an amazing son. I don't want to be a peripheral part of his life – I want to mean something to him. I want him to call me "Dad". I want the world to know he's mine. Not yet,' he says hurriedly. 'We need space first without the press harassing us.'

I shake my head and look away. 'No. Just you saying that reminds me of how it is.' I still remember being hounded by the paparazzi one time when I drove Johnny's Porsche and they thought I was him. 'I don't want that for Barney,' I add.

'You don't have a choice. The press are going to find out about him sometime, whether you like it or not,' he states. 'At least in LA you'd both have protection; you know my security guys are some of the best in the business. Wouldn't it be better for Barney to grow up with this life from the start, so he doesn't know any different? Wouldn't that be better than him getting thrown in at the deep end when he's older?'

'Like me?' I say with a wry smile.

He mirrors my expression. 'Think about it. Please, Meg.' I notice he's not calling me Nutmeg. He must be serious. 'Just think about it.'

Chapter 27

'It is so good to see you again, Miss Stiles.'

I smile ahead at the driver, who's grinning back at me in his rear-view mirror. 'It's good to see you too, Davey.'

'I don't know, I just had a feeling about you, that something was different. I see now that I was right!' he exclaims, jabbing his thumb over his shoulder at Barney, who is strapped into a brand-new and very smart car seat.

I shrug, embarrassed. 'What can I say?'

He chuckles with amusement and shakes his head. I peer out of my window at the skinny-as-a-beanpole palm trees towering overhead. The sun beats down from a hazy blue sky. I'm thankful for the air-conditioning in the limo. Even in October, LA is warm and muggy.

Did I just say LA? That's where we are: the City of Angels. My head is still spinning about the fact that I agreed to Johnny's crazy suggestion.

My parents weren't too pleased about it. It took only a few hours of being back in Grasse with them for me to make up my mind, and once that was done, there was no turning back.

They've accepted it now. But they did make me promise I would tell Susan and Tony the real reason behind Johnny's visit back in August. I still haven't got around to it.

Davey drives through the gates into Bel Air, past Elvis's old house and countless other mansions belonging to the rich and famous. We climb upwards into the hills – the journey taking longer than I remember from when I used to live here – and then we reach some imposing wooden gates, equipped with intimidating security cameras. Davey speaks into the intercom and the gates slowly open, then it's along a winding driveway until, finally, there's a break in the trees and there, in front of us, is Johnny's house.

I stare out at the modern, white concrete, two-storey architectural masterpiece and feel slightly breathless.

I flashback to the first time I was here . . . The enormous front door swung open to reveal a short, plump, pleasantly smiling Hispanic-looking woman. Rosa. It's not going to be the same here without her.

Davey takes me to the front door with our suitcases and presses the buzzer. As butterflies swarm around my stomach I realise I feel almost as nervous as I did three years ago. Who's going to open the door? The new cook? Lena? Dana? I hope not Dana – I'm not ready for that yet. I jig Barney up and down in my arms and try to channel my nerves into excitement. It doesn't work.

There's a click behind the door and it starts to open. I'm holding my breath, and then suddenly I'm face to face with Johnny and my face breaks into a smile.

'Hey!' he exclaims, patting me with affection on my back and then opening his arms to Barney. I pass him over, stupidly delighted that he's here to welcome us. I feel like I need familiar right now. 'You can put those up in her room,' Johnny says to Davey, leading the way inside. He's wearing a long-sleeved white shirt with dark-grey Bermuda shorts and bare feet.

I follow him into the living room and halt in my tracks, even though I've seen this view hundreds of times. Floor-to-ceiling windows look out onto the city of LA in the distance, and before that is a beautiful infinity pool, far more spectacular than the one in Barcelona with Bess.

Aah, Bess. She went nuts when I told her. We spoke on the phone last week . . .

'How are you?'

'Pretty damn good,' I replied with a smile.

'What's happened?' she asked drily.

'Johnny's asked us to go to LA with him.'

'WHAT?'

'Not like that, you ninny,' I said flippantly. 'As friends. As the mother of his child. He wants to spend more time with Barney and I just thought, why the hell not?'

'I'll tell you why not.' She cut straight to the chase. 'Because you fell madly in love with him and went to hell and back!'

'That's not going to happen again,' I said patiently.

'How on earth would you know?' she exclaimed.

'Because I'm different now. I won't let myself get into a situation like that ever again.'

'It's not up to you!' she squawked. 'It's up to your bloody heart! That's the problem.'

Anyway . . . She'll get over it.

* * *

'Where's Dana?' I ask.

'She's coming over this afty. Giving you time to settle in before she descends.' He winks at me.

I force a smile. 'How is she?'

'Fine,' he says with a shrug.

'Did she relapse?'

'Nah.' He shakes his head. 'Relax, babe,' he says annoyingly.

'Don't call me babe.'

'Don't call me babe, don't call me Nutmeg . . .' he teases in a sing-song voice. 'Jesus, what can I call you?'

'Meg would be a good start. Mummy will also do.' I try to keep a straight face as I look at Barney in his arms.

'Hello!'

At the sound of a voice, I turn around to see a tall, tanned woman with dark blonde hair coming into the living room from the direction of the office.

'Aah, Lena,' Johnny says. 'Come and meet Meg.'

'We meet at last,' she says with a smile, walking towards me with her hand extended. She has an accent. I think I remember Christian once saying she was from Holland.

'Hi!' I falter before smiling back and shaking her hand. She's unnervingly stunning. Her eyes are green, almost as green as Johnny's, and her hair is straight and falls to just below her chin. She's taller than me – I would guess five foot nine without her heels on – and she looks like she's in her late twenties, early thirties. She actually resembles Johnny in an uncanny way – she could almost be his sister.

'I can't believe you're finally here!' She smiles warmly and folds her arms in front of herself, casually rocking back on her heels.

'Neither can I,' I reply, shifting from foot to foot. She seems nice, even if she is far too beautiful to be human.

'And *you* must be Barney!' She reaches over and pinches one of his chubby cheeks between her thumb and forefinger. He smiles back at her before holding his arms out to me. I take him from Johnny and he nestles into my neck, shyly, before peeking back out at her again.

'We have *lots* to talk about,' she says to me. 'But right now I imagine you just want to sit down with a – what do they say in England? A cuppa!'

I laugh. 'Actually, that'd be great. Still no cook?'

'No. In fact,' she turns to Johnny, 'I must talk to you about that.'

'Later, Lennie,' he replies.

She crossly wags her finger in his face. 'I mean it, Johnny, if you keep calling me that I'll quit.'

'You won't quit,' he replies with amusement.

'Why are you so sure?' she snaps.

'You like me too much.' He grins and leans against the back of the sofa.

'Argh!' she cries with frustration before storming off to the kitchen, which is behind a curved, frosted-glass wall.

I give Johnny an inquisitive look. 'I thought you told me you didn't give her a nickname because her husband wouldn't approve.'

'I didn't say husband,' he replies with a smirk.

'What do you mean by that?'

'I'M GAY!' Lena shouts from the kitchen.

I look at Johnny with widened eyes. 'Seriously?' I mouth.

'I CAN HEAR YOU!' Lena shouts again.

221

'She didn't say anything!' Johnny exclaims with mock outrage.

Lena appears at the door of the kitchen with a mug in one hand and a carton of milk in the other.

'I know what you're saying,' she says through narrowed eyes, brandishing the milk at us.

'Did Johnny know you were gay when he hired you?' I ask.

Johnny gives me a wry look. Lena smirks. 'No.'

'No, I didn't think so,' I reply, giggling. Lena's face breaks into a smile. 'I like her,' she says to Johnny.

'Oi,' he warns. 'Don't get any ideas.'

I grin at Johnny. I thought she was nice before, but on this evidence, I think we could actually become friends.

A few minutes later, Lena returns to the sofas with a tray laden with cups and snacks.

'These are new.' I reach back to stroke my hand across the dark-brown leather. Johnny had sofas before, but these are enormous and form a long V-shape facing the windows, so everywhere you sit you're faced with a view of the city and pool.

'Barney, come back here,' I say as he starts to climb along one of them.

'He's fine, man, he's fine,' Johnny brushes me off.

'Let me take off his shoes.'

'He's fine, Meg,' Johnny reiterates, helping Barney climb over his lap.

'Johnny thought this place could do with cosying up,' Lena says with a knowing look at Barney.

He got these in for our little boy's benefit? That's, well, kind of sweet. Didn't think I'd ever use that word to describe the man.

'Here, Barney,' Lena says, getting up and going to a cream-coloured, oversized, golf-ball-type thing. She lifts off the lid and I see that it's full to the brim of brand-new toys. My mouth drops open as Lena pulls out Buzz Lightyear.

'To infinity and beyond!' Buzz shouts. Barney climbs down from the sofa and makes his way towards her with as much enthusiasm as a five-year-old on Christmas morning.

I turn to Johnny. 'Been shopping?'

He chuckles. 'Lena.'

She glances my way with a grin.

'Thank you,' I say sincerely.

'It was fun!' she replies, then her face falls. 'Hey, I'm sorry we didn't get the pool done in time.'

'The pool?' I look at her with confusion.

'I mean, the pool gate.'

'Oh!'

'We're getting the best guys in the business to do it, but they're working on a Tom and Katie installation at the moment. They'll start with us tomorrow, so we'll just have to keep the doors locked until then.'

'Of course! Don't worry,' I tell her, feeling bad that the beautiful infinity pool is going to be marred by a ghastly vision of iron bars.

Johnny pulls his phone out of his pocket. It's vibrating.

'Hey,' he says into the receiver, getting to his feet and going to the outside door. He slides it shut behind him. I see him reach back into his pocket for his fags. He lights up while talking to the person on the other end of the line. I have a feeling it's Dana.

'Well,' Lena says, interrupting my thoughts. 'You don't need a tour of the house, but do you want to see Barney's room?'

'Ooh, yes!' I gush, jumping up. I try to ease Barney away from Buzz Lightyear, but he's having none of it, so we bring the Space Ranger with us. I follow Lena up the stairs, giving Johnny a reluctant glance over my shoulder as I go.

Chapter 28

'Now, you're still in the white room,' Lena says, turning right at the top of the stairs.

'Brilliant!' I reply.

She smiles at my delight and takes me on a detour to my room first. Aah, my lovely room . . . The windows look out at the autumnal trees at the back of the house, but aside from the suitcases that Davey has put just inside the door, burnt orange is the only colour you can see because the rest of the room is white. I go to look in the en suite, just to remind myself of its beauty. Numerous halogens overhead light up the room to display an enormous spa bath at the back alongside a huge shower, and double basins to my right, all of which are formed out of dazzling white stone. Fluffy white towels adorn the towel rails. I sigh happily.

Lena laughs. 'Barney's room?'

'Go on, then,' I say grudgingly, tearing myself away.

Barney's room is next door to mine. The walls have been wallpapered in subtle blue and yellow pinstripe. There's a cot over by the far wall, and a green grass-like rug underfoot, plus a small table and chairs and enough toys to fill Hamleys spilling out of more of those strange golf-ball-type toy boxes on the floor. A white storage system of drawers, cupboards, wardrobes and shelves stocked with children's books runs along the left-hand wall. There's also a door which leads to an enormous en suite.

'I'm sorry it's a bit bare,' Lena says and my eyes open wide in disbelief. She continues, oblivious, 'I wanted to get some more things in, but Johnny said you'd want to do that. Which reminds me . . .' She reaches into her pocket and pulls out a folded white envelope. She hands it over. 'Johnny wants you to have this.'

I open it up, curiously. There's a credit card inside with my name on it.

'No limit,' she says with a grin.

I meet her eyes, taken aback. I open my mouth to speak.

'Don't argue,' she interrupts. 'Johnny said that you would. But he owes you child maintenance, so, please, don't think twice about using it for whatever you and Barney need.' I close my mouth again, feeling distinctly like a goldfish. 'You've also got a Porsche Panamera arriving tomorrow. Again, sorry I couldn't get it here in time.'

'Please tell me you're joking.'

'Can't fit a car seat in the Bugatti,' she replies flippantly. 'Can't fit them in the McLaren, Gullwing, Ferrari or Carrera, either – although,' she thinks aloud, 'it might fit in the front of some of them if it was just you and Barney going out. Maybe I'll get another car seat just in case. You don't want to be swapping them over all the time; that would drive you nuts.'

226

I stare at her, gobsmacked. 'I'm sorry, but are you actually a real person? You even know the names of his cars.'

She laughs. 'Katya is into mean machines.'

'Katya?'

'My girlfriend.' She slaps her hand on her forehead. 'I mean, wife. We got married as soon as it became legal – you know, before it became illegal again.' She smiles wryly. 'But I still can't get my head around the term.'

'Congratulations,' I reply with a smile.

'Thanks.' She shrugs. 'Shall we head back downstairs?'

'Sure.'

I follow her out of Barney's room and back along the landing towards the stairs. Johnny's room is at the far end and I remember that it's massive, spanning from the front to the back of the house so he has trees at one end and a view of the city at the other. His music studio is next to his bedroom, and between that and Barney's room are three more spare rooms.

'So where do you stay?' I ask curiously as we start to walk down the stairs.

'Not here,' she replies. 'Katya would kill me.'

'I bet she hates it when Johnny goes on tour?' Where is he, by the way? I can't see him outside.

'She comes along.' Lena flashes me a grin over her shoulder.

'Really?' I try to focus on our conversation. 'What does she do?'

'She's a stylist.'

'She works for Johnny?'

'On tour, yes. She helps out. Very handy.'

'I'd like to meet her sometime.' We reach the living room and I look around distractedly. Where has he gone?

'Oh, you will,' Lena replies ominously. 'She can't wait to meet Barney. And she's dying to meet you. The one that got away . . .'

I blush and Lena laughs. 'Seriously, I'm so glad you're here,' she says, and I return those feelings. To think I was worried about her. 'It'll be nice to have female company around the joint again. Since Rosa quit . . .' She sighs.

'That's very sad.'

'You're telling me. Poor old girl.'

I'd almost forgotten that Johnny overdosed. That night when I found out he was in hospital . . . how I scoured the internet for information about him and Dana . . . It seems like a long time ago.

'What's Da—' I'm about to ask Lena about Dana when Johnny comes out of the office.

'You wanted to talk to me about the cook?' Johnny says and I wonder how much of our conversation he heard.

'Yes,' Lena replies, unfazed. She walks straight past him into the office. I follow with Barney, for want of anything better to do. Lena goes to what used to be my desk and pulls out a chair. Johnny slumps down in the black Eames chair to her left and edges in closer. It's what he used to do with me, and suddenly, however much I do like Lena, I feel uncomfortable about being here.

'These are the ten that I've narrowed it down to,' I hear her say as I quietly step away from the door. I lead Barney back to the toy box in the living room.

'Meg?' Johnny calls from the office door a couple of minutes later.

'Yep?' I call back.

228

'Can you come here?'

Barney seems happy enough playing with the brand-new wooden Brio train set that I've just unpacked from its box, so I get up and go to the office, feeling curious.

Johnny is sitting back down in the Eames chair when I arrive at the door. Lena stands up and indicates her – formerly known as my – chair.

'Would you mind having a look at these?' Lena asks, putting a pile of what I now see are CVs in front of me. I look up at her in surprise, and then glance at Johnny with confusion.

'I want your opinion,' he says, leaning back in his chair.

I check Lena's expression again, but she doesn't seem put out. 'I'll keep an eye on Barney,' she says lightly, leaving the room. Still a little taken aback, I lean forward and pick up the first CV.

Out of the corner of my eye I can see Johnny's foot jigging, but he says nothing, waiting patiently. After a while I relax and concentrate on the job at hand.

'They've all got excellent experience, but I would invite these three in for interview,' I decide at last, patting the small pile of nominated CVs.

'Done.' He gets up and takes them from the desk, then goes to the door. 'Lena?'

'Er, don't you want to know why?' I stutter after him.

'Nope,' he replies over his shoulder. Lena re-emerges. 'These three,' he says, handing them over.

'Great stuff,' she replies, giving me a warm smile.

Does she seriously not mind me stepping on her toes? Maybe she's worked with Johnny long enough to not give a toss. I know myself that any help with getting him to agree to something is appreciated.

'Meg can sit in on the interviews,' he says, going to walk out through the door.

'Er, hello?' I interrupt. He turns around, frowning. 'Since when did I go back on your payroll?' I ask indignantly.

Johnny regards me for a moment, not saying anything, then: 'Didn't you get the credit card?'

'Ha!' I reply, outraged. 'If those are your terms and conditions, I don't want it!'

Lena regards us with wariness, but then Johnny's face breaks into a smile. 'I'm joking, Nutmeg. I didn't think you'd mind doing me a favour. Do you?' he asks when I don't immediately reply.

'No, I suppose not,' I tell him.

'Good.'

I look at Lena and purse my lips. She starts to laugh and I find myself doing the same.

Johnny and Barney are nowhere to be seen when I walk out of the office, but I can hear the distant sound of music playing. I follow the sound up the stairs and into Johnny's studio. Barney is sitting on Johnny's lap in front of the mixing console, determinedly pressing all the buttons he can reach. I stand at the door and watch them for a moment, smiling. Johnny senses my presence and turns around.

'Do you think he's going to be like you?' I ask.

'I hope not.'

I smirk. 'I mean, into music.'

'That I could handle,' Johnny replies looking down at his blond-haired boy. 'You want to play guitar like your old man?'

Barney babbles and flips a switch. The base suddenly sounds really loud.

Johnny chuckles and flips the switch back again.

'Are you alright with him for a little while?' I ask.

'Of course.'

'I might go and unpack.'

'Sandy can do it, if you want? She'll be here soon.' Sandy's the maid.

'No, no, it's okay,' I brush him off. 'I'd rather do it myself so I know where everything is.'

'Control freak.'

'That's me,' I say brightly, flashing him a grin and walking out of the studio.

I heave the first suitcase onto the bed and unzip it. I take out my cosmetics bag and go straight to my beloved bathroom with the intention of unpacking it, but when I'm greeted with the sight of the beautiful big spa tub, the urge to relax in it overcomes me. I decide to unpack later. I put in the plug and turn on the taps, then open the cupboards under the sink so I can start to put away my things. I gasp with amazement as tiny light bulbs inside the cupboard reveal the most divine selection of beauty goodies I think I've ever seen. Glass bottles of expensive bubble bath in an array of colours sparkle at me like glittering jewels, and top-name brands of moisturisers, facial scrubs, eye creams – you name it – are lined up in neat little rows. Lena, Lena, you have truly outdone yourself. First things first, I reach for a bottle of ruby-red bubble bath and pour some under the tap.

This is bliss, I think to myself a little while later, immersed up to my neck in warm water peaked with fluffy white bubbles. I could get used to this.

Christian . . .

My mood instantly turns sombre. What would he say if he could see me now? Nothing. I think he'd say nothing. He'd regard me with disgust and walk away. I get out of the bath soon after that.

Chapter 29

I poke my head out of the bedroom door and can still hear music coming from the studio. I haven't been in the bath for long, so I've probably still got a little time to unpack. I open the wardrobes and find that I'm face to face with an old friend of mine.

A sheepskin sheep stares out at me from one of the shelves in the wardrobe. This was my Christmas present from Johnny when we went to the Dales the first time. I still remember laughing about it, because that Christmas other personal assistants were being given cars by their celebrity bosses. But this bloody sheep meant more to me than any car ever could. I left it here when I quit. I hoped Johnny would see it, but assumed Sandy would throw it out. It's strange finding it here again. It looks the same, it's in the same place, but everything around it has changed and moved on. Especially me. It's a weird feeling.

I pick it up and almost expect it to baa at me. On an impulse I leave the packing unfinished and walk back down the landing to the studio. Movement at the corner of my eye as I pass Barney's bedroom brings me to a standstill. I peek inside and see Johnny cradling Barney in his arms, singing softly. He has his back to me. Barney *would* be tired. He's obviously trying to get him to sleep – something I rarely manage during the daytime without four wheels and motion.

The front-door buzzer sounds loudly and Barney jolts in Johnny's arms. He lifts his sleepy head and sees me, and then all of Johnny's hard work is undone. Barney starts to rub his eyes and cry, and Johnny smiles wryly and goes to relocate him to my arms. I hold up the sheep.

'I cannot believe you still have this.' I put it down on a table and take Barney.

'I can't believe it either.' He picks it up and turns it over. 'Where was it?'

'In my wardrobe. I thought Sandy would throw it out.'

'Mmm.' We meet each other's eyes.

'Well, ain't this a happy little family!'

Startled, I spin around to see Dana standing in the doorway. She's tiny, shorter than me by a couple of inches, and skinnier. She's dressed all in black – black rock-chick T-shirt and black leggings with black peep-toe wedge heels. Her long, dark hair is tied up into a high, backcombed ponytail and she's wearing a lot of make-up, even in the daytime.

'Hey, little dude!' She makes a beeline for Barney. 'What's with the tears?'

'He's tired,' I reply on his behalf. Unpleasant goose pimples have formed all over my body. Her perfume is overpowering.

Barney stops crying for a moment to look at this strange, over-the-top American woman. Dana peers closely at his face. 'Jesus, you do look like your daddy.' She turns to Johnny. 'Hey, baby,' she says warmly, giving him a kiss, followed immediately by a longer one, straight on his lips. Then she faces me.

'Dana, this is Meg,' Johnny says.

We exchange hellos and she extends her hand so I give it a perfunctory shake. I notice her nails are short, and her blood-red nail polish is chipped. I wonder if she bites them.

'What's with the sheep?' she says to Johnny. 'That is one fucking ugly toy.'

I flinch at her language, but don't say anything.

Johnny chuckles. 'I bought it for Meg as a Christmas present when she worked for me.'

'Fucking cheapskate.' She laughs and I glance irritably at Johnny. Is he going to tell her off? Nope.

She reaches down and ruffles Barney's hair. 'So you're the little dude that's been keeping my man away.'

Barney starts to whinge.

'I should get him to sleep,' I say abruptly to Johnny. 'I usually use the buggy.'

'Throw him in his bed and be done with it,' Dana says.

I can't keep the annoyance from my face.

'I'm joking!' she cries with amusement. 'I thought you British were supposed to have a sense of humour.'

I force a laugh.

'Come on, Johnny, I'm starving. Are we going out to eat or what?'

Johnny glances at me, then back at her. 'Let's see what's in the kitchen.'

'Have you got a new cook?'

'No, not yet.' He leads her to the door.

'Bum. I could really do with a fucking Rosa quesadilla special right now. Fucking bitch.'

I reel backwards in horror.

'Joke, chick!' Dana calls back at me, before cracking up laughing.

As soon as they've gone, I let out a long breath and realise I've been holding it. The smell of Dana's perfume is lingering. I lean down and sniff Barney's hair – he smells of her, and I bloody hate it.

I don't want to go back downstairs to find Barney's buggy so I persevere and manage to get him to sleep in my arms. He's exhausted after our inter-continental flight, so it's not hard. I lay him in his cot and pull the covers over him, then stroke his hair back away from his face and stare down at him for a while. I turn and see the sheep on the table. I pick it up and scrutinise it. What is she talking about, saying it's ugly? No, it's not. As sheep go, it's not bad. In fact, it's pretty damn attractive. Dana's clearly deluded.

Lovely Lena has already installed a baby monitor so I don't need to go and dig one out from my suitcase. I take the parent handset and wait until I'm outside the room before switching it on. I don't want the interference to make a loud screeching noise and wake Barney up.

I'd much rather hide out in my bedroom and continue with my unpacking, but it feels rude not to go and chat to Dana. Mind you, she was planning on going out, so she's obviously not bothered about conversing with me. I hesitate. No. I should make an effort to get to know her, even if she would prefer me to steer clear.

I find them outside on a couple of sunloungers. They're both smoking and Dana has her hand in a bowl of peanuts. Couldn't be bothered to cook, I'm guessing.

'Hi,' I say, sliding the glass door shut behind me.

'Alright?' Johnny replies. Dana lifts her cigarette in a half wave and chucks some peanuts in her mouth.

'He's asleep,' I tell them.

Johnny nods. Dana tilts her face up towards the sky. I stand there feeling awkward and then make myself go and sit on a sunlounger nearby.

'So, Dukey's hangin' out at Marmont tonight,' Dana says casually. 'We should go.' I assume she's talking about Chateau Marmont: celeb heaven.

Johnny glances at me before looking away again and taking a long drag on his cigarette. 'I don't know,' he replies before exhaling.

Dana sits up and glares at him. 'What? Why not? He'll be pissed at you if you don't show.'

'Why should he care if I go or not?'

'You know what he's like. He'll be bustin' his ass to make sure the PR machine's running like a dream. You're his money shot.'

'And you think that makes me want to go?'

'Come on, Johnny, they need the publicity. Do it for me.'

'Who's Dukey?' I interrupt.

Dana huffs and lies back down again. Johnny turns his head towards me.

'Dana's manager.'

'Oh, right. What's he publicising?'

'A new band he's signed.'

I remember the last time a girlfriend's manager tried to swing on the coat-tails of Johnny's success. It didn't end well. Johnny doesn't like being manipulated. I'm surprised Dana's manager doesn't know this already. Is it wrong to feel smug?

Johnny is still looking at me, but I can't see his eyes behind his dark shades. It's disconcerting. He looks away.

'Alright,' he says in Dana's direction.

Hey?

'I'll go.'

'Cool,' Dana replies indifferently, throwing another handful of nuts into her mouth. I no longer feel so self-righteous.

'Come if you want,' Johnny says offhandedly to me as he stubs out his cigarette.

Dana screws up her nose. 'It won't be much fun.'

'No, you're alright, thanks,' I reply. 'I'll be jet-lagged anyway, and I wouldn't leave Barney on his first night here.'

'Haven't you got a fucking nanny?' Dana asks.

'No.' I give Johnny a pointed look.

He leans over and pats Dana's thigh. 'Can't swear anymore, babe.'

'Why the fuck not?'

'Barney.'

'The little dude's not even here!' she exclaims, sitting upright. I hate how she's already found her own nickname for him.

'Yeah, but you've gotta get out of the habit. Unless you want to incur Meg's wrath,' Johnny drawls, glancing my way. Dana meets my eyes for a long moment and then looks away herself. I have a horrid feeling she couldn't care less about upsetting me.

'What's that?' She points at my hand with her lit cigarette.

'Barney's baby monitor.'

She gets another cigarette out of the packet and lights it from the stub of her current one. 'What, like some kind of walkie-talkie?'

'Yes. I'll hear him if he wakes up.'

She hands Johnny the new cigarette and lights another for herself. Chain-smoking by its very definition. Nice.

'That's a bit Big Brother, isn't it?' She blows a puff of smoke in my direction.

I'm unable to keep my laugh from sounding derisive. 'He's only a year and a bit old.'

'Wrestle control early,' she replies, unaffected by my tone. 'That's what I'd do, too. Not that I plan on getting knocked up.' She kicks Johnny gently with her peep-toe wedge. 'So if you fancy yourself as some kind of Baby Daddy you'd better look for a different girl.'

Johnny smirks and nudges her foot away.

I don't want to be here anymore.

'Where are you going?' Johnny asks when I get up.

'Going to finish my unpacking before Barney wakes up.'

'Have fun,' Dana says, not even bothering to look at me.

I'll have a hell of a lot more fun than if I stay here, that's for sure.

Chapter 30

When I worked for Johnny, I made friends with another CPA – Celebrity Personal Assistant – called Kitty. We stayed in touch for a while after I quit, but, as time went on, our contact dwindled. I've been in LA for a few days before I decide to call her, but I still have no idea what to say. The thing about this business is that people have to be discreet; it's part of the job description. I think I can trust Kitty. I never confided in her at the time about what went on with Johnny – I was constrained by the privacy agreement I'd signed. When I left so suddenly, Kitty knew better than to ask if anything had happened between us, but I'm sure she had her suspicions.

This town is too small to stay hidden for long. Kitty is going to find out on the celebrity circuit that I'm back, even if we do manage to keep Barney a secret from the press for a while. People talk. I'd rather she heard it from me. I just hope she's the same person she was when I left.

I call her on a Saturday morning. Her number is the same; so she's still working for Rod Freemantle, a middle-aged actor who has had almost as many wives as Brad and Angelina have children. He's currently on his fifth.

She answers the phone: 'Rod Freemantle's office.'

'Kitty.'

'Yes, can I help you?'

'It's Meg.'

'Meg!' she cries, dropping all formality. 'Long time no hear! How's it going?'

'Good! Really good.'

'How's your little boy?'

'Barney is great,' I say, just in case she's forgotten his name. 'He's almost one and a half, can you believe?'

'Jeez, no, I can't believe it. I'm so ashamed that I haven't met him yet.' I'm about to tell her she can make up for lost time, but she moves on. 'How's Christian?'

'Er, not so good,' I reply.

'What's wrong with him?'

'We split up.'

'Oh, man!' she exclaims. 'That sucks. What happened?'

'It's a long story . . . Too long to explain on the phone.'

'Well, I ain't coming to London anytime soon . . .'

She doesn't even know I've been living in France. 'Just as well I'm in LA, then,' I reply.

'Are you kidding me?'

'Nope.'

'What are you doing back here?'

'That is part of the long story. Listen, when can we hook up?'

'I'm free this arvo?'

I hesitate for all of two seconds. Johnny's going out tonight, so he can hardly have a problem with me going out today. He's got Dana for company – and that's something I won't fight him for.

'Sounds good.'

Kitty and I meet on Melrose Avenue at one of our old haunts, an Italian coffee shop which does some of the best pasta dishes I've ever tasted. She's already there when I walk in, struggling to carry Barney and my oversized bag.

'Oh my God!' she cries, getting to her feet and rushing over. 'I cannot believe you gave birth to that!'

I laugh. 'He wasn't this big when I squeezed him out.'

She checks me over. 'You look amazing!'

'I tried not to let myself go,' I joke. I'm wearing skinny jeans, brown leather boots and a fitted navy-blue military peacoat, which Mum bought for me as an early birthday present.

'Here, let me help you.' She relieves me of my bag and leads the way through the cramped space to our table. I sit Barney on my lap because there are no high chairs. He immediately reaches for the salt and pepper shaker.

Kitty still looks the same, albeit a little older. She's wearing a stripy chocolate, beige, army-green and hot-pink dress, teamed with a purple cardie and a chunky green belt. She must be thirty-three now; she was thirty when I met her three years ago, and I was only twenty-four then, so she's always been older and wiser than me. She stares at Barney and shakes her head, her dark-brown ringlets bouncing around her shoulders.

'He's so big now! He has your hair.'

'And Johnny's eyes,' I say. I wasn't planning on dropping the bombshell in quite such an offhand fashion, but it just sort of came out. It takes a few moments for the news to sink in, and, when it does, her jaw practically hits the table.

'Pardon?' I've never heard her say pardon before.

'He's Johnny's,' I tell her. 'Strictly confidential, of course.'

'He's . . . He's . . . *Johnny Jefferson has a son?*'

'Yep.' I lift my fingers up and point at the top of Barney's head.

'Holy shit, Meg!'

'Oops, no swearing.'

She clamps her hand across her mouth and her wide-open eyes stare at me. 'He's *Johnny's?*'

'Yep.'

'What about Christian?'

My nonchalance dries up. I take a deep breath and sigh. 'I thought – hoped – Barney would be Christian's. But as you can see, he looks nothing like him.'

'Is that why you split up?'

'It's a pretty good reason, don't you think?'

'So what are you doing back here?' Again she clamps her hand over her mouth. 'You're not back with Johnny?'

'No, no,' I brush her off. 'No, he's with Dana, hook, line and sinker. But he didn't take the news about Barney as badly as I thought he would. He wanted us to come here and spend some time with him.'

Bump goes her jaw on the table again.

'Sorry, are we talking about the same Johnny Jefferson?'

'Yeah, I know,' I smile wryly. 'It came as a surprise to me, too.'

'Hang on, hang on, let's backtrack a bit. What happened? Was it just a one-night stand?'

'No, it was more than that.' I explain to her about the whole

243

shebang and finally come to the part about him asking me to go and live with him in LA.

'And you said no?' She looks at me like I'm mad.

I screw up my nose. 'You wonder why?'

'But he's Johnny Jefferson, Meg! How could you have said no to him?'

'I didn't manage to say no to everything.' I indicate Barney with my fingers once more. 'As you can see by Exhibit A.'

'Holy shit! Sorry.'

The waitress belatedly comes over to take our order. We've been too busy talking to realise we've been ignored all this time. I haven't had a chance to look at the menu so I order an old favourite – lasagne – plus some penne pomodoro for Barney.

'What's been happening with you?' I ask casually when we're alone again.

'No. Uh-uh.' She shakes her head. 'Nothing's been happening with me. Nothing that even remotely compares to what's been happening with you.'

'I'm sure that's not true. Still working for Rod?'

'Yep, but who cares, right? You've got Johnny Jefferson's son on your lap! I cannot believe this hasn't hit the press yet.'

'Shh! It's only a matter of time with you talking that loudly!'

'Sorry!'

I giggle, then fall serious. 'Really, though, I'm sure it is only a matter of time. Not something that I'm happy about.'

'Jeez Louise, are you ready to be flung into the spotlight like that?'

'What do you think? Don't you remember that time Johnny took me to the Ivy when I was just his PA and the paps thought

I could be "somebody"? I looked like a rabbit in the headlights!'
I shudder at the memory. 'No, I am definitely not ready to be
flung into the spotlight.'

When I get home, Johnny has already gone out. I put Barney to
bed and go downstairs. Lena doesn't work on Saturdays unless
there's an emergency, so I'm on my own. I wander into the
kitchen and aimlessly look in cupboards, even though I'm not
hungry, before making myself a tea and heading to the office. I
stand inside the door. It really doesn't look any different to how
it was years ago; there are even a couple of sacks of fan mail
propped up against the wall. I never managed to make a dent in
them. More letters would always replace the ones I'd dealt with.
It's actually insane that Johnny doesn't have a fan club. Maybe
he thinks that's a bit too 'pop' for him. I might try to convince
him otherwise, because I'm sure Lena has enough on her plate
without replying to his often demented fans.

I have a weird urge to tackle some fan mail now. I know
Lena wouldn't mind. If anything she'll be grateful – I would be.
I put down my tea on the spare desk and try not to remember
how Christian once sat there working on his Johnny Jefferson
biography. I dig into the nearest sack and pull out a handful of
letters.

I work quickly and quietly and find it's soothing being back in
this frame of mind. I locate standard fan-mail responses on the
server and adapt them appropriately, then print them out, attach
a signed photograph and stuff everything into addressed enve-
lopes. The time flies and I don't even notice Johnny at the door
until he clears his throat.

'Hello, there!' I say. 'What are you doing home so early?'

'Couldn't be arsed,' he replies with a shrug and I remember he always did have the attention span of a gnat.

'Is Dana with you?'

'No, she wanted to stick around.'

I stifle a sigh of relief. I haven't enjoyed my encounters with her these last few days. Luckily she hasn't been here too much.

'What are you up to?' Johnny asks, standing by my desk.

'Sorting through fan mail, would you believe?'

'Are you billing me for this work?'

'Consider it a freebie.'

I may have been irritated initially about Johnny's credit-card comment, but, in all seriousness, I do want to earn my keep. I'm not, and have never been, a freeloader. I didn't like relying on Christian to bring in the dough once we had Barney, but it was preferable to paying someone else to look after him while I went out to work. In any case, what was I going to do? I dallied with waitressing for a while when I returned to the UK, but, in truth, I was a good PA. Organisation has always been my forte. I just couldn't bear the thought of running anyone else's life for them after I left LA.

Johnny pulls up a chair and sits down next to me, just as he used to. I lean back in my chair and put my arms on the armrests.

'It's weird seeing you here,' he says.

'It's a bit strange being back,' I admit. 'But everything's different now. It's the way it should be.'

'Definitely different,' he agrees, looking away and raising his eyebrows. I don't know what he means by that so I move on.

'I sat in on those interviews with Lena yesterday.'

'For the cook?'

'Yeah.'

'Opinion?'

'Honestly? I liked Eddie.'

'The guy?' He sounds surprised.

'Yeah.'

'What was he like?'

'Very grounded, young and upcoming. He can turn his hand to different styles, but it's all good home-cooking, not too wanky.'

'Wanky?' He looks amused.

'Not wanky, I said.'

He laughs. 'What did he look like?'

'I should have known that would be your next question.'

'And?'

'He was alright.' I play it down, because, actually, he was pretty damn fine.

'I want to meet him before he starts.' Shame. 'Not that I don't trust you,' he adds. 'On hiring a cook, at least.'

I purse my lips at him and he gives me a slightly defiant look. 'That was a bit below the belt,' I say, because I'm sad to have lost his trust, even if I deserve it. 'I won't lie to you again,' I add seriously.

He leans forward in his chair. 'You won't lie to me again?'

'No.' I stare back at him, confused.

'I am *so* going to use that against you.'

My face heats up and he chuckles. I look away to the desk. 'I think I'll call it a night.'

'Change the subject . . .'

I glance back at him and smirk. 'Can you blame me?'

'Did you fancy the cook?'

'He was alright.'

'You've already used that word to describe him.'

'Because it's true. Not a lie, you see.'

'Yeah, but would you?'

'Would I what?' I laugh, outraged.

'You know.' He whistles to signify naughty business.

'Get out of here, Johnny Jefferson.' I poke him on his arm.

'I thought you were leaving?' he says.

'Maybe I've got a bit more work in me, but hey, if we're both staying, let me show you this one.' I riffle through the stack of fan mail and pull out a red envelope. 'It's freakin' hilarious.' I'm already sounding more American. I open it up and show Johnny the photographs that one bonkers fan has enclosed of her five previous boyfriends. Each and every one of them has a strikingly bad resemblance to Johnny.

'Check out this guy.' I show him a picture of a skinny forty-something dude with wiry dyed blond hair and leather trousers.

'Fuck me,' Johnny says, studying it.

We both crack up laughing.

'Is this the best you've got?' he asks when we've calmed down.

'It takes some beating,' I reply, digging into the stack for another one of my favourites, this time from a foreign fan who tries to describe what she'd like to do with him in bed, but who can't speak English to save her life. I put on a silly accent and read it to him and soon we're both in hysterics again.

'That is fucking funny,' he says. 'We should be drinking while reading these.' He looks at me. 'Actually, I could do with a whisky and a fag. Come to the terrace with me?'

I hesitate.

'Nutmeg, you're not going to be able to stop me from drinking,' he says. 'So you may as well join me.'

I sigh and smile. 'Alright, then.' The truth is I could do with some down time with Johnny. And a drink wouldn't go amiss, either. I haven't had one for ages.

I follow him out to the terrace and in the direction of the outdoor bar. The pool fence has been fitted – if you can call it a pool fence; it's so far removed from the metal bars that I envisaged. It's clear glass with very few joins so there's hardly any interruption to the view. No wonder Lena thought these installers were worth waiting for.

Johnny opens up the outdoor fridge and light spills onto his face.

'What're you having?' he asks. 'Bubbles?'

'Ooh, yeah, that sounds good.'

He cracks open a bottle of Dom Pérignon Rosé without even blinking. I shudder to think of the cost.

'What do you want me to do about the car, by the way?' It's a question I've been meaning to ask for ages.

'Which car?'

'The GTI.' I left it with my parents in Grasse. It was such a manic time getting ready for our trip that I forgot to ask Johnny if he wanted me to sell it.

'Oh, that. Nothing. Your parents can have it.'

'No, Johnny, that's too much.'

'It's fine. Darn sight better than that shitty pile of junk that they drive.'

I smile. 'Well, if you're sure.'

'Yep. How do you like the Panamera?'

'Amazing. Seriously amazing.' I drove the family-sized Porsche this afternoon when I went to see Kitty. Scared the hell out of me at first – it's properly powerful and there's a weight behind it that I'm not used to – but I loved it. 'Thank you so much, again.'

'S'okay. Wanted my boy to be safe.'

I smile at him. 'You're an old softy, really.'

'Shut the fuck up and pass me the whisky.'

I shake my head and pass it to him while he lights up. He takes a swig straight from the bottle then chinks it against the champagne bottle.

'Am I not getting a glass?' I ask him drily.

'Come on, Nutmeg, you're what – twenty-six?'

'Twenty-seven next week.'

'So live a little.' He chinks the bottles together again before taking another swig. I follow his lead and drink straight from the champagne bottle. The bubbles hit the back of my throat and immediately add warmth to the heat that's already inside my stomach because he remembered what age I am. He grins at me and indicates the polished concrete bench table overlooking the city. We walk over there, bottles in hand, and sit down beside each other.

'So what do you think of Dana?' he asks.

'She's nice,' I reply.

'You said you wouldn't lie to me again.'

'Hmm . . .'

'She has a good heart,' he says. I don't know why he's trying to convince me. 'You'll get to like her.'

Another swig, another drag on his cigarette. I take a deep breath. The night air is warm and the scent of pine trees mingles with the smell of Johnny's smoke. The lights of the city blink and twinkle in the haze and far away a police car whizzes around the bends on a hill, its sirens blazing. A cricket chirps in the

250

undergrowth. Johnny scratches at his stubble and gazes sideways at me before straddling the bench seat and facing me full-on.

'You're different,' he says.

'Am I?' I change position so I'm also facing him. 'In what way?'

'More confident. You're not blushing like a schoolgirl with every word I say.'

I take a drink and raise one eyebrow at him.

'Only every second word,' he corrects himself.

'Bugger off.' I kick his leg.

'There,' he says. 'You see? More confident. I'm serious!' he insists when I roll my eyes.

I rest my elbow on the table and prop my head against my hand. Thinking about it, he's right. I'm no longer just his PA, an employee who fell in love with him. I can no longer be accused of being the same as all those nameless groupies. I'm the mother of his child. We are forever tied to each other. I guess that thought gives me comfort – and security, in a weird kind of way. That's why I'm more relaxed. He might be one of the world's most famous people, but he's also just a man. A parent. And in that respect, at the very least, we're equals.

He takes another swig and stares across at me. The way he's looking at me is starting to make me feel a little funny. I take another drink myself, but don't break eye contact.

'Do you ever think about that day?' he asks.

'What day?

'London, two years ago.'

He doesn't say 'Christian's house', but I know what he's talking about. The last time we slept together.

251

I nod and he lights up another cigarette, scrutinising me. The alcohol has made him more blatant. It's making me feel warm and fuzzy and somewhere, deep inside, I know this is a bad thing, but I don't want him to stop looking at me. I want to go to bed with him.

Meg! What the hell are you thinking?

He jolts suddenly and reaches into his pocket for his vibrating phone, and like a bombed submarine, my heart sinks.

Dana . . .

'Hey,' he says into the receiver, looking away from me. 'Just having a drink with Meg.'

He never calls me Nutmeg in front of her. I wonder if she has a nickname. I haven't heard him use one.

'No, we're outside on the terrace,' he says. 'Sure.' Pause. 'Okay, see you in a bit.'

He hangs up.

'Dana?' Although I know I don't have to ask.

'On her way over,' he says.

The bubbles go flat. What a waste of good champagne.

I yawn. 'Well, I'm knackered.' I don't want to see Dana, not at the best of times, but definitely not when I've been thinking dirty thoughts about her boyfriend.

Johnny gets up and follows me inside, stubbing out his fag in one of the tall steel cylindrical ashtrays on his way past.

'See you tomorrow,' I say, not looking back as I head towards the stairs.

'Nutmeg,' he calls and I turn reluctantly to face him. He's standing there in the middle of the room, clutching a half-empty bottle of whisky. His eyes are intense, even from this distance, and he looks hurt, like he's in pain. Suddenly I want to run to

252

him, to throw my arms around him, to kiss him, but I don't. My feet stay rooted to the spot.

'I'm glad you're back,' he says in a gruff voice.

I nod, and then I turn and walk up the stairs.

Chapter 31

I wake up early the next morning and glance across at the monitor. Barney has just started to stir. We're both still jet-lagged. I climb out of bed and drag on my dressing gown, then go to the bathroom to take two Ibuprofen. My head hurts. That'll teach me to drink champagne on a practically empty stomach. I stand there in the bathroom for a while, remembering my conversation with Johnny last night. I hate that I still have feelings for him. Bess was right: it's my heart that's the problem.

It's a bright sunny day and even though there's a chill in the air, after breakfast I decide to take Barney for a swim in the heated pool. I don't imagine Johnny and Dana will emerge for some time. We splash about for twenty minutes and are just about to get out when a familiar figure walks around the side of the house in khaki board shorts and a red T-shirt. Santiago! He stops in his tracks and then his face breaks into a grin.

'Hello, stranger!' he shouts. 'How the hell are you?'

'I'm good!' I beam, getting out of the pool and wrapping Barney in a towel before seeing to myself. 'How are you?'

'Still the same.' He shakes his head and stares at Barney. 'I can't believe it.' He meets my eyes and I shrug.

'Mmm.'

'They made me sign another privacy agreement.'

'Did they?' I laugh. 'Probably for the best.'

'Jesus, the shit's really going to hit the fan when this comes out.' My face falls and he apologises. 'Sorry, I didn't mean . . .'

'No, it's okay. I know you're right. Guess we'll cross that bridge, hey?'

He looks older and broader – he must be twenty-four or twenty-five now. But he has the same olive skin, short jet-black hair and pearly white teeth. He always was good-looking, if a bit short.

'What's his name?' Santiago asks, referring to the bundle in my arms.

'Barney,' I tell him and he holds out his arms to take him so I hand him over. I remember now that Santiago used to babysit his little brother when his mum – a nurse – had a shift.

'How old is your brother?' I ask.

'He's thirteen now.'

'Not so little anymore.'

'Still little compared to me.'

'That's true.' I laugh. 'Hey, listen, let me go and get us dressed and then we'll come and keep you company. I want to know all the gossip.'

'Oh, and there's plenty,' he says with a wink. 'Let's go out back to the hedges so we're out of sight.'

'Sounds like a plan.'

I throw on some clothes and see to Barney and then root around in his downstairs giant golf-ball toy box for some children's gardening gear I saw in there the other day. Then we go out of the front door and up the back of the garden to the hedges, where Santiago is already at work.

'Tell me everything!' I command, plonking Barney on the grass with a plastic spade.

'You've met Dana, I take it?' Santiago asks with an unamused look.

'Not keen?' I turn the tables on him.

'Hell, no. Demented crazy bitch.'

'Eesh.' I sit down on the grass and cross my legs, staring up at him as he clips away at the greenery.

'That's putting it mildly,' he says. 'You know Rosa quit?'

'She found Johnny after the overdose, right?'

'Yeah, that's not the only reason she left, though. She couldn't stand Dana.'

'Really?' I sit up in anticipation.

'Bad influence. You know it was her dealer that got them into that mess? So much for rehab.' He snorts.

'God.'

'She was also always getting Rosa to do stuff for her.'

'Bossing her about?'

'No, that was the thing. She tried to wheedle her way into Rosa's affections, batting her eyelashes at her, giving her shoulder massages, but Rosa was having none of it.' He puts on a silly voice. '"Rosa, baby, you couldn't do us some popcorn, could you?" There's a friggin' popcorn machine in the private cinema! All you've got to do is switch it on,' he rants.

'How do you know all this?' I ask, because Rosa was no gossip.

'Sandy told me.' The maid. 'She's a friend of my aunt's and we caught up at a barbecue recently.'

'Can sign a privacy agreement, but can't stop the staff from talking, hey?'

'Exactly. Everybody's gotta blow off steam.'

'Have you spoken to Rosa?'

'Nah, not me. We didn't work together much. But I liked her. She was a nice lady.' He looks down at Barney and then back at me. 'So what about you? Are you going to tell me how this happened? I mean, Jesus, it was pretty obvious you were into each other. That time he flipped out when I gave you a cigarette? Jealous as hell, I knew that straight away. But a *baby*? A frickin' *baby*, Meg? How did that happen?'

'Didn't your mum tell you about the birds and the bees?' I ask sardonically.

He rolls his eyes at me. 'Okay, so you ain't gonna talk, but, Jesus,' he says again, shaking his head. 'I never would have known.'

'He's surprised me,' I admit honestly. 'I didn't think he'd take it as well as he has.'

'I can't believe you're here again,' he says with a grin.

'Neither can I.'

Dana emerges around lunchtime looking like a bear with a sore head. She's wearing a white vest with a black bra underneath, skimpy white shorts and holey black tights. I wonder if she went out looking like that last night. Probably.

Barney is trying to feed himself chicken pasta with a spoon. It's not pretty.

'Morning, Mary Poppins,' she says drily as she goes to the fridge.

I frown. 'Mary Poppins was a nanny, not a mother.'

'Technicalities.' She opens up the fridge and looks inside before slamming the door in disgust. 'Still no fucking cook?' I flinch. 'What the fuck has Lena been doing all week?' she snaps.

'Can you watch your language around my son, please?' I ask tetchily. 'We interviewed some new cooks on Friday.'

'What do you mean by "we"?' She pulls up a chair at the table and sits down. Not that I want company. Not hers, anyway.

'"We" as in Lena and me.'

'Why did you get involved?' She looks confused.

'Johnny asked me to.'

She gives me a hard stare for a moment and then shrugs. 'Guess you did use to work for him. And you haven't got much else to do around here. Except for looking after this little dude.' She peers at Barney too closely and then laughs when he glances at her indifferently and carries on eating.

'Where's Johnny?' I ask.

'In bed. Had a big one last night.'

'Did you go out?'

'No, we partied at home,' she replies with a smug smile. 'Drank the rest of your champagne.' She raises her eyebrows at me disapprovingly and then tuts. 'Leaving it outside on the terrace going flat . . . Didn't figure you for the wasteful type.'

'Were you just drinking?' I find myself asking.

'As opposed to doing hard drugs?' She laughs. 'You're not going to lecture me, are you, chick?' I open my mouth to speak, but she continues, 'Because I don't oppose this little guy being here, but I'm sure as hell not going to take any crap from *you*.'

The way she says 'you' makes my mouth clamp shut again.

She glares at me and then gets up and goes to the door. 'I'm gonna shoot. Tell Johnny I'll catch him later.'

She walks out, not leaving me time to reply, even if I could come up with some suitably scathing words.

I'm still in a foul mood when Johnny emerges an hour later. I can barely look at him.

'What's up with you?' he asks, sensing the bad atmosphere. Barney is asleep in his cot.

'Can you tell your fucking girlfriend to stop swearing?'

'Christ, Nutmeg, pot calling the kettle black.'

'I mean it, Johnny. I'm angry.'

'I can see that,' he says, scratching his head. He looks rough. He has clearly been burning the candle at both ends.

'What was she swearing about?'

'About the cook . . .' I falter, not really knowing what else to add. 'What do you want to do about that?' I ask, leaving the Dana conversation alone for the moment. 'Shall I get Eddie in tomorrow so you can meet him?'

'No, I don't need to meet him. If you like him, hire him.'

'Are you sure?' I'm surprised after his initial reservations. Now he doesn't seem to care.

'Yeah, yeah, go ahead. I'm gonna head down to Big Sur for a few days.'

I went to Big Sur with him once. He'd gone there to do some writing and I'd joined him. I still remember being with him in the pool overlooking the ocean. That was the first time I felt a spark between us that wasn't one-sided.

259

'Is Dana going with you?' I ask casually, and am stung when he replies.

'Yeah, she could do with a break.'

'Oh, right. I'll get Eddie in, then, yes?'

'Go for it.'

Chapter 32

I'm standing in the studio – alone. It's late at night and I don't feel tired. I turned twenty-seven today, but there were no celebrations. Johnny has been gone for four days. I feel like I did in France: isolated and lonely. Only this time it's Johnny who's left and not Christian. I miss him. Christian, I mean. He was going to take me to Barcelona for my birthday. I wonder if he remembers. I wonder what he's doing right now.

I sit down on the chair and stare into the studio, remembering the first time I saw Johnny standing at the mic with his band behind him. He looked straight into my eyes and I felt like time stood still as he sang to me. Christian had invited me in to listen. What would he think now if he knew I was here? He'd hate me even more than he already does.

'MUUUMMMMMYYY!' Barney cries out on the monitor so I hurry out of the studio and go to his room. I put my hand on his chest, hoping to settle him, but instead I find that he's unusually hot. He continues to cry, unsettled, as I press my hand to his forehead – again too hot. Worriedly I lift him out of his cot and put the lights on low, then go to the cupboard to retrieve his medicine. I administer some infant paracetamol and strip off his clothes, trying to cool him down. He stops crying, but continues to whimper and rub at his eyes and ears. Could this be an ear infection? I peer into his ear cavity, but can see nothing. I wonder if Mum would know. I spoke to her this morning, but what's the time in France now? They're ahead of us so it should be their morning. I call her, full of hope, but she doesn't answer the home phone and the mobile goes straight through to voicemail. I feel like crying because right now all I want is *my* mummy.

I eventually bring Barney into bed with me at about four o'clock in the morning, after hours of going back and forth to his bedroom like a yo-yo. As soon as it's light, I take him downstairs and hunt out Lena's home number. I want to call Johnny's doctor, but I don't know if he's aware of Barney's existence and I'm not sure how to handle it. It's exhausting, this – people not knowing. I know it's going to be hard when it all comes out, but in a sense there should be some relief in the truth.

'Hi, Lena, it's Meg. I'm sorry to wake you,' I say when she answers.

'Are you okay?'

'Barney isn't well.'

'Oh no, what's wrong with him?'

'He has a high temperature and has been unsettled all night. I think it may be an ear infection. I wanted to call Johnny's doctor, but I didn't know if he knew . . .'

'He does. Let me get you the number.'

'It's okay, I have it here. Is it still Dr Navigo?'

'That's right.'

'I'll call him now,' I tell her.

'I'll come straight in,' she replies.

'Don't worry, go back to bed.'

She doesn't, of course. In fact, she arrives before the doctor does. I'm sitting on the sofa, cradling a teary Barney in my arms and watching children's TV.

'You look tired.' She touches my arm. 'Did you get hold of Dr Navigo?' she asks sympathetically.

I nod. 'He'll be here within the hour, he said.'

'I'll make you a cup of tea.' She doesn't wait for me to reply before going to the kitchen.

The doctor comes and confirms my suspicions. He's professional and discreet, and doesn't mention Barney's relationship to Johnny. He writes out a prescription for antibiotics, which Lena promptly takes from me, and informs me that I should continue to dose him up with constant pain relief. Lena has already set off to the chemist by the time he leaves.

Barney doesn't improve that day, and he's even more unsettled that night. I finally get through to my parents, but feel worse than I already did when my mum demands to know what Johnny is doing having a jaunty little holiday when his new family is in town. I start to feel angry about his absence, but the next morning my anger turns to fear when I discover a blotchy red rash all over Barney's body. Dr Navigo comes again and on examination he diagnoses a reaction to the antibiotics. He writes out a new prescription.

With no Lena here, I strap Barney into the Panamera and take him with me to the chemist. It's an overcast day, but the air is deceptively muggy. I feel prickly and uncomfortable in my jeans and jumper and my eyes are stinging from lack of sleep. To my dismay, Barney starts to doze off on the way there and is far from happy when I have to get him out of his car seat to go into the chemist. His cries turn into full-on wails as I stand in the queue, struggling to hold him in my arms. I don't want to wait until we get home to give him a dose of medicine, in case he falls asleep again; but he refuses to comply so eventually I have to force it into his mouth, and I'm at my wit's end by the time that's done. He's still whimpering even as he nods off, but the moment he does, I pull over onto the side of the road and burst into tears.

My mum is right. What the hell is Johnny doing, buggering off to Big Sur when we've just arrived? I hate him! And I hate his fucking girlfriend! Even their fucking swearing is rubbing off on me.

Christian . . . Christian would never have left . . .

Oh, who am I kidding? He couldn't even make it home for Barney's first birthday. I can't look at our life together through rose-tinted glasses. I won't.

I'm alone in this world. Well, not alone. I'm with Barney. It's just him and me. I wipe my tears from my eyes with steely resolution and set off for home.

By the time Johnny returns after almost a week away, Barney is much better. My little boy welcomes his biological father home with open arms, but I don't even want to look at him, much less speak to him. Maybe this is me being irrational, but I feel like I've been to hell and back these last few months and I'm starting to accept that it's not entirely my own doing.

'Alright?' Johnny asks. He looks knackered – even more so than he did before he left.

'How was Big Sur?' I ask without smiling.

'We didn't go there in the end,' he replies indifferently.

'Where did you go?'

'Up to San Fran. Caught up with some friends.'

So that's why he looks whacked. Instead of R&R in Big Sur he went for sex, drugs and rock 'n' roll in San Francisco. My simmering blood reaches boiling point.

'What's up with you?' Johnny asks, sensing my mood.

'Barney hasn't been well.'

'He looks alright to me.' He reaches down and squeezes Barney's shoulder, but his cutesy gesture has no effect on me.

'He had an ear infection and then a bad reaction to his antibiotics. I had to call the doctor in twice.'

'You did the right thing,' he says, which I find extremely patronising. I stand there glaring at him, but he's seemingly oblivious. 'Had a hard few days. Going to hit the sack.' He turns to walk away and I stare after him in disbelief. 'Probably still going to do Big Sur this week,' he adds.

'Are you kidding me?' I practically screech.

He turns around, confusion etched across his brow.

'You're not going anywhere!'

Even I realise I sound slightly demented, but I've had it up to my ears.

'Excuse me?' he replies, slightly sinisterly. Lena hurries out of the office and gives us both a wary look before ushering Barney outside with her. Somewhere inside I'm grateful, but my emotions are mostly anger.

'What's your problem?' he asks.

'You! You are my problem!' Now there's no end to my ranting. 'What the hell am I even doing here?'

'Where would you rather be? Back in France, living with your parents?' he says cuttingly.

I ignore that comment. 'You wanted to spend some more time with Barney, yet you're buggering off with your druggy nut-job girlfriend left, right and centre!'

'Hey!' he warns. 'You're out of line.'

'Why?' I screech. 'It's true!'

'Fuck you.'

'Fuck you!'

'Fuck you!' He raises his voice and points at me. 'I won't have you talking about Dana like that!'

His words cut like a knife and, to my horror, my eyes fill with tears. I turn and flee up the stairs to the relative safety of my bedroom. I slam the door shut and lean up against it. I'm shaking. Tears pour down my cheeks and I angrily brush them away, furious with myself for not being able to argue my own corner. How can he still reduce me to a quivering wreck? I used to be strong. I somehow found the strength to leave last time – but it took too long. Way too long. I still despise myself for it.

Oh, God. My life is a wreck. I used to like myself. I haven't liked myself for a long time. Johnny has always made me feel weak and out of control – ever since I first came to work for him.

There's a knock on the door. I pause, wondering if it's Lena with Barney.

'Yes?'

'Open up,' Johnny says.

'Go away,' I respond angrily.

He starts to open the door.

'I said, GO AWAY!' I shout, pushing back against it like a crazy teenager.

'Open the fucking door,' he says gruffly. 'I want to talk to you.'

I'm about to reply, 'I don't want to talk to *you*', when I reel my fifteen-year-old self back in. It's time to regain control.

I step away from the door and he stumbles into the bedroom.

'What?' I snap, defiantly staring into his piercing eyes.

He roughly pushes his hair away from his face. Suddenly the enormous room feels too small. The bed we slept on together is there, right there.

'What do you want from me?' he demands to know, his chest heaving underneath his black T-shirt.

I let out a sharp laugh. 'Are you taking the piss?'

He frowns.

'*You* were the one who wanted us to come here, Johnny. If you're going to keep buggering off—'

'For fuck's sake, I've only been away for a few days.'

'Almost a week! And you want to go away again.'

'Aren't you happy here? I've done what I can to make it as nice for you as possible . . .'

'I appreciate that. But it's not why we came.' I take a deep breath. 'We came so you could spend some quality time with your son, not so you could go off on little holidays with your girlfriend.'

'That's what the issue is, here, isn't it?' He gives me a look. 'That I'm going away with her?'

'What are you implying?' I ask crossly. 'Because if you think I'm still in any way interested in you, you're out of your mind.'

'Fine.' He puts his hands up to stop me talking. 'So you'll be happy as long as I spend time with Barney?'

I sigh and turn my back on him, facing the bed. 'Yes. I guess so.' I don't want to look at him, even though I feel his eyes on me. 'I'd better get him.' I start towards the door.

'Lena has him.'

'I know that, but she'll have work to do.'

'Just chill out for a minute, would you?' he says with irritation. 'You look knackered.' I hesitate and then nod, defeated. He leans against the wall and folds his arms. 'So he hasn't been well?'

I shake my head. 'No. He had an ear infection. He got it on my birthday,' I add miserably.

'Shit! Your birthday.'

'Yep.' My bottom lip goes out.

'I forgot.'

'I know.'

'Anyway,' I continue, 'he's been in a lot of pain and has barely slept so I've had a tough time of it with no one to help me.'

He stares at me and I wonder if he knows I'm missing Christian. 'You need a nanny,' he says at last.

'I don't want a frigging nanny!' I say crossly.

'You said you needed help.'

'Not *hired* help. I don't want to hand over my son to someone who's paid to look after him. I want people to *want* to look after him – friends, family . . .'

'Damn, you're difficult.'

'I don't think that's me being difficult.'

'It is. What about using an agency just so you can go out for a night? Celebrate your birthday? I've got tickets to the premiere of that new martial-arts flick and the after-show. You and that PA – what's her name? Kerry?'

'Kitty.'

'You and Kitty could go.'

I narrow my eyes at him. 'When?' I'm not massively keen on martial-arts movies, but a premiere's a premiere.

'Thursday night.'

'Because I can't go out tonight. I can't leave him so soon after he's been ill.'

'Like I said, Thursday night.'

I nod. 'I'll think about it.'

He rolls his eyes at me.

'I said, I'll think about it!' I exclaim.

'Yeah, yeah, whatever.'

He walks out of the room, leaving me – annoyingly – feeling foolish.

I wait a minute before following him out. He's nowhere to be seen. I go downstairs and out through the sliding doors to find Lena playing with Barney under the shade of a large white umbrella.

'Sorry about that,' I say. 'Thanks for looking after him.'

'No problem,' she replies. 'We're having fun.'

Barney beams up at her as if to accentuate that point.

'You want to talk about it?' she asks tentatively.

I shrug. 'Not really.' She nods, but I continue anyway, 'He thinks I should get a nanny. But I'm not having one,' I add defiantly. 'He said I should at least use an agency so I can go out. He's got premiere tickets to some new martial-arts film on Thursday night.'

'We'll look after Barney!' she bursts out. 'Katya and I!'

I regard her for a moment before shaking my head. 'No, you've got enough on. I'll use an agency. I'm sure it'll be alright.'

'Meg,' she says firmly. 'I would love to look after Barney. We'll stay in the house so he's in familiar surroundings, and he knows me. Plus, as I've already told you, Katya is dying to meet him.'

I pause. 'Are you sure?'

'I'm sure.'

My face breaks into a smile. 'Thank you. Thank you. I'd better go and call Kitty!'

Chapter 33

Davey, Johnny's driver, picks Kitty up from Rod Freemantle's mansion and we travel to the premiere together.

'Champers?' I offer when she climbs into the back of the limo wearing black jeans and a frilly red top.

'You look stunning!' she exclaims with wide eyes.

'Thank you!' I smile and pour her a glass before putting the bottle back in the mini-fridge.

The first time I came to one of these things I remember getting dressed up to the dozen and I was a bit embarrassed when Kitty turned up wearing jeans. I soon learned my lesson. But tonight I'm throwing caution to the wind. I haven't been out properly since way before Barney was born – and I'm damn well going to make the most of it. Plus, I have an excuse. Johnny gave me a silvery-gold Rodarte dress as a belated birthday present. Maybe he got Lena to buy it, but I don't care. It's beautiful.

I'm wearing glittery grey eye shadow and lashings of mascara and my blonde hair is piled up into a tousled bun on top of my head. I'm also wearing strappy gold heels, which I can totally get away with thanks to Davey dropping us practically at the door.

'You look lovely, too.' I clink her glass and take a sip before collapsing into giggles.

'How much have you already drunk?' she demands to know.

'Nothing! This is my first one.'

'I don't believe you.'

'I swear! I'm just so bloody excited to be going out for a night!'

'What's Johnny doing tonight?' Kitty asks casually.

'I don't know. Hanging out with Dana, probably.'

'So Lena's looking after Barney?'

'Yes.' Kitty knows Lena through the CPA circuit, although not well. I don't think Lena goes out very much, which is a shame because Johnny gets so many free tickets to premieres and parties and they'll be going to waste.

'That's nice of her,' Kitty says.

'You're telling me. Her partner is helping out.'

Katya is lovely. Very pretty, just like Lena, but with short black hair, dark-blue eyes and a petite frame. Her nose is pierced with a diamond stud.

'Johnny's plans with Dana were too important, then?'

'What do you mean?' I ask.

'For him to look after Barney?'

All of a sudden I feel a bit funny. Why didn't he offer to look after Barney? He's his father, after all. All he could think about was a nanny or a babysitting agency.

'Er, yeah, I guess so,' I reply.

On second thoughts, would I actually want Johnny to look after Barney? And Dana? No. No way. I can imagine the two of them getting drunk, stoned or worse. I shudder at the thought.

'Are you okay?' Kitty asks with concern.

'I'm fine. Drink up!'

Davey drives the limo right up to the entrance to the red carpet on Hollywood Boulevard. We step out, camera bulbs flashing like strobe lights around us, and my heart starts hammering with adrenalin. The screams from the crowd are deafening as the stars in front of us walk down the red carpet, signing autographs and posing for pictures. We're mostly ignored and that's fine by me, but it's amazing to soak up the atmosphere. I don't even feel like an idiot dolled up like this. I've been let out for a night! I should be wearing my hair down, not up . . .

We make our way into Grauman's Chinese Theatre and take our seats, and then settle down to watch the action on the big screen. A camera crew outside is filming interviews with the stars as they arrive, so this part is even more fun than the film itself.

'Look, there's Will Smith!' I say.

'Good old Will. Phwoar, Jared Leto is looking pretty hot these days . . .' Kitty comments.

'Mmm, yes,' I agree. 'Isn't that the blond bloke from *Glee*?' I ask.

'Ooh, yeah! I so fancy him. Hey, and there's Scott from Contour Lines!' Kitty says. 'Who's that new bird on his arm?'

But I'm not looking at the girl he's with; I'm scanning the crowd for Christian. My whole body is tense. Is he here? Will I see him face to face? He'll be shocked to find me in LA. Will he refuse to speak to me? I wonder how he'll feel when the news about Barney hits the press. It's only a matter of time. I can't even imagine how horrendous that will be for him. I have to get hold of him before that happens, whatever it takes.

Christian is nowhere to be seen, but two hours later, when we climb back into Davey's limo and head to the after-show party, I'm still wrought with anxiety. I eventually confide in Kitty.

'I didn't even know he was writing their biography,' she says. 'I thought he was writing novels?'

'He still is. Kind of,' I explain. 'His first book didn't do so well. So he's gone back to his roots.'

'I read his Johnny Jefferson book,' she tells me. 'It was good.' She grins. 'Amusing reading about you in there.'

'I wasn't in it that much.'

'Not as much as you should have been,' she says with a knowing wink at my tummy. 'Open up the fridge,' she instructs. 'No more thinking about the bad stuff. You need more champagne.'

I don't disagree with her.

The after-show party is being held nearby at a trendy new rooftop bar. We take the lift up to the top floor and relieve the hunky, bare-chested kung-fu serving staff of a couple of champagne cocktails. I'm feeling tipsy again after a top-up in the limo, but I'm not here one hundred per cent. One eye is always scanning the room for Christian.

'Canapés!' Kitty chirps, eagerly reaching for a tray of mini-spring rolls. I follow her lead. They're delicious.

'God, I miss this,' I exclaim suddenly.

'Do you?' She beams at me.

'I do!'

'I missed you when you left,' she confides. 'It's so cool that you're back.'

'Do you still go out a lot?' I ask.

'Sometimes. But it gets a bit tiring after a while. Same old people again and again. I'd rather hang at home.'

'Are you seeing anyone?' I forgot to ask her this the last

time we caught up – we were too busy talking about my eventful past.

'No,' she replies. 'It's all too hard. I live with Rod so I can hardly bring men back. Living with a famous actor kind of stuffs up your love life.'

'Aren't you lonely, though?'

The corners of her lips turn down. 'I'm kind of getting used to it.'

'When was the last time you had a boyfriend?'

'Oh, God, it was years ago.'

'You realise that you've been with Rod longer than any of his wives have?'

'Don't tell me that!' she cries.

'You may as well be married to him,' I point out, giggling.

'Jeepers creepers.' She shakes her head in horror.

I try to ignore the fact that she just said 'jeepers creepers'. Nope, I can't.

'Did you really just say, "jeepers creepers"?'

'Yes, why?' She looks confused and I start to laugh. 'Should I say "bollocks" instead?' Her English accent is truly terrible and we both burst into laughter.

'Having fun?' A sexy, bare-chested waiter interrupts us. He's wearing nothing aside from black kung-fu style pants and a bandanna across his brow.

'We'd have more fun if you left us the whole tray.' Kitty indicates the vast array of dim sums in front of us. The waiter grins at her. 'On second thoughts, you can stay,' she adds with a smile.

'I wish I could,' he replies flirtatiously.

'Well, maybe we could hook up later,' she suggests with a raised eyebrow.

'Maybe we could.' He winks at her and moves on.

'Bloody hell!' I exclaim. 'That Rod comment must've really got to you.'

'Marriage is far from my mind. But a night of hot sex really wouldn't go amiss.'

'Well, as long as you don't say, "jeepers creepers", you could be in luck.'

We laugh again. 'Ooh, prawn toasts!' she cries, running after a tray.

I suddenly sense someone standing beside me and I whip around, expecting it to be Christian. It's not; but my relief is short-lived.

'Meg Stiles.'

'Hello, Charlie.'

Charlie used to be a CPA back when I worked for Johnny. I disliked her the moment I met her – which is unusual for me. She's shorter and skinnier than me, and her long, dead-straight chestnut hair has been cut into a bob. She's wearing tight black leather leggings with heels, and a black and white asymmetric top. She has a sprinkling of freckles around her nose and cheeks and would be considered pretty, but there's something unpleasant about her eyes – there always has been.

'I didn't know you were back in LA,' she says. 'Who are you working for?'

'No one,' I reply, trying not to give anything away in my facial expressions. 'I'm here for pleasure, not business.'

'Oh?'

Kitty returns, her face falling when she sees who has joined us. 'Hello,' she says unenthusiastically.

'How's Rod?' Charlie asks.

'Fine.'

'Still married?'

'Yes.'

'That's a novelty.' She sniggers before returning the subject to us. 'I wasn't aware you two had kept in touch.'

We both nod indifferently. Kitty will know that the last person I want finding out about Barney and Johnny is standing right in front of us.

'Does Johnny know you're back in town?' she asks pertinently.

My heart skips a beat. 'Yes,' I reply honestly. 'I'm staying with him.'

'You're . . . you're staying with him?' Charlie stutters. She wasn't expecting that response.

I shrug. 'We're mates.'

'Mates? But what about Dana?'

'His girlfriend doesn't mind him having female friends, you know.'

'But . . . but . . . I thought it all ended badly with you?'

'Whatever gave you that idea?' I ask flippantly. 'Oh, he was a nightmare to work with, but no hard feelings. It's cool hanging out at his house, and Dana's really nice.' Okay, so that part's a lie.

'Wow.' That's all she can say.

'Who are you working with now?' I ask pleasantly.

'Isla,' she replies, still distracted by my revelation. I bet she thought she knew everything about Johnny and me. She couldn't be more wrong.

'Is she back in LA?' Isla Montagne is a silly young socialite who Charlie worked for before she moved to the UK to be with her boyfriend. Who turned out to be gay. Whoops.

'She's been back for two years. Have you been living under a rock?' she asks scathingly.

I laugh it off. 'I haven't really been keeping up to date with matters of celebrity . . .' I say in a plummy voice.

She gives me a weird look and walks off without saying another word.

'That was short and brief,' I say, taking a gulp of champagne.

'Not short and brief enough,' Kitty replies.

'My feet are killing me,' I admit. 'Can we go and find somewhere to sit down?'

'Sure.'

We squeeze our way through the crowd and find a bunch of tables and chairs near the swimming pool. A rooftop bar in LA is not a rooftop bar without a swimming pool. There are a fair few vacant seats – most of the people here would rather be working the room than sitting on the sidelines. I collapse on a chair with a sigh and stretch my legs out in front of me.

'I'm not used to wearing high heels.'

'Aren't you?'

I turn sharply to see who asked this question and find myself face to face with an absolutely, totally and utterly gorgeous man. He has short black hair and his eyes are the darkest brown. My heart flips.

'Excuse me?' I reply, wondering if he's even talking to me.

'I was just wondering why you're not used to wearing heels.'

'You're British,' I say, cocking my head to one side.

'So are you,' he replies with an easy smile.

Kitty's outstretched palm appears beside me. 'I'm Kitty,' she says with a smile.

'Joseph.' He shakes her hand and then takes mine.

'Meg.' I suddenly feel all flustered.

'What are you doing in LA?' he asks, not releasing my hand or taking his gorgeous brown eyes from mine.

'Catching up with friends,' I reply, nodding at Kitty and gently extricating myself.

'Did you enjoy the movie?'

'It was okay,' I reply.

'Just okay?' he says with amusement.

'I'm not really big into martial-arts movies.'

'Oh!' Kitty clamps her hand over her mouth. 'You were in it, weren't you? I recognise you!'

I stare at him with horror as he nods.

'Only a small part,' he reveals with a smile.

I don't remember him at all.

'It was when you went to the bathroom,' Kitty tells me, causing me to blush again. That'll teach me to drink too much champagne in the limo.

Joseph leans back in his chair. He's wearing a black suit with a pristine white shirt, unbuttoned at the top. I catch a glimpse of his extremely fit chest and suddenly see myself in bed with him. I shake my head to rid myself of the image. It doesn't work.

'You had some mean moves on you,' Kitty continues and he looks down modestly.

'Do you do kung fu?' I ask, starting to warm to the idea of the bed thing.

He nods.

'Do you have a black belt?' I raise one eyebrow at him as my nerves oddly evaporate.

He hooks his thumb through his belt loop. I look down to see a black leather belt.

'Smart arse,' I say with a grin. He grins back at me. God, he's sexy.

'Ooh, there's the canapé guy,' Kitty says, getting to her feet and hurrying over to him. Joseph doesn't remove his eyes from mine.

'Which part of England are you from?' I ask him.

'I used to live in London.'

'Really? Where?'

'All over. North, south, east, west, I wasn't fussy. You?' he asks.

'I lived in Belsize Park for a while, and London Bridge before that.'

'Cool.'

'How long have you been in LA?' I ask.

'Not long.'

'Is it going well?' It surely must be with looks and a body like his.

He shrugs. 'Alright so far.' He leans forward and stares straight into my eyes.

'What?' No one has looked at me intensely like this for quite some time. Well, not since Johnny the other day.

'You never answered my question,' he says.

'Question?'

'Why don't you wear heels?'

'Um . . .' I tuck my feet back underneath my chair and give him a funny look.

'They suit you,' he adds.

'Er, thanks,' I reply. 'Well, you never answered my question about being a black belt.' I deflect him. I don't want to reveal yet that I'm a mother and the last thing I want to do is rush around in high heels when I'm dealing with a toddler.

He scratches the corner of his lip. Still, his eyes are on mine.

'Yes, I am. Your turn.'

'Um . . . I run around a lot. I'm very busy.'

'Doing what?'

'Looking after my one-and-a-half-year-old,' I admit.

He reels backwards. 'You have a baby?' Here we go. Bye bye, beautiful man.

'Yes. A son.'

'Are you married?'

'No.'

'Do you have a boyfriend?'

'No.'

He leans forward again and casually knocks his forefinger on my knee.

'So let's hook up.'

I nod. Only because I'm rendered speechless. He reaches into his jacket pocket for his mobile phone. A shiver goes through me. I want him to touch me again. 'What's your number?' he asks. I tell him and he punches it straight in. My phone starts to vibrate in my purse and he ends his call. 'Now you have mine,' he adds.

'Joseph!' We both jolt away from each other and look in the direction of the voice. A blond-haired man in his late forties is standing on the other side of the tables. 'Nicky's been looking for you.'

Joseph nods and the man checks his watch. He turns back to me.

'Nicky's my agent,' he explains, standing up. 'It's been nice talking to you, Meg,' he says with a small smile. 'I'll be in touch.'

'Cool,' I reply, but he's already started making his way between the tables. I look around for Kitty. Right on cue, she bounds over to me.

'Got his number!' she says triumphantly, referring to the canapé guy.

I take my phone out of my bag and waggle it in front of her. 'Me too.'

'Nice work,' she says, impressed. 'About time you got back on the horse.'

Johnny and Christian's faces flicker through my mind, one after the other, before settling on Johnny's. Then I see Dana.

'You're right.' I turn to Kitty. 'I know you're right.'

Chapter 34

'Has he called you yet?' Kitty asks me the next day.

'It's only midday,' I reply. 'How's your head?'

'My head's fine after my nice sleep-in.'

'Cow.'

She laughs. 'How's yours?'

'Not so fine,' I admit. 'But damn, it was worth it.'

'It was a fun night,' she agrees. 'We should do it more often.'

I look across at Barney, making a mess of his cheese sandwich. We're in the kitchen.

I came home last night to find a note from Lena on the landing saying that she and Katya were sleeping in the green room and that I could go in and get the monitor. I crept into the bedroom, trying not to stare too much at the sleeping bodies snuggled up together under the covers, and retrieved the device. They joined me earlier for breakfast before Katya went home. The babysitting went well – Barney slept through – and I feel strangely free as a result. I really could do this more often.

'Sounds good to me,' I reply. 'I've decided to check out some babysitters.'

'Really? Good for you!'

'Yeah.' I look across at my son. 'Last night I started to feel like my old self again.'

Johnny and Dana went out last night. I gather they stayed at hers because Barney is having his afternoon nap and Johnny's still not home. Lena is working in the office, but the place feels empty. The new cook can't start soon enough. I go into the office.

'When is Eddie starting?' I ask Lena.

'Monday!' she replies with a wide smile. I'm guessing she misses the extra company as much as I do.

'Brilliant. I can't wait.'

'Me neither.'

'I wonder if he does cookies . . .' I think out loud.

She laughs. 'He'd better.'

'Hey,' I have a sudden thought. 'Can we check out the premiere pics from last night?'

'Sure.' She indicates the chair next to her. I sit down and stare at the computer with anticipation as she goes to a well-known picture-agency website. Images start to fill the screen. I peer closely, trying to hunt out Joseph.

'Him,' I say with a start. 'Can you enlarge it?'

She does, but it's not Joseph.

'No,' I reply.

'Are you looking for anyone in particular?' she asks with curiosity.

'Just a guy I met last night.' I try to keep a straight face, but fail.

'Ooh,' she says with a smirk. 'You kept this quiet this morning. Tell me all about it.'

'It was nothing,' I reply, before having a brainwave. 'Check out the imdb!'

The Internet Movie Database lists practically every movie, director and actor there is. We look up the name of the film and scroll down the cast list. A 'Joseph' appears near the bottom.

'That one!' I say excitedly. She clicks on his name and his page comes up.

'Joseph Strike,' she reads. 'Sexy.'

His cast shot is a snapshot of him on a nondescript red carpet. He looks very much like he did last night in a slim-fitting dark suit and a white shirt. Phwoar.

'Did you get his number?' Lena asks.

'Yes. And he's got mine.'

'Are you going to call him?'

'No!' I reply, aghast. 'He'll call me if he wants to.'

She shakes her head at me. 'It doesn't work like that anymore.'

'How would you know?' I ask teasingly.

'I just do,' she replies.

'No. I'm waiting,' I say firmly.

'Waiting for what?'

I jump out of my seat at the sound of Johnny's voice.

'Where did you come from?' My heart is hammering.

'Waiting for what?' he asks again, ignoring my question.

I ignore his. 'You're always appearing out of nowhere and scaring me.' Two can play at that game.

'No, I'm not,' he scoffs, coming into the room. 'Who's the dude?'

Lena answers for me.

'Some guy Meg met last night,' she says with a knowing look. 'She was telling me all about it.'

'Tell us both,' Johnny says, sitting down on another chair and giving me a penetrating stare.

'Like I told Lena, it was nothing.'

'Yet here you are, checking him out on the internet.' He leans in closer and reads the text. 'Trained in martial arts. Nice,' he adds sarcastically. 'Did he show you any of his moves?'

'Hopefully he will when we next meet,' I reply sweetly, disliking his tone.

'You're going on a date?' His eyes widen and he leans back in his chair.

'Why is that so surprising?'

'Didn't figure you for such an easy lay.'

'I am *not* an easy lay!'

'Take it outside, guys,' Lena interrupts.

Johnny shrugs, then gets to his feet and walks out of the office.

'Bastard!' I spit.

'He's just jealous,' Lena says casually.

'No, he's not,' I reply. 'He's just a wanker.'

'So,' she says, smiling at me expectantly. 'You're going on a date, are you?'

'Bloody well better be now,' I mutter.

'You should call him,' she reiterates.

'Damn you!' I exclaim, brandishing my finger in her direction. She smirks. I snatch up my phone from the desk and give her a look, then go upstairs to my bedroom.

I stare down at his number. Should I? Light-bulb moment: I could text him!

No. Coward's way out and then I could be waiting forever for him to reply. Bugger it. I press dial and wait for it to start ringing. I've been through much worse than this. If he isn't interested in the cold light of day, who cares?

He answers almost immediately.

'Meg.' I can tell he's smiling. 'You called me.'

'You gave me your number,' I reply flippantly.

'How are your feet?'

'My feet?' My brow furrows, then it clicks. 'Oh! They're not too bad. They thank you for being concerned for their welfare.'

'Tell them they're very welcome.'

'I'll pass that on.'

He chuckles. 'So, are you free this afternoon?'

'This afternoon?' I ask in shock. 'I only saw you last night!'

'Why wait?'

'So keen? You weren't even the one who called me.'

'Would you believe me if I told you I had my phone in my hand and was about to press dial?'

'No.'

'Guess I have to earn your trust.'

I hesitate, then tell him straight because I can't be bothered to play games: 'I can't meet you this afternoon. I have to look after my son.'

'Bring him.'

'Bring him?'

'That's what I said.'

I sigh. Surely it's too soon to be introducing the family. Could I ask Johnny to look after him? Erm . . .

'I'll sort something out,' I tell him. 'Where and when?'

'Santa Monica beach? We could take your son on the Ferris Wheel?'

287

I pull a face which he can't see. 'I'm not sure I'll bring Barney,' I reply.

'Why not?'

'Don't you think it's a bit soon to be meeting my offspring?'

'Meg!' He laughs. 'We're not talking marriage, here. I need to spend some time with a fellow Brit. And the more the merrier, quite frankly. Do you want me to come and pick you up?'

'No!' I say quickly. 'I'll meet you there. Car seats,' I add lamely.

'By the pier in a couple of hours?' he suggests.

'Perfect.' I look at the time on my phone. 'See you at three.'

We end the call and I stare ahead, thoughtfully. Santa Monica beach is where Christian took me once when we went out for the day in Johnny's Bugatti Veyron. I don't really want to be faced with those memories, but I couldn't come up with another plan on the spot. I'm sure it will be okay. Barney will like the fairground – I'll do it for him.

My earlier nonchalance turns to nerves by the time we're walking along the boardwalk past the ever-present palm trees towards the pier. I whip Barney to one side as a rollerblader whizzes by us. It's 18 degrees today, but it's cooler down at the beach so I'm glad I packed an extra jumper for Barney. I'm just about warm enough in my black leggings and red maxi cardie.

In the distance I can see Joseph waiting by the pier. As we get closer he spots us too and starts to walk in our direction. My pulse quickens as he flashes a smile at us. He is so gorgeous.

'Hey,' he says warmly, his eyes twinkling.

'Hi,' I reply. 'This is Barney.'

'Hello.' He smiles down at him. Barney hides behind my leg.

'He's not usually shy,' I say.

I couldn't be sure of his height yesterday because he was sitting down, but now I'm thrilled to see that he's quite a bit taller than me – probably about Johnny's height.

'Shall we go to the pier?' he asks.

'Sure.' I pick up Barney. 'Look!' I point. 'Ferris Wheel!' He follows the direction of my extended finger. 'Can you say Ferris Wheel?'

'Pess will,' he tries and I hug him to me with adoration and kiss his little forehead. Joseph glances away and I suddenly feel awkward about my open display of affection. Maybe I was right about this being too much too soon.

I put my son down on the sand and we start our slow walk towards the pier. Slow because Barney keeps stopping to play in the sand.

'Come on, honey,' I urge, taking his hand. 'We're going to go on the big wheel.'

He's never even been on one so I doubt he understands the urgency.

'Shall I give him a piggyback?' Joseph asks me.

'Um . . . You can try.' I'm not sure how Barney will take to a stranger picking him up and throwing him onto his shoulders, but, to my delight, he starts to giggle as Joseph jogs across the sand away from me. I run after them, laughing.

I'm out of breath by the time we reach the pier, in total contrast to Joseph. He glances at me and my face starts to burn. I look at the ocean, at the waves crashing against the sand. Hopefully he hasn't noticed me blushing. It's so strange, being on a date. I'm not used to it.

'Did you have a good time last night?' I ask him.

'It was okay,' he shrugs. 'As these things go.' He's still carrying Barney. 'Did you?'

'Brilliant. Loved it. Already having withdrawal symptoms. I clearly need to get out more.'

'You don't go out much?'

I laugh and nod meaningfully at Barney. 'No.'

'Who looked after him last night?' he asks.

'A friend.'

'No family?'

'My parents live in France.'

'What about his father?'

'Oh . . .' I try to act casual. 'Yes, he's around, but he's sort of a bit useless.' I try to laugh it off. 'Ooh, candy floss!'

He follows my gaze.

'Or cotton candy, as they call it here,' I continue.

'Aah. You want some?'

'Hell, yeah!'

He chuckles and deftly gets his wallet out of his pocket while holding onto Barney one-handed.

A few minutes later, pink spun sugar is melting on my tongue. I sigh with delight and offer him the bag.

'No, thanks. I'd never work again if I got into that stuff,' he says with a grin. I glance at his biceps and suddenly it doesn't seem quite so important that he shares my indulgence for calorie-laden sweeties.

'So is that your thing?' I ask. 'Martial arts?'

He shrugs. 'I can act as well. Or so I'm told.'

'That's cool,' I say. 'Have you been in any other films?'

'A couple. Nothing too exciting. I've got an audition on Monday, though.'

'Oh, wow. What's that for?'

'A sci-fi flick. Adrian Reigler's at the helm.'

'Ooh.' I try to sound impressed.

'You don't know who that is, do you?'

I look sheepish. 'No, sorry.'

He grins. 'He's a new and upcoming director. Think the next James Cameron, but younger.'

'He's not going to paint you blue and dress you up like an Avatar alien, is he?'

He laughs. 'I hope not.'

'Well, good luck with it. Is that what your agent wanted to talk to you about last night?'

'It was, actually.' I think he's impressed that I remember. 'He gave me a rap on the knuckles for not working the room more.'

'How long had you been sitting there before we arrived?'

'About half an hour,' he admits.

'And you didn't even have the excuse of sore feet,' I tut.

'True.' He glances down at my black ballet pumps.

'Flats today,' I tell him.

'They suit you too,' he says with a grin.

The image returns of the two of us in bed together, although it's quickly quashed when I look up at Barney on his shoulders. Next time, I think to myself, I'll get a babysitter.

We meet each other's eyes and I wonder if he can read my mind. Right now, I don't particularly care. Like Kitty says, it's time to get back on the horse. And sooner rather than later would be really rather lovely, thank you very much.

Chapter 35

I'm still on a high when I get home at six o'clock that night, even though Barney has grizzled the entire way back because he's tired and hungry. I fed him snacks in the car, but we're an hour late for his dinner. Of course I feel guilty, but not that guilty. I feel kind of dazed – in a good way. I waft into the house and go straight to the kitchen to prepare him some beans on toast. I can't wait for Eddie to start on Monday. We'll eat proper food again! Hurray.

Lena comes in a minute later.

'Are you off home?' I ask her.

'No.' She gives me a wary look. 'Johnny wants to talk to you.'

'What about?' I ask, alarmed.

'Today,' she says meaningfully.

I pull a face. 'Joseph?'

She nods. 'I'll feed Barney.'

'No, you should go,' I reply. 'It's the start of the weekend.'

'No, I'll feed Barney,' she insists, and I know at that moment that I'm in for a hard time of it with Johnny.

'Okay,' I reply with a heavy heart, and I go to find him. As it turns out, he finds me.

'Meg!' He comes out of his room and jogs down the stairs. To my annoyance, Dana follows him, although with far less urgency.

'Did you take Barney with you on a date?' He's angry and my hackles are immediately raised.

'You know I did. What's your problem?'

'This guy could have been a serial killer!' he exclaims.

'Ooh, yes,' I reply sarcastically. 'A simple kick to the head with one of his karate moves should do it.' Okay, so Joseph does kung fu, but really, what's the difference?

'You're out of line!' he shouts, gesticulating furiously. I hear Lena close the kitchen door in the background.

'Why are you getting angry?' Dana interrupts calmly from beside him. 'What's the big deal if Meg has a boyfriend?'

What the—? I wasn't expecting her to stick up for me.

'I'm not angry,' Johnny snaps back, kind of illustrating her point. He glares at me. I raise my eyebrows at him challengingly. He exhales loudly. 'Look,' he says, sounding slightly calmer, 'I wouldn't expect you to let me take Barney out with anyone you didn't know.'

'I wouldn't want you to take Barney out with anyone I *did* know.' I look pointedly at Dana.

'Oh, I've got no interest in babysitting.' She brushes me off. 'Sorry,' she adds flippantly.

'Don't be,' I say through gritted teeth.

She continues, unperturbed, 'Johnny, can I borrow the silver car to go pick up Nina?'

'Sure,' he replies, still looking at me.

She pecks him on the cheek, raises one eyebrow at me over her shoulder, and then walks out.

Johnny is still staring angrily at me. 'What I said stands,' he reiterates firmly. 'I don't want anyone looking after Barney who I don't know.'

'Since when did *you* become a protective father?'

'Don't you DARE!' he shouts at me. 'I didn't have a fucking choice, remember? You took that away from me!'

I spin on my heels – well, flats – and head up the stairs. I'm not hearing this again.

'Where are you going?' he shouts after me.

'Away from you,' I reply.

'I mean what I said!' he continues.

'Yeah, yeah.'

'AND I WANT HIM TO CALL ME DADDY!' he blares.

I turn around and stare at him, then I can't help it: I crack up laughing.

'What?' he asks crossly, his face flushed with rage.

'You!' I can barely get the word out.

'What?' he asks again, really annoyed now.

'You!' I'm almost crying with laughter. 'Shouting "DADDY" after me.'

His face softens. I collapse on the stairs and laugh so hard I have to clutch at my chest.

'Fuck you,' he says, but his face breaks into a grin. He walks up the stairs and sits down next to me, resting his elbows on his knees. Eventually my laughs subside. I look across at him, but he's staring down at his fingernails. I look at them, too, then my eyes travel up his hands to his wrist and his latest tattoo. It's black and twirly. I don't know what it means, if it even has any meaning. I bet it hurt, though, I think distractedly.

I realise Johnny is now looking at me so I meet his eyes. My heart skips a beat. He's too close. I force myself to speak, hopefully without shaking.

'Okay, you can meet him.'

Something changes in his expression, I'm not sure what. It should be relief, but I don't think so.

'Good,' he replies. He rests his chin on his forefingers and stares straight ahead.

In the kitchen, Barney starts to cry.

'I'll go,' I say, getting to my feet and going to him. Lena is just cleaning up. He's tired. 'Thanks,' I say to Lena. 'I can take it from here. You should go home.'

'Cool,' she replies. 'I just have to finish up a few things in the office.'

I get Barney out of his high chair and carry him back through to the living room.

I notice with surprise that Johnny is still where I left him. On impulse I carry Barney up the stairs and sit back down next to Johnny. Barney shifts his head to my other shoulder and stares straight at his father. Johnny smiles and ruffles his hair. Warmness seeps through me.

At that point Dana appears at the bottom of the stairs. We both start with surprise and I'm instantly cold again.

'Meg,' she says. 'How do you get out the fucking car seat?'

'Can you *not* swear?' I say irritably, looking pointedly at Barney.

'Yeah, yeah, apologies, Snow White. Car seat. I can't pick up my friend because there's a goddamn car seat in the front.'

'Unbuckle it, then,' I say.

'What, unbuckle the seat belt?'

'Yes.' I look at her like she's dim, because, quite frankly, she clearly is. 'Unbuckle the seat belt,' I say slowly, 'remove it from the back of the car seat, and lift out the car seat. Hey presto.'

'No need to be so fucking patronising about it,' she snaps, storming out.

I didn't even know Lena had fitted a car seat into the Porsche Carrera GT. I remember finding out that Johnny bought the Carrera new a few years ago for almost half a million bucks. If I was going to use a car other than the Panamera, I wouldn't risk borrowing that one. Dana clearly doesn't have the same hang-ups.

I glance at Johnny and raise my eyebrows disapprovingly.

'Okay, okay, I'll talk to her again,' he says wearily, getting to his feet.

'That would be helpful,' I say primly, standing up myself. I follow Johnny up the stairs and suddenly, desperately, wish he'd come with me to bath Barney. My heart sinks as he turns left and goes into his music studio. I go right and head into Barney's en suite.

Bloody Dana, I think to myself as I turn on the taps in the huge bathtub. I don't know why she couldn't just take something else. There are enough cars in the garage to choose from. I don't like the thought of her taking the Panamera, though. She wouldn't, in any case. Not attention-grabbing enough. I bet the silly cow loves it when the paparazzi snap her in Johnny's cars . . .

Realisation hits me. Jesus! The paps could have snapped Barney and me in one of Johnny's regular cars! They could have put two and two together and then our secret would have been out. Damn, that was close. I'm glad I realised in time. The Panamera is new. Nobody has linked it to Johnny because he never drives it. It even has a fairly indiscriminate number plate. Still wide-eyed with relief, I get up and go to the top of the stairs, just in time to catch Lena leaving for the weekend.

'We nearly had a close shave,' I call down to her.

'What?' she asks with alarm.

'I can't drive any of Johnny's other cars.'

'Why not?'

'The press might spot us and find out about Barney!'

'Oh.' She looks down and adjusts her bag on her shoulder. 'Well, you know the Panamera is booked into the garage tomorrow . . .'

'No? I didn't know that.'

'That light on the dash. I thought we should get it checked out.'

'Oh, right. Yes, I guess we should.' Bummer. I was planning on going to see Kitty.

'I installed the spare car seat in the Carrera so you'd still have wheels,' she explains, telling me what I already know.

'Yeah, Dana took it out so she could pick up her friend,' I tell her with a wry smile.

'Did she?' She frowns. 'Couldn't she use the 911 or one of the others instead?'

I shrug and Lena surreptitiously rolls her eyes before nodding towards the door.

'See ya,' I say.

'Have a good one,' she replies.

I smile and go back into Barney's bedroom. It's the first time I've seen Lena openly diss Dana since we arrived. She's usually so professional. I'm pleased, though. It's nice to have some solidarity on that point.

Chapter 36

I call Bess the next morning, when it's Saturday evening in the UK. I couldn't call her the night before because of the time difference, but I desperately want a friend to help me dissect my date with Joseph, and only Bess will do.

'How are you?' I ask warmly.

'Oh, not so good,' she replies.

'What's wrong?'

'I lost my job yesterday.'

'Oh, Bess, I'm so sorry. What happened?'

'Cutbacks. They're closing the London office. Half of us lost our jobs, the other half are being relocated.'

'That sucks.'

'You're telling me.' Poor Bess, she sounds defeated.

'What are you going to do now?'

'I don't know. Look for another job, I guess. But I don't know who's going to want to employ a fat, ugly marketing manager.'

'*Bess!*' I exclaim. 'You're not fat *or* ugly! I don't want to hear you talking about yourself like that.'

'I've just had a rubbish couple of days,' she replies flatly.

'What can I do to cheer you up?' I ask, although I have absolutely no desire to tell her about the shiny new premiere I went to and the sexy man I met.

'Fly me out to LA?' she jokes.

My heart jumps. 'I could,' I say.

'I was joking,' she replies.

'But I could!' I sit up on my bed, my head tingling with excitement. 'Bess, why don't you come over? You could come this weekend!' I cry. 'You could literally get on a flight tomorrow and come and stay with me!' I'm getting totally carried away by this idea.

She doesn't speak, then she says, 'I can't afford it.'

'I'll pay for you, you ninny!' I scoff. 'Well, Johnny will. You know he gave me a credit card with no limit?'

'Get out of here,' she says with disbelief.

'I'm serious! I haven't used it yet. But he won't care! He'll be pleased I've got someone to take my mind off the sexy kung-fu actor I met the other night.'

'Excuse me?' she says and I know her face has broken into the biggest grin.

'I'll tell you all about it. Tomorrow. In person.'

She cracks up laughing and I know I've sold it to her. We both start to scream with hysterics, and when we've calmed down I take the phone with me to the office and together we check out her flight options.

I'm still buzzing with excitement two days later when Davey takes Barney and me to collect Bess from the airport. In the end we had to settle for Monday, because it was already Saturday evening for Bess when we talked and she thought she could do with Sunday to pack – and get a bikini wax, she told me with a giggle.

Johnny spent all of Saturday and Sunday morning with Dana, so I had to wait until the afternoon to reveal my plans. As predicted, he was cool with the idea. He's never met Bess, to her dismay. She's been dying to meet him for three years – no, longer than that. She's been dying to meet him ever since he became famous. When I worked for Johnny the thought of her meeting him used to slightly terrify me. I was shamefully embarrassed by the idea, but now I don't care. Now he's just Johnny. Bring it on.

Bess and I are still chattering away animatedly when Davey pulls up at the gates. He's hardly been able to get a word in, which is odd for him, but he's smiled the entire time. He's never seen me so completely and utterly beside myself.

'Oh, wow,' Bess exclaims as the house appears in front of us.

I watch her with delight, remembering how I felt when I first came here. It's so nice to witness someone else's thrill. I can't wait until she sees the outside view.

'*Wow!*' she says five minutes later, from the terrace. She's jiggling Barney in her arms and her eyes are wide with amazement as we look down at the LA skyline. 'No wonder you found it hard to leave last time.'

'The view wasn't what was keeping me here.'

'No, I know.' She puts her hand on my arm and meets my eyes. 'How's it all going with him?'

'Alright,' I reply, looking away.

'Meg . . .'

'No, it's okay.' I look back at her. 'I don't like Dana,' I admit.

'Hardly surprising,' she scoffs, smiling down at Barney. 'Silly moo.'

'You can't be rude to her,' I warn.

'As if! Don't worry about me. I'll be nice as pie.'

'Don't be too nice,' I say with a laugh.

'Where is Johnny?' she asks as Barney wriggles in her arms and points to the ground. She puts him down and he wanders over to the sandpit that Lena organised last week.

'He's asleep,' I tell Bess, and her eyes light up, almost as if she weren't expecting him to be here. 'This is far too early for him,' I add. 'Are you excited about meeting him?' I grin, knowingly.

'Nah,' she replies indifferently, before jumping up and down on the spot, her face stretched into the biggest, craziest, most ridiculous smile I've ever seen. I burst into laughter and her expression reverts back to deadpan. 'Not in the least bit bothered,' she adds casually as I laugh harder.

Bess and I have been friends since secondary school. Even though she went to university in Bristol and I went to Nottingham, we never lost touch or drifted apart. The only dodgy time in our history of friendship was when I first came to work for Johnny. I found myself unable to confide in her – partly because of my confidentiality clause and partly because I felt like her new flatmate, Serena, had replaced me, but mostly because I was going through the strangest, most exhilarating, out-of-this-world time of my life and it was impossible to convey these emotions to someone who wasn't already along for the ride. But we got through it. I decided I'd rather get sued for breach of contract than lose my best friend, so I opened up my heart and told her everything.

She doesn't even see Serena anymore. One of those flash-in-the-pan friendships in the end. Can't say I mind much.

Bess grins at me. 'So what are we doing for the next two weeks?'

'Whatever you like. Sunbathing—'

'Is it hot enough?' she interrupts.

'It was twenty-two degrees yesterday.'

'No shit? Wow.'

'Shopping—'

'Can't afford it.'

'I don't know, then . . . seeing the sights, we could go for a drive to check out the Hollywood sign, maybe go to a showcase or a premiere or something.' I really do need to get onto a babysitting agency. 'Today our new cook starts,' I add.

'Ooh, I've definitely arrived at the right time, then.'

'Absolutely. He's pretty cute, too.'

'He? Cute? Fab.'

'I'd also love you to meet Kitty.'

'Yeah, that would be great,' she says.

'And I guess we'll just hang out a bit and soak up the atmosphere. God, it's so great to have a friend here to share all this with.'

'Thank Christ I got fired, eh?' She nudges me.

'You didn't get fired; you got made redundant,' I point out.

'Who gives a shit right now? I mean, *really* . . .'

We both giggle. 'Want to see inside?'

'Hell, yeah.'

'Come on, Barney . . .' I lift him out of the sandpit and dust him off.

Eddie arrives just as we're finishing the tour and I have to remind myself not to step on Lena's toes. Because I played a part in hiring him, it feels strange to not be the one to show him around and settle him in, but it's Lena's job to do that, not mine. So Bess and I introduce ourselves and go back outside to the terrace.

'What time does Johnny wake up?' Bess asks.

'Unusual for him to emerge before eleven,' I reveal.

She checks her watch. It's nine fifteen now.

'Shall we take Barney for a walk around the grounds?' I ask.

'Sure. And I want you to tell me all about this sexy actor you met last week.'

By the time we decide to go inside for a coffee, the smell of freshly baked something or other is wafting through the house. I lead the way expectantly into the kitchen.

'Mmm, something smells good,' I say as Eddie spins around to smile at us. He's twenty-four, is about five foot ten or eleven and has short blond hair, blue eyes and a cheeky smile. I liked him immensely at the interview, and from the smell of whatever it is baking in the oven, I like him even more now.

'You're just in time,' he says, grabbing an oven mitt and retrieving a tray full of muffins.

'Wow,' Bess says, her mouth falling open.

'White chocolate and raspberry, dark chocolate and orange, banana and bran . . . Anything take your fancy?' Eddie offers.

'One of each, please,' Bess jokes.

'Sure,' Eddie replies earnestly. 'Who wants a coffee? Tea? Hot chocolate?'

'A coffee would be great,' I say, sinking down onto a chair at the table and sighing with delight. At last we're going to eat well again!

'I'll go and ask Lena what she wants,' Eddie says. 'Do you think, er, Johnny will come down soon?'

It strikes me that he's nervous. He would be; he never met Johnny at the interview stage.

'Probably not for a while,' I tell him with a smile. 'So you can relax and enjoy the fruits of your labour.'

The five of us – Bess, Lena, Eddie, Barney and me – are sitting around the table having a good old chat when the front-door buzzer sounds. Lena goes to answer it. I come out of the kitchen to see Dana breaking away from Lena to go up the stairs. She ignores me.

'Dana's here,' I turn around to tell Bess and Eddie as Lena rejoins us.

'What does that mean?' Bess asks.

'You won't be meeting Johnny anytime soon.'

Both their faces fall, but they do well to cover up their disappointment. 'In that case,' Eddie says with a small smile, 'I'd better get on with lunch.'

Bess looks knackered so I suggest she has a bath and chills out for a bit because there's no point in hanging around waiting for Johnny.

'Come and get me if anything interesting happens,' she says meaningfully.

'I promise,' I tell her.

I put Barney down for his nap and go into the office to research babysitting agencies. I speak to a couple and arrange to meet this afternoon with the one I like the sound of most. I feel much more relaxed with the idea of leaving Barney so I can have the odd night out with Bess during the two weeks that she's here.

Lena puts a stack of press releases in front of me.

'Events for the next couple of weeks,' she says with a smile. 'Take your pick.'

'Aah, brilliant,' I say, riffling through them. A fortieth-birthday party for some Hollywood scriptwriter – nope, feels a bit weird going to a birthday celebration for someone I don't know. A premiere for an indie flick – not likely to be that star-packed. A showcase for an upcoming female pop star at the Mondrian's Skybar. Okay, so the music is undoubtedly likely to be more my cup of tea than Bess's, but the venue is fun – I've been there a few times for various things. I come to another invite – one that's black and sparkly and shaped like a bat. I read the silvery, spider-web-style writing. A Halloween party being held by Sylvester Middleman, one of America's top music producers. A quick search on Google reveals that he and his wife have four children aged between one and seven, so this should be good. I put it to one side, along with the showcase invite, and carry on looking.

When Bess comes searching for me an hour and a half later, I've RSVP-ed to five events for the next couple of weeks, including a film premiere for a romcom, a gig with backstage passes and an after-show party for a band Bess absolutely loves. She's beside herself.

But that's nothing compared to the look on her face when Johnny comes into the office a few minutes later.

'Alright?' he says to Bess, bending down and kissing her on the cheek. 'Don't get up.'

She stays where she is, but her face turns bright red and I can see her hands are shaking.

'How was your flight?' he asks. He's wearing a tight black T-shirt and black pants with his trademark metal-studded belt.

He looks like he could have stepped off the front cover of a magazine.

'Fine, fine, it was fine,' she replies nervously.

'Eddie's here,' Lena tells him.

'Aah, cool. In the kitchen?' He points in that direction.

'As you'd expect,' Lena replies with a wry smile. 'Come on.'

'He's so good-looking in real life!' Bess whispers through clenched teeth as soon as they've gone.

'He's not bad,' I reply indifferently.

'You've shagged him!' she screeches quietly.

'Shh!' I say with alarm, but then I can't help but giggle at the look on her face. 'Let's go, too,' I decide suddenly, so Bess and I head out of the office and into the kitchen. Johnny is leaning against a countertop with his arms folded, while Eddie stands in front of him. He seems on edge as he runs through the menu options for the next week.

'All sounds great,' Johnny replies. He's not really big into food. Booze, on the other hand . . .

'Johnny, you've got to try one of these,' Lena says enthusiastically, taking a muffin from the tray and putting it on a plate for him.

'Have you got one for Dana, too?' he asks.

'Of course,' Eddie replies. 'Actually, would you both like lunch? I'm just finishing up some pizza bases to put in the outside oven.' It's a wood-fired oven on the terrace.

'Sounds good,' Johnny says, putting the muffin back on the countertop. 'Let's all go. Is Barney asleep?' he asks me.

'Yes, but he needs to wake up soon.'

'Shall I get him?'

'You can, if you like,' I reply.

'Cool.' He turns around and exits the room, leaving a buzz in the air. I forgot that Johnny has the ability to do this. A room always lights up in his presence. It's just as obvious when there are four people as when there are four hundred.

Eddie picks up a couple of trays of pizza bases. 'To the terrace?' he asks.

Lena, Bess and I lift up the remaining trays and follow him. I go to the outdoor bar and start to sort out drinks. Bess joins me.

'You've shagged him,' she quietly exclaims again through clenched teeth.

'Stop it,' I hiss.

She grins at me and then she freezes as her eyes fall on something behind me. I turn around to see Johnny sliding shut the outside door. He's carrying Barney in his arms and my little boy is still half-asleep as he presses his face into his father's neck.

'Oh my God,' Bess whispers slowly as Johnny walks towards us. 'That is the cutest thing I've ever seen.'

Barney lifts his head and looks at me, then opens up his arms, so Johnny hands him over. We lock eyes for the duration of this exchange and a flutter goes through me. It's not healthy for me to witness Johnny's attractiveness through someone else's eyes.

Dana slides the door open and steps over the threshold. She immediately lights up a fag, not bothering to close the door behind her.

'Johnny,' she calls abruptly. He turns around and goes to her, taking the lit cigarette from her fingers as she lights another one for herself. They go to a sunlounger away from us and sit facing each other. Dana suddenly leans forward and kisses Johnny passionately on his lips. Bess and I look away, awkwardly.

'Christ,' she whispers.

'Yep. She's a corker.'

'Mmm.'

'Grub's up!' Eddie calls.

Bess laughs as we wander over. 'That's a very English saying.'

'Thought I'd better practise some, considering my boss is from "across the pond"!' He says the last bit in a posh accent.

'No, you've got it all wrong,' Bess tells him. 'He's from Newcastle originally, so you've got to learn things like, "Eh up, lass."'

'What's this?' Johnny asks, stubbing his cigarette out on his way over.

'Bess is just teaching Eddie some Geordie sayings,' I explain.

'"Eh up, lass" is from Yorkshire, ye divvy,' Johnny says in a thick Geordie accent. 'Whey aye, man,' he adds. We all crack up laughing. In the background, Dana reluctantly gets to her feet.

'Divvint ye knaa owt?' Johnny adds to much hilarity. Dana joins us and he turns to her: 'A'reet, pet?'

'What the hell are you saying?' she asks, unimpressed.

'Talk from the toon,' he replies.

'Talk from the where? Oh, whatever,' she brushes him off. 'I'm fucking starving.'

I glare at her before leading Barney to the table. I don't want to make a scene in front of everyone. I fix Barney's highchair to the edge of the stone table. Bess comes to help.

'Just as well he can't talk yet,' she murmurs.

'It's only a matter of time before "duck" becomes part of his vocabulary,' I reply. She grins at me. 'It's good to have you here,' I say quietly, grinning back at her.

The others join us and we tuck in to Eddie's truly incredible pizzas. After a while, my phone starts vibrating in my pocket. I pull it out and look at the screen: Joseph.

'Hi!' I say warmly.

'Hey,' he replies. 'How's it going?'

'Good. Great, in fact. My best friend from the UK arrived this morning.'

'Really? I didn't know you had a pal coming to stay.'

'Neither did I until Saturday. Bit of a last-minute plan. Have you just come from your audition?' I notice Johnny's conversation halts briefly as his eyes flick towards mine.

'You remembered,' he replies, and once again I'm sure he's smiling.

'Of course. How did it go?'

'Aah, you know, it's hard to tell with these things. So I was going to see if you wanted to catch up for dinner, but I guess you're busy with your friend . . .'

'Kind of,' I say, 'but we're going to a gig tomorrow night. Saldo Sorvie. Maybe we could get an extra ticket?' I glance at Bess to check she doesn't mind him gate-crashing, but she nods happily.

'That'd be great,' Joseph replies.

Johnny puts his fork down noisily and pointedly, and glares at me across the table.

'What?' I mouth with annoyance.

'You're using my name to get him a ticket?'

I cover the receiver with my forefinger. 'You wouldn't normally care.'

He doesn't reply. Everyone else around the table eats their food and tries to act invisible. Everyone except for Dana, who's watching this exchange intently.

I remove my finger. 'Sorry, Joseph,' I say. 'Just having a discussion with my . . . housemate.'

Johnny angrily gets to his feet and storms off.

Dana stares after him, slightly taken aback. Lena gives me a look, but I'm not sure what it means, while Dana puts down her cutlery and gets up from the table. 'That was spectacular, dude,' she says to Eddie, although it sounds far from genuine to me, and probably to the rest of us around the table – with the exception of Barney, who hasn't learned about false sincerity yet. She follows Johnny inside.

'Hello?' I hear Joseph say in a tinny voice. I realise I've dropped the receiver from my ear.

'Sorry!' I say again.

'Is this a bad time?' he asks.

'We're just in the middle of lunch. Can I call you back?'

'Sure.'

We end the call. Eddie is already tidying away after Johnny and Lena.

'Well, that was short and sweet,' I say of our getting-to-know-each-other meal. 'That was Joseph,' I say, indicating my phone.

'I gathered,' Lena replies knowingly.

'Who's Joseph?' Eddie chips in. 'If you don't mind me asking,' he adds.

'No, no, of course not,' I brush him off. There's no point in keeping secrets from a staff of this size. 'A guy I met last week.'

'Doesn't Johnny like him?'

Lena laughs sharply and I furrow my brow at her as I reply, 'He hasn't met him.'

'He doesn't want to,' Bess replies, 'from the way he acted there.'

'Why's that?' Eddie pries.

'Jealous,' Lena interjects.

'Jealous of what?' I feel slightly put out. Why does she keep coming out with comments like that? Because he's not still interested in me. I can tell her that, right now. He wouldn't rub his feelings for Dana in my face if he were.

She shrugs, but doesn't expand.

'I think we can safely assume Johnny doesn't want to get Joseph another ticket to the gig tomorrow night.'

'He might be able to get one through his agent,' Lena suggests.

'Maybe,' I reply, but I'm thinking it's better to leave it on this occasion.

Chapter 37

'Is he going with you?' Johnny asks me the next day, with a fair amount of attitude.

'Might be,' I reply. 'You know he's perfectly capable of getting his own ticket, don't you?' I don't know why I'm doing this, but I want to wind him up for some reason. As it turns out, I told Joseph the gig thing might be a bit too complicated and that I'd call him tomorrow – Wednesday – so that we could make a plan then.

'Who's looking after Barney?' Johnny demands to know.

'A lovely girl called Esther from an agency.'

'You're getting an agency in?' he spits.

'On your suggestion!' I point out. 'Why, do *you* want to look after him? You know, seeing as you're his father and all that?' I say sarcastically.

He stares at me angrily for a long moment. 'Yeah, I do, actually.'

Really? Damn.

'Dana and I don't have any other plans,' he continues.

Oh, shit. Not her. Him, I can handle, but I don't – I *really* don't – want her looking after Barney. Hopefully he's not serious. I call his bluff.

'Fine.' I shrug and walk out of the office. Dana is sitting on the sofa reading a magazine.

'You're fine with it?' Johnny asks, hot on my heels.

'Yep. Better check with Dana, though,' I say, looking across at her.

'What's up?' she drawls.

'Johnny wants you to babysit tonight.'

'Fuck that,' she snorts, throwing the magazine down.

'Dana!' Johnny erupts.

'I told you, baby, I ain't got no interest in being a mummy.'

My hackles go up. Mummy? You've got to be kidding me. But I stay quiet so she can dig her own hole.

I look pointedly at Johnny. He's glaring at Dana, but she's not biting. 'I guess I won't cancel the babysitter, then.'

No one says anything as I leave the room.

Bess is in the kitchen taste-testing Eddie's latest concoction: roasted pumpkin soup with melted Gruyère cheese and Parmesan croutons.

'That is ridiculously yummy,' she tells him.

'Should help get us in the mood for Halloween,' he replies with a grin.

'Ooh, yeah. Hey, we need to go costume shopping,' I say to Bess. 'We'll need to get something for Barney, too.'

Just then, we hear Johnny's raised voice coming from the living room.

'I don't give a shit,' he growls at Dana. 'Either you pull your weight or we don't have a future.'

'Is that an ultimatum? Because I ain't a girl for ultimatums, Johnny. You should know that about me.'

Eddie, Bess and I stand stock-still, staring at each other.

'I guess you'd better go, then,' comes Johnny's reply. My heart lifts with hope. Is he breaking up with Dana? I shouldn't care, but, God, I do, I really, really do.

There's no sound coming from the living room. Very slowly and carefully, I poke my head around the corner, just in time to hear the front door slam shut.

'Meg!' Bess whispers, trying to pull me back.

Johnny is standing alone in the living room. He turns and stalks up the stairs. Is it wrong that I want to go and comfort him? Silly question, I know the answer.

'She's gone,' I say to Bess and Eddie.

'What was that about?' Eddie asks.

I shrug. Small staff and everything, but this time I want to stay silent.

'I'll be back in a minute,' I tell them, walking out of the room.

'Meg . . .' Bess calls after me, a warning tone to her voice. She knows what I'm up to. I feel guilty, but I can't stop my feet from taking me up the stairs. I turn left at the top, but before I can reach Johnny's room, he comes out, a stony expression on his face.

'Cancel the babysitter,' he says with resolution. 'I'll look after Barney.'

'But I thought—'

'I said I'll do it.'

'What about—'

'Dana's gone,' he interrupts me again.

'Are you okay?' I ask tentatively.

314

'Oh, I'm fine,' he replies with a slightly menacing undertone. 'Now you go and have a good time with your boyfriend. Although why you'd want to go on a date when your so-called best friend has just come all the way from England . . .'

I sigh. 'Joseph isn't going tonight.'

'Then why did you say—'

'To annoy you.'

His green eyes meet mine for a long moment. He nods briefly, but doesn't smile and I find I haven't got the words to say anything else. It's like he understands, and even though I should deny whatever conclusion he's coming to about me and my feelings for him, I just can't.

He's the one to break eye contact and it makes me feel wretched.

'I've got work to do,' he mutters, and turns towards the studio. I stand there on the spot for a while, silently cursing myself.

Bess is not impressed later when I tell her what happened.

'You should totally have invited Joseph along tonight.'

'No.' I shake my head. 'Johnny's right – three's a crowd.'

'No, it's not,' she scoffs. 'I want to check out this hot kung-fu guy. I assume you're not going to be humping his leg in front of me, or anything like that.'

I laugh. 'No.'

'Then it's not a problem.'

'It's fine. Tonight I think I need some girl time.'

'That suits me, too,' she replies. 'But for God's sake, put Johnny out of your mind. He's bad for you.'

I know she's right, but tonight I can't. He's all I can think about. Bess enjoys every minute of the Saldo Sorvie gig, and while I dance along like everyone else in the crowd, all I can think about is Johnny's eyes, while my heart flips over and over and over. He's consuming me again, but, if he's finished with Dana, that no longer seems like such a bad thing.

I don't want to go to the after-show party – I just want to get home to 'my boys' – but I can't do that to Bess, so we go and I pretend to have a good time. I'm a pretty good actress when I need to be. Maybe I could look into that as a career?

'Stop pretending to have a good time,' Bess says at eleven o'clock.

Maybe not, re the actress thing.

'I'm not pretending.'

'Yes, you are. You can't fool me.'

Okay, definitely not, re the actress thing.

'Stop thinking about him,' she adds.

'Thinking about who?' Nope, won't work. 'I can't,' I come clean.

'Jesus, you don't even seem miserable about the fact.'

'He's split up with Dana!' I point out, my eyes wide with excitement.

'You don't know that for sure.' She brings me down to earth with a bump.

'I do.' My tone is resolute. 'I feel like it's over. They're not right for each other. She's a silly cow and she's no good for him.'

'The press seem to think she's The One.'

'Don't believe everything you read.' The phrase trips off my tongue, but Bess devours the tabloids regularly . . . 'Why, what have you heard?' I ask curiously.

She sighs. 'You really should read the papers more.'

'I'd rather you just fill me in, thanks.'

She hesitates before continuing. 'You know the pair of them were snapped looking at rings in San Francisco recently?'

Nausea swamps me. 'That doesn't mean anything,' I reply.

'Maybe not,' she agrees. 'But they looked pretty loved-up to me.'

'Let's not talk about this anymore,' I suddenly decide. 'I think we need another drink.'

But half an hour after that, we call it a night and go home.

The sickness in my stomach is replaced by a jittery feeling as we walk through the front door. I wonder if he's still awake. Should I go to his room to retrieve the monitor? The lights are on low in the living room, but it's deserted. Hang on, the terrace doors are open. I turn back to look at Bess.

'Night, night, then.'

'Meg . . .' It's that warning tone again.

'Please,' I beg. I don't want her to make this harder for me. I can't stay away from him. Not now. Not ever.

She gives me a sad look and heads up the stairs. I watch after her, waiting until she's in her room before I walk to the terrace doors. It's dark outside, so I look for the light of his cigarette. I can smell smoke, so he's out here somewhere, but I can't see anything. And then I hear her. I freeze on the spot as my eyes adjust to the darkness. I stare in the direction of the tiny gasps which are punctuated by low grunts, and then I see Dana, her naked back visible in the moonlight as she rocks on top of Johnny on a sunlounger beside the pool.

Bile rises up in my throat. I turn and flee into the house, my heart pounding. I run up the stairs, thankful only that she had her back to me as she screwed the one-time love of my life, and then I hide in the safety of my bedroom. I stand against the door, breathing heavily, hot tears in my eyes, and finally my pulse calms down and I remember my son. I angrily brush away my tears, knowing full well that my anger is directed at myself as much as at Johnny and that stupid cow out there, and then I walk out of my bedroom and down the landing to Barney's room. I go inside. He's sleeping peacefully, his low murmur audible only to me. I reach down and push his hair away from his face and then bend down to kiss his brow. The tears return, only this time they're full of sorrow. I straighten up as a shadow is cast across the doorway. I spin around and my heart stops when I see Johnny standing there. I compose myself and go to the door. He steps aside to let me through and then I close it behind me and turn to face him.

'I heard something on the monitor,' he explains, not meeting my eyes as he hands it over.

I stare at his face as I take it from him. Is he going to tell me she's back?

No need. I hear the terrace door sliding shut. Johnny finally meets my eyes and I don't know what it is I see in them as Dana's footsteps sound on the stairs. She appears behind him and he looks away again, but not at her.

'Can we go to bed now the Baby Whisperer is home?' she drawls into his ear. I can't even be bothered to look at her.

'I'll be there in a minute,' he replies in a gruff voice, staring at the wall.

She turns and walks away. 'Don't keep me waiting long, baby. You've got to finish what you started.' She giggles and pushes open his door. He looks at me again.

'Nice,' I say quietly and sarcastically. I give him a look of contempt and then head along the landing to my bedroom.

'Hey,' he whispers after me. I don't wait to hear what he has to say before going into my bedroom and firmly shutting the door.

Chapter 38

'Take your bloody time,' Joseph jokes. 'I didn't think you were ever going to call.'

I didn't want to. Bess made me. She said I had to get back on the horse, which was funny because those were the exact same words that Kitty used.

'Sorry, it's been a busy few days. Listen, I wondered if you'd fancy coming to a Halloween party on Saturday night? It's being held by Sylvester Middleman – I don't know if you know him?'

'I know *of* him. How did you get an invite to that?' He sounds impressed.

'Barney's dad is kind of well connected.'

'Aah, I see,' he replies, thankfully not asking who Barney's dad actually is. 'Do you have a spare ticket?'

'I'm pretty sure I could get one.' And I don't give a crap if Johnny is annoyed about it.

'Cool, well, don't put yourself out.'

'Oh, it won't be any trouble at all,' I tell him.

With Dana back on the scene and clearly keen to make

her mark on the matter, Bess and I spend more time out of the house and keeping busy so the weekend comes around quicker than expected. On Friday we go fancy-dress shopping, and after much hilarious deliberation, Bess opts to go dressed as Minnie Mouse, and somehow or other she manages to talk me into wearing a slinky black cat suit so I'm going as a cat. Barney, we're dressing as a pumpkin because it's the only costume he doesn't immediately try to take off. We're sitting in the kitchen having a laugh with Eddie, when Johnny saunters in. Our easy conversation halts, as it tends to do in his presence.

'You still here?' he asks Eddie.

'I'm just finishing up,' Eddie replies.

'Any plans for the weekend?' asks Johnny.

'Nope. Just hearing about Bess and Meg's fancy-dress costumes. Sounds like it's going to be a blast.'

'What's going to be a blast?' Dana asks with fake enthusiasm as she bounds into the room.

'Halloween,' Johnny replies shortly as she kisses him on his cheek and throws her arm around his neck. She's clearly in an annoyingly good mood.

'Fuck me, I forgot it was Halloween! What are we doing?'

'Hey,' he warns softly, glancing at Barney and me.

She clamps her hand over her mouth and looks at me. 'Sorry, Maria!'

'Maria?' I ask, unamused.

'The nanny from *The Sound of Music*,' she replies with a shrug.

'Can you stop calling me names?' I ask with irritation.

She just laughs. 'Shit, you should totally go dressed as a nun. I bet you'd look great in a habit.'

321

'Oh, bugger off,' I mutter.

'Meg.' Johnny frowns, glancing at Barney as if I'm the one who's being out of line.

'Are you taking the piss?' I'm about to lose it, and my son being in the vicinity isn't going to change that.

Bess gets up and goes to take Barney, but I stop her.

'Forget it,' I say calmly.

'So, anyway,' Dana moves on brightly. 'Who's doing what for Halloween?' She glances at each of us, but neither Bess nor I speak. 'Johnny? We gotta do something to celebrate our first Halloween together . . .'

'Are you going to Sylvester's do?' he asks me.

'Mmm,' I nod, non-committally.

'Sylvester?' Dana asks. 'As in Middleman?'

Johnny nods.

'Shit, we should totally go to that! Everyone will be there.'

'Really?' Johnny asks her with surprise. 'You want to do Halloween?'

'Hell, yeah!'

My heart continues its descent into the pit of my stomach.

'Hey, you should come, too!' she says to Eddie. 'Staff party!' She laughs.

'Sure, Lena will be able to sort you out with another ticket,' Johnny says.

'Lena's left for the weekend,' I point out, then, like the martyr I am, add: 'I'll do it.'

'This is going to be awesome!' Dana enthuses, ruffling Barney's hair. 'What are you going dressed as, buddy?'

My skin prickles with annoyance. Buddy? That's what Johnny calls him, not her.

She looks at me, expecting me to reply. 'A pumpkin,' I answer shortly.

She snorts. 'A pumpkin? Does that mean you're going as Cinderella?' She embarks on a giggling fit. Bess raises one eyebrow at me.

'What's Joseph going dressed as?' Bess asks me. Johnny's eyes dart towards mine.

'Who's Joseph?' Dana chips in, conveniently forgetting the other day on the terrace when he called me.

'Meg's hot new martial-arts-trained boyfriend,' Bess explains.

He's hardly my boyfriend, but I don't think I'll bother correcting her.

'Is he coming?' Johnny asks me quietly.

'Yep,' I reply bluntly. 'Right, I'll go and RSVP for the lot of us.'

I feel his eyes on my back as I walk out of the room.

Because there are children involved, the party starts at four o'clock on Saturday, but that's too early for Dana and Johnny, so Bess, Eddie, Barney and I travel there together. The party is being held at Sylvester's enormous mansion on Mulholland Drive. We offered to go on a detour to pick up Joseph, but he's hitching a ride with a couple of actor friends who are going. He's already waiting out at the front when Davey pulls up, paparazzi flashbulbs going off all around us as celebrities and industry insiders exit their limos.

'There he is,' I say with a smile.

'Which one?' Bess asks, leaning forward.

'The guy in the Karate Kid costume.'

She bursts out laughing. 'That's funny.' Then her laughs die. 'Oh my God, Meg, he's *gorgeous*!'

'Hey!' Eddie smacks her on her thigh. 'Give a guy a complex, why don't you?'

I just smile wider.

'Hello!' I exclaim, climbing from the car and almost forgetting to bring my tail with me.

He sucks the air in through his teeth. 'Look at you,' he says.

'Meow,' I reply, but can't say it sexily so I start laughing instead.

It's probably the stress, but somehow or other I've managed to keep the figure I obtained from walking up the hills in Cucugnan, so my skin-tight costume doesn't look too bad – it helps that I'm wearing high-heeled boots. I've tied my blonde hair up into a high, tight ponytail, which goes strangely well with my velvet black cat ears, and my eye make-up is dark grey and glittery. I'm wearing a slick of pink lipgloss and a touch of peachy blusher.

I turn around to take Barney from Bess, hooking my long cat tail over my arm. I briefly admire my fingernails, painted dark cherry red – Bess and I went for a manicure earlier and I'm wearing black finger-less gloves to show them off.

'Cute,' Joseph says with a smile at Barney the Pumpkin, before his eyes fall on Bess.

'This is my friend, Bess,' I introduce them.

'Hi!' she says with a cheeky grin. Behind us, Batman climbs out of the car.

'This is Eddie,' I explain to my perplexed date.

'Are you . . .' Joseph glances at Eddie.

'No, he's not Barney's dad,' I reply quickly. 'Although . . .' I hesitate before answering truthfully. 'He is supposed to be coming later.'

Bess gives me a wary look. Can I trust Joseph? I don't think I have a choice. But for now, my news can wait.

I turn to the others. 'Shall we go in?'

It's not dark yet, but everywhere we look there are candles burning – inside dozens of carved pumpkins lining the winding footpaths, hanging from the olive trees, floating in the enormous swimming pool. I think about the army of staff members it will take to keep them burning as the night wears on; but when darkness hits, it will be breathtaking. The inside of the house has been decorated with fake spider webs and giant sparkly spiders and there are glass bowls full of Halloween-themed sweets on practically every surface. I'm in my element as I grab two jelly snakes and hand one to Barney. Everyone here is dressed in the most extravagant costumes – I dread to think how much they cost. Someone actually *has* come as Cinderella, with her blonde hair up in a bun and a diamond tiara to finish off the most spectacular, glittering, silver and white meringue I've ever seen. I'm actually quite jealous, if I'm honest. My cat costume is looking meagre in comparison.

'Did you see that witch?' Bess asks me with amazement.

'No, where?'

'She's gone into the other room. Seriously impressive warts and I swear she must've had a professional make-up artist construct her nose and the hairs on her chin.'

'She probably did.'

'I feel like a right tit in my Minnie Mouse get-up.'

I laugh. 'Don't be ridiculous, it's not a competition.'

'Actually, it is,' Eddie points out. We follow the direction of his gaze to a poster on the wall. 'Winner and runners-up announced at nine o'clock.'

'Bummer,' I say. 'Oh, well, hopefully no one will notice us if we hide away in a corner and snaffle the canapés as they come out of the kitchen.'

'Did I just hear someone say canapés?'

I spin around with a huge grin on my face as a sexy red devil comes over to give me a great big hug.

'Bess, this is Kitty,' I introduce them. Kitty told me earlier on in the week that she and her boss were coming to this do. It feels like the whole of Hollywood is here.

'I swear I just saw Brad Pitt!' Bess suddenly squeals.

I shake my head. 'Nah, he won't be here.'

'He looked just like him!' She's convinced.

'He and Ange might bring the kids,' Kitty muses.

'I'm on serious celeb-watch in any case,' Bess tells us.

'You'll do well to spot anyone with their costumes on,' Kitty points out. 'Hello, Joseph,' she adds with a smile.

'Hey,' he replies. She turns to give Batman an inquisitive look.

'Oh, sorry,' I come to my senses. 'Kitty, this is Eddie.'

'Hi, Eddie.'

He lifts up his face mask and shakes her hand.

She narrows her eyes. 'You look familiar.'

'Oh,' he shrugs modestly as he puts his mask back on. 'You might've seen me on morning TV.'

'You're a chef!' she exclaims. 'Yes, I have seen you! So you're working for Johnny, then?' She puts two and two together.

'That's right,' he nods.

'Who's Johnny?' Joseph asks.

'Johnny Jefferson,' I reply, glancing at him to gauge his reaction.

'Oh, right. Eddie works for him?' He looks interested, but not overawed, which I'm pleased about.

'Sure does.' Tell him about Barney. 'Shall we get a drink?' Nope. Maybe later.

I see Dana before I see Johnny. It's hard not to because she's lit up like a frigging Christmas tree.

'An angel,' Bess says wryly.

'Can you believe it?' I reply.

She's wearing a cascade of white silk and her wings and halo are actually glowing from within. It's an impressive costume, I'll give her that much.

People turn to stare, which is exactly the reaction she was seeking, but when the room suddenly falls silent before the noise pipes back up again, I'm pretty certain it's because Johnny has arrived. Is he really here already? It's only seven o'clock. I crane my neck to look for him before I reel myself back in. I don't want to look like I care. I realise everyone else in the room is probably doing the same thing.

'Your boss is here,' Joseph says to Eddie.

'Yeah,' Eddie replies, glancing at me with a strange expression on his face. He clearly thinks I should tell Joseph the truth.

I spy Johnny behind Dana and he nods at me briefly before turning to greet someone else.

'Do you know him, too?' Joseph asks me.

'He's Barney's father,' I reply, turning to look at him.

'No shit,' he murmurs, dragging his eyes away from Johnny. 'You managed to keep that well hidden from the press – and from me,' he adds quietly.

'I'm telling you now,' I say.

'I'll keep your secret safe,' he replies seriously.

'Thank you,' I mouth, just as Johnny interrupts us.

'Eddie,' he says, shaking Eddie's hand. 'Kitty.' He leans down to give her a kiss on her cheek and then does the same to Bess. Both blush furiously. Even though Kitty works in showbiz, Johnny is on another level of fame to most, so even she feels daunted by him. He nods at me and then sweeps Barney up in his arms. For a split second the room falls silent again and my heart momentarily clenches with fear. What is he doing? Johnny Jefferson is hardly known to be kiddie-friendly – so why would he do that? He turns to look at Joseph.

'Johnny, meet Joseph. Joseph, Johnny.'

Johnny nods, but doesn't shake his hand because he's carrying Barney. Or perhaps that's *why* he's carrying Barney – very tactical.

'Hello.' Dana beams at Joseph as she steps forward. 'I like your costume.' She giggles.

'Not very inventive,' he replies. 'Yours is pretty impressive.'

'I was being ironic,' she points out smugly, as if everyone in this room isn't already aware of that fact.

'I gathered that,' Joseph replies with an easy grin.

'I think she looks like a glow-worm,' Bess mutters in my ear and I stifle a snort.

Johnny's gaze hardens.

'What did you come as?' I ask him innocently.

'I don't do fancy dress,' he replies bluntly.

'No, really? I was being sarcastic.' I nod at Barney in his arms. 'Is that such a good idea?'

Johnny shrugs and puts him down on the floor. Barney turns around to face Johnny and jumps up and down on the spot, desperate to be picked up again. A few people in the vicinity look amused. I lift up Barney myself, hoping to dispel the attention, but then I realise it might look even odder to the strangers here. What's Johnny doing carrying my son? Who am I? It occurs to me that some people might actually recognise me – I did use to work as his PA, after all. The bad feeling inside me grows stronger.

'Let's go to the bar,' Johnny says to Dana.

'Christ, I didn't think those words were ever going to come,' she replies with relief, before following him without a backward glance.

'Alright?' Joseph asks me, sensing my trepidation.

'Mmm,' I reply, glancing nervously at the other party-goers. 'Do you mind if we go outside?'

'Lead the way.'

I head outside to the rolling gardens overlooking the city lights. It's already dark, but the gardens are lit with fairy lights and hundreds of the aforementioned candles. There's a children's play area inside a giant pumpkin coach and it suddenly clicks.

'Aah!'

'What?' Bess asks me.

'Cinderella must be Sylvester's wife.'

'She is,' Kitty confirms. 'You know Sly's dressed like the Prince?'

'Really? Genius,' I reply. 'What about his kids?'

'Ugly sisters?' Eddie suggests.

'Rats?' Bess pipes up.

'Rats?' Eddie asks, pulling a face.

'Yeah, you know,' Bess explains. 'Doesn't the Fairy Godmother turn mice and rats into horses and footmen or something like that?'

Eddie shrugs and Bess punches his arm. 'Don't you know anything?'

'I know that I need another drink,' he replies with a wink. 'Come with me to the bar?'

'Okay.' Off they head.

'I'd better check on the Rodster,' Kitty tells us, making an obvious exit for our benefit. God knows why – my seventeen-month-old son is right there so we're hardly going to copulate in the bushes.

I wander over to a bench and sit down so I can keep an eye on Barney in the pumpkin. A pumpkin in a pumpkin. I wonder if that's doing anyone else's head in.

'Heels again,' Joseph points out with a grin.

I smile back at him. 'How was your audition?'

'Pretty good, I think. Hard to tell, though. So much bullshit in Hollywood.'

'You had a bit of a West Country twang, then.'

'Really? I spent some time there as a kid,' he explains.

'Did you? Which part?'

'Er, Dorset, mainly.'

'I used to go to Somerset when my ex-boyfriend lived there.'

'Is that right?'

'It's beautiful,' I comment.

'I haven't been back for a long time.'

'You lived in London, right?'

'I did, but I'm pretty settled here now. At least for the time being. We'll see if it gets me anywhere.'

'Have you always wanted to be an actor?' I ask.

'Hell, no.' He laughs. 'I kind of got into it by accident.'

'Really? How?'

'A film crew came in to do a documentary about kick-boxing. The director saw – I don't know,' he looks a little awkward, 'something in me and cast me as a small part in a British film.'

'I thought you were trained in kung fu?'

'I am, now. But I started off as a kick-boxer.'

'Cool.'

He laughs. 'What about you? How did you end up with a . . . rock star?' he asks in a funny voice.

'I used to be his PA.'

'Aah,' he replies ominously. The whole business suddenly feels sordid.

'It was complicated,' I try to explain.

'These things usually are. It makes you wonder how many other illegitimate children of celebrities there are around the world.'

That uneasy feeling again.

'I think Barney is Johnny's only child,' I tell him. Why would anyone else keep it a secret? I had my reasons for staying quiet. Then again, I guess I'm not the only girl to cheat on her boyfriend . . . I bet plenty of Johnny's groupies were in relationships when they slept with him. What a horrid thought.

'Cheer up,' Joseph says brightly, patting my leg.

'Yeah, let's change the subject,' I reply, screwing up my nose. 'You don't have a girlfriend, do you?'

331

He laughs. 'I wouldn't be here with you if I did.'

I smile at him, embarrassed. 'Okay, so that was a silly question,' I admit. 'But seriously, why not? How can someone who looks like you be single?'

He laughs again. 'I thought we were changing the subject? We don't really want talk about our exes, do we?'

'No, maybe not.' Definitely not. Christian comes to my mind and I realise how much he would have loved this party with all its bowls of sweets.

A wail comes from the pumpkin coach.

'Barney,' I tell Joseph as I hurry over to my son. He's on the floor and has clearly fallen over or been pushed, but his sobs seem like a pretty big overreaction.

'He's tired,' I say when I return to the bench. Barney snuggles into my chest and I pray silently that he's not snotting on my outfit. Black is the worst colour to wear when you have kids – I should have worn white. But then I would have looked like Dana. I scan the crowd. Where's everyone else we know? It's a big place, so even though she's lit up like a beacon, I can't see Dana anywhere. An image of her screwing Johnny the other night pierces my mind. I try to blot it out, without any joy. I glance at Joseph.

'We should go on a proper date,' I say suddenly. 'Without . . .' I glance down at Barney.

'That'd be nice,' he replies. 'How long is Bess sticking around?'

'Two weeks, but it might be longer. She's got nothing to rush back to the UK for.' I tell him about her job. 'She won't mind me going out one night, though. In fact, she'd probably offer to babysit.'

'Sorry,' he says with a frown. 'I know we were changing the subject and everything, but doesn't Johnny babysit?'

I smile wryly. 'Not really. He did the other night, but Dana turned up and I don't want her anywhere near Barney.' My tone sounds venomous and I can't help it.

Joseph raises his eyebrows. 'Not keen, hey?'

'Nope.' I look down at the ground.

Suddenly Bess pushes through the crowd. She looks anxious.

'What's wrong?' I sit up in my seat.

She glances at Joseph and obviously feels awkward.

'Refill?' he asks me tactfully.

I hand him my glass. 'Yes, please.'

He gives Bess a concerned look before walking away.

'What is it?'

'*I just snogged Eddie!*' she bleats.

'Really?' My face breaks into the hugest grin. 'That's good, isn't it?'

'No, no, no, it's terrible,' she says mournfully. 'I was flirting with him, you know, as you do, because he's quite hot, and then I . . . I forced him into it, Meg! It was awful. He didn't want to snog me! I *made* him do it!'

I scoff. 'You can't make someone snog you, Bess.'

'Yes, I can. I just bloody did!' she erupts before looking apologetically at Barney. 'Can we leave?' she pleads. 'Well, no, you can stay, but can I leave? I'll take Barney home; he looks exhausted.'

'Don't leave,' I try to convince her, but she's having none of it, and while I definitely want her to stay, I'll have to leave within an hour myself, before Barney hits meltdown. The thought of being here with Joseph . . .

'Are you sure?' I ask her.

'Yes, please.' She nods her head fervently.

'Okay. I'll call Davey.'

Joseph returns before Bess and Barney leave. 'I got you one, too,' he tells her, handing over a glass of orange punch.

'Thanks, but I'm off,' she replies.

'You're leaving?' he asks with surprise.

'Going to take Barney home.'

He glances at me.

'I'm staying,' I tell him with a small shrug. 'I'll walk Bess out,' I add. 'Meet you at the bar.'

'Don't worry about Eddie,' I tell Bess at the kerbside. 'It's just a drunken snog; there's no harm in it.'

'If you see him, tell him I apologise.'

'I'll tell him no such thing,' I reply hotly. 'Why should you apologise for kissing someone? He's a lucky git, if you ask me.'

She smiles a small smile. 'See you in the morning.' She gives me a sly grin. 'Or maybe not,' she whispers.

My face heats up.

'Seriously,' she adds. 'Don't rush home. Get back on—'

'Do not mention the hoofed animal again,' I interrupt.

'Whatever.' She laughs and climbs into the limo. Barney is already fast asleep in his car seat.

'Call me if you need me.' I nod at Barney. 'I'll come straight home.'

'We'll be fine,' she assures me. 'Have fun!'

That's exactly my intention . . .

334

Chapter 39

I feel nervy as I walk back through the crowded mansion in search of the Karate Kid. I find him at the bar, chatting to a beautiful blonde princess, and my heart sinks, but he turns and smiles and introduces us.

'Meg, this is Penny. She shares the same agent as me,' he explains.

'Hi,' I say. 'Are you an actress?'

'And a waitress,' she replies with a grin. 'Gotta make a living somehow, right?' She smiles at Joseph and gives him a meaningful look. 'I'll leave you to it.'

'Nice to meet you,' I say to her departing back. I turn back to Joseph and take a sip of my drink. I have no idea what's in this tasty orange punch, but it's making me feel warm and tipsy, so it's doing something right.

I lean up against the bar and look at him, in his white cotton outfit with a bandanna tied around his forehead. I can't help but smile. 'You know, you do look remarkably like Ralph . . . what's his name? Macho or something.'

'Macchio,' he replies with a grin. 'I hope my hair is better than his.'

'Oh, it is,' I assure him. 'And your muscles are an improvement, too.' Unable to help myself, and certainly aided by that cheeky little punch, I reach over and squeeze one of his biceps. He flexes it for a joke before laughing.

'Whoa,' I say, removing my hand and not for the first time wondering what his chest looks like. I have a mad urge to slip my hands inside his costume. Down, girl. I take a large gulp of my drink and force myself to look away from his dark eyes, which still manage to twinkle even though they're as black as night.

White light on the other side of the room rouses my attention and I look around to see Dana and Johnny standing there. Johnny is chatting animatedly to a guy I recognise from somewhere or other and Dana has just thrown her head back and laughed, while clutching onto the arm of another man. She buries her face in his shoulder, still laughing. That's a bit flirty, I think to myself. I look at Johnny to see if he's reacting. He's not. He must be used to it. Maybe that's why he likes her: she's not clingy. That's one way of putting it, in any case.

I glance back at Joseph. He's watching me intently.

Glow White starts to move so I turn to see Dana as she's led, laughing, out of the room. More people begin to follow.

'What's going on?' I ask Joseph.

'I don't know.'

'Fancy-dress time!' someone shouts behind us.

'The competition,' I say to Joseph.

'Shall we go and see?' he asks.

'Sure.'

He leads the way, and because I'm walking so closely behind Joseph, I don't see the person who grabs my hand and turns me round until I'm face to face with him.

'Where's Barney?' Johnny demands to know.

I turn to call after Joseph, but he's already left the room.

'He'll wait for you outside,' Johnny tells me firmly. 'Where's Barney?'

'Bess took him home,' I reply, removing my hand from his grip. He hooks his thumbs through his belt loops and regards me unhappily.

'How can you have a problem with that?' I ask him with annoyance.

He shrugs and turns his back on me. I hurry after Joseph and for a split second think that I see bitchy Charlie out of the corner of my eye, but when I turn around she's nowhere to be seen. Joseph is craning his head to look back into the room.

'Sorry,' I tell him. 'Let's go.'

He gives me an inquisitive look, but says nothing.

By the time Dana is announced as the winner of the fancy-dress competition, Johnny has joined her in the garden. She squeals with irrational delight and leaps off the platform into his arms. Even he looks taken aback by her actions, but somehow manages to keep his cool. She gives him a passionate kiss on his lips as the crowd whoops and cheers. I feel a warm hand take mine and turn to look into Joseph's dark eyes.

'Let's go for a walk,' he suggests, squeezing my hand briefly before letting it go.

I nod and follow him, my hand now feeling a chill despite the outdoor heating.

'I wonder how many staff it's taken to keep those pumpkin candles burning all night,' he wonders aloud.

'I was thinking the exact same thing when we walked in!' I exclaim.

'Great minds,' he says.

'Can you really do kung fu?' I ask with a smile.

'Yeah.'

'I can't believe I missed your part in the movie.'

He chuckles. 'You didn't miss much.'

'How did you get into martial arts?'

He glances at me and then looks away again. 'I wanted to know how to fight.'

'Why?' I ask with a frown.

He shrugs. 'Something to do.'

I know that's not the real reason, but he's not opening up to me. And why should he? I'm not opening up to him, either. I've barely told him anything about Johnny, and I sure as hell am not going to be mentioning Christian anytime soon. He'd run a mile if he knew what sort of a person I really was – the lies I'm capable of. I suddenly feel deflated. Almost as though sensing my mood, he turns to face me. We're alone. We've left the party-goers back at the mansion and we've wandered along this winding path for some time. There's no one else around – even the pumpkin lanterns have dried up.

I look down at his lips and then back to his eyes. Neither of us says anything for a very long time, and then he's kissing me.

I feel drunk, giddy. His hands are on my waist. I do what I've wanted to do for what seems like forever and slide my hands inside his uniform. Oh my God, he feels so hot and warm and so deliciously toned. I want him. I really, really want him. Everything else has flown far from my mind.

'Come back to mine,' he murmurs into my mouth.

'Yes,' I gasp.

He wrenches my hand away from his chest and leads me along

behind him as we hurry back towards the house, his phone to his ear as he arranges for his friend's car to be waiting.

We reach the mansion and hurry through the rooms. Somewhere along the way I become vaguely aware of Dana's glow, but I don't look back to see if she's accompanied by Johnny. I don't want to see his face. I don't want anyone to ruin this moment.

Out at the front, a vaguely bored paparazzo takes a couple of lazy snaps, but no one's interested in us when there are so many A-listers still inside. Joseph grips my hand hard and my heart is pounding as much from rushing through the house as from the adrenalin of kissing him. His car pulls up and he yanks open the door and climbs in after me. The heat of his hand in mine is scorching, but apart from that he doesn't kiss me or touch me on the journey home to God knows where. I couldn't concentrate on geography right now if my life depended on it. All I can think about is him.

Finally, we're there.

'It's nothing fancy,' Joseph warns as he unlocks the door.

'I won't be looking at the furniture,' I reply and then he's kissing me again and I can barely take in my surroundings as we trip and stumble our way to his bedroom.

'I can't get this bloody knot undone!' I gasp, grappling with his black belt.

'Fuck that,' he says. 'Where's the zip?'

'Here. Mind my tail!' I cry. 'I don't want to pay for the repairs.'

He just laughs and unzips me and the look in his eyes as he grins down at me makes my heart flip. I want to kiss him again. So I do.

I slide his top off and butterflies swarm in my stomach when I see what I've been dying to see ever since I first laid eyes on him at the premiere party. He's beautiful, so beautiful. It's not right that he's not a big-screen star already so other woman can share in his glory.

Oh, God, and he's such a great kisser. I go to take my cat ears off.

'Leave them on,' he says with a grin as he pulls me onto the bed. 'Sex kitten.'

I laugh and lie down on top of him. A split second later I'm underneath him and his lips are on my neck. His hands cup my breasts and then I'm pulling him into me, hot and urgent and utterly desperate to be back on the . . .

Johnny.

Christian.

GO. AWAY.

And then it's just Joseph, Joseph, Joseph . . .

'That was mind-blowing,' I say with a small laugh afterwards. My head is still tingling, and as for the rest of me . . .

'Mmm,' he murmurs, his eyes closed.

I lie there for a while in his warm arms, and I desperately want to stay there, but reality keeps tugging away at me. Finally I shift in his arms and sit up.

'I should go.'

'Really?' His voice is tinged with disappointment.

'Barney,' I explain. 'I don't want him to wake up without me.'

He nods and sits up himself. I look around for my cat costume.

'I'm going to feel like a right tit going home in this,' I say.

He laughs. 'Do you want one of my shirts?'

'No, you're alright. At least it's still dark.'

I smile at him and he raises one eyebrow at me sexily before pulling me back down again. We kiss, long and languidly.

'Don't, you're making me feel drunk again,' I say.

'Without the hangover,' he replies.

'That's true.'

More kissing. I pull away and stare down at him.

'Did you use to have your eyebrow pierced?' I ask. I can just make out two tiny holes there.

'Yeah,' he replies. 'A long, long time ago.'

'Can't have been that long,' I reply.

'Feels like forever to me.'

'Back when you had a West Country accent and wanted to know how to fight,' I say with a smile, but his has faltered somehow.

He kisses me perfunctorily on the nose and goes to sit up again. Something has changed in him, but I don't know what.

'I'll call you a cab.'

'Don't worry, I'll ring Davey.'

'Are you sure?'

'Yes. You'd better tell me your address, though. I wasn't exactly paying attention in the car.'

He makes me tea while I wait for Davey. He lives in an apartment block with two other wannabe actors. It's a bit of a tip.

'Where are your flatmates?' I ask him.

'Out and about. Networking, probably,' he replies.

'You don't seem to do much of that.' I try to ignore his naked torso – he's wearing black PJ bottoms and nothing else.

'No.' He grins. 'Not as much as my agent would like me to. It's not really my thing.'

'Yet here you are, wanting to be an actor.'

'I'm not that desperate.'

I smile and stare at him for a long moment.

'You're going to be huge one day.'

He raises one eyebrow at me. 'Is that right, Mystic Meg?'

I crack up laughing. 'Oh my God, do you remember her from the National Lottery?'

'Yeah, I do. Did she ever predict the winner correctly?'

'I have no idea.'

My phone buzzes. Davey is here.

'Gotta go,' I say and stand up. 'Thanks for having me.'

'It was my absolute pleasure,' he replies with a cheeky twinkle in his eye. 'Thanks for having me.'

I laugh. 'Oh, that was a pleasure also.' I place my hands on his beautiful chest one more time, just for luck and all that.

He kisses me softly on the lips.

'You can go back to bed now,' I say.

'I'll call you,' he replies, but I recognise something in his eyes – a sadness. As I walk out through the door I wonder who it was that hurt him.

Soon my thoughts gravitate towards Johnny and Christian, and my earlier euphoria dissolves into dust.

Chapter 40

'What the—' I murmur out loud. 'What's going on?' I ask Davey with alarm.

We've pulled through the gates to Johnny's house and now I see that the whole driveway is lined with cars.

'I think the boss is having a house party,' he replies chirpily. 'I thought you knew?'

The hell I did. I can hear the music pounding before I even climb out of the limo. It's almost one o'clock in the morning. I hope Barney is alright.

'Thanks, Davey.'

'Will you be needing me again tonight?' he asks.

'No, no. Sorry I called you out again,' I say apologetically. I should have rung for an ordinary taxi – I don't know what I was thinking.

'Of course, it's no problem if you do,' he says graciously.

'I'm pretty sure we'll be in for the night, now,' I tell him unhappily, looking at the house. It's practically vibrating with the noise. I must check on Barney.

I hurry to the front door and get there seconds before a group of

Goths. No, hang on, they're vampires. I recognise a couple of them from Sylvester Middleman's Halloween party. What are they doing here? I hurry through the door and see Dana almost immediately, standing a few feet away with a couple of guys. One of them turns around and laughs while pointing at someone behind me.

'Look what the cat dragged in!' he shouts gleefully. I turn to see who he's pointing at.

'Fuck off, Derek,' a vampire guy jokes, giving him the finger.

'That's fucking HILARIOUS!' Dana screams, hooting loudly. *'Look what the cat dragged in!'* she repeats the joke, pointing at me and almost crying with laughter. Is she on something? It wasn't that funny.

'You've lost your ears,' she says suddenly, looking at me with odd surprise. She wobbles slightly and one of her companions holds her up. I feel sick as I notice her pupils are dilated.

'Where's Johnny?' I demand to know.

'WHEEERRRREEEE'S JOHNNY?' Derek shouts to much hilarity. They're all off their faces. I turn and look around, wildly scanning the room for him. I see with disgust that a blond-haired knight in shining armour is snorting a line of coke off the coffee table, but Johnny is nowhere to be seen.

Barney.

I run up the stairs, bumping into you know who at the top.

'JOHNNY!' I shout.

'Nutmeg!' he cries with unbridled delight, trying to put his arms around me. I push him away.

'Where's Barney?'

His face falls. 'I thought he was with you?'

I feel sick, horribly sick. I shove him out of the way and run to Barney's bedroom, pushing down the handle. It doesn't budge.

I urgently knock at the door, dread filling every part of me. The door opens and a grave-faced Bess is standing there with Barney in her arms.

'Oh, thank God,' I say, hurrying inside and shutting the door behind me.

'Mummy,' Barney says sleepily, reaching out for me. I take him and cuddle him into me.

'What's going on?' I ask Bess.

She shrugs. 'I don't know. They all appeared out of nowhere. Barney woke up with the noise so I came in to settle him, but he wasn't going to go off again with that racket.'

'No, of course not,' I reply.

'I locked the door so they wouldn't come in.' She shivers.

'Why has he invited this lot back here?'

She doesn't respond. Someone pounds on the door.

'NUTMEG!'

'It's Johnny,' I say. 'Ignore him.'

But the pounding doesn't stop. I hand Barney back to Bess and she takes him to the other side of the room, making shushing noises. I open the door a crack.

'*What are you doing?*' I screech in a loud whisper at Johnny.

'Why didn't you let me in?' he demands to know, pushing the door wide open and sauntering in. He's had way too much alcohol – and God knows what else.

'I didn't want you to disturb Barney!' I exclaim.

'Aah, Barney!' he says happily.

'Stop it!' I shove him out of the room and follow after him. 'Go away!' I whisper angrily once we're on the landing. A few revellers at the top of the stairs turn to look at us. I drag Johnny down the corridor.

'Whoa, whoa, whoa,' he says with a grin as I push him inside my bedroom. 'Nutmeg, I didn't think you cared.'

'Fuck off, Johnny!' I snap. 'What the hell are you doing inviting all these people over? There's someone snorting coke off the coffee table! Dana's off her face – so are you – and YOUR SON is in the house!' I'm practically screaming the last part.

'Oh . . .' Something dawns on him in the way that things do when you've drunk your own body weight in booze. 'Sly broke his foot.'

'What?'

'Sly.'

'Sylvester, yes?'

'Broke his foot. Fell down the stairs. Party got called off.'

'So you invited everyone here?' I ask with disbelief.

He shrugs. 'Dana did.'

'That's totally inappropriate!' I cry.

'No stopping her,' he says cheerfully. 'How long have you been back? I thought I saw you leaving with whatshisname.'

'Joseph. I did leave with him. I've just got back now.'

'Aah,' he says knowingly, leaning up against the wall and folding his arms. 'Good shag, was he?'

'None of your bloody business,' I reply hotly, wrenching open the door and shoving him out.

'Don't be cross with me, Nutmeg,' he laments.

I slam the door in his face and wait a minute before hurrying back to Barney's room.

It's a long night. We decamp to my bedroom because the noise seems more manageable somehow and the bed is big enough for the three of us. Barney does eventually doze off, with me covering one ear with my hand, but he's awake again and ready for breakfast well before the last person has left. Luckily I have a small kitchen in my room, so none of us has to venture outside yet. Bess didn't have much sleep either, going by the bags under her eyes. As for me, I've still got all my make-up on and probably look like someone has punched me in the face. At least I managed to get out of my cat costume and into my PJs.

'What a night,' Bess murmurs.

'What a nightmare, you mean,' I reply.

She nods. 'He really was wasted, wasn't he?'

'That was nothing. You should have seen him when we went on tour.'

She sighs and looks at me sadly.

'What are you thinking?' I ask after a while because the curiosity is killing me, even though I'm no longer a cat.

'He really is a shit, isn't he?'

'Yep,' I reply, deflated.

'You know, I kind of thought . . . I don't know.'

'What?' I press.

'I thought there might have been a happy ending in it for you two—'

'Fat chance,' I interrupt angrily. Then I'm the one who's sighing. 'I don't know what I'm doing here, Bess.' She keeps staring at me sadly. 'I don't know what I'm doing with my life. What have I achieved? Nothing. I'm nothing.'

'That's not true,' she butts in, nodding pointedly at Barney. 'You've achieved more than me.'

I shake my head, hopelessly.

'How was last night?' she asks, changing the subject.

'Good,' I reply, and can't help smirking.

347

'Was he?' she asks with a cheeky grin.

'Was he what?'

'Good?'

I giggle. 'Just a bit.'

'Are you going to see him again?'

'I hope so!'

We doze off again after breakfast, but after a while I get up and get ready. I ask Bess to stay with Barney in my room while I go downstairs into the unknown. I wouldn't like to say it's worse than I imagined – because what I imagined was pretty damn horrendous – but it certainly comes close. It reeks of alcohol, smoke and vomit. I can see from my view up here on the landing that there's broken glass in at least three different places, and I dread to think of the cocaine dust on the coffee table and God know what – and where – else. I can't see any people so hopefully they've all gone home, although I haven't been outside yet. And right now, I don't intend to.

I return to my room and call Sandy, Johnny's maid. She says she'll organise a team of professional cleaners.

'They've been here before; they know what they're doing,' she reveals.

'Have they been here before?' I ask. Johnny never had house parties like this when I worked for him.

'Three times since March,' she says pointedly.

That was when Johnny met Dana. Another non-fan of the girlfriend . . .

The cleaners arrive within the hour. We stay upstairs and out of sight, but my anger has been steadily brewing since last night

348

– and especially since Sandy's revelation. I'm trying to keep a lid on it, but finally I can stand it no longer.

'Are you alright here?' I ask Bess, who's watching a DVD with Barney on the flatscreen in my bedroom.

'Where are you going?' she asks.

'I have to speak to him.'

She nods, her face serious. 'Take your time.'

I go to his bedroom door and knock loudly. No answer, as I expected. I pound harder and harder, until eventually I give up and try the door. It's not locked.

The stench I smelled earlier – smoke, booze, vomit – has started to evaporate from the rest of the house, thanks to the cleaners and fresh air, but now it oozes out of the room. Dread replaces some of the anger as I suddenly wonder what I might find inside. I take each step with trepidation until I round the corner and the bed comes into view. Dana is lying naked on her back and sprawled across the bed diagonally. There's a pool of vomit on the floor beside her, but she is breathing. I feel sickened at the sight; but as for Johnny, he's nowhere to be seen. I try the en-suite door – it's locked. I pound on the door and call his name, but there's no answer.

'What the fuck?' Dana calls groggily from the bed.

'Is Johnny in the bathroom?' I shout at her. She shrugs and collapses backwards, not even bothering to cover up her skinny frame.

I slam my hand on the door in frustration and then look at the lock. He may be a millionaire, but he's still only got one of those locks that can be opened quite easily from this side, with a coin.

'Have you got any coins?' I demand to know from Dana.

349

'What?' she asks. She's totally out of it.

'Damn you!' I erupt. I run from the room to my bedroom and burst inside.

'What? What is it?' Bess asks fearfully.

'Money, I need money,' I say in a tizz. I grab my bag and get out a coin. 'Stay here,' I tell her, running out again.

Dana appears to have fallen back into unconsciousness so I unlock the door, full of nausea and fear. Is this how Rosa felt? My heart jumps as I see him lying in the bath, naked from the waist up.

'Johnny? JOHNNY!' I run to him and feel his pulse. It's there. I shake him roughly. 'Johnny, wake up!'

He moans and I feel like slapping his face – hard – again and again. He half opens his bloodshot eyes.

I sink down on the floor, full of despair tinged with relief. The anger, for now, has diluted.

'What are you doing?' I whisper.

He stares at me, but says nothing. He's still in a drug-fuelled daze.

'Barney is in the house.' Tears fill my eyes. 'We can't stay here.'

He shakes his head, but still words fail to come.

'I'll call the doctor.' I get to my feet.

'Meg . . .' he says in a croaky voice, reaching out his hand to me.

I stare at him sadly for a moment before leaving.

Bess is standing on the landing looking alarmed when I re-emerge.

'He's alive,' I say as I walk towards her. I nod at my bedroom door and we go back inside. 'We'll have to leave,' I tell her.

She says nothing.

'I can't put Barney at risk like this.' And then the anger returns. 'How dare he!' I glance quickly at Barney, who's still engrossed in his DVD, and as I look back at Bess I'm fervently shaking my head, tears in my eyes.

'We could go to a hotel?' she says hopefully. 'Until it all blows over?'

'Yes,' I agree. 'That's a good plan.'

Chapter 41

It's not until Monday morning that it occurs to me that Joseph hasn't called. It's the first time I've thought of him since Saturday night, but before I rouse enough energy to care, something else happens.

'Meg, you must ring me as soon as you can . . .'

I automatically jump to the conclusion that this voicemail message from Lena is to do with Johnny, but I soon find out that it's regarding his son.

'I got wind of it last night,' she informs me. 'I tried to call you, but your phone was switched off and Johnny didn't know which hotel you'd gone to.'

It's what I've always feared. A journalist has found out about Barney and they're breaking it in one of America's biggest tabloids.

'Is there anything we can do?' I ask.

'No. It's already been published.'

'In this morning's paper?' My tone is incredulous.

'Yes. And tomorrow, it will be everywhere . . .'

After I hang up, I stare at Bess, shell-shocked.

'What is it?' she asks.

'The press know about Barney.'

She gasps. 'Barney? I thought that phone conversation was about Johnny!'

'No.' I shake my head, gravely. 'I'm afraid our secret is out.'

We have to go back to the house because it's the only place we'll be safe – for now. But I know I have to come up with a long-term plan, and staying with Johnny and his screwed-up girlfriend is no longer an option.

We took the Panamera when we left yesterday, and I've been thankful because all the paps know Davey's car. However, when we pull around the corner to Johnny's gates, I deeply regret my decision. There must be thirty paparazzi photographers and journalists all camped out there, and we have no protection. Our windows are tinted, but not blacked out.

'Cover Barney's face!' I shout at Bess. She starts to scramble into the back seat. 'No, wait,' I change my mind. That could look even worse. 'Oh, God,' I moan. 'We're just going to have to go in with our heads held high.'

They don't pay too much attention at first, but when they realise that this is the car belonging to Johnny's former lover and his illegitimate lovechild, the pack becomes frenzied.

'Mummy!' Barney wails as bulbs start going off like strobe lights in his face.

I beep my horn to get them to move, but they won't. They pound on the windows, screaming questions and taking photos, until suddenly the gates open and Johnny's security team – which seems to have quadrupled overnight – swarms out and pushes back the crowd so we can slowly move forward into sanctuary.

'Holy shit,' Bess murmurs under her breath.

But I know – God, do I know – that this is just the start of it.

I don't bother to park in the garage, pulling up instead right in front of the door. I clutch Barney to me protectively as we hurry into the house. I'm close to tears because he's distraught and has no idea what's going on or how his life has just changed dramatically. There are people milling about in the living room who I don't even know. I regard them warily, then suddenly Lena appears.

'Meg,' she breathes.

'Who are they?' I ask quietly, stupendously aware of their eyes on me, but particularly on my son.

'People from the record companies, publicists . . .'

'I didn't even know Johnny had a publicist.' He always hated that sort of thing. 'Record companies?' I acknowledge the plural.

'Dana's also. They want to minimise the damage.'

'Or maximise it,' I say under my breath.

She gives me a sympathetic smile and pats my arm. 'It'll be okay.'

I recognise Bill Blakely – Johnny's manager – as he steps away from the crowd and comes over to me.

'Meg Stiles,' he says knowingly in his inimitable cockney accent.

'Hello, Bill.'

We don't see eye to eye. He never forgave me for whisking Johnny off to the Dales on a 'rehab adventure' when he should have been at his end-of-tour party. Loads of important people from the industry and the media had given up their Christmas Eves to be there.

'Didn't think I'd be seeing you again, darlin',' he says.

'Surprise,' I say wryly.

'So this is the little chap?' He looks at Barney.

'It is indeed.' I swivel Barney around to face him.

'Jesus,' he mutters under his breath. 'He does look like him. The pics don't do it justice.'

'Pics? What pics?' I ask with alarm.

'In the paper.'

'There are pictures?'

He looks at me like I'm mad. 'Of course.'

I shake my head manically. 'I haven't seen the piece yet. Excuse me, Bill.'

I hurry over to Lena, waiting a few feet away. She ushers me into the office.

'I'll take Barney,' Bess offers, but I hug him tighter.

'No. Thank you,' I add. 'I want to keep him with me.'

She sinks down onto a chair and looks over my shoulder as Lena passes me the paper.

It's front-page news. A whole front page. The photograph they've used is one of me carrying Barney out of the Halloween party. My heart clenches. He's dressed as a pumpkin, the little soul. We must've been caught in the background of another shot – the resolution is grainy and a touch blurry. I scan the article. They know about me; how I used to work as Johnny's PA. Inside the paper there's another photograph of Johnny and me from when we got snapped at the Ivy one time. There was nothing in it – he just wanted to go out for a bite to eat and it was my job to accompany him – but even I have to admit that we look suspicious, arriving together on his motorcycle. No wonder his girlfriend at the time was angry. Now this journalist is making out that we had a sleazy affair while she was still on the scene. I read on and my nausea triples. I put down the paper and stare up at Lena.

'Our lawyers are on it,' she quickly assures me.

'It's already been printed,' I whisper with horror.

Apparently I'm living here now as Johnny's second wife . . . Dana, him and me, all under the same roof as one big happy, sordid household. The journalist has spun a tale of debauchery – he seems to know all about the drug-fuelled party on Saturday night – but nothing of the facts. Bess has been painted as our live-in nanny, hired to give me more time to devote to my lovers . . .

I nod at Bess. She can take Barney now, because I don't have the strength to hold him. She leaps up and relieves me. Just then, Johnny walks into the room.

'Nice bit of bedtime reading,' he says jauntily, nodding at the paper.

'I don't know how the' – I almost say 'fuck' – '*hell* you can joke about this!'

Bess, thankfully, takes Barney out, which is a huge relief because then Dana appears and there's no way I'll be able to contain my anger now.

'What the hell are YOU still doing here!' I practically scream at her. 'Haven't you caused enough trouble?'

'She couldn't leave now, even if she wanted to,' Johnny drawls.

'I do want to,' she points out.

'Why? Have you got an appointment with your drug dealer that you just can't cancel?' I ask bitterly.

She laughs and it makes me so angry I could slap her. None of this is bothering her at all. She feeds off the drama. I get the feeling that that's what she thrives on in life. Trouble and strife. That's cockney for 'wife', I think distractedly to myself. Is there something in that? Back to the present.

'You're pathetic,' I say through gritted teeth. 'Both of you. One of your fucked-up friends leaked this story—'

'Who's to say it was one of our friends?' Johnny interjects sinisterly. 'What about that Joseph?'

'Yeah, your boyfriend could have spilled the beans,' Dana adds with a sly grin.

My pulse quickens. Really? No. But he hasn't called me . . .

No. He wouldn't. I'm a better judge of character than that.

Aren't I?

The two of them watch me, watch my reaction. My face has given away my doubt and they see this with satisfaction. I remember Charlie and wonder if she might have been to blame. Who knows?

I look back at Johnny, his green eyes challenging mine as Dana smirks.

'You make me sick,' I whisper at him, and a flicker of something passes over his face. Dana laughs, but I ignore her. 'We're leaving,' I tell him resolutely.

'No, you're not,' he replies.

'Oh, yes,' I nod and I suddenly feel very, very calm. 'Yes, we are. And until you sort yourself out and get rid of your fucked-up—'

'Language,' Dana butts in merrily.

'. . . druggie girlfriend,' I continue, while she sucks the air in through her teeth but pretends not to care, 'we'll have nothing more to do with you.'

'You're not going anywhere,' Johnny reiterates, but his conviction is waning.

I raise my eyebrows at him and walk out of the office.

I head upstairs to my room, where Bess is waiting with Barney.

'Your phone has been beeping,' she says, handing me my handbag, which she helpfully carried up along with my son.

I take it from her and pull out my phone. Eleven missed calls, mainly from Mum and Dad, and – oh, hell – there are a couple from Susan.

I never did tell her . . .

Christian. I never told him, either.

I cover my mouth with my hand. 'Can you entertain Barney in his room?' I ask Bess, tears welling up in my eyes.

'Of course,' she replies with concern.

'Thank you,' I call after her. 'I don't know what I would have done without you here.'

'It'll be okay,' she tells me.

But she's wrong. It will never be just okay from now on. Okay is not a word that can be used to describe our lives anymore. Nor is normal, or average, or run-of-the-mill. From now on, our lives will be – and will forevermore be – extraordinary. I'm no longer an ordinary girl and Barney is no longer an ordinary boy.

I get a flashback to being with Johnny in France – him being there for me when it all came crashing down – and for a moment I feel tender towards him. But then my heart reverts to steel. Steel which turns molten when I remember why I asked Bess to leave.

Christian.

I dial his number. And for the first time since he left me, he answers.

'Christian,' I whisper.

Silence.

'Christian?'

'What?' he asks quietly.

'You've seen the news?'

'Bit hard to miss.'

'I'm so sorry.'

He snorts. 'Sorry for what, exactly? Because the list is growing longer, Meg. I'm finding it hard to keep tabs on it.'

He sounds so bitter and twisted. So unlike the man I once loved. Still love. 'My family send you their regards,' he says nastily and I feel even more wretched than I already did.

I swallow. 'What did Vanessa and Anton have?'

'A boy,' he replies; then adds, his voice dripping with sarcasm: 'At last our family has a little boy we can call our own.'

'Please . . .' I beg and then I'm on a roll. 'I tried calling you before. I've tried you time and time again. I wanted to tell you we were coming here. He wanted to get to know Barney – it's not like they've made it out to be in the papers . . . That party on Saturday night, that was Dana's doing. I was sick about it. We took Barney to a hotel on Sunday. I've told Johnny we're leaving. We can't stay here with him if he's going to put Barney at risk like this.'

He says nothing and, for a moment, I wonder if he's even there at all.

'Christian?' I ask.

'I'm here.'

Has his tone softened? I hear him swallow.

'Do you know what?' His volume is low.

'What?' I ask hopefully.

'It would be easier if you were dead.'

He hangs up on me.

I lie on the bed and sob my heart out for what feels like a long time. I have no idea that Johnny has entered the room until he's standing right over me.

'What the hell are you doing, walking in like that? Don't you knock?'

'I don't have to knock in my own house,' he says non-chalantly.

'I hate you!' I hurl the phone at him. Call it an ironic ode to Christian, who did the same thing to me not that long ago.

'Whoa! Calm down.'

'Don't you fucking tell me to calm down! I just spoke to Christian.'

He tenses.

'It's the first time I've managed to speak to him since . . .' My voice trails off. 'He hates me,' I say painfully.

'Even more than you hate me?' he asks drily.

'I don't hate you,' I sniff.

'I know. And Christian doesn't hate you, either,' he says firmly. 'No one could hate you, Meg.'

'Christian does,' I say fervently. 'He definitely does.'

'He doesn't!'

'We're not going to have an argument about this as well, are we? We're going,' I tell him determinedly. He puts his hand up to stop me speaking, but I continue, 'This isn't going to work.'

'Stop,' he says. 'Don't say that. I know Saturday night was fucked up—'

'And Sunday morning . . .'

'And Sunday morning,' he concedes. Finding him in the bath is a memory that won't quickly leave me. 'But it won't happen again.'

'How can you say that?' I stand up. 'How can you ever say that to me, ever again? I've been through this already with you, Johnny! How many more times are you going to—'

'I'll get help,' he interrupts.

'You *got* help! Then you met Dana! Fat lot of good that did both of you!'

'You can't blame her.'

'I don't,' I tell him calmly. 'I blame you.'

I meet his eyes for a long moment before looking away again.

'Stay another week,' he begs quietly.

'No.'

'Just one more week.' His words pick up speed. 'If you still want to leave, I'll arrange it for you. You can have the jet – go anywhere you want to go.' He takes my hand and presses it. 'But you can't go back to a normal life now,' he says gently. 'You'll need security, protection . . . Barney is a kidnap threat.'

Fear grips me once more.

'I'll make sure you and Barney are set up with a house – a safe house,' he adds. 'If you still want to leave after a week . . .'

I stare up at him, and for the first time in what seems like a very long time, I feel like I see him again. He's blurry when he's with her.

'Please, give me another chance to make it right for you here,' he adds.

'What about Dana?' I ask flatly.

'She's leaving.'

'For good?' My eyes widen and my heart quickens.

'No,' he says edgily, and my senses return to dull. 'Just for now. But she'll be out of your way.'

'Okay,' I nod. 'I'll give it a week. But only so we have time to sort out security and everything else. We'll still be leaving at the end of it.'

'If that's how you feel, so be it,' he says bluntly, releasing my hand and taking a step backwards. He stares at me with his piercing green eyes and I feel uneasy. 'As long as we've got a week.'

Chapter 42

Eddie is the last person to leave that night and I breathe a sigh of relief as the house at last falls silent.

'I'll join you in that,' Bess says, exhaling loudly. I suddenly remember something.

'Oh, God! Bess, I forgot about you and Eddie!'

'It's alright,' she brushes me off. 'Small fry compared to what's going on now.'

'No, no, no, it isn't.' I sit up with urgency. 'Have you spoken to him? Did he say anything to you?'

She laughs it off. 'Meg, seriously, it's fine. We don't need to dissect the whole thing. It really is fine. We had a bit of a laugh about it in the kitchen earlier.'

'Did you?' I ask with relief. 'What did he say?'

'Neither of us said anything,' she replies. 'We just gave each other a bit of a look and then laughed. It's done. Over. What about you?'

'What about me?'

'What happened with Johnny earlier?'

I fill her in on the details. 'Aah, that's good.' She sighs, putting

363

her feet up on the coffee table. 'I wasn't ready to swap LA for miserable old London just yet.' I nudge her roughly on her arm and she laughs. 'You know I'm joking. I'll go whenever you want me to.'

'I want you to stay,' I say.

'Really?'

'As long as I'm staying.'

'We'll be out of here in a week, then,' she says.

I nod. 'That's the plan.'

My phone beeps.

'Message from Joseph,' I tell Bess.

'About time! What's he saying?'

'He's asking me if I'm okay.'

'Better call him back. I'll look after Barney,' she tells me, 'you know, seeing as I'm your live-in nanny, and all.'

We smirk at each other and I take my phone upstairs to my bedroom.

'Hey,' he says upon answering.

'Howdy, stranger,' I reply jovially.

Pause. 'Sorry I didn't call you yesterday.'

'Don't worry about it, we were a bit busy doing drugs, having threesomes and drinking each other under the table.'

He chuckles. At least he has the same sense of humour.

'You've read the papers, I presume?'

'Afraid so.'

I sigh. 'It was going to happen, but I didn't think they'd make it out to be quite so tawdry.'

'That's the tabloids for you.'

'You'll have to deal with it, too, when you're a huge Hollywood A-lister.'

He laughs. 'I doubt that very much.'

I don't.

'So,' he says. 'I guess you won't be free for dinner anytime soon?'

'Afraid not. Can I call you when it all blows over?'

'Of course you can.'

I know he's smiling, and as I hang up I smile, too, but mine is tinged with sadness. If I'm honest with myself, I may never see Joseph again – face to face, at least. Not if we're leaving. But I've got enough on my mind without dwelling on that as well. I'll try not to think about it.

I have to wait a few more hours, with the time difference, before I can tackle my European calls, and then it's a question of who first: Mum and Dad or Susan? Urgh. I decide to get my sister out of the way.

'About bloody time!' she squawks before I even have a chance to say hello. 'How do you think I felt reading about THAT in the papers?'

I stifle any retort. She's right: she deserved to know the truth from me. 'Not great, I imagine. I'm sorry, Susan.'

'Yeah, well, thankfully Mum had already told me.'

'What?'

'What did you expect? She said she'd asked you time and time again to fill me in – I'm your sister, Meg – and you didn't.'

True again. I can hardly blame my mum for doing what I should have done myself.

'Alright,' I sigh. 'I'm glad you know the truth. I'd better go and call Mum and Dad.'

'Oh, no, you don't!' she erupts. 'I want to know everything. All of the details. How did you end up with *Johnny Jefferson's* son?'

An image comes to me of her sitting on the edge of her seat, pressing the phone eagerly to her ear. She's such a gossip-monger. But I don't have it in me to even care anymore so I fill her in, skimming over anything I don't want to go into. At the end of it, she's satiated. I hang up with barely enough energy to speak, let alone the strength to talk to my parents, but I know I have no choice. I keep our conversation as short and sweet as they'll allow, but I reassure them that I don't condone Johnny or Dana's behaviour and that I'm going back to England as soon as we can sort everything out. They accept, with worry, that our lives are different now.

'Why don't you come to France?' Dad presses.

'I don't know, Dad,' I reply. 'I'll have to think about it.'

We could go back to France – but staying with my parents? No. It's long, long overdue, but I think it's time I did this on my own.

Chapter 43

True to Johnny's promise, Dana doesn't return to the house over the next few days. Bess and I spend our time watching movies, or, if we're feeling brave, out by the pool, trying to ignore the sound of helicopters persistently buzzing like flies overhead. Sometimes Johnny joins us, and sometimes he takes Barney off to spend some time with him alone.

I've heard Lena and Eddie muttering to each other about the state of things outside the gates. It's hard for all the staff to get in or out with the hordes of paparazzi out there.

The degrading stories about me being Johnny's 'second wife' have kept coming throughout the week. I've stopped reading the papers now, and I've asked my parents to do the same. I know there's no use in asking Susan to comply – she's addicted to the tabloids.

On Friday, Bess and I are sitting out by the pool. It's an unusually warm day for November. I couldn't be bothered to change out of my jeans when I realised how hot it was, but Bess is in her tankini and wearing the largest, darkest pair of shades I think I've ever seen.

'I can't stand this,' I snap, out of the blue.

'What can't you stand?' Bess asks me lazily.

'This! Being stuck here! I feel like I'm marooned!'

She lifts up her sunglasses and gazes at me. 'There are worse places you could be, you know.'

'I know.' I sigh and try to enjoy the sunshine, but I can't. I've got itchy feet.

Johnny comes out to the terrace. 'What's up with you?' he asks me curiously. I've started to hop on the spot.

'Sort her out, Johnny,' Bess says casually.

'What is it?' He frowns.

'I'm *fed up* with being stuck in this goddamn house!' I explode.

He stands and stares at me for a moment. 'So let's get out of here.'

'Ooh, you sounded just like Johnny from *Dirty Dancing*, then!' Bess says gleefully.

Johnny gives her a weird look, not understanding the reference. 'Are you okay looking after Barney for a couple of hours?' he asks her, moving on.

'Sure . . .'

'Come with me.' He grabs my hand.

'Where are we going?'

'Out,' he says shortly.

I glance back at Bess. She raises her eyebrows, smiling.

He drags me all the way around the outside of the house to the garage. I could have shaken his hand off ages ago, but for some strange reason I've let myself be pulled along by him. It felt kind of nice, somehow. A break from the norm. And I'm bored – so bored – of the norm.

He flicks on the lights in the garage and stalks determinedly to the Ducatti. He passes me a helmet and a jacket. I hold them up and look at him with a grin.

'Really?'

'Really,' he says firmly as he shrugs on his biker jacket. He straddles the machine and looks over his shoulder at me. I climb on behind him and then he starts up the engine with a roar and we ride out of the garage. He lifts his hand at his security team up ahead and they open the gates and hold back the crowd with perfect timing. The paps don't know what has hit them. I can barely hear anything over the noise of the engine as we shoot past them and down the winding roads, but I know what a frenzy they'll be in as they scramble into their cars to try to follow us in hot pursuit. They'll never get close. They've got no chance. I hold tighter to Johnny's waist and scream with delight. I can feel his stomach tensing as he laughs.

I have no idea where we're going, but the freedom of this is mind-blowing. Johnny keeps to the hills and out of the city, but after a while we head to the ocean.

'Hungry?' he asks over his shoulder as we approach a petrol station.

'Always room for chocolate,' I reply.

'I should've known you'd say that.'

He pulls in and fills the tank, while I run inside to pick up some snacks and pay. The man behind the desk gives me a funny look and I wonder if he recognises me from all the press this week, but we're out of there and on the road again before he can do anything about it.

Eventually we arrive at a cliff overlooking the ocean. Johnny climbs off and helps me down and for a moment I feel like we've flashbacked to a few years ago when everything was new and exciting and far less complicated. He meets my eyes and I wonder if he's also remembering back then, when I was merely his employee, or even a few months later, when he claimed he was in love with me. But as quickly as it appeared, that look in his eyes has gone again. We walk as close to the cliff edge as we dare and then sit down on the grass, taking off our jackets. I lean back on my elbows and tilt my face up to the sun. Contentment settles over me. Johnny lies down beside me. Neither of us says anything and it's perfect; just what I needed. I rest my head down on the grass. I find myself taking a series of deep breaths and the weight I've been feeling inside seems to lift a little. For a brief moment I remember the lone blonde doing yoga on the hill in Cucugnan. Next to me, Johnny moves and I feel alert again. I open my eyes and turn my head. He's propped up on one elbow, looking down at me. My heart flips.

'Better?' he asks.

'Yes,' I reply, feeling vulnerable and exposed in a strange way.

He reaches over and pushes a strand of hair off my face, doing nothing to alleviate this feeling.

'It's going to be okay,' he says quietly, and for a while I'm lost for words. I just stare back at him until my pulse begins to quicken.

He starts to hum a tune and I muse to myself that if any other guy did this it would seem corny, but that's not a word that could ever be used to describe Johnny.

'What's that?' I ask. 'Something you've been working on?'

'Mmm.'

'Sing it to me?'

'I don't have all the words yet.'

'Hum it to me, then.'

'I am.'

I smile across at him and he winks at me. My heart flips again and for once I don't chastise myself for the feeling. Right now, I just want to be. I'll be back to reality soon enough – I can't be in danger of losing myself in the space of an hour, surely?

'Aah, Meg . . .' His voice trails off and hearing him say my real name instead of Nutmeg makes the butterflies swarm around even more.

'I suppose we'd better get the chocolate out before you fade away.'

'And before it melts,' I add.

He reaches for the plastic bag and delves inside. 'What have you got for me?' he asks.

'Crisps. You're a savoury boy, through and through. That's why it could never have worked between us,' I tease.

'Oh, that's why, is it?' he asks, drily. 'See, I disagree.'

'Oh?'

'Think about it,' he says, lying back down on his side, food forgotten for a moment. 'If we went to the movies, I'd have salt popcorn and you'd have sweet. You'd be able to have it all to yourself, none of this annoying nicking business.'

'You've got a point,' I reply with a grin. 'But I like my popcorn mixed.'

'Sweet *and* salted?' He screws up his nose. 'Your taste buds are sick and twisted, girl.'

'I can't disagree with you there,' I reply jokily. 'I have very bad taste. Terrible taste in men, too, as it turns out.'

'Ouch.' He nudges my arm and my heart flips.

Yep, again.

We're still smiling at each other. Up this close I can see the freckles on his nose – the ones they airbrush out in magazine shoots. I could never understand why anyone would want to do that. They make him more . . . human, somehow.

'Pass. Me. The chocolate,' I say in a monotone voice. He grins and sits back up. He's wearing a light-grey T-shirt with pink graphics on the front. The muscles on his arms flex as he moves, and at that very moment, I want nothing more than for him to hold me tight in his arms.

We will be leaving in two days . . .

I've found a place near Henley in Oxfordshire. We're renting to begin with. There wasn't enough time to push a sale through, and anyway, I didn't want to rush into buying anything. It's bigger than I wanted it to be, but both Johnny and Lena insisted it had to be of a certain size to accommodate the security staff. Plus, it needs its own garden with private access and you don't get too many tiny cottages that meet those kinds of requirements.

'Have you heard from Joseph?' Johnny asks, out of the blue.

'Yes, I have. It wasn't him, Johnny. He didn't leak it to the press.'

'If you say so.' Pause. 'Are you seeing him again?'

'I don't think I'll have time to before we leave.'

He looks down and then starts to pick at the grass between us. I can hear the sound of the waves crashing against the rocks below.

'How's Dana?' I ask.

'Fine.'

'What's she been up to this week?'

'Recording.'

I'd almost forgotten she was allegedly the Next Big Thing in music. It makes me dislike her even more.

'You must be missing her . . .'

Please say no, please say no . . .

He shrugs. Very non-committal.

'When are you going to see her again?' I press.

'When you leave, I guess,' he replies and it stings.

'Is she the one?' I find myself asking and holding my breath at the same time.

He glances at me. 'I don't know. But there's something about her that I'd find hard to give up.'

I didn't think it would hurt this much to hear him say that.

I sit up and put the rest of my chocolate bar back in the plastic bag. I don't feel like eating anymore. 'Do you think we should head back?' I ask.

'Guess so.' He gets to his feet and holds his hand down. I feel resentful about taking it – now I don't want him to touch me – but it seems wrong to shun his help. He pulls me to my feet and for a split second I want to forget everything he's just said.

I want him to kiss me, and he knows it.

He cups my face with his hand and I feel dizzy.

I want to forget everything he's just said . . . But I can't.

I step away from him and reach down to pick up my jacket. 'Come on,' I say. 'Let's go.'

I sit behind him on the way home with my arms wrapped around his waist and I feel like this is the last time I'll ever be close to him. He can't see the tears in my eyes, or feel the deep aching sadness in my heart, but both are a clear indication to me that I need to get away from here. Fast.

Chapter 44

'I'm so sad you're leaving,' Lena says to me on Friday evening, just before she leaves for the weekend. We won't still be here on Monday when she arrives for work. 'Are you really going to go?'

'Yes,' I nod. 'We have to.'

'But do you?' she presses. 'Do you really? I thought all this was just a smokescreen.'

'A smokescreen?' I'm confused.

She looks away, edgily.

'What?' I press.

She shrugs. 'I thought maybe to get Dana out of the picture.'

I laugh sharply. 'Dana's going nowhere, and why you keep saying things like that is beyond me. It's like you think Johnny and I are somehow, ooh, I don't know, destined to be together.' My tone is sarcastic and I expect her to smile, but she doesn't. 'Lena?'

'I do think you're meant to be together.'

'Oh, stop it,' I brush her off.

'I do!' she insists. 'You're good for him.'

I look at her seriously. 'Well, he's no good for me. You know that, don't you.' It's not a question.

'I thought he might've been,' she says quietly. 'It didn't work out the way I thought it would.'

'The way you thought it would,' I repeat with a roll of my eyes.

'The way I planned it,' she adds quietly.

'What?' I glance at her.

'If he hadn't had that stupid party,' she spits.

'What are you talking about?' I don't know why I suddenly think of the car seats in Johnny's supercars, but there they are: a picture in my mind. Then it hits me. She wanted me to drive Barney around in his cars . . . She wanted me to be spotted by the press . . .

'You were the one who leaked the story,' I whisper with horror.

She doesn't deny it.

I cover my mouth with my hand. 'How could you do such a thing?'

She looks deflated. 'I thought it would work out differently,' she reiterates, more dully this time.

I sit down and put my head in my hands.

'Please don't tell Johnny,' she begs.

'I can't believe you did that.'

'I'll lose my job.'

I look up at her. 'I know you will. How could you violate his privacy like that?'

'I had good intentions.' She sits down next to me.

'Which were?'

She sighs. 'I thought if it was all out in the open . . . I don't

375

know, that you and Johnny might get back together . . . I can't stand Dana!' she adds bitterly.

'Oh, Lena.' I look at her sadly. 'How did you do it?'

'Anonymously. I put the thought out there and the journalist pieced together the rest. Except he didn't piece together the right facts.'

'I can't believe you expected him to.'

'I was naive,' she admits. 'Oh, God, I'm going to lose my job. Katya will kill me.'

'Katya will forgive you,' I say. 'And Johnny will too.'

'You're going to tell him?'

I stare at her. 'I think you should. But I won't.'

'You won't have to,' he says from the doorway. 'I can't fucking believe it!' he shouts at Lena. 'I trusted you!'

She looks terrified.

'Get out of here!'

'Johnny,' I interject.

'GO!' he shouts, his chest heaving.

I jump to my feet. 'You're being too rash! Think about it.' I turn to Lena. 'Go home for the weekend. Johnny will be in touch.'

'No, I fucking won't,' he says angrily.

'Yes, you will,' I reply firmly, putting my hand on his chest. He glances at me sharply. 'Let her go home for the weekend. Talk about things on Monday.'

I feel his chest shudder under my touch as he takes a deep breath. He nods. Lena is out of there like a shot, murmuring sincere apologies and leaving the two of us standing alone in the office staring at each other.

'I'll make you a coffee.' I take my hand off his chest. He follows me into the kitchen. Eddie has already left for the day.

Johnny slumps down in a chair and stares ahead dejectedly. I know this will hit him hard. Lena has worked for him for over two years. That's a long time in Johnny's world.

I turn around and put his mug on the table. He gazes up at me. He looks broken.

'It'll be okay.'

'Don't go,' he says quietly, reaching for my hand.

'We can't stay,' I reply. 'Not like this. We both need space.'

'But I need you.' I'm shocked to see his eyes glistening.

'Don't fire Lena,' I implore. 'Whatever she's done. She's good for you. She's the best.'

'No, you were the best.'

I squeeze his hand gently and let it go. 'Do you think Davey will be okay taking us to the airport tomorrow, with all the fuss outside the gates?'

'He's not taking you,' he replies in a monotone voice.

I give him a look because I assume he's making a joke about not letting us leave.

'You're going by helicopter,' he adds.

'Helicopter?' I ask with surprise. 'Where's it going to land?'

'On the roof.'

'You have a helicopter pad on your roof?' How did I not know this?

'No,' he replies with a sigh. 'But it's flat. They've landed there before.'

I nod. 'Fair enough.'

'It'll fly you to the airfield and from there the jet will take you to the UK.' He stares straight ahead.

'I meant to ask what you want me to do with all of Barney's toys?'

'Take them with you.'

'We can't take everything.'

'Leave them here, then. He can play with them when he comes to visit.'

'He will have grown out of them by then.'

He looks even more miserable and I wish I hadn't said that.

'I'll have everything sent over,' he says flatly.

'You'd definitely better not fire Lena, then.'

He doesn't smile so I nudge him. 'Cheer up,' I say. 'It'll all be okay.' He doesn't answer. 'I'd better go and get on with the packing.' I leave the room before I get upset.

I so wanted it all to work out. I wanted Barney to have a good relationship with his father – his real father. Instead he's going to be like all the other children of celebrities out there – the ones whose parents didn't stay together. He'll see his dad on the telly and in the papers and he'll know about him that way, along with everyone else. But he'll never *truly* know him, in as much as you can know your own parents. Their relationship will only ever scratch the surface. Once again my heart aches for Christian and everything that he's lost. Whenever things have got hard, I've missed Christian terribly. I know that I have to let him go before I can move on with my life. I never let Johnny go, and that's why it was never one hundred per cent with Christian. Even if I hadn't had Barney, Christian and I wouldn't have lasted. I think I know that for certain.

My phone rings. It's Kitty.

'Hey there,' I say into the receiver.

'How's it all going?' she asks sympathetically.

'It's all a bit shit, to be honest,' I reply with a teary laugh. I fill her in about Lena.

'Unbelievable,' she says when I've finished. 'She seemed so professional and above board.'

'I know. Don't tell anyone,' I add. If Johnny doesn't keep Lena I don't want her CPA career to be ruined by this getting around, but I know I can trust Kitty.

'You know I won't.' Pause. 'I have some news also,' she says.

'Really? What?'

'I've handed in my resignation.'

'No!' I gasp. 'Why?' I'm shocked. 'You've worked for Rod for years.'

'Exactly. I've known him longer than several of his wives put together.'

I remember I joked about something similar when we went out to the premiere that night.

'I hope it wasn't anything I said.' I feel guilty.

'No, no,' she brushes me off. 'I've got to move on. I have no life, no boyfriend, and I'm not getting any younger.'

'What are you going to do?'

'I'm taking a year out,' she says excitedly. 'I've saved quite a lot of money,' and she's right because she's been living under Rod's roof for years with no overheads, 'so I'm going to go travelling,' she explains.

I smile. 'Good for you.'

'Thanks. And you know I'm coming to stay with you in England.'

I laugh. 'You'll always be very welcome. I'm going to need my friends around me.'

When we've said our goodbyes I wonder if I should call

Joseph. It was only a week ago, but that Halloween night seems like another lifetime. I haven't been able to think about him for days – I've had too much else on my mind – but I owe it to him to say goodbye. I dial his number.

'Mystic Meg,' he says with a grin which I can't see, but I know it's there.

'Hi,' I reply with a sad smile.

'You okay?'

'As well as can be expected.' Pause. 'Barney and I are leaving on Sunday.'

'Leaving?'

'Flying back to the UK.'

'Oh.' He exhales loudly. 'That's sad.'

I feel teary again. 'I'm sorry I didn't get to see you.'

'Me, too,' he replies.

I feel compelled to talk about something a little less heavy. 'Hey, you never did tell me the outcome of your audition?'

'Aah,' he says with a half-hearted laugh. 'I got the part.'

'Did you?' I ask, unable to contain my excitement for him. 'For the sci-fi movie?'

'Yeah.'

'No way? Is it a big part?'

'Kind of,' he replies, and I sense that he's being modest. 'It's the male lead.'

'That's fantastic!' I enthuse. 'I know it's going to work out for you.'

'You too, Mystic Meg.'

Now that I know it was Lena who leaked the story, I feel sorry that I ever doubted him. Another place, another time, it might've been different. But I have no room for men in my life at the moment, and I sense that if I'd stayed, Joseph might not have had room for me in his. There was something in his eyes that night – I know he has issues of his own with an ex or exes, and it's a tiny bit of an understatement to say that I do, too.

I've never been in a helicopter before. Neither has Bess, and even though we know one is coming for us, it's still a bit of a shock when one of those persistent blowflies buzzes in and lands on Johnny's roof. We've been so used to the sight and sound of them high up in the sky over the last week.

Most of our bags went to the airfield earlier, so now all that's left is for us to say goodbye. Bess says hers first before climbing in and buckling herself up, then it's just Johnny, Barney and me standing on the roof.

'Well, this is it,' I say, trying to sound breezy. I don't want Barney to pick up on the sombre mood. He's had enough of an upheaval recently and I feel terrible about it. I usher him towards Johnny.

'Give Daddy a cuddle.'

Johnny looks at me quickly as he lifts him up.

'What?'

'You just called me Daddy.'

'First time for everything,' I say flippantly. God knows how that just popped out.

'Don't make light of it,' he commands.

I nod, silently.

'Daddy will see you soon,' he says seriously to Barney, hugging him tightly before putting him in the helicopter along with the sheepskin sheep that he's clutching. He found it in my cupboard when we were hiding out in my room last weekend and he took quite a liking to it.

'Can you entertain my boy while I say goodbye to his mother?' he asks the pilot.

'Sure.'

Johnny turns around to face me for the last time. 'I told her not to throw it out,' he says dully.

'What?'

'The sheep, the fucking sheepskin sheep,' he snaps, pointing in at Barney.

So Johnny did ask Sandy to leave it in my wardrobe.

'You're a loser,' I tease, wanting to make light of the situation so it doesn't hurt so much.

He stares at me seriously. 'I'm sorry I fucked everything up.'

'Language,' I chide.

He smiles and looks down.

I turn away from him and climb into the helicopter. The pilot lifts Barney into the back so I can strap him in between Bess and me.

'Don't forget me, buddy,' Johnny says through the open door.

'I hated it when Dana called him that,' I admit.

'I know,' he replies.

He shuts the door, but he doesn't take his eyes from us until we're in the air and he's a speck in the distance.

Chapter 45

'Get this down ya.' Susan hands me a cup of tea.

'Another one?' I ask.

'Can never have too much tea,' she replies. 'Especially in times of crisis.'

I sigh. 'I'm used to it now. It's hardly a time of crisis.'

'Near enough. The same goes for chocolate biscuits.'

She hands me a tin of posh ones that she brought with her.

'You're right,' I say, opening up the tin and peering inside. 'Times of crisis indeed.'

I choose one and hand back the tin. We smile at each other.

I never thought I'd say this, but Susan – formerly known as My Annoying Older Sister Susan – has been a gem since Barney and I returned to the UK. At first I turned down her offer of help, but she insisted on taking time off work to come to Henley and help me unpack and settle in. I thought she'd drive me around the bend, but she's seriously surprised me. She's been here every weekend since, offering tea and sympathy. And chocolate biscuits. I don't know what I would have done without her.

I'm especially glad she's here today. There's been a new story about Johnny in the tabloids. He and Dana were snapped hanging off each other and looking utterly wasted in the early hours of yesterday morning as they exited a club.

I've spoken to Johnny a couple of times in the last few weeks, but he seems to have lost all of the tenderness he showed me in the week before we left. Dana's influence, I imagine. Or maybe he's just hardened up towards me because it's his only way to cope. That's what Lena says. Yes, she still works for him, although it's going to be a long time before he trusts her again. Silly, really, because she was only trying to help him in her own, funny kind of way. She certainly won't risk messing up again.

Christmas comes and goes, as does New Year's Eve. Mum and Dad manage to get here after a day's delay when the airports close due to snowfall, and Susan and Only Slightly Less Annoying Tony also join us for the holidays. Our new home can more than accommodate everyone. It's truly beautiful: a large, six-bedroom Georgian house with white rendered walls, a slate roof and French windows. The garden is south-facing and full of promise for the approaching spring. When we first moved here I used to walk into Henley with Barney and go to tea shops and visit the playground by the river. He loves nothing more than feeding the multitude of swans, geese and ducks, and watching the boats as they pass by. We've even made a couple of new friends. But it's been a bitterly cold December and January, so we've huddled up a bit and made the most of the real log fire. I've become a dab hand at stoking it.

My evenings are lonely, though. The only adult conversation

I have is when one of our two security guys – Alan or Smithy – does their final check. After that I only have the television for company. But I can't complain about it.

One day in the middle of February I get an unexpected call from Christian. I texted him when we returned because he refused to answer my calls, but I didn't know if he'd ever make contact.

'Are you at home?' he asks me.

'Yes,' I reply with anticipation.

'I'm in Marlow,' he says of the nearby town, also on the river. 'Visiting friends,' he explains. 'I thought I might pop by.'

'Yes, please do!' I exclaim, trying not to scare him away with my enthusiasm. I can't quite believe I'm hearing this. I give him my full address and end the call before he changes his mind. He arrives less than half an hour later. I've been pacing the hall nervously, wondering if I should wake Barney from his nap so he's there to welcome Christian. In the end I leave him. It would be awful if their reunion were spoiled by an overtired and tearful toddler.

Security buzzes to announce Christian's arrival and I venture outside into the cold to greet him. He drives up the gravel drive-way in a dark-grey Audi and climbs out. His hair is longer and I'm surprised to see that he's grown a beard – not a big one, not like Santa's or anything like that, but it's more than merely designer stubble. He's clearly committed to it.

'Hello,' I say shyly.

'Hi.' He slams the door and comes to meet me. I stare up at him, not quite sure if we should kiss or hug. In the end we do neither.

'Shall we go inside?' he suggests. 'You must be freezing. Where's Barney?'

'Asleep.'

'Does he still have his daytime nap?'

'Yes. He needs it otherwise he's a terror.'

He looks around. I don't expect him to comment on the house, not when he'll know Johnny is financing it.

'He hasn't changed that much,' I tell him, wanting it to be true, but knowing that it's not.

'I'll be the judge of that,' he replies, and it hurts. 'Sorry,' he says. 'I don't want this to be unpleasant.'

I look at the floor.

'That didn't come out right,' he tells me. 'I mean, I just want to move on now. Okay?'

'Yes. Yes,' I say again, just to be sure. 'Tea? Coffee?'

'Tea, please.'

'Chocolate biscuit?'

'What do you think?'

He smiles at me for a brief moment before looking away again.

'Susan brought them,' I explain.

'Did she?' he asks with surprise. He never had much time for her, either.

'She's been great, you know.' He follows me into the kitchen and I tell him about her. We take our teas and biscuits through to the living room. 'How's it all going with your work?' I ask him.

'Not bad. Book two coming out next month.'

'Wow. I remember talking to my dad earlier last year about that one coming out in March. God, it's been a long year.'

'I know what you mean.'

The baby monitor indicates that Barney has started to stir.

'Do you want to go?' I ask tentatively.

'No, you'd better.'

I nod and head up the stairs. Actually, that wasn't a smart suggestion. Who knows how Barney will react to seeing Christian again. He won't remember him, surely? Not at his age. My nerves return. I hope he doesn't cry. Please don't let him cry.

'Hey,' Christian says gently as I carry him into the living room. Barney lifts his head and peers down at him. He stays sitting on the sofa. I almost say, 'Go to Daddy', but I catch myself in time and my head spins at the thought of what would have been a horrendous faux pas. Christian doesn't attempt to take him from me, so I decide against handing him over for the moment.

'He's grown,' Christian comments as I sit down again.

Barney wriggles out of my arms so I put him on the floor and he walks over to his toys.

'Walking!' he exclaims. 'But of course he would be by now.' He doesn't say it in a terrible way, but I still feel tense.

'He says quite a lot, too,' I reveal. 'Barney, what are you playing with?'

'Tains,' comes the response.

'Trains,' I say to Christian.

'I gathered that,' he replies with a wry grin.

We both fall silent.

'How's your Contour Lines biography coming along?'

'Done and dusted. In the editing stage at the moment.'

'Brilliant. Are you happy with it?'

'It's not bad. Considering.'

Considering what you've been through and you still managed to write a book . . . We leave that unsaid.

'When does it come out?' I ask.

'September.'

'It should do well. Great Christmas present for Contour Lines fans.'

'Let's hope so.'

Again we fall silent. He watches Barney playing with his train set and sips at his tea. I hand him another chocolate biscuit.

'I like your beard.'

'Er, thanks,' he replies, embarrassed.

I do. It actually suits him.

'You haven't changed,' he comments, glancing at me. 'Looks-wise, in any case.'

We meet each other's eyes before looking away again.

'I didn't know if we'd ever see you again,' I say after a while.

'I just needed some time.' He stares at Barney. 'He's grown so much.'

I watch him for any sign of tears, but he seems remarkably calm. I wonder if he has anyone in his life, if that's why he appears so strong. I daren't ask.

'You seem so, I don't know . . .' My voice trails off.

'I've come to terms with it.'

'Have you?' I ask hopefully.

'I didn't have a choice.'

'No.' Please don't hate me forever.

'I don't hate you, Meg.'

Did I say that out loud?

'If that's what you've been thinking,' he adds.

Okay, then, so no, I didn't.

'I didn't want to feel bitter anymore,' he explains. 'It's . . . exhausting. I couldn't go on like that.'

I take a deep breath.

'That's not to say I forgive you,' he continues, glancing at me.

'No, of course not,' I reply quickly.

'But I've missed him.'

He gets down on the floor and starts to put together some more pieces of the wooden train track. Barney 'helps' him by unhelpfully taking it apart again.

'Oi, you! Give that back!' Christian says in a funny voice. Barney's face breaks into a toothy smile. 'Oi!' Christian says again and Barney starts to giggle as he tickles him.

It's hard not to laugh at the sight. It's hard not to feel hope. So I do laugh. And I do hope. And I pray for happier times ahead.

Chapter 46

Christian comes to visit again a week later – and a week after that. Soon it's his publication day and he invites us to his launch party in London. We go – Bess comes, too – and we're so proud to hear his editor talking about him and what a pleasure he is to work with. He gave me a proof copy of his book to read before it came out and it's nail-bitingly gripping. I'm crossing all my fingers and toes that it sells well so he can get on with the thing he loves most: writing crime fiction instead of following disturbed celebrities around the world and watching from the sidelines as they get up to all manner of grief.

Dana is back in rehab.

Johnny is not.

He wasn't involved in her latest attempt to sink into the depths of depravity. He was away in Big Sur, writing. The press made out that she was angry with him for leaving her alone in LA – that this was her way of getting back at him. Of course, I shouldn't believe anything the press says, but Lena confirmed it. Quite happily, in fact. She also said that, to her knowledge,

Johnny has been teetotal for almost two months. But that's the key, you see: *to her knowledge*. I can't believe it. I want to, but I can't.

He tried to come and visit us over Christmas, but I was so angry about the stories I'd seen in the press and the photos of him and Dana looking absolutely rat-arsed, that I told him quite strongly to stay away. I said I didn't want to hear another thing from him until he'd changed. He hasn't contacted me since, but Lena has. The cynical side of me wonders if he's put her up to it.

At the beginning of April, Dana checks herself out of rehab. I do what always makes me feel sick and dirty and scour the internet for news and gossip about Johnny and her, but, to my surprise, there's very little about them. I don't know if it's because everyone has become bored with their tawdry lives or if it's because there genuinely isn't much to say. Three nights in a row I torture myself by doing this, and by the fourth night I'm so confused by what I'm seeing – or not seeing – that I seriously consider calling Lena for the lowdown. Somehow, I'm still not sure how, I manage to restrain myself. The next day, Christian comes to visit, and for the first time since we started on our tentative journey towards friendship, he asks me about Johnny.

'Do you hear much from him?'

'No,' I reply. 'Not much at all these days. He called occasionally when we first moved here,' I explain. 'But he was angry with me for leaving LA, and then I was angry with him for all the crap he gets up to with Dana, so I told him to stay away from us for a while.'

'I saw she's out of rehab,' he comments.

'Mmm. We'll see how long that lasts.'

'What did you think of her?'

'What do you reckon? I couldn't stand her! She was always winding me up, calling me names and swearing in front of Barney.'

'I'm surprised you lasted in LA as long as you did.'

'I bet you thought we were crazy to go there in the first place,' I muse aloud.

He says nothing for a while, then: 'No, I understood it.'

I glance at him. 'You did?'

'I didn't want to, but yes, I did.'

'I bet you knew it wouldn't work out, too.'

He raises his eyebrows, but doesn't answer. That's a yes, then.

'Shall we go for a walk into town?' he suggests instead.

'That'd be nice. Is it warm out? Do we need our coats?'

'No, it's lovely.'

'Aah, I so hope we have a decent summer . . .'

'Me, too. Hey, we could hire a rowboat on the river!' he suggests excitedly.

'Ooh, yeah!' I enthuse. 'We haven't done that yet.'

'Wicked! Let's go.'

It's so nice to have him back in our lives. I was right: he is seeing someone. She's called Sara and she works at his publishers doing the publicity for his books. I met her at his book launch and immediately sensed there was something going on. She's very pretty, with long dark hair and extremely blue eyes. She's about my age – give or take a year. I don't want to ask too many questions about her for fear of him thinking I'm in any way jealous. He deserves to be happy.

It's four o'clock by the time we get back to the house. Christian is carrying Barney on his shoulders because it's hard enough pushing the buggy across the gravel driveway without the weight of my son in it. He's pretending to be a horse and Barney is laughing his head off as he rears and neighs. I jolt to a stop when I see Johnny standing on the doorstep, a lit cigarette in his hand. Christian carries on playing, oblivious, but my feet are rooted to the spot. I put my hand on Christian's arm and he follows my gaze, tensing suddenly when he realises what I've seen. He lifts Barney down from his shoulders, but Barney immediately starts to whinge and complain, jumping about in front of him and wanting to be picked up again. Instead, I whisk Barney up into my arms and Christian carries the buggy. We walk together to meet Johnny, who is stony-faced as he watches us.

'Hello,' I say.

'Alright,' he replies curtly.

'You should have told me you were coming.'

'I wanted to surprise you,' he says, glancing at Christian.

Barney wriggles in my arms so I put him down and he runs over to Johnny.

'Hey, little buddy,' he says warmly, ditching his cigarette and swooping him up. Christian averts his gaze.

'I guess I should go,' he says to me.

'Please stay,' I say.

'No, please go,' Johnny interrupts.

'Hey!' I warn, crossly, promptly taking Barney from him. 'Enough of that. Budge over so I can let us in. I didn't think security would leave you standing out here like this.'

'They didn't,' he replies. 'I needed a smoke.'

'Aah, so you've seen inside, have you?'

'I've been staring at your lovely walls for three hours,' he replies sarcastically.

I tut, but don't wind him up further.

I usher Johnny inside.

'Come in,' I say firmly to Christian. He tentatively follows me over the threshold. 'I'll put the kettle on. Tea? Coffee?'

'Tea, please,' Christian says.

'I'll come with you,' Johnny insists, not wanting to be left alone in a room with his one-time best mate. I hand Barney to Christian, and Johnny stares after them as they go into the living room. I lead the way to the kitchen.

'I didn't know you were seeing him again.'

'He contacted me a couple of months ago,' I explain.

'Are you seeing him? *Seeing* seeing him?' he asks with surprise.

'No, don't worry,' I brush him off. 'He's got a girlfriend.'

'Why should I be worried?' he retorts over the noise of the kettle boiling.

'Okay, so you're not worried,' I reply with frustration. 'But I'm glad he's back in our lives again. I want him to have a relationship with Barney.'

'Does anyone actually care what *I* want?' he asks in a low tone.

I slam the teaspoon I'm holding down on the countertop. 'No, actually,' I say angrily. 'And if you've come here to cause any trouble whatsoever you can bugger off. I *told* you, Johnny, I told you that I didn't want anything more to do with you until you'd sorted yourself out!'

'Hey!' He holds his palms up at me and I feel myself calming down. I pick up the teaspoon again and stir sugar into Christian's tea. Johnny comes and stands next to me. I feel uneasy with him so close, but I carry on stirring and ignore him. 'Maybe I have sorted myself out,' he says quietly. I glance up at him, but I have to step away a couple of paces before I can look at him properly.

'Lena said you haven't touched a drop of booze since January.'

'New Year's Day,' he confirms.

'Had a rough time the night before, did you?' I glance at him, unamused. He shifts on his feet. 'How is Dana?'

'She's alright, so I hear.'

'So you hear?'

'We split up.'

My stomach turns over. 'Did you? When?'

'After her last stint in rehab.'

'I heard she was back in rehab.' I can't believe Lena failed to call me with this new information! How has this not been in the press? I ask the question.

'She's been back in Montana, recuperating.' That's where her parents live. 'Off the radar.'

'Is it definitely over?' I hate myself for hoping.

'Definitely.'

I'm not sure I believe him. She's surely capable of getting her claws back into him. I try to ignore the jittery feeling inside. I turn and stare at Johnny. 'Be nice to Christian,' I command. 'He's the injured party in all of this. Remember that.'

He pushes himself off the wall and starts to follow me. 'He didn't look too injured to me when he was prancing about with my son on his shoulders,' he mutters. He's jealous, of course.

'You know, you still should apologise.' I know exactly what response I'm going to get.

'I'm not apologising!' he snaps. Yep, I was right. 'You were my girl first, remember.' My heart skips a beat, but he continues, unaware: 'If he hadn't nicked you from me in the first place, I wouldn't have had to try to get you back.'

I force a roll of my eyes at him, but it's disconcerting hearing him speaking as frankly as this. I lead the way back through to the living room.

'How are your book sales coming along?' I ask Christian.

He grins. 'Really well. Really, really well. Better than expected.'

'Oh, Christian, that's brilliant!'

'I've been offered another book deal.'

'Have you?' I squeal, getting to my feet. He gets to his and we both hug each other happily.

Christian glances over his shoulder at Johnny, but he's steadfastly ignoring us. We both sit down again, but I can't stop beaming. 'What did your dad say?' I ask. 'I bet he's proud of you.'

'He's thrilled.'

I know from a previous conversation with Christian – after I'd finally built up the courage to ask – that his family haven't forgiven me for deceiving them about Barney. They can, however, understand Christian's desire to have a relationship with him. It hurts a great deal, but I hope that time will heal their wounds and that one day they'll want to spend time with Barney themselves, if not with me.

Barney starts to whinge, so we both turn around. He's trying to take one of his toys from Johnny, a pull-along caterpillar that breaks into three pieces.

'I'm fixing it for you, buddy,' Johnny murmurs. Barney just whinges more.

'He likes it like that,' Christian chips in, a frown on his face.

'Excuse me?' Johnny asks, challengingly.

'He prefers to bang the bits together. He doesn't like pulling it along.'

'Don't try to tell me what's good for my son,' he warns.

'You're a piece of work,' Christian says darkly. 'I swear to God, if Barney weren't here . . .'

'Enough!' I hiss. 'I'm not having this anymore! We've all been through enough over the last year. It's time to move on. Time for us all to move on. Barney wants both of you in his life, so you're going to have to deal with each other whether you like it or not. You both claim to want the best for him – well, this is it! So get on with it.'

Johnny, Christian and Barney all freeze and stare at me. I get to my feet and go over to Barney.

'I'm going to make him his dinner. You two: talk. Sort it out. Don't break things, for God's sake, but when I come back with Barney in half an hour I want you to at least know how to be civil to each other.

'No, I . . . I should get off.' Christian starts to get up.

'Sit. Down,' I command. 'Do this for me. No, not for me. Do it for Barney.'

With that I walk out of the room.

I return to the kitchen and secure Barney in his highchair before getting on with his dinner. I can't hear anything for a while, but then come the raised voices. It gets very heated at one point and I have to resist going back through to mediate, but I know this is necessary. Finally I can't hear anything and that almost makes me more nervous. Dinner over, I clean up Barney and tentatively walk back through to the living room.

'Is it safe to come in?' I ask from the doorway.

They're both sitting on the sofas, facing each other. Christian gets to his feet. 'I should be going.'

'Don't you want to stay for dinner?' I ask him, disappointed.

'Not if you're cooking.'

I cast my eyes heavenwards at this much-abused joke. Barney leans out of my arms to go to Christian. I sense Johnny watching as Christian hugs him goodbye. 'See you soon,' he says, kissing him on his nose. Then he hands him down to Johnny on the sofa. 'Go to Daddy,' he says.

Startled, Johnny glances up at him. I'm also in shock.

'Walk me out,' Christian says to me, touching my arm.

I follow him in a daze.

'See you soon,' Johnny calls after us. We turn around. 'Seriously,' he says. 'We should catch up again.'

Christian pauses and then nods.

'I'll be in touch,' Johnny says.

'Was that okay?' I ask Christian when we reach the hallway.

'Not as bad as it could have been,' he replies, before qualifying it. 'No, it was alright.'

'Did he say sorry?'

He laughs. 'What do you think?'

I shake my head.

'Thanks for having me,' he says.

'You're always welcome. Very welcome. When will you next come?'

'Sara and I are going to a wedding next weekend.' It's not often he speaks about his girlfriend and it still makes me start to hear him say her name. 'But the weekend after? Maybe go for a picnic in Hurley, if the weather's nice?'

'That'd be great. You know, you could always bring Sara along,' I say, wanting to make amends in any way possible.

'Maybe sometime.'

I wait until he's in his car and has driven out of the gates before I return to the living room. Johnny is tickling a giggling Barney on the sofa. I stand at the doorway watching them for a moment, remembering a time last year when I saw Christian doing a similar thing. I recall how sick I felt, seeing the dissimilarities between them – Christian with his dark hair and dark eyes, and Barney the polar opposite. Now, witnessing Johnny and Barney face to face like this as they laugh at each other, I know this is the way it's meant to be.

Johnny senses my presence and looks up.

'Where are you staying?' I ask him.

'I thought I might stay here?' he replies hopefully.

'Of course you can. Not like we don't have enough room.' I start to tidy up.

'Want me to do anything?' he asks.

'Actually,' I pause. 'You could take Barney upstairs and get on with his bath.'

'Sure thing.'

He whisks Barney up into his arms and carries him out of the room. I look after them. The whole time we were in LA he never offered to help with basic parenting chores. But then I never asked him to. It could never have worked because we never gave it a chance.

I toy with the idea of staying away, to see how Johnny gets on with bath time, but then I see sense. Even Christian, when we were together, still managed to forget to do simple things like wash Barney's face and brush his teeth, and Johnny won't have the foggiest about where to find pyjamas or nappies. So I go up the stairs and head towards the noise. Johnny is on his knees, leaning over the side of the bath. He's pushed his sleeves up and is zooming a toy boat around, crashing it into my hysterical son's legs. Chuckling, Johnny glances up and sees me.

'Having fun?' I ask.

He looks back at Barney and exhales deeply. 'He's grown.'

'Children tend to do that.'

'I didn't think he'd change this much in the space of a few months.'

I sit down on the toilet seat and rest my elbows on my knees. 'You've got a new tattoo,' I muse, staring down at Johnny's arm. It's a 'B'. 'Wait . . .' I frown. 'Is that for—'

'Barney,' he interrupts a touch awkwardly.

'No way.'

He shrugs.

'I didn't figure you for the sentimental type.'

'Didn't you?' he asks, giving me a cheeky grin. The song he wrote for me comes to mind and I find myself blushing. Then it occurs to me to wonder how many songs he wrote for Dana. I stand up.

'Would you get him out and dry him off? I'll go and get his PJs ready.'

I walk out of the room and down the corridor towards Barney's bedroom.

I'm standing on the cliff and Johnny is cupping my face with his hand . . .

I shake my head. Then I see a naked Dana on top of him outside by the pool. I shake my head again, more violently this time.

'Got something in your ear?' Johnny asks drily from behind me.

I jump. 'That was quick. Oh, he's still wet.'

Bloody men.

'Thought I'd get him dry in here,' he explains.

'Better to keep him in the warmth of the bathroom in future.'

He says nothing, but I feel bad for nagging. It's not like he's going to do this much – I should let him make his own mistakes.

'Do you want to read him a story while I get his milk?'

'Okay.'

This is all very domesticated, I think to myself as I whack Barney's sippy cup full of milk in the microwave. I don't like to admit it to myself, but I miss having a man around.

Oh dear. It's so not healthy for me to have Johnny here.

He does seem different, though. More stable, somehow.

Definitely not healthy if I'm thinking things like that. Where's that image of Dana again? That'll sort me out. Urgh, yes, there it is. Job done.

I go back upstairs and hand over the milk. 'What do you want for dinner?'

'Happy with beans on toast.'

'Are you being diplomatic?'

He grins up at me and the room shrinks. 'No. I'm just not very hungry. I'm still on LA time, remember.'

'In that case, toast it is. Breakfast is the most important meal of the day, and all that . . .'

In the end I make us both an omelette and we eat it in the opulent dining room under the low-level light of a chandelier. It feels fraudulent – a five-course meal would have felt more apt

– but it's nice to sit across the table from someone and have a conversation that doesn't involve talking about yourself – Mummy – in the third person.

'Do you like living here?' Johnny asks me.

'I do. I really do, actually.'

'You sound surprised.'

'I guess I am a little bit. But I haven't felt this happy or more at home in a house or an area for a long time. Possibly ever. Mum and Dad moved abroad while I was still at university, so I lost my family home then,' I explain. 'Bess and I lived in a student hovel, obviously, then I came to stay with you—'

'My crib wasn't good enough for you?' he interrupts.

'Your house is lovely. But, as you well know, Johnny Jefferson, being in LA with you was not without its complications.'

'Go on,' he urges.

'Anyway, Christian's house was always Christian's house—'

He interrupts again. 'Even though you lived there for two years?'

'Even then.'

'France – lovely, but, again, somebody else's house. Mum and Dad's place, and then back at yours.'

'My place could have felt like home.'

'No. Your place could never feel like home.'

It's true, I never did feel like anything more than a house guest. We were always visitors – never permanent residents.

He frowns. 'Why not?'

'Don't be annoyed with me.' I try to explain: 'It's incredible – you know I love it – but it has too many bad memories. It would never feel like my home. It would always feel tainted.'

'I'm sorry to hear you say that,' he says quietly. 'But now this place feels like home?'

'Yes. Even though it's not. Henley does, too. I've made some friends here. I never had that in France. I've met a couple of other mums down at the playground. We've been to toddler groups together.' He nods, watching me. I shrug. 'It might sound trivial . . .' I pause. 'I do feel bad about not working, though.'

'You can't put Barney in a nursery because it wouldn't be secure enough if anyone found out who he was.'

I nod. 'I know.'

'Still against the idea of a nanny?'

I nod again. 'I couldn't cope with someone else being as important a part in his life as I am.'

'No one will ever be that,' he says, the unusual voice of reason.

'Maybe not, but I thought . . .'

'Go on.'

'I thought I might do some charity work.'

He leans forward and rests his elbows on the table. 'That's a good idea.'

'I wouldn't use your name.'

'You can, if you want.'

'No, I mean, amazingly, no one's found out about us here, yet. I'm enjoying my return to anonymity.'

He sighs. 'You know that won't last.'

I look down at my hands. 'I know.'

'Have you told any of your friends who you are?'

I laugh. 'Who I am? You mean, who Barney is.'

He shrugs.

'No,' I admit. 'No one's been back here, either. I don't really want to explain how I came to live in a house like this.'

'You could say you won the lottery,' he suggests with a grin.

'I don't want to lie anymore.'

He smiles sympathetically. 'I was joking.'

'I know.'

'Well, I'm glad you're happy.' He starts to get up. 'I'm going to get myself a drink. Want anything?' He sighs at the look on my face. 'Water, not whisky, Nutmeg.'

'Oh, okay. Sorry.' I smile shamefacedly after him as he leaves the room. I get up and clear the plates, taking them through to the kitchen. Johnny is looking in the fridge.

'What are you after?' I ask him.

'Water,' he replies.

'The tap's over there.'

'Don't you have any bottled water?' he asks.

'No!' I grab him a glass and fill it from the tap. 'Bloody celebrities,' I mutter under my breath. He grins and takes the glass from me, leaning up against the countertop. God, he's gorgeous.

'What are you thinking?' he asks with amusement.

'Let's go through to the living room,' I reply, my face heating up.

'That's not what you were thinking,' he says, raising his eyebrows.

'How long are you planning on staying?' I ask over my shoulder, ignoring his tone of voice.

'Couple of days?' he replies and I experience a surge of disappointment.

'Just a couple of days?'

'Don't want to outstay my welcome.'

'You're not. You can stay longer, if you want.'

'Maybe next time,' he replies, and I wish I hadn't said anything.

I sit down on the sofa and Johnny takes an armchair. Barney cries out on the monitor and Johnny is out of his seat like a shot. 'I'll go,' he says, before I even have a chance to move. I stare after him in surprise as he leaves the room. He's never done that before. He returns a few minutes later.

'Okay?' I ask, still slightly in shock. I know I shouldn't be – he is his father and everything.

'Fine.' He collapses in his chair and stares up at the ceiling.

'You do seem different, you know,' I find myself saying.

'I've missed him,' he admits. 'I thought I could kill the pain with drugs, but I can't. The ache is still there.' I hold my breath. Johnny rarely opens up like this. 'I don't want to be a fuck-up forever, like my dad,' he adds.

Johnny's mum died when he was thirteen, and he moved down to London to live with his dad. Back then his dad overdosed on drink, drugs and women, and even though Johnny's mum warned him not to end up like his father, he always worries that he has.

'I thought your dad had changed since he got married?' It was almost three years ago.

He laughs bitterly and shakes his head. 'He's getting a divorce.' He meets my eyes. 'Shelley is pregnant,' he explains.

'No! But how old is she?'

'Forty-five, something like that. Dad has been having an affair for the last year with some bimbo from the social club. So now my half-brother or half-sister is going to grow up having a shitty excuse for a father, just like I did.'

'Oh, no, Johnny, I'm sorry.'

'Just like Barney has,' he adds.

'Hey,' I say warningly. 'You're not a shitty excuse for a father.'

He puts his head in his hands and moans. 'I can't believe I let all those fucked-up losers come over when he was in the house.'

I say nothing. I still can't believe he did that either.

He glances up at me. 'I didn't take drugs that night.'

I avert my gaze.

'I know you don't believe me.' He stares at me, anguished. 'But it's true. Not knowingly. Someone spiked my drink.'

I stare at him, not sure whether or not he's telling the truth.

'I swear to you, Meg. I was only drinking. That night, at least,' he admits, because he can't fool me that he was only abusing alcohol on the nights in December when the paps kept snapping him for the papers.

'Who spiked your drink?' Dana?

He looks down. 'I don't know.'

Neither of us says anything for a while.

'I just wanted to explain,' he tells me. 'I really need you to understand.'

I shake my head. 'I'll never understand you.'

He regards me sadly. 'No. I guess not,' he says quietly.

'Dana understood you,' I point out, as sick nerves start to plague my insides.

He shakes his head. 'No.'

'More than I ever have.'

'No,' he says resolutely. 'No, that's not true.'

I pause. 'I thought there was something about her that you couldn't give up?'

He looks at me for a long time with those piercing eyes and I struggle not to look away. 'Turns out I was wrong.'

'You think,' I say wryly.

'If she's capable of hurting herself like that to get back at me, then I'm as bad for her as she is for me. I assume you saw the stories in the press.'

I nod. 'What if she changes?'

'She won't.'

'You don't know that.' Why am I playing devil's advocate?

'Believe me, I do. Even if she gives up the drink and drugs she won't change. There's a darkness inside her. She's not a good person to be around. For anyone to be around, not least my son.'

'I never thought I'd hear you talking about her like that.'

He stares at me directly and I try to ignore the swirling nerves. 'I had a lot of time to think about things while she was in rehab.'

Seconds pass before I tear my eyes away. 'I think I'm going to go to bed.'

He nods and stands up before I do. 'Me, too.'

He holds his hands down to me. I hesitate for a split second before taking them. His grasp is warm and firm as he pulls me to my feet, and then I'm standing right in front of him, holding his hands and looking up into his troubled eyes. It's the second time this evening that a room has felt too small. I want to step backwards but the sofa is there. My heart starts to beat quicker, but I can't look away. And then he lets go of my hands and puts his arms around me, pulling me into his chest. He rests his chin on the top of my head and my pulse starts to return to normal. This is just a hug. He's not going to try to kiss me. I relax into him as he holds me tenderly and it feels like the most natural place in the world for me to be. Neither of us speaks, but I know he's sorry. I know he regrets what he's done to me. Eventually he lets

407

me go and smiles down at me sadly. I feel at peace with him for the first time, possibly ever.

'Night, night, Nutmeg,' he says softly, squeezing my hand one last time before letting it go.

I smile up at him before pulling a funny face. 'Hang on, you don't even know which room you're sleeping in.'

He pulls a sad face. 'I thought I was sleeping in yours?'

'Oi!' I whack him on his arm. 'You can't give me one nice cuddle and then expect to get into my pants.'

He laughs. 'Can't I?'

'No, you bloody can't!' Obviously he's joking.

'Come on, then. See me to my room.'

'You can see yourself there. Up the stairs, down the corridor, second one to your right. I've got to clean up the kitchen.'

'No, you don't.' He frowns, taking my hand again. 'The kitchen can wait until the morning.'

'What, when you get up at seven and come downstairs with your rubber gloves on?'

'I might surprise you,' he teases.

'Alright, then,' I concede as he leads me to the stairs, switching off lights as he goes. 'I'll have a lie-in.'

He chuckles softly. We reach his bedroom door. 'This is you,' I say.

'Where's your room?' he asks.

'I'm not telling you.'

'What, in case I can't keep my hands to myself in the middle of the night?'

'Exactly. Not like that hasn't happened before,' I reply with a knowing look. He leans against the doorframe. Butterflies flit around my stomach, the earlier sickness a distant memory.

'Give me another hug,' he says, out of the blue. I giggle as I allow him to wrap his arms around me and hold me tight. It feels so right to be this close to him. I've missed him. Hang on, I've never felt this close to him. He gives me one last squeeze and then pulls away and opens his door.

'Sleep tight,' he says with a grin.

'Goodnight, Johnny Jefferson,' I reply and turn away. He spanks my bum.

'Ow!' I squawk to the sound of his laughter as he shuts the door in my face.

I go to bed that night feeling warm and happy and drunk with contentment. But in the middle of the night when I wake up, as I have done every night since I met that famous green-eyed rock star, my happiness turns to unease and I know that I have to be careful if I don't want to get hurt again.

Chapter 47

'Didn't George Harrison use to live in Henley?' Johnny asks as we pass a gated mansion. It's Sunday, late morning, and we're going for a walk into Henley.

'I don't know, did he?'

'Yeah, you know George Harrison,' he says facetiously. 'Used to be in The Beatles.'

'Who are The Beatles?' I ask innocently. He smirks down at me. He's always teasing me about my lack of taste in – and knowledge about – music. 'I also remember that Morrissey used to be a member of The Smiths.'

'Oh, well done,' he says.

I still recall the time when I first went to work for Johnny in LA, going outside onto the terrace to hear him singing a song by The Smiths. I asked him if it was one he'd written. He wasn't too impressed.

'How far away is this playground?'

'A bit of a walk. You need the exercise,' I tease.

* * *

'MEG!' I hear a shout as we walk along the river. There's a small fun fair in the local park and we're on our way to let Barney go on the carousel.

'Oh, God,' I moan under my breath. It's one of my new friends, Liz, who I met at Barney's weekly playgroup. Johnny stops and turns around, distracting Barney with some bread for the ducks.

'Hello!' I say as she approaches.

'I thought that was you!' she calls, with a big grin on her face. She's with her husband, Guy, who I've met a couple of times, and he's carrying their two-year-old, Sam, on his shoulders. 'Where's Barney?' she asks, looking around and then spotting him. 'Oh, there he is. Hello, Barney!'

I realise with a sigh that there's no escaping this. Johnny turns around and follows Barney over. The look on Liz's face when she sees him is a picture.

'This is my friend—' I start to say.

'John,' Johnny interrupts, holding out his hand.

'Oh, er, hi!' Liz replies, taken aback, her gaze flitting between us. She's clearly confused.

'Hi, there,' Guy says when the introductory handshake comes his way. 'You all enjoying the sunshine?'

'Oh, aye, it's grand,' Johnny says with a wink. Liz looks even more disconcerted.

'We're about to take Barney on the carousel,' I tell her.

'We've just come from there,' she says with a smile, her eyes going up to Johnny's again.

This is silly. I'm going to have to tell her. But not now; next time.

'Are we still going to Monkey Music on Tuesday?' I ask casually.

'Absolutely,' she says, backing away. 'See you then.'

'We'll be there!'

'See you again,' Guy says merrily. 'Enjoy the weekend.' He's still none the wiser.

'You, too!' Johnny and I reply before turning away. I look down to see Barney's shoelace is undone. I bend down to tie it.

'Have they gone?' I ask under my breath.

'Yes. Oh, no,' he gives me a running commentary. 'No, she's just said something to him and now he's looking over his shoulder.' He starts to whistle under his breath as though completely unaware of the attention.

'What are they doing now?' I whisper up at him.

'His jaw has just hit the ground.'

'Look away! Look away!' I exclaim. He grins down at me.

'Don't worry about it, Nutmeg. People were going to find out sooner or later.'

'I was hoping it would be later.'

'They might keep it quiet,' he says reasonably.

I stand back up and sigh. 'I suppose they might just assume you look like him. Surely she wouldn't really think I was with Johnny Jefferson.'

'Exactly,' he says chirpily. 'Come on, let's go on the merry-go-round.'

'You're not going on, are you?'

'Course I am.'

'Are you *trying* to draw attention to yourself?' I ask with amazement. He just shrugs. We set off in the direction of the fairground.

'I can't believe you said your name was John,' I mutter under my breath.

* * *

All too soon, Johnny is gone again. April turns into May, but this time we keep in touch by phone. Soon it's Barney's second birthday, and Johnny takes a break from recording his new album to pay us a visit. We have a small party for our son at home – my parents come over from France, and Susan, Tony and Bess join us as well. But Christian's presence is what really makes my day. He missed Barney's first birthday, and the fact that, one year on, we can all be here together – Johnny, too – and no longer be living a lie . . . I feel lighter than ever.

But even though I want him to stay, Johnny goes back to LA to carry on with his recording.

'How's it all going?' I ask him during one Skype session, when Barney has got bored with sitting in front of the computer and looking at his father's face, and has gone off to play with his toys.

'Pretty well, I think,' Johnny admits, leaning back in his chair.

'Have you got all your songs ready to go?' I ask.

'I've written them all, yes,' he says. 'A few about Barney in there.'

'Really?'

'A few about you, too,' he adds.

'No!' I can't help smiling even though I feel shy. Then it's back to reality with a bump. 'And Dana?' I try to sound offhanded, but fail.

'Yeah, she's in a couple,' he says and my heart sinks. 'Not very flattering, mind.'

'Oh, good,' I say, perking up.

He chuckles and leans in, putting his elbows on the desktop. I sit back in my seat. This may be only a virtual chat and he may

413

be five and a half thousand miles away, but I still need my personal space.

'I was thinking about coming over at the end of June, beginning of July,' he says.

'Really?'

'I want to go to the Goodwood Festival of Speed,' he explains.

'What's that?'

'A motor-racing event. I've been asked to display my new Bugatti and to drive.'

'I didn't know you had a new one.'

'It's being flown in from France in time for the event. It's a convertible.'

'Nice.' He always did fancy himself as a bit of a racing driver.

'Anyway, I wondered if you and Barney might fancy coming with me. He'd like the cars,' he says.

'Oh, right, yes! Of course,' I say. 'It sounds pretty high-profile, though, doesn't it?'

'If you're worried about blowing your cover,' he says, staring at me through the computer with his penetrating eyes, 'then yes, it will probably do that.'

'Oh, right.'

'But maybe it's time?' he says with a shrug.

'Maybe.' I look down at the keyboard and then back up at him. He's still staring at me. 'I'll think about it.'

Christian calls the next day to arrange a visit and I ask him what he thinks.

'Go,' he says straight away.

'Really?'

'You can't hide out forever,' he says. 'It's about time. Dana's off the scene, so you shouldn't get the level of press disruption you got last time. It's your last hurdle and then you can get on with your life without living in fear the whole time.'

'I'm hardly living in fear,' I scoff.

'It's on your mind, though, isn't it?' he presses. 'Being discovered.'

'Well, yes.'

I never did tell Liz about Johnny, and, incredibly, no one else paid him any attention while he was sitting on a tiny car going round and around with Barney on his lap. Liz did comment, wide-eyed, that my friend – because that's all I said we were – looked like Johnny Jefferson. I just laughed it off and said she wasn't the first person to say that. It wasn't a lie – it just wasn't the whole truth. I know she'll understand my need for privacy when it does come out.

'You should go,' he says again, more resolutely.

'Maybe you could come,' I suggest. 'It might be something you'd enjoy.'

'I'm on holiday with Sara,' he replies.

'Aah, nice. Where are you going?' I try to sound casual and interested, as a friend would be. I haven't met her since Christian's book launch. I get the feeling she doesn't like me much. And why should she? I wouldn't like me either if I knew what she knew.

'Tuscany,' he replies. He pauses. 'Did Johnny tell you I saw him in LA last week?'

'No?' God knows why not.

'I was over there tying up some loose ends for the Contour Lines biography – my editor wanted an epilogue before it went to print,' he explains. 'I gave him a call and we caught up.'

'Wow.' After everything they've been through, is there really hope for their friendship?

'He apologised.' He laughs.

'No way!'

'Yes. He really did.'

I'm aghast.

'He seemed well,' he continues. 'Better than I've seen him in a long time.'

'He's still sober, then?'

'Surely you know that,' he chides. Of course I should do, if I believe it.

'I guess so,' I reply non-committally.

'He certainly is as far as I can tell,' he says kindly.

'Have you forgiven him?' I ask.

'I don't know. I don't think so. But it's harder to hate. It's harder on me,' he qualifies.

'I know what you mean. Look at poor Robbie.'

'Robbie?'

'Robbie Williams. There was so much animosity between him and the rest of Take That, it really screwed him up. Now they're all friends again and I've never seen him so happy.'

He says nothing for a long moment, then he cracks up laughing. 'I cannot believe you're comparing Johnny and me to Robbie and Take That.'

'Sorry.'

'Don't be. You've made me laugh. That's always a good thing.'

'Oh, bugger off,' I joke.

'I've got to go, anyway. Sara's on her way over.'

'Say hi to her from me.' I try to sound flippant.

'You know I won't,' he says and I know he's grinning as he hangs up.

Chapter 48

I'm excited. I've got our bags packed for a three-night stay and Johnny is coming to pick us up at any moment. He called me from the airfield to say he was on his way. I'm nervous for some reason. I haven't seen him since Barney's birthday in May, weeks ago, but we've spoken on Skype every few nights since. I've felt closer to him this last couple of months. At peace with him, in a weird kind of way. I'm able to admit to myself that I can't wait to see him again.

The doorbell goes and I literally run down the corridor and swing it open, half out of breath.

'Alright?' Johnny says.

'Hello!' I exclaim, resisting a wild urge to throw my arms around him and hug him half to death. He gives me a funny look. 'Come in!' I say, moving out of the way. I'm unable to wipe the enormous smile from my face as he steps warily across the threshold.

'You're in a good mood,' he comments.

'And? Is that a crime?'

He shrugs. 'Not at all. Are you all set?' He glances down at the bags in the hall.

'We certainly are.' I turn and call down the corridor, 'Barney! Daddy's here!' Johnny heads off in search of his son. 'He's in the living room,' I say. 'Do you want a drink?'

'Nah, let's get on the road.'

'Okay.' I beam at him again. I think that my enthusiasm is entertaining him. Or maybe it's just freaking him out.

'Hey, little buddy!' he says warmly when Barney appears around the corner.

'Daddy!' Barney shouts. Johnny still hasn't got used to him saying it, even though he says it all the time. Literally, all the time. I can barely get a word in when Barney is in the room during our Skype sessions.

Johnny lifts him up for a cuddle, but Barney twists around and holds his hand out to me, so I step in.

'Family hug,' I joke, as Johnny wraps one arm around me and looks down at me with amusement. I rest my cheek on his chest and close my eyes for a second before gazing up at a giggly Barney.

'Famwee hug,' Barney repeats. Johnny and I glance at each other and laugh.

With the traffic on the M25 the journey takes a long time, but Johnny makes up for our delays once we hit the country roads. It's a perfect English summer's day. There are just a few white fluffy clouds in the sky, and the sunshine manages to find us even when the roadside is densely populated by leafy green trees.

'I forgot how fast you drove,' I say as I clutch onto the armrest. Barney is fast asleep in the back. We've had time to catch up on each other's news, and I've just found out that, sadly, Shelley has had a miscarriage. 'How is your dad taking it?' I ask.

'He's bloody delighted,' he mutters with disgust.

'Is he still with that other woman?'

'God knows. I don't want to hear anything about it.'

'Fair enough.' I exhale loudly. 'Argh!' Another corner; too fast.

'Chill out, babe.' He reaches across and pats my thigh, completely unaware that his touch has left me tingling.

We're staying at a hotel about twenty minutes' drive from Goodwood. The organisers at the Festival of Speed have booked us two rooms right across from each other – one of which is the hotel's spacious signature room, with a four-poster bed, vaulted ceiling and a wood-burning stove. A travel cot has been placed in the second, smaller room, but Johnny immediately wants to swap Barney and me to the larger room.

'Don't be ridiculous,' I say. 'We've got more than enough space.'

'I feel bad, though,' he replies.

'You? Feel bad? You've got to be kidding me. We'll be fine. More than fine. Anyway,' I say with a smirk, 'we couldn't possibly deny you the luxury that you've grown so used to.'

He gives me a look and I laugh as I bustle Barney into our room. Johnny stands at the doorway. 'Shall we go for a walk?'

'Sure. I'm just going to unpack, because I'm anal like that.'

'Come on,' he moans.

'Patience . . .' I warn. 'I'll only be a few minutes. Not like I've brought the house with me.'

He comes in and sits on the bed.

'Why don't you take Barney down to the garden to see the peacocks?' To our son's delight there were a couple wandering around earlier. 'I'll be there in a sec.'

'Alright,' he says glumly. 'Come on, buddy.'

'Can you take the buggy?' I call after him.

'I told you before, I don't do buggies.'

'Oh, for God's sake.' I give him a comically withering look. 'What will you be like if you get married one day and have more kids? What's your poor wife going to do?'

Even though I say this flippantly, the horrible thought of him settling down with some strange woman and having children with her suddenly makes me feel quite sick. I avert my gaze. 'Don't worry, I'll bring it.'

'I'll take it,' he says abruptly, looking around. 'Where is it?'

'Actually, it's still in the car,' I realise.

He rolls his eyes at me. 'Trouble-causer. See you downstairs.'

'Okey-dokey!'

'And get a bleedin' move on!' he shouts on his way out.

We wander through the hotel's thirty acres of private parkland with its moat, streams – and peacocks – all the way to an unspoiled beach. The walk should feel blissful, but my comment earlier has unsettled me and I can't shift from my mind the idea of Johnny's future partners. If his dad almost had a second child at the age of sixty-two, I've got years and years of worry ahead of me. Maybe I'll get married myself and have more children; but I don't like that thought, either. Lovely as it was being with Joseph, I haven't had any desire to date again.

I know what's happening, but I don't want to fall for Johnny again. I don't want to re-experience that level of hurt.

Only it's too late. It's always been too late.

Johnny is quieter than usual and I wonder if he knows what's going through my mind.

We sit down on the pebble beach. Johnny lights himself a

cigarette and throws stones into the water while Barney plays in a nearby rock pool. I stare ahead at the waves gently lapping against the shore. I wrap my arms around my knees and hug them to me for comfort. Johnny leans back on his elbows and glances across at me.

'Penny for your thoughts?'

'Cheapskate.'

We manage a small smile at each other.

'I don't want anyone else,' he says as my heart begins to thump more prominently inside my chest.

'What do you mean?' I ask warily.

He hesitates. 'I don't want to end up with another woman, have more kids.'

I stare back at him, into his green, green eyes, but all I feel is pain.

He reaches over and takes my hand, but I snatch it away.

'Nutmeg . . .' he says.

'No.' I shake my head vehemently. 'No. I can't do this.'

'I won't hurt you again.' His voice is almost a whisper.

'You can't promise me that.'

'I can and I will. I do,' he insists.

'Stop it.'

Barney makes his way back over to us and our conversation is cut short. 'Let's talk later,' he says.

'No,' I reply. 'I don't want to talk about it anymore.'

He doesn't look at me as he gets to his feet.

We have an early dinner that night before heading to our rooms.

'Can I help with bath time?' he asks outside my room.

'No, it's okay.'

'Come on, I don't get to do it much. Go and chill out in my room or something.'

'Okay,' I agree. He heads into my room and I into his. I stand there for a minute, looking around. His ever-present guitar is lying on the bed – he must've been playing it earlier. I climb up onto the bed myself and gently run my fingers across the strings. The ache in my heart has been replaced with jittery nerves. I've been getting this sensation a lot lately. I remember it well.

What am I doing? What is *he* doing? He's toyed with my feelings before and I couldn't bear it if he were cruel enough to do it again.

Can I trust him? No. I don't trust him. That's the God's honest truth.

I climb down from the bed and walk determinedly to my room.

'I'll take over from here,' I say firmly.

His brow furrows. 'Are you sure?'

'I'm sure.'

I don't look at him as he steps away from the bath. 'Out we get.' I try to sound bright and breezy as I lift Barney out of the bath and wrap him in a fluffy white towel.

'Meg . . .' His tone is disappointed.

'Night, Johnny.'

It's a long moment before I hear the bedroom door close and then the pain returns tenfold. I try to swallow the lump in my throat as I read a bedtime story to Barney and then settle him in his cot. I just want to get him to sleep so I can shed a few tears in peace. I'm all set and ready to go when my phone beeps.

Come through. We need to talk.

Can't leave Barney.

Yes you can. Bring monitor.

No.

Yes.

No! Bugger off!

Not taking no for an answer.

I don't reply. He sends me another text a minute later:

I mean it.

Oh, for God's sake. Then I remember something:

Can't. Didn't bring monitor with me.

My phone starts to ring. It's him.

'Leave your phone there,' he says firmly. 'I'll put my phone on speaker so you'll be able to hear him if he wakes up.'

'No, Johnny.'

'Meg, stop fucking around,' he snaps. 'Come through or I'll drag you in here.'

'Alright, then, you bully.' But our feisty exchange lightens my mood. I place my phone in Barney's cot and go out of the

424

door. Johnny is waiting for me. He gives me a wry look and I smirk up at him as I pass under his arm, which is holding the door back. He closes the door behind me and I turn to face him.

'What?'

'What do you mean, what?' he says.

'What do you want to say?'

'Jesus, babe, don't make it easy for me.'

'Don't call me babe,' I snipe.

'Why not?'

'You've probably called a hundred other girls "babe", maybe more. I don't want to be like them.'

'You're not,' he says simply.

'How do I know that?' I ask pointedly and he stares at me for a long moment before sighing. I find it slightly unnerving. He sits down on the bed and looks up at me.

'I think you do know it,' he says quietly.

I look away from him. 'No. No, I don't.' I glance back at him and he's still staring at me. It's not like he's telling me he loves me, or anything like that.

Suddenly I feel exhausted. 'I'm going to bed.'

'Don't go,' he murmurs.

I hesitate, but still no declaration of love.

'Argh!' I snap, heading towards the door.

'Meg, wait,' he says, standing up. I pause with my hand on the doorknob. 'You know,' he says.

'I know what?' He's going to have to spell it out. I'm sorry, but he owes me that.

'You know you're special to me.'

A feeling of déjà vu hits me. 'You've said that to me before,' I tell him flatly as the memory clearly hits him, too. He said it and afterwards hurt me so badly I thought I'd never recover. I shake my head and go back to my room, switching off the phone in Barney's cot before he can say another word.

Chapter 49

The next day it's Saturday and Johnny is driving at the Festival of Speed. The event takes place in the grounds of Goodwood House, a stunning country mansion owned by the Earl and Countess of March, and it's effectively one very large garden party, populated with racing royalty, celebrities and members of the general public.

Johnny and I barely speak on the way there, aside from general forced chit-chat with Barney.

He's taking part in a demonstration drive at eleven o'clock, so he goes off to get changed into his racing gear while I wander around the grounds with Barney. My mind is never far from our conversation last night, but it's easy to get distracted by the sights. We stare with gaping mouths at the incredible soaring car-sculpture outside Goodwood House and then we go to check out Johnny's new Bugatti Veyron convertible, which is on display in the supercar compound nearby.

A crowd has already gathered around it, and even though I've been in this situation a thousand times, it still freaks me out hearing people talk about 'Johnny Jefferson'.

'This one Daddy's?' Barney points happily.

'Yes!' I whisper, stifling a giggle.

'You know Johnny Jefferson is here this weekend,' one man enthuses to his wife.

'Isn't he doing the hill-climb at eleven o'clock?' she asks with a frown as she consults the programme. The hill-climb is the demonstration run of all the classic, historic and new high-powered sports and racing cars they have here this weekend.

'Eleven o'clock?' the man gasps. 'Quick, we're going to miss it!' They rush away.

I realise that we'd better get a move on, too.

We've got special VIP enamel badges that allow us into the house so I decide to go to the balcony to have a glass of champagne and watch the action from there. I pause for a moment at the bottom of the stairs, wondering how I'm going to carry up the buggy, but a good-looking young man in racing overalls jogs down them and offers to give me a hand.

'Thank you so much,' I say when we reach the top, me huffing and puffing, him barely out of breath.

'No problem,' he replies in a foreign accent, before flashing me a pearly white grin and heading back down the stairs. I stare after him curiously, wondering who he is, because he looked kind of familiar with his olive skin and dark curly hair, but I've never really been a motorsport fan so I haven't got the foggiest. Johnny was right about Barney, however: he loves the racing. I've never heard him say 'car' and 'brum brum' so much in my life. We watch on a big screen situated down on the grass below as a camera crew films Johnny getting into the second car he had flown over, a Ferrari 599 GTO. He looks pretty cool in his racing helmet and overalls, and despite everything I can't help but feel proud, even if all we get to see is a blurry red car shooting past at one point.

'Daddy!' Barney says when the cameras film Johnny climbing out of the car in the pits afterwards. A couple of people turn to look at us and I shift on my feet and manage an embarrassed smile.

This could be my life . . .

Could it? Could things ever work out between Johnny and me? Could we be a family? A tiny ray of hope sparks life into my insides.

At that moment, my gaze falls on a beautiful brunette standing behind a group of strangers. She's staring straight at me, I realise with surprise, but then she ducks back into the house and I'm left feeling lost and confused. I know her. Then it hits me: Paola. Johnny's PA before me.

He had an affair with her, too. She was a nice girl, Christian once told me, and he treated her like dirt, just like he did me.

He'll never change. It's not in his blood – just look at his old man.

'Come on, Nutmeg,' Johnny chides on the drive back to Goodwood later that night. We've been to the hotel to get changed because we've been invited to a ball at seven p.m. at the house. There will be dinner, dancing, fireworks and even a rock concert. Of all the musicians and rock bands in the world, Contour Lines happen to be playing tonight. It's just as well Christian has finished his book, otherwise his poor girlfriend might've had to forgo her holiday to Tuscany.

Barney has been left with a babysitter. Surprisingly, I'm not nervous about leaving him, possibly because I still feel unsettled about seeing Paola.

'Cheer up.' Johnny has been pretty jolly today, full of buzz from the racing. It's like our conversation last night didn't even occur.

I've asked him before about Paola and he refused to answer me.

That's it! Consider this a test.

'Did you know Paola's at Goodwood?' I ask him, out of the blue.

He glances across at me sharply. 'My PA, Paola?'

I nod.

'Is she?' The look on his face tells me that he had no idea.

'Yes.'

He meets my eyes for a moment before returning his attention to the road. 'Are you okay with that?' he asks and I'm taken aback that he actually sounds sympathetic.

'Not really,' I admit, jolting slightly at my own candour. He stares ahead at the road.

'What the hell is she doing here?' he murmurs under his breath.

'When was the last time you saw her?' I press.

'Years ago. That time at the Skybar when you were there.'

I feel like he's being truthful with me and the uneasy feeling begins to settle.

'It's okay, Nutmeg,' he says, placing his hand on my knee.

This wasn't how I expected him to react. Not at all. He knows the thought of her hurts me – has hurt me in the past – and he's trying to help. This isn't the Johnny I thought I knew.

He returns his hand to the wheel. I stare ahead in contemplation.

'You look beautiful, by the way,' he says when we get out of the car. I'm wearing a long, black, designer evening gown that skims the floor, even in heels. I've curled my blonde hair slightly so it's got that tousled look and have partly tied it back with diamanté clips.

'Thanks.' I look away awkwardly. 'You don't scrub up half bad yourself.' He's wearing a slim-fitting tux. He grins at me as he closes the door behind me and then he runs his fingers down my bare arm and squeezes my hand briefly before letting me go. A shiver goes through me.

We don't speak much during dinner because the other guests at our table in the beautiful Tapestry Marquee are quite taken with Johnny and he's consequently the centre of attention. Later, though, we wander outside to the lawn to watch the fireworks before the concert starts. I notice the man who helped me up the stairs earlier.

I lean into Johnny's ear. 'Who's that?' I ask curiously. 'Don't make it obvious!' I urge.

He glances to his right and then looks back at me with a grin. 'Luis Castro,' he explains.

'Should I know who that is?' My brow furrows.

'F1 driver. Leading the championship.'

'Oh, right. He helped me up the—'

My voice cuts off. Paola has just joined him.

'What?' Johnny turns around and freezes. At that same moment, Paola and Luis spot us, too.

'Hey!' Johnny exclaims. Paola glances uneasily at Luis and then they come over.

'Hello,' she says, her eyes flitting between the two of us. I try not to take the deep breath my lungs need.

'It's been a long time,' Johnny says warmly. 'Hi.' He reaches over and shakes Luis's hand. 'I'm a big fan of yours.'

'Thanks,' Luis replies with a grin. 'Saw your hill-climb earlier. Nice work.'

'I'm Meg,' I say to Paola as Johnny and Luis talk cars.

'Hello,' she replies, shaking my hand. 'I know that, of course.'

'And of course I know who you are.' We smile at each other and something passes between us. An understanding.

'I helped you on the stairs!' Luis interrupts with sudden realisation.

'You did.' I laugh.

'Where's your little boy?' he asks loudly as fireworks start to explode over our heads.

'At the hotel, with a babysitter.'

Johnny folds his arms. 'My son,' he shouts at Paola.

'I know,' she shouts back with a raised eyebrow.

Johnny reaches out and rubs the small of my back. I notice Luis does the same thing to Paola. Both of our men comforting us under strange circumstances.

'We should go back and join the others,' Luis says to Paola. 'I don't think we'll be having a late one,' he tells us.

'British Grand Prix next week.' Paola nods at Luis: 'Needs his R&R.'

'Good luck, mate,' Johnny says as they shake hands again.

'Thanks. Looking forward to hearing the new album.'

'Bye,' I say to Paola.

'Bye.' She smiles at me and they turn away. I watch them for a few seconds until Luis kisses her temple and then I turn back to Johnny.

'She's happy,' he notes. 'I'm glad for her.'

Maybe I should feel jealous, but I don't.

'Are you alright?' he asks in my ear as glittering explosions light up the sky over our heads.

'Yes. I'm fine.' We stare at each other for a long moment. He reaches across and strokes my cheek with his thumb.

'People will talk,' I say as the pyrotechnics come to an end.

'So?'

I shake my head and look away. 'I don't think I can go there again.'

'Why not?' He looks hurt.

'How long is it going to be before you get bored and need to . . . I don't know, add another notch to your belt?' I glance up at him unhappily.

He gives me a hard look. 'Without wanting to sound crass, I've been there and done that. I don't need to do it again.'

'How do you know?'

'I know. I don't need anyone else. I was too fucked-up to admit that to myself, but it's true.'

I smile a small smile. 'You've really got to stop swearing.'

'Fuck off,' he says with a grin and kisses me right on the lips. I start with surprise. He pulls away and stares straight at me. 'You know I'm far from perfect. And I know that, too. But all that shit . . . all that stuff . . . It's in the past. I don't want to be that person anymore.'

'Hey, Johnny!'

We both turn to see Scott, the lead singer from Contour Lines, walking towards us.

'Alright, mate, how's it going?' Johnny says, shaking his hand and patting his back. 'Aren't you guys on stage soon?'

'Yeah, man, that's what I wanted to talk to you about,' Scott replies, glancing at me.

'This is Meg.' Johnny puts his arm around my shoulders.

'Hi,' I say, feeling awkward. Maybe Christian never mentioned me, but they spent so much time together . . . Scott won't think much of me if he knows. 'I'm going to nip to the ladies',' I say, hurrying away.

I stand in front of one of the basins and look in the mirror. My face is flushed and I run my hands under the cold-water tap and then press them to my cheeks. I can hear the band has started to play in the marquee. I walk back out into the throng, but Johnny is nowhere to be seen.

'Excuse me, Meg?' A female roadie appears in front of me. She's dressed all in black and is wearing an earpiece.

'Yes?' I ask, confused.

'Johnny's agreed to do a number.' She indicates the stage where Contour Lines are playing their latest single. 'Can you come with me?' I nod and follow her through the crowd to the backstage area. We climb the stairs and she leaves me in the darkness. I feel a hand on my back and spin around to see Johnny.

'Do you mind?' he shouts in my ear as a soundman hooks up an amp to an electric guitar and hands it over.

I shake my head and smile at him as he puts the guitar strap over his head. He swings the instrument behind him so the strap is pulled tight against his chest. I have a sudden desire to put my hands on his hips, but then Scott introduces a 'special guest' and Johnny raises his eyebrows at me before striding out on stage.

I still remember the first time I saw him play a stadium, the sound of eighty thousand people chanting and banging like tribal warriors before the concert had even started. When he launched into one of his greatest hits, the crowd roared . . . I'll never forget the sight of tens of thousands of people jumping up and down as one. Of course, here and now there are fewer than one and a half thousand, but they still go absolutely bonkers as he steps up close to the mic and speaks into it.

'I wrote this song for the love of my life. The mother of my son. She's here tonight.' He looks backstage at me, and I stand stock-still in shock as he starts to sing my song. His voice fills up the marquee, deep and soulful as he closes his eyes, and when he turns and stares at me again, I feel like he's piercing my soul.

I don't have the strength to resist him anymore. I know I have to let go and give in, even if it ruins me. But I wouldn't be me if I didn't give it a try. I'd just be a shadow of myself, never truly knowing happiness, only pain.

He comes off stage to stupendous applause and then his hands are cupping my face and he's kissing me. I kiss him back, passionately, as the world around me spins. He pulls away, but it's me who speaks first.

'Let's go.'

We practically run to the car together, hand in hand, as I try not to giggle. He revs up the engine and screeches out of the car park.

'Slow down or Lord March won't invite you back next year,' I squeal, but he just laughs.

I'm full of butterflies during the entire journey. Neither of us says a word, but the anticipation doesn't die. I follow him to his room and he unlocks the door. The babysitter is right across the hall, but we're back early; we have time. He shuts the door behind me and then he just stares at me. Is he going to kiss me or what? I stare back at him, warily, wondering why he's not sweeping me off my feet; because I'm a goner, I haven't the will to resist him anymore.

I cock my head to one side in confusion. There's a strange look in his eyes. Has he changed his mind? Oh, God, has he?

He gets down on one knee and takes my hand. My jaw hits the floor.

'I love you,' he says as tears fill my eyes. 'I never want to be without you. I never want to spend another day, another minute, without you and Barney by my side. I've been thinking about doing this for a long, long time. Meg Stiles . . .'

I cover my mouth with my hand and laugh tearfully.

'Will you marry me?'

I nod down at him.

'Yes?' he checks.

'Yes.'

Then he's on his feet and I'm in his arms and he's holding me so tight, and I never want him to let me go. He pulls away and looks down at me and then he's kissing me passionately and I'm melting into him and tears are running down my cheeks as I realise that this is it. *I* was the one to change him. He fell for *me*. He loves *me*. And I love him right back. I'll love him till the day I die.

Epilogue

It's not George Harrison's former house, but we do live in Henley in an enormous gated rock-star mansion. I couldn't go back to LA. That house – that city – had too many bad memories, and, God knows, we needed a fresh start.

I was terrified about the press's reaction to our relationship, but they've astounded me. Hilariously, I've been painted as some sort of angel: Johnny's saviour. It appears that even the blood-thirsty media love a happy ending: the ordinary girl who hooked one of the most famous men in the world. Poor Dana, though. She's still the devil's spawn. But she has resilience – she'll bounce back, I'm quite sure of it.

I still feel guilty about Johnny's staff losing their jobs, especially Santiago, who has finally got a computer and emails me occasionally with the latest Hollywood gossip. But Johnny wrote everyone excellent references and gave them fantastic severance pay, so they'll be okay.

Johnny still doesn't have a PA. At the moment I'm handling things, and the first job on my list was to set him up with a proper fan club. I figure I've seen enough freaky letters to last me a lifetime.

Lena took a placement with Rod Freemantle, believe it or not. She's worked for him for three months now, which is longer than any of his PAs lasted after Kitty. I think he's still mourning her. It's a shame there wasn't any sexual chemistry between them, because they were perfect for each other. Rod split up with his fifth wife and will no doubt be onto his sixth soon. I think he's trying to break some sort of record.

As for Kitty, the last I heard from her she was travelling around Thailand with a couple of hot American boys. She sounds like she's having a whale of a time. I hope she drops in on us again soon.

Bess is the same as ever. She had another drunken snog with Eddie at our wedding. Did I forget to mention that Eddie came with us? He's our full-time cook and he really does make the best chocolate-chip cookies I've ever tasted.

Sorry, I'm getting ahead of myself. Wedding. That's right! We actually did tie the knot. We got married at a local church before coming back here to the house for the reception. All of Johnny's former staff flew over for the ceremony, including dear Rosa. It was so good to see her again, and for Johnny it was particularly therapeutic. In fact, I think it was quite therapeutic for her, too. Kitty also put aside her backpack to join us for a few days, and even Liz and Guy came along. Liz nearly fell off her chair when I finally came clean about Johnny. It's been a relief to have everything out in the open.

Christian and Sara were invited, although sadly they had other plans that weekend. Perhaps it was a bit too much, too soon. But Christian's Contour Lines biography was a huge success and he's writing his third crime book at the moment, so he's in a good place, all in all.

Johnny and I got married in December and it snowed. The whole place was lit up with fairy lights and candles and it truly was magical. I always used to dream of a summer wedding, but I wanted to get married before I started to show. That's another thing I forgot to mention. I'm pregnant. Again. But this time there's no uncertainty, no hurt or pain or fear. Only love. Love, love, love. Just like The Beatles said – and yes, I do know who they are – that's all you need.

Acknowledgements

Thank you – always – to my lovely, *lovely* readers. Your Facebook messages and friendship requests make me smile so much that my face aches – and I'm not even joking! I hope you continue to enjoy reading my books as much as I enjoy writing them.

Thank you to my brilliant editor, Suzanne Baboneau – it's such a pleasure to work with you and the whole team at Simon & Schuster. Believe me, I know how lucky I am.

Big thanks to Jo Willitt for all her help with the Goodwood-related questions. Thank you to Giles Wright and his mother Ann for the Newcastle low-down. Thanks also to Zoe Paramor for the book title brainstorming session – and the alcohol that went with it . . .

Thank you to all my friends and family – but especially my parents, Jen and Vern Schuppan and my brother Kerrin and my parents-in-law, Ian and Helga Toon.

And thank you to my darling husband Greg and my beautiful children, Indy and Idha. This winter threw all sorts of 'fun' at us, from chicken pox and seemingly never-ending sleepless nights to sickness bugs and four bouts of tonsillitis, but – phew! – we got there in the end. I love you all so very much.

Read on for an excerpt of
the next summer page-turner from

Paige Toon

THE
LONGEST
HOLIDAY

Chapter 1

He's smiling down at me with tears in his eyes as I say my solemn vow:

'*I, Laura Rose Smythson, take thee, Matthew Christopher Perry, to be my lawful wedded husband. To have and to hold, from this day forward . . .*'

I thought I would never feel like this about anyone ever again. Not after Will, my first love . . . Not after the heartbreak and the loss and the trying to pick myself back up again . . . Then I met Matthew, and I know that he has my heart forever: my perfect, gorgeous, adoring Matthew.

And then I wake up. And I remember that he's not perfect. He's so far from perfect that my heart could surely collapse from the pain that engulfs me.

'Sorry for waking you,' my friend Marty apologises from beside me as she vigorously rubs at a damp patch on her jeans with a paper napkin. 'Bridget knocked my effin' drink over with her fat arse,' she mutters. I groggily come to and look across at Bridget. She's fast asleep and partially curled up towards the window, her offending arse anything but fat. Feeling like I'm still in a dream

445

– or, more accurately, a nightmare – I bend down to retrieve my bag from under the seat in front of me. Tissues are the one thing I *did* remember to pack. I would have forgotten my passport if Marty hadn't reminded me.

'Thanks,' Marty says, while I use my Kleenex supply to help mop up the spilt gin and tonic on the tray table. 'How are you feeling?' She gives me a sympathetic look and regards me over the top of her ruby-red horn-rimmed glasses.

'Don't,' I warn, but it's too late. The lump returns to lodge itself firmly in my throat.

'Sorry, sorry!' she says hurriedly before I cry again. 'Here, quick!' I take the gin and tonic that she's proffering – what remains of it, anyway – and throw it down in one gulp. 'Think happy thoughts!' she urges. 'Think of the sun! Think of the sea! Think of the cocktails on the beach and all the hot men!'

Bridget sighs loudly with annoyance at the noise, her back still turned towards us.

Marty purses her lips at me and I mirror her expression, tears kept at bay. For now.

'Laura? Do you want another one?' my friend asks in a loud whisper, pressing the call button on her armrest before I can reply.

'Sure, why not?' I nod.

'I'm going to,' she says, as I knew she would. 'May as well, seeing as they're free and all.'

'Is everything okay, ladies?'

We look up at the air stewardess hovering in the aisle.

'Could we get another couple of these, please?' Marty asks.

'Gin and tonic?' the air stewardess asks frostily.

'Them's the ones,' Marty replies jauntily, adding, 'snooty

cow,' under her breath as soon as the woman turns her back. 'So I reckon, when we arrive, we'll just get the car and drive straight up to Key West.'

'Down,' I correct. Her geographical knowledge is probably on a par with a seven-year-old's, which is funny, considering her job as a travel agent.

'Whatever. You don't want to see Miami this afternoon, do you? I know Bridge is desperate to go, but we can always do a day trip.'

'It's six hours there and back,' I remind her.

'So we'll check it out on the return journey, like we'd planned. What do you think?'

'Sure,' I reply. 'It will be good to get to our hotel and—'

'—and get into our swimming costumes and head to the beach-slash-bar,' she finishes my sentence for me, although that wasn't what I was going to say.

'We could unpack first,' I suggest.

'No. No,' she says firmly. 'You are not unpacking. Not this time. On this holiday you are going to throw caution to the wind. There will be no unpacking, no trawling through the tourist brochures, no writing of shopping lists, or anything like that. I'm not having it.'

I roll my eyes at her and say thank you to the air stewardess as she returns with our drinks.

Bridget shifts in her seat on the other side of Marty and sweeps her wavy, medium-length brown hair over her shoulder as she tries in vain to get comfortable. It's been a long flight and we had an early start.

'Have you managed to get any kip?' I ask Marty quietly.

'No. I'll sleep on the beach. Cheers.'

We chink glasses. Matthew's face appears in the forefront of my mind and I wince. I take a gulp of my drink.

'Stop thinking about him,' Marty snaps.

'I wish I could,' I reply, not taking offence at her tone. Any thing but sympathy.

She changes the subject. 'How long until we land?'

I check my watch. 'Two hours.'

'Just enough time to watch a movie.'

'Good plan,' I agree.

She reaches into the seat pocket in front of her for the entertainment guide and then presses the call button once more.

'You haven't finished your last one!' I exclaim.

She sniggers like a naughty schoolgirl. 'I know. I thought I'd ask the snooty cow if she has any popcorn . . .'

For all her bravado, Marty doesn't last long before she falls fast asleep in the front passenger seat of our hired red Chevy Equinox. Bridget is driving and I'm relieved because we'd barely turned out of the airport car park before we'd had two near misses – the drivers here all seem a bit nuts.

We're on a long, wide, straight road heading away from Miami and towards the Florida Keys. I stare out of the window at the fat palm trees planted in the central reservation. It's a bright, sunny afternoon and in a rare uplifting moment, I think to put on my sunglasses, but then I remember that I packed them in my suitcase and I can't even be bothered to feel irritated. It's hard to care about anything much these days.

Jessie J comes on the radio and Bridget turns up the sound. We haven't said more than two words to each other since Marty crashed out. We're not friends.

That sounds wrong. What I mean is, she's Marty's friend, not mine. It's not to say that I don't like her. I do. Sort of. But Marty and I have been best friends since childhood. Bridget only dates back to Marty's early twenties, when they shared a flat together in London. They're great friends, but not old friends. When it comes to longevity, I win. And yes, it does feel like a competition.

I wasn't supposed to come on this holiday. Bridget is a travel writer and Marty, as I've already mentioned, is a travel *agent*, and between the two of them they had this holiday sewn up long before I came along and ruined it.

That's not strictly true. Marty invited me. And Bridget couldn't exactly say no, considering 20.10.12.

20.10.12. The date of my hen night, the date of Matthew's stag do, the date that popped up on one of his Facebook messages just two weeks ago:

Are you the Matthew Perry who was at Elation on 20.10.12?

'There it is!' Bridget interrupts my dark thoughts with a gleeful cry.

Before she fell asleep, Marty challenged us to be the first one to spot the ocean. Bridget thinks she's the victor.

'That's not the ocean, is it?' I say doubtfully from the back seat, although I think I can smell salt water, even through closed windows. 'It's a lagoon.'

'A lagoon . . .' From her side profile I can tell Bridget is looking thoughtful. 'Do you know, I have never said that word out loud.'

'Neither have I, come to think of it.'

'Don't suppose there are many lagoons in London.' That's where we live. 'Or England, for that matter,' she adds. 'Probably the whole of Europe. Mangroves!' she exclaims, her blue eyes widening as they look at me in the rear-view mirror. 'Don't they grow in swamps?'

I laugh. 'I have no idea. But swamp or lagoon, it's still not the ocean.'

'I'll beat you yet,' she says in what I *think* is a joke serious voice. Perhaps she's more competitive than I thought.

We pass a palm tree farm on our left, followed on our right by a tangled sprawl of multicoloured bungalows with boats in their back yards.

I'm struggling to keep my eyes open, but I feel bad about abandoning Bridget. She may have nabbed the driving just so she could sit in the front seat with Marty, but I won't hold that against her. Don't want her to fall asleep at the wheel and kill us all – much as it's hard to imagine how I'll ever live with the humiliation of what my husband is putting me through.

'There!' she shouts as we pass a huge expanse of water.

'Nope.' I shake my head. 'Still a lagoon. Look, you can see land over there.'

'Shit,' she mutters.

I smile to myself. The sunlight on the water is blinding, but I force myself to look at it. I need some light in my life. The last two weeks have been *dark*.

'Hang on,' Bridget snaps. 'We're in Key bloody Largo! You can't tell me that's not the ocean.'

'Okay, you win,' I concede. I told you, it's hard to care about much these days.

Four white sails project out of the mangrove swamps as they

make their way towards open water. We pass a bank of houses on stilts and I can see the water glinting beyond them. The houses and shop fronts are painted in colours of blue, green, aqua, yellow and cream, and in front of some flies the American flag on a gentle breeze. Polystyrene buoys hang like garlands on strings over fences and outside bars, and there are a lot of scuba-diving and bait and tackle shops. I keep catching flashes of the ocean through the lush, tropical vegetation. And all the time, the long straight road goes on. How strange that it will come to a permanent stop in Key West, the southernmost point of the USA. Then all that will be left in two weeks' time is for us to get back on this same road and come home again. The thought depresses me. Maybe I'll hitch a boat ride to Cuba instead.

Marty lets out a loud – and I mean LOUD – snore, and Bridget and I crack up laughing.

'What? *What?*' Marty jerks awake.

'You were snoring,' Bridget says.

'No, I wasn't,' Marty scoffs.

'Yes, you damn well were! You sounded like a whale. Didn't she, Laura?'

'Whales don't snore,' Marty retorts, before I can answer.

'A pig, then,' Bridget says.

'I'd rather be a friggin' whale!' Marty exclaims.

We all crack up and then Bridget lets out a huge snort at the end of one guffaw, which only makes us laugh more.

'God, I'm tired,' she says when we've all calmed down.

'Do you want me to drive for a bit?' I offer.

'No, it's okay.' She brushes me off. 'I slept on the plane, so I'm alright.' She yawns loudly. What a martyr.

'What have I missed?' Marty demands to know, wriggling in her seat.

'Bridget spotted the ocean first,' I tell her as we drive onto a massive bridge with ocean all around us.

'Wow, exciting stuff,' she replies sardonically.

I guess this is why they call it the Overseas Highway, I think to myself as I look out of the window. The Atlantic on our left is choppy and sparkling, while the Gulf of Mexico on our right is glassily still. Two pelicans glide over the road ahead, huge and grey with an enormous wingspan, and then we're back on land again.

We pass a dolphin rescue centre with a sign out at the front saying: 'Have you hugged a dolphin today?'

'I want to hug a dolphin!' Marty shouts at the top of her voice, making Bridget jump out of her skin. Marty and I giggle. And then I see another sign on someone's front gate, saying: 'Wish you were here', and for a brief moment I imagine Matthew sitting on the empty seat beside me and I miss him so much it hurts.

The urge to get out of the car overcomes me.

'Can we stop for a moment?' I ask, trying to keep the desperation out of my voice.

'What's wrong?' Marty whips her head around to look at me.

'Sure,' Bridget replies, nonplussed, indicating left. She pulls off the road into a small car park next to a white sandy beach. A middle-aged couple sits at one of the picnic tables, but other than that it's deserted.

'Don't know if there's a loo here, though,' she adds, misunderstanding my needs.

'I just want some air,' I explain, opening the car door and

climbing out. I hear the sound of Bridget's car door opening, too, but Marty says something to her in a quiet voice, so they stay in the car. My oldest and dearest friend knows me well.

Head and heart pounding in unison, I walk to the water's edge and kick off my shoes, stepping into cool, clear, turquoise-coloured water. Then I take a deep breath and momentarily close my eyes before opening them again and staring out at the nothingness of the vast ocean.

On his stag do, my husband-to-be got wasted beyond recognition and ended up kissing a random girl at a club. He didn't tell me this before marrying me a week later. Nor did he think it would be wise to confess to it during our first seven months of marriage. He probably wouldn't have confessed to it at all except that, two weeks ago, I saw a message on his Facebook page from a pretty girl called Tessa Blight. It soon transpired that she'd been messaging every Matthew Perry she could find – trying to track down *my* Matthew Perry. My Matthew Perry, whose kiss with a random girl at a club called Elation had somehow developed into dirty sex in the club's toilets. And now that random girl is having Matthew Perry's – *my* Matthew Perry's – baby in less than two months.

My husband is going to be a father to another woman's child for the rest of his life. There's no getting away from that. No getting away from the crippling humiliation of all of our friends and family knowing that he had sex with another woman a week before marrying me, the so-called love of his life. He's sorry, of course he's sorry. He's not a terrible person, but it was a terrible, terrible mistake. He didn't mean to hurt me, he didn't mean to do it at all – he was so drunk, it just happened. And he will do anything he can possibly do to make it up to me.